MW01006853

An Accidental Messiah

The Dry Bones Society

Book II

DAN SOFER

Copyright © 2017 Dan Sofer

All rights reserved.

First edition: October 2017

This book is a work of fiction. Any resemblance to actual events or persons, living or dead, is entirely coincidental.

ISBN: 0-9863932-5-8
ISBN-13: 978-0-9863932-5-9

www.dansofer.com

Cover Design: Damonza Book Cover Design

CHAPTER 1

The tour guide had just welcomed his first group of the day to the Mount Herzl National Cemetery when he saw the naked man. Among the bushes at the edge of the Jerusalem Forest, the pale streaker scratched his head and stroked the stately brown beard that fell to his chest.

Despite having been trained to handle this exact situation, the tour guide choked up, and his group of Japanese tourists, with their matching yellow hats and oversized cameras, chattered among themselves and eyed their catatonic guide with concern.

He had approached the rumors with a healthy dose of skepticism at first—after all, dead people didn't spontaneously rise from their graves—until early one morning a fellow guide had discovered a man, naked and alone, among the tombstones of the military cemetery. The former soldier had saved his brothers-in-arms by diving onto a grenade during the Second Lebanon War. A camera crew had arrived to immortalize the moment of his return, and the number of visitors to the park had spiked—resurrection tourists mostly—but after a few days life on Mount Herzl had returned to normal.

Over the following weeks, however, more casualties sprouted from their graves: shell-shocked tank drivers of the

Yom Kippur War; commando fighters of the Six Day War; and then the waves of gaunt Eastern Europeans mowed down during the War of Independence.

The phenomenon, bizarre and surreal by any standard, soon became routine, and they no longer bothered to notify the media when a long-deceased Jew turned up among the hedges. They did notice one trend: as time progressed, the arrivals returned from further back in the past, and the guides placed bets on which of them—if any of them at all—would welcome back to the land of the living the personage enshrined at the heart of the national park.

Today was this guide's lucky day.

"One moment," he told the Japanese tourists in English, as he hurried over to the bushes.

The naked man looked him over with suspicion. *By God, it's him!* the guide thought. He had seen a hundred photos of the man and studied his life in detail, but today the statesman had stepped out of the pages of history—and the grave—and into the present.

The man held his head high, despite his embarrassing state of undress. "*Wo bin ich?*"

"Pardon me?" For the first time since graduating from university, the guide wished that he had studied German as a third language instead of Arabic.

The man sighed and switched to English. "Where am I?"

The guide delivered the good news with glee. "In Jerusalem, sir, the capital of Israel—the Jewish State!"

A satisfied smile curled the man's lips and a fire burned in his dark eyes. "We *did* it!" He clenched a victorious fist in the air. Then he winced and massaged his temple. "*Mein kopf!*"

Remembering his training, the guide reached into his shoulder bag and tore open the DBS First Responder Kit. He helped the man into the thick spa gown with the words Dry Bones Society sewn onto the back and then handed him the two Acamol tablets and the small bottle of mineral water.

The man popped the pills and washed them down, then blinked as cameras flashed. The Japanese had caught up and were documenting the historic event.

"Friends," the guide said to his audience. "I present to you Mr. Theodore Herzl, the Visionary of the State!"

Herzl stepped out from the bushes, bowed his head, and posed with the guide for the cameras.

Then he gazed at the sculpted gardens and stone paths. "What is this place?"

"Mount Herzl, the national cemetery named after you. Your tomb is over there, in the center." The guide pointed. "I'll show you."

Herzl slipped on the pair of spa slippers, also courtesy of the DBS, and they walked along a path of rock slabs.

"When was the State established?"

"1948."

"So late?"

"The road to nationhood was long and winding, but I think you'll be proud of the result. The land has thrived, the desert bloomed. Jews have returned from all over the world. We have an Israeli government and army, technology and culture."

"And yet you do not speak German?"

"Hebrew is the official language, along with Arabic and English. English has become the language of science and culture."

"English? How strange."

"Times have changed. You died over a hundred years ago."

"A hundred years? Incredible!"

They arrived at the large central plaza of white Jerusalem stone and approached the prominent slab of black granite in the center of a circle of grass. The name Herzl was etched into the tombstone.

Herzl sucked in a deep breath. A summer breeze ruffled his hair as he stared at his own grave. Tearing up, he turned to the guide and shook his hand. "I thank you for fulfilling my wishes and bringing my remains to the Jewish State. But how did you revive me?"

Once again, the guide leaned on his training. The instructor from the Dry Bones Society had warned the guides not to overwhelm the new arrivals with information. "You have many questions," he said, using the instructor's words. "We will answer them in time as best we can."

"A hundred years," Herzl repeated. "My children must have passed on already. Their children too. Tell me—what role did they play in the founding of the State?" A hopeful smile made his lips tremble. "Was my son the first chancellor?"

The guide swallowed hard. He had hoped to avoid that topic.

"Tell me, please," Herzl continued. "Are they buried here as well?"

The guide grasped at the shred of positivity. "Yes, they are. Over there."

Herzl gripped the guide by the shoulders. "Show me!"

This was a very bad idea but how could he refuse the Father of the Jewish State?

He led the newly resurrected visionary along another stony path. He needed to call the Dry Bones Society to arrange a pickup but stopped himself. The instructor had warned against using modern technology such as mobile phones, which might disorient the new arrival.

He stopped before a row of three plaques. "Here they are. Paulina, Trude, and Hans."

Herzl appraised the markers in solemn silence. "The dates," he said, startled. "Paulina and Hans died in the same year—and so young!"

The guide hesitated. "Paulina suffered from depression. She overdosed on heroin. Hans shot himself on the day of her funeral."

"Depression," Herzl muttered. "The scourge of our family. And little Trude? Died 1943. Did she, at least, live a happy life? And why does she not have a gravestone?"

He was right. Behind the plaque with Trude's details, and between the two large rectangular gravestones of her siblings, lay a gaping empty space.

The guide shook his head. He had already said too much.

"Tell me!" Veins throbbed on the forehead of the resurrected statesman.

"We don't have her remains. She died in the Holocaust."

"Holocaust? What Holocaust?"

"During World War Two."

"A world war—and two of them? Please continue. I must know."

There was no holding back now. "The Germans and their collaborators systematically murdered Jews throughout Europe."

"The Germans? If you had told me the French I would have believed you, but the Germans? How many Jews died?"

"A great many."

"Tell me, boy—a thousand, ten thousand?"

"Six million."

Herzl ran his fingers through his mane of hair. "Dear God. 1943. But you said that the State was established in 1948—only five years later. Five years too late! We didn't work fast enough."

He lurched backward and the guide steadied him. He called on two of the Japanese who had followed them to support the distraught man. He should never have shown him the Herzl family plot.

"Wait here, sir. I'm going to call for help and I'll get you something to eat."

He dashed off toward the snack store and called the Dry Bones Society on his way. A team of their volunteers was on the way.

Theodore Herzl himself! The guide's skin prickled all over. The recent resurrection had raised hopes for the dawn of a new utopian era, and who better to lead the nation into a brighter future than the spiritual father of the modern Jewish State? The Visionary of the State had returned with perfect timing.

When the guide returned to the Herzl family plot with a

handful of Mars bars and a covered paper cup of sugared tea, however, Herzl had vanished.

"Where is he?"

The Japanese chattered excitedly and pointed toward the forest. The guide shielded his eyes with his hand and scanned the thick press of trees. In the distance, between the tall trunks, a bearded man in a white gown sprinted and disappeared.

CHAPTER 2

"We should set a date for our wedding," Moshe Karlin's wife said as she drove her white Kia Sportage down Emek Refaim Street early Tuesday morning.

"Right," said Moshe Karlin, who sat in the passenger seat.

Outside the window, Egged buses hissed and growled through the heart of Jerusalem's German Colony. Cars honked their horns as commuters rushed to their jobs.

Ordinarily, a man was not required to marry his wife twice, but these were not ordinary times and, technically, their first marriage had terminated with his death.

"This time," Galit continued, "I think we should try a different venue."

Moshe agreed. Three months ago, Moshe had awoken in the Mount of Olives Cemetery to discover that his best friend, Avi, had invaded his home and taken over his family business. Make that *ex*–best friend. Moshe's struggle to win back his life had culminated in a dramatic attempt to stop Avi from marrying Galit at the Ramat Rachel Hotel in South Jerusalem, the very same venue where Moshe and Galit had first tied the knot. The time had come to paint new memories on a fresh canvas.

"What do you think of Mamilla?" Galit asked.

Moshe almost choked. A ceremony at the luxury Mamilla

Hotel across the road from the Old City would be a beautiful and memorable affair. The bill, on the other hand, would empty their bank account ten times over. Their savings had run so low that, if he didn't deposit a paycheck soon, Moshe, Galit, and little Talya would have to get used to life without electricity and flowing water.

"That would be wonderful," he said, when he could draw breath.

Despite serving as the CEO of a thriving organization, Moshe was penniless. As a pre-deceased man in bureaucratic limbo, he was still unable to draw a salary. He could not vote or drive a car either. But today, all of that would change.

On the street, store owners rolled up the security gates of cafés and boutiques, while pedestrians hurried about the errands of their daily lives. At 9 AM today, finally, Moshe would join their ranks, and not a moment too soon.

"I can speak with Rabbi Yosef," Moshe said. "I'm sure he'll be happy to officiate."

The neighborhood rabbi had taken Moshe off the street and into his home despite fierce opposition from both his wife—the rabbanit—and the ultra-Orthodox rabbinate. That good deed had cost the rabbi his teaching position at Daas Torah Primary, and so Moshe had hired him as Spiritual Counselor at the Dry Bones Society.

"Sure," Galit said. "I'd like that."

"Good," Moshe said, and crossed off one expense from his mental list. The kindhearted rabbi would probably conduct the wedding pro bono.

Galit maneuvered the car into downtown Jerusalem and along the quaint back roads of Nachlaot.

Moshe felt his pockets for his cue cards. In the mad rush of preparations ahead of today's event, he had not found time to rehearse his speech.

"Nervous?" Galit asked.

He found the cards. "A little. So much is riding on today. And we'll be on national television." Butterflies had roamed his stomach that morning and killed his appetite at breakfast.

"You'll be great. Like last time." She was referring to the Channel Ten documentary about the Dry Bones Society, the non-profit that Moshe had founded to assist the influx of newly resurrected Israelis.

This broadcast would be different, though. This time, he was making history.

As they descended the ramp to the parking bay beneath Clal Center on Jaffa Street, the butterflies launched from his stomach into his rib cage and his breath caught in his lungs. Seeing that Moshe's first life had ended in cardiac arrest, the sudden pain in his chest did not bode well. *Not again! Today, of all days?*

"You OK?" Galit said, her face tight with concern. She had just parked in a spot marked DBS when she noticed him cramp up.

Moshe lowered his hands from his solar plexus.

"Heartburn," he said. "That's all." He managed to produce a reassuring grin. "Couldn't be better."

His heart pounded like a battle drum, but the pain had subsided. There was no need to scare her. After today's event, he'd be eligible for medical aid and he'd see a cardiologist pronto.

Reassured, Galit turned off the ignition and winked at him. "Time to conquer the world."

CHAPTER 3

The hubbub of excited human activity echoed down the central pier of Clal Center on Jaffa Street, and the decaying shopping mall seemed to quiver with anticipation.

Moshe and Galit took the small, cranky lift to the third floor, and the murmurs grew louder as they made their way down the corridor. Moshe ran his fingers over the proud silver lettering on the frosted glass of the door: The Dry Bones Society. The sign had once read, "Karlin & Son."

"There you are!" Irina hurried over to them. The tall Russian with the short blond locks and sparkling fairy eyes had been Moshe's closest friend in the darkest hours of his early afterlife.

"What do you think?" She pointed to a table dressed in blue and white at the edge of the cubicles of the call center.

Behind the table, a man in a black suit and fedora stood on a plastic chair and taped a banner to the wall above a large Israeli flag. The large black letters read, "The Ministry of the Interior and The Dry Bones Society."

"Looking good," Moshe said. "Great job, guys. Morning, Rabbi Yosef."

The rabbi stepped off the chair and shook his hand. "And well done to you, Moshe," he said. "This is all thanks to you."

Moshe picked up the single printed page that lay on the

table beside two ballpoint pens, and reviewed the copy. The Minister of the Interior's secretary had mounted the revised text on official ministry stationery and forwarded the declaration to Moshe's email yesterday. With a few strokes of a pen, Minister Dov Malkior would change the lives of all resurrected Israelis forever.

Moshe returned the sheet to the table. "All set."

A tap on the shoulder made him turn. "Moshe!" Shmuel, retired reporter and fellow founder of the Society, shook his hand. He patted the remaining strands of gray hair on his head and looked unusually formal in his blue suit. "Can you believe the day has arrived?"

"Almost," Moshe said. Another middle-aged man stood beside Shmuel, a press card clipped to his shirt pocket. "Eran, thank you for joining us."

Shmuel's former colleague shook Moshe's hand. "Thank *you*, Mr. Karlin, for another exclusive."

Men in Channel Ten T-shirts adjusted large video cameras on tripods and set up microphones.

The flat-screen television on the wall read 8:45 AM, and indicated that two callers—resurrectees in need of help or donors eager to support their cause—waited in line for the operators.

Moshe nodded greetings at the clump of volunteers and Society members who hovered beside the cubicle dividers, and he slipped his speech from his trouser pocket. The cue cards trembled in his hands. *A historic day*, he read, *for our brothers and sisters across the nation—*

"Moshe, dear," said a grandmotherly voice. "Have some breakfast. You need your strength for the big day." Savta Sarah, Galit's grandmother and the Society's in-house caterer, peered up at him, her sad eyes filling the lenses of her thick glasses, as she shoved a plate of gefilte fish at him. The sharp scent from the purple swirl of chopped horseradish cleared his sinuses at two paces.

"Thanks, Savta, but I'll eat later."

Galit came to his rescue. "Savta," she said, "I wanted to

talk to you about catering our wedding," and she herded her grandmother toward the buffet tables. Early wedding preparations had their benefits after all.

Moshe returned to his cue cards. *To you, Minister Malkior and your dedicated staff, our thanks and heartfelt appreciation.* But ten seconds of uninterrupted speech rehearsal was too much to expect.

"Moshe!" Samira, the young, olive-skinned woman in the green *hijab*, was the third resurrected Israeli they had discovered and the first Arab. "Will we receive our identity cards at the ceremony?"

"Not yet. But within a few days Minister Malkior will set up special procedures to speed up the process."

Samira smiled and wandered off.

Moshe cleared his throat and continued his rehearsal. *For allowing us to start our lives anew with dignity and with hope—*

"Mazel tov, Moshe!" This time Rafi's rasping voice had interrupted Moshe's speech. At this rate, he'd have to ad lib at the podium, which would probably make for a far shorter speech. There was a bright side to everything.

The Yemenite taxi driver gave his hand a vigorous shake. "Your father would be so proud." Moshe's father had jump-started Rafi's career decades ago, and now his replenished fleet of transport vans shuttled the newly resurrected to the Dry Bones Society's Absorption Center every morning.

Moshe found a quiet corner and studied his cue cards. *To become equal participants in society.* He pulled a pen from his pocket and tagged on the words "once more."

"You'll be fine," said a voice. Irina had sidled up to him.

Moshe sighed. "I hope I'll do us justice." He was used to speaking to a roomful of employees but he had never addressed government ministers on television.

"You already have. Today is a big deal."

A sadness had crept into her smile, and he knew what she was thinking. Three months had passed since her resurrection and still she remembered nothing of her former life, not even her real name. Having no clear identity, she could not apply for an identity card at the Ministry of the Interior.

"Your turn will come soon enough," he said. "I'm sure the minister will work something out for you."

Her eyebrows rose and fell without conviction. "I hope so."

"Moshe," called Rabbi Yosef from a nearby cubicle. He held a desk phone to his ear and covered the mouthpiece with his hand. His trademark ecstatic grin split his face.

"Donors," the rabbi said, "from the United States. They flew in this morning especially to speak with you. They're on their way to Jerusalem now. When can you meet with them?"

Foreign donors—another first. Word of the Dry Bones Society was spreading across the globe. "In an hour or so. After the ceremony."

Rabbi Yosef nodded and spoke into the receiver. "Alo," he said in heavily accented English. "Dis morning. Yes. Yes!"

Moshe fled to his corner office and returned to his speech. His change of tactic worked. He rehearsed the full text twice without interruption, then pocketed the cards and walked over to the large office windows. The ceremonial table stood at the ready. The microphones and cameras waited in position. Only one very significant detail was missing.

He pulled out his mobile phone, property of the Dry Bones Society, and read the time. 9:07 AM. He had pawned his wristwatch—the Rolex that his grandfather had handed down—to escape the slave labor camp run by Boris, a Russian mobster. Now he got by with his phone.

He stepped out of the office, glanced at the assembled reporters, volunteers, and onlookers, and gave them reassuring smiles.

Shmuel walked over, an edginess in his gait. "Is he on his way?"

"I'm sure he's just stuck in traffic."

Shmuel frowned and paced the room.

Moshe's shirt collar itched against his neck. He opened the top button and loosened his tie. Minister Malkior had been friendly and cooperative in their meetings. He had shown

genuine interest in the plight of their new and unlikely demographic. He wouldn't stand them up, would he?

At 9:11 AM, Moshe dialed the minister's personal mobile
number. After ringing twice, the call cut to voicemail. He
dialed the office number.

"Mr. Karlin," said Tzippi, the minister's helpful young re-
ceptionist, "I was just about to call you." Her voice, usually
casual and friendly, had become formal and defensive in tone.

"We're all good to go here. Is everything all right?"

She drew an audible breath. "The minister regrets that he
won't be able to join you."

The floor fell out of Moshe's stomach. "I'm sorry to hear
that. Would he prefer this afternoon?"

Silence on the line. "I'm afraid not," Tzippi said. "He
won't be able to participate. Not today. Not ever. I'm sorry."

She ended the call.

Moshe stood there for a few moments, then slipped his
phone back into his pocket, his cheeks cold, his forehead
damp. A room full of anxious faces watched him in silence.

"The minister won't be joining us today," he said. "Sorry
for all the trouble."

The camera crew exchanged glances and began to disman-
tle their equipment.

Shmuel whispered in Eran's ear, then marched over.
"What happened?"

Moshe kept his voice down. "He backed out."

"What the hell?"

"Where does that leave us?" Samira asked. Fear flickered
in her eyes and in the eyes of the half-dozen Society members
who now gathered around Moshe.

He had given them hope, he had promised them a future—but now the iron doors of government bureaucracy
blocked their path and refused to budge. They didn't deserve
this. At a minimum, they deserved an explanation.

"I don't know," he said, balling his hands into fists. "But
I'm going to find out."

CHAPTER 4

Moshe stormed down the corridor of the Ministry of the Interior, the letter of intent in hand and a fire in his heart. Malkior would sign the agreement today, as he had promised, press conference or not. Too many lives depended on the wave of his pen.

Shmuel and Irina followed him in a V formation. Rafi had dropped them off at the government buildings on Safra Square. Over the last few weeks, they had gotten to know those corridors well and this time they were not going to leave empty-handed.

At the sight of the charging delegation, the minister's secretary placed a hand on her desk phone. One wrong move and she'd call security.

"Tzippi," Moshe said, his voice calm and amicable. Angry words would not help them here. He glanced at the large wooden door behind her. "We just need a few moments with the minister to understand why he changed his mind. I'm sure we can work things out."

Her cheeks turned pink, and her mouth tightened. This was difficult for her. She had always spoken kindly with them. "He can't see you today. He's in meetings."

"That's OK. We'll wait."

"You'll be waiting a long time."

"We don't mind. We're right over here."

They settled on the set of four joined chairs opposite. Bureaucrats strolled the corridor, holding documents and paper cups of coffee, and glanced them over.

After all he had experienced in his second life, Moshe should be used to the floor disappearing beneath his feet.

"It doesn't make sense," he said. "More registered citizens means more taxes. More grateful voters. Elections are a month away. It's a win-win deal."

"The whole thing smells rotten," Shmuel said.

Moshe had to agree.

"But he seemed so understanding," Irina said. "He seemed to really care about us."

"All politicians do," Shmuel said. "When it serves their agenda. As a reporter, I saw that a lot."

They cooled their heels for half an hour before the door handle turned. A dozen men in black suits, hats, and gray-streaked beards left the office, chuckling and nodding. The tallest wore a silky suit and tidy bowler hat. When his eyes met Moshe's, he smiled and touched the brim of his hat.

"Oh, no," Moshe said.

"You know him?" Shmuel said.

"Rabbi Emden, Rabbi Yosef's old mentor. He introduced us to the Great Council." They had appeared before the rabbinic aristocracy within the immense Belz Synagogue in the heart of Chassidic north Jerusalem. The frenzied chant of the horde of followers still rang in his ears. *Sitra Achra! Sitra Achra!*

"The ones who claimed we're the evil Other Side?"

Moshe nodded. He had a bad feeling about this. "Let's go."

They rushed forward and slipped through the door before Tzippi could protest.

Framed photos of the Prime Minister and the President hung on the walls of a richly decorated office, the office of a man who intended to stay there a very long time. Minister of the Interior Dov Malkior looked up from his large wooden desk.

"Moshe," he said, rising from his seat as though greeting a long-lost friend. He shook his hand, then frowned at circumstances beyond his control. "I am truly, deeply sorry for having to cancel."

"Not as sorry as us," Shmuel said.

Moshe motioned for Shmuel to stand down. "Dov," he said. They had moved to first names early on. "We'd like to understand what your concerns are. I'm sure we can work something out."

Malkior returned to his seat behind the large wooden desk. "These are difficult times, Moshe. Elections are close. The coalition is in disarray. Let's speak again in a few months and we'll see what we can do."

Moshe smelled an evasive maneuver. Cab operators had used the same tactic when he approached them to sign with Karlin & Son while other dispatch agencies were courting them. "It's the rabbis, isn't it?"

Malkior blew air through his lips and threw up his hands. "What can I say? You've made some powerful enemies."

"Let me guess—if you drop the agreement with the Dry Bones Society then they'll join the new government?"

Malkior continued to smile but said nothing.

Moshe leaned his knuckles on the desk. "People are suffering, Dov. Hundreds, if not thousands, of people. Us included. We can't rent an apartment or support our families or even see a doctor. Some of us are being roped into slave labor, right now, as we were. You can help them." He placed the document on the desk. "All you have to do is sign."

Malkior leaned back in his puffy leather chair as if to distance himself from the agreement. "My hands are tied. Let's speak later, after the elections have blown over." He chuckled. "If I'm still in this office. This isn't personal, Moshe. It's just politics."

The deal was done and Malkior would not budge. Moshe turned to leave. "It is for us."

CHAPTER 5

Boris Poddobni was used to fear and panic. Usually, he elicited those responses in others, but as he waited outside a private home in the quiet suburbia of southwest Jerusalem, his pulse galloped. Depending on how his meeting went, today he might breathe his last.

In the valley below the row of houses, rose the square of the Malcha Mall and the towers of the Malcha Technology Park. Birds sang in the trees. The house betrayed few clues to the dangers that lay within. The front door of carved white wood had a silver knocker shaped like a grasping gloved hand. A security camera eyed him from a corner.

He patted his bushy gray hair and moustache and knocked twice.

Boris avoided meetings with the boss. The man was a genius, yes, and Boris had learned much from him, but he could never predict his next move. The boss had little tolerance for failure, and Boris's tidings would not make him happy.

The door opened.

"*Pree-vee-et*," Boris said. Hello. From here on, he would speak Russian. The bald man in the doorway was built like a cement truck and wore black jeans and a black T-shirt. Boris regretted having to leave his own muscleman, Igor, in the car, but not even Igor could save him in here.

The bald man looked Boris over, his face expressionless, a nasty, jagged scar down his left cheek, and indicated for him to enter with a jerk of his head.

Marble covered the entrance hall, white and shiny. The life-size statue of a young woman greeted him. A blindfold covered her eyes, but she had cocked back her head to steal a peek, and her cheeky breasts pushed through the folds of her flowing toga. In one hand, she held a square tablet, a raised lance in the other, a gesture of defiance. Or warning.

The door closed behind him.

Boris turned to the doorman. "Is The Jew here?" Boris said.

"Downstairs. And I wouldn't call him that anymore."

"No?" The nickname had commanded respect in the Russian underworld. When The Jew had moved to Israel, he had quickly swallowed up the local gangs to rule the largest network of organized crime in the country.

"He goes by Mandrake now."

"Mandrake. Like the magician? A fitting name."

The henchman glared at him.

Boris nodded. He passed the statue woman and her raised lance, glimpsed a well-furnished living room with large windows facing the mall, the technology park, and Teddy Stadium, and descended the rounded staircase to the basement.

His shoes squeaked on marble tiles as he sank deeper into the dark belly of the house, then plastic sheeting crinkled underfoot as he stepped onto the landing. A spotlight fell on an overturned wooden table at the far end of the basement. Black tape outlined the crude shape of a human form on the round red surface, like chalk marks at a crime scene.

"Boris, my friend," a sonorous voice said.

As his eyes adjusted, a bald man emerged from the gloom. He stood in the middle of the den, his back to the stairs. Muscles bulged on his shoulders beneath his black T-shirt.

The friendly tone did not comfort Boris. Cheer and sympathy could turn to violence in an instant.

The man reached into a small briefcase on a stool and withdrew a large knife. Grasping the tapered blade between two fingers, he raised the knife in the air. Then, with a movement as fast as a striking viper, he flung the knife, burying the blade between the eyes of the outline with a metallic twang.

"Business is booming, from what I hear," Mandrake said, without turning.

By "business" he meant the labor camp that Boris managed in the Talpiot industrial zone. In return for manual labor, he offered illegal aliens, ex-cons, and other unemployables board and lodging in his warehouse facility. The workers soon found themselves buried in debt for expenses hidden in the fine print of their contract.

The promise of deportation helped keep them in line, along with the threat of grievous bodily harm. Revenues had skyrocketed three months ago thanks to the sudden crop of resurrected Israelis that sprung up each morning at cemeteries around the country, providing a glut of easy prey.

Boris cleared his throat. "It was, sir, until recently. That's why I've come to see you."

Mandrake lifted another blade from the box. "Continue."

No turning back now.

Boris spoke and Mandrake listened, the blade hovering beside his ear.

"So," Mandrake said, when Boris had finished, "you collect these dead people as they wake up in the cemetery each morning?"

"Yes." Boris swallowed hard. He had not believed the tale either at first. Would Mandrake? "They are real. They've appeared on television. We picked them up by the busload until the Dry Bones Society came along."

"The Dry Bones Society?"

"A bunch of do-gooders led by Moshe Karlin, a resurrected Israeli himself. They get to the new arrivals before we can and take them in." He did not mention that Moshe Karlin had once worked for him and that Boris had let him buy his way out. Unflattering details like those would not aid Boris's chances of survival.

Mandrake held the next throwing knife in the air for a few seconds. Then his arm became a blur and the blade slammed into the wooden target, piercing the outline's heart.

The plastic sheeting crinkled beneath Boris's shifting feet and a sudden thought made him freeze. The knives. The plastic sheeting on the floor. The red paint of the target. *He's already seen the numbers!* Mandrake had been expecting him, and only one scenario required covering the floors in plastic sheeting.

Boris braced for the worst. There was no running from a man like Mandrake. Not for long. He only hoped that Mandrake had run out of throwing knives, and would opt for a quicker and cleaner death by gunshot.

Mandrake reached down and lifted a third blade from the box.

Derr'mo! Crap!

Boris closed his eyes.

"Do you believe in magic, Boris?"

Boris opened one eye. The knife still hovered at Mandrake's ear. What was the right answer? What kind of magic did his boss have in mind? Boris closed his eye again. His answer wouldn't matter. He knew the drill. Any moment, Mandrake would spin around and skewer him for his failure.

Three long seconds passed, however, and he was still breathing.

Bam!

Boris clenched up but felt no pain. He opened his eyes. The third knife quivered hilt-deep in the groin of the outline.

"I'd like to learn this magic trick," his boss said. "The leader of this Society, this Moshe…?"

"Moshe Karlin, sir."

"We should get to know him better. Find out how he operates. From the inside. And then"—he raised his hand and curled the fingers into a fist—"we will crush him."

Boris exhaled a pent-up breath. *We.* He might survive the

meeting after all.

"Sir," he said, hoping that he was not pushing his luck. "Karlin knows me and my men. I'll need fresh faces to get close."

Mandrake turned to face him, and Boris swallowed the knot of fear in his throat. Stupid, stupid, stupid! He should never have opened his mouth.

Mandrake considered him with a pair of sympathetic eyes above the largest hooked nose Boris had ever seen.

"Don't worry, my friend," he said. "I have just the man for the job."

CHAPTER 6

Eli lay in bed Tuesday morning, listening to the sounds of his new life. A girl showered in his en suite bathroom. The mattress felt warm where she had slept and her sweet scent clung to the sheets. The murmur of traffic far below seeped through the windows.

He had everything a young man could desire: an amazing girlfriend, a penthouse, his own business, and more money than he could spend.

Then why don't I have the energy to get out of bed?

Was he still adjusting? Sharing his apartment took some getting used to, as did his new identity, and the idea that he was, one day, going to die.

How did people do it? Wake up each day. Brush their teeth. Get dressed. Go to work. It seemed like a lot of effort when your life was going to end in a few years. Mortality sucked.

As Elijah the Prophet, he had had—literally—all the time in the world. The fate of humanity had depended on him. Eli Katz the man of flesh and blood, on the other hand, had numbered days and questionable purpose. But he did have one thing that even Elijah the Prophet would envy. He had Noga Shemer. Without her, he would have stepped off the window ledge a long time ago.

Noga padded into the room in her underwear and a T-shirt. She pulled on her jeans and fastened her sandals, and looked him over with a playful smile that almost hid her frustration.

"Going out today?" she asked.

He shook his head.

"Let's go for a walk when I get back. Get some fresh air."

Since his return from the hospital, Eli had spent most days on the living room couch, staring at the Jerusalem skyline.

"Change out of your pajamas, at least? Tonight we're celebrating, remember? This is my big day."

He reached for her and gave her a mischievous smile. "We can celebrate right here."

She stepped away quickly to avoid his grasp and giggled. "We celebrate here often enough. I put years of work into this. It deserves. A night. Out."

"Years of work," he repeated.

"Yes," she said, and leaned in for a parting kiss. "Out. Tonight. Understand?"

"I understand," he said. "You want to get me out of my pajamas."

She waggled a finger at him and left the room. Moments later, he heard the front door close, and she was gone.

Noga. Venus. His goddess of love. His guiding star. Today was her big day. For her, he'd make the extra effort.

He counted to ten and rolled out of bed. After a shower and a shave, he padded barefoot down the parquet of the corridor in a robe. He had done his part; he had gotten out of his pajamas. In his designer, open-plan kitchen, he poured a cup of coffee and moved to the couch of cream leather. The furry carpet tickled the soles of his feet.

He sipped his morning espresso, sunlight warming his legs. The city sprawled in the French windows. The offices of downtown Jerusalem. The fancy hotels. The ancient walls of the Old City.

He put the mug down beside the laptop on the glass coffee table and pressed a key. Lines of computer code displayed on the screen. OpenGen, the genealogy website he had founded, ticked along and paid the bills. Recording the chains of ancestry had been Elijah the Prophet's obsession and his way of tracking lineages ahead of the End of Days. He had cranked out new features and honed his marketing techniques for hours on end, and even set up a telephone support team in Bangladesh.

Eli closed the lid of the computer and slumped back on the cushioned upholstery. The next app version could wait.

He reached for the remote and turned on the television in the corner. He had not had time for television in his deluded former life, and he had a lot of catching up to do.

A bearded face filled the screen. "We are witnessing the fulfillment of prophecies in the Bible," the smiling rabbi said. "The Resurrection is one stage of the Final Redemption."

"How does the Resurrection process work?" asked an earnest, gray-haired reporter.

"It is a great miracle," the rabbi explained. "Our ancient writings talk of the Dew of Resurrection, which recreates the physical body from the Luz, a small, indestructible bone in the spine."

Eli fired the remote and the television went blank.

Prophecies. The Resurrection. His chest heaved. The remote trembled in his hand. He knew that bearded face. The man had hovered over him as Eli had lain bleeding on the ground. The rabbi from the Mount of Olives. The End of Days. He had to tell him. To complete his mission. The Thin Voice had commanded him!

He shot to his feet. "No!" he said aloud. "I'm done with that." He clutched his head in his hands and shivered. His breath came in short, fitful bursts. If he relapsed into delusion, he'd lose Noga, he'd lose the only thing of value in his life.

Calm down. He sat on the couch and sucked in air.

That isn't real. It's only in your mind. He raised the remote and pressed the button.

The screen blinked to life. A podgy man in an expensive

suit pushed through a crowd of reporters like a penguin. A penguin with bodyguards. He had a smug smile on his face. "He calls his new party Upward," the narrator said. "The breakaway has sent ripples through the political world, causing defections and havoc, with only a month until general elections, elections that Mr. Gurion initiated when he toppled the government by withdrawing his former party from the coalition."

Eli turned off the television and breathed a lungful of relief. Treacherous politicians and election fever. Reality. There was no Resurrection. No End of Days.

He had turned his back on his false memories, but now the madness had returned to tap him on the shoulder. Was that why he never left the apartment—not depression but the fear that, once again, he would lose his mind?

A new resolve launched him to his feet. He marched down the corridor and opened the one door he had not dared to touch since his discharge from the hospital. He turned on the light.

Items of various shapes and sizes lined the walls of the sanctum and the sunken den in the center, like the walls of a museum: a shaggy fur cloak, a leather shield, a sword in a leather scabbard, a rounded clay urn, an oriental rug, a clunky pistol with a rounded handle. The mementos from his imagined past were also doorways to insanity.

He rolled up the sleeves of his gown. To seal the tomb of his delusions he needed to purge every trace of his old life.

And now he knew how.

Yosef reached out a hesitant hand, hoping to make a good impression. "Welcome," he said in his shaky English. "Welcome."

The tall, silver-haired stranger in the tailored suit gave his hand a mighty double-handed squeeze and shake. "Rabbi Lev, I presume." He spoke with an oily southern drawl.

"Yes." Yosef kept his words to a minimum to avoid accidentally insulting his guest. Moshe had yet to return from the Ministry of the Interior and so Yosef would have to entertain the honored guest in his stead.

"The name is Adams but you can call me Henry." Mr. Adams entered the Dry Bones Society with the momentum of a charging buffalo and the regal posture of an American Indian chief. A lanky suited associate followed in his wake, carrying a leather briefcase.

Adams looked around the call center, his broad, white smile and suntanned skin radiating health and confidence. He seemed to like what he saw.

"And you can, eh, call me Yosef. How was your, eh, flight?"

"As long as it needed to be, Rabbi. So this is your call center. And the volunteers?"

"In the field."

"The field?"

"At the cemeteries. For collection." Yosef had looked up English words on the Internet before the potential donor's arrival.

"Ah. Extraction teams across the country, welcoming home the returned souls."

"Yes!" Yosef could not have said it better, even in Hebrew.

"And Mr. Karlin?"

Yosef swallowed. "He had to go out," he said. "An emergency. I am, eh, very sorry."

The American frowned only for a moment. "No problem. Is there somewhere we can talk?"

Yosef ushered him to Moshe's corner office.

"We're big admirers of the work you're doing," Mr. Adams said, when they were seated. "And we want to help you however we can." He nodded at his associate, who opened the briefcase and handed Yosef a check.

Yosef inhaled sharply when he read the amount. "Ten thousand dollars?" The sum, worth about forty thousand shekels, was more money than Yosef had ever handled.

"A modest contribution to get us started."

To get us started! "Thank you, sir!"

"You'll need more of that to continue your good work."

"Yes. More supplies for the new arrivals. And, eh, more teams in more cemeteries. Yes."

"Good, good." Their benefactor seemed less interested in the operational details. "The money is yours to spend as you see fit. All we ask in return is an update now and then to see how things are progressing. I understand that the number of your Society members has been rising steadily."

"Yes. More and more each day."

"Good." Adams cleared his throat. "Now that the Resurrection is in full force, you wouldn't happen to have heard from a charismatic young man, would you?"

Yosef racked his memory. "A resurrected man?"

"Hmm. Yes, but not recently. Mid-thirties with long hair,

probably. Speaks Aramaic."

Yosef shrugged. None of the returnees spoke Aramaic.

"I see." Adams seemed disappointed. "Is it true," he continued, "that, as time goes by, the resurrected have been returning from farther back in the past?"

Surprise delayed the words in Yosef's throat. "Yes," he said. "I didn't think anyone outside knows this."

"We like to keep informed," Adams said. "How far back are we now?"

"Well, we get a lot of soldiers now. British soldiers."

Adams leaned in. "From the British mandate era?"

"Yes. Some die in the fighting. Some die from, how you say, malaria. And then some from even before! That why we start lessons."

"Lessons—you mean training courses?"

"Yes. Training. They know nothing. Nothing! No cars. No electricity. No cell phone. Need to learn everything."

Adams raised his eyebrows and exchanged a meaningful glance with his associate. "And how far back do you think this will go?"

Yosef shrugged. "God knows."

The two visitors exchanged another glance and smiled.

"We're very serious about our continued support. In fact, our organization has created a wholly owned subsidiary just to manage your funds. We'll be in touch soon about our next contribution, so please go ahead and send us the Society's bank details." Adams got up to go. His voice dropped to a whisper. "And keep an eye out for that young charismatic friend of ours. It appears that he'll be arriving when his generation returns, so I'd appreciate it if you'd call me when we reach the Roman Period."

"The *Roman Period?*" Yosef repeated. Had he heard correctly? The benefactor's words had sped by so fast and some of them had raised red flags. "Wait—what organization?"

Adams handed him a business card. The credentials read:

Rev. Henry Adams, Managing Director
The Flesh and Blood Fund

A division of the New Evangelical Church of America

Yosef almost swallowed his tongue. The words of the sages of the Great Council echoed in his ears. *Sitra Achra!* The Other Side.

Yosef had ignored their warnings, siding with his conscience, and now he was joining forces with a fundamentalist Christian organization! Had the sages been right all along? Were they falling into the grip of the unholy Other Side?

He reread the card, hoping that he had misunderstood.

"Flesh and Blood?" he said.

Adams smiled with one side of his mouth. "You're the Dry Bones, right?"

"Yes?"

"Well, we've got you covered." He chuckled, patted Yosef on the shoulder, and charged out of the room, his associate in tow.

Yosef stared at the check and the card in his hands. Drops of sweat slipped down his brow. The check would go a long way to helping people in need, but was he allowed to accept their money? For all Yosef's good intentions, his new partners might have very different motives.

He could stand the uncertainty no longer. He ran after his guests, catching up with them at the front door. "Mr. Adams," he said. "Why are you helping us?"

Adams turned and flashed his confident smile. "We've been waiting for this day a long time, Yosef," he said. "Our Daddy's coming home."

CHAPTER 8

Noga stepped onto the train on Jaffa Road and swiped her *Chofshi Chodshi* monthly pass over the sensor. For once, everything in her life was going well.

Weeks ago, she had completed the data collection phase of her thesis, the longest and least stimulating part of her research project, and submitted the batch of DNA samples for processing at a private lab. Her doctoral degree, forever in the distant future, had finally inched within grasp. Today she would return to the Shaare Zedek Medical Center to collect the results. All that remained was to analyze the raw data and make them pretty for her paper.

She found a vacant window seat and rested her laptop bag beside her. On Jaffa Street pedestrians dragged their shopping carts toward the Machaneh Yehuda market as the train pulled off.

Shaare Zedek. She smiled to herself. The hospital had provided the other new development in her life. At Shaare Zedek, she had met Eli Katz.

Within a week, Eli had swept her off her feet and she had helped him overcome his delusions. A fair exchange, in her opinion. By the time of his release from the hospital two months ago, they had become inseparable, and when the lease on her apartment had expired two weeks ago, Noga had moved in with him.

The tram veered left onto Herzl Boulevard toward the Mount Herzl military cemetery and the Yad Vashem Holocaust Remembrance Center.

She had been single and miserable for so long that she found her recent good fortune hard to believe. Eli was the love of her life, he was gorgeous, and he adored her. He also happened to be very rich. She had found the fairy-tale Happily Ever After to a bumpy early life. She only hoped that at twelve o'clock her chariot wouldn't turn into a pumpkin and her Prince Charming into a frog.

Stop worrying, girl, and enjoy your life. Those irrational fears belonged to her old life. Why shouldn't she be happy?

After two and a half months together, it was time to introduce him to her parents. Her adoptive parents. Why had she waited so long? At first, she had kept a wary eye on Eli, expecting him at any moment to explode into another impassioned rant about the End of Days or claims of immortality. Eli had done nothing of the sort. Instead, he had sunk into a sluggish routine of inactivity, and now she wasn't sure which boyfriend she preferred—the manic delusional or the depressed couch potato.

Had he grown bored with her? Noga remembered Eli's words that morning and she smiled. He still wanted her around, that much was sure. He was still adjusting to his new life. Maybe a warm extended family was the support and encouragement he needed.

The train stopped and she got off.

Inside the hospital, she passed by the Steimatzky bookstore and the flower shop. Glimpsing a glass door out the corner of her eye, she changed direction and pushed through the exit.

The secret green courtyard had not changed much. She sat on the bench, the spot where one fateful afternoon Eli had presented her with a jewelry box. She had thought that he was going to propose. Instead, he had given her the entrance code to his apartment and made his confession. He was

Elijah the Prophet, ancient and immortal, and Noga had a role to play in the End of Days. She had stormed out on him, of course, and they had never come so close to losing each other. A cold shiver crept down her spine.

That was then, this was now. Today, she wouldn't mind receiving another jewelry box from Eli Katz, and this time, a ring.

She snapped out of her memories and continued to the elevator. Her results waited for her at the Medical Genetics Institute on the fifth floor, but as the slow doors of the large metal elevator closed, she pressed the number four. She couldn't resist one more stroll down memory lane.

The linoleum corridors of the neurology ward had not changed. She waved at Nadir, who rose to greet her at the nurses' desk. Noga complimented her on her new head covering, and Nadir smiled and said, "I'll call Eliana. She won't want to miss you."

"Noga, dear," a man's voice said.

Noga stiffened. "Dr. Stern."

The department head, an older man graying at the temples and in a white medical cloak, drew near. "Lovely to see you again." His icy blue eyes scanned her. "And how is our mutual friend?"

Dr. Stern had once threatened to ship Eli off to the Kfar Shaul Mental Health Center, and his ongoing interest in his former patient triggered her defenses. She relaxed. The doctor had only been trying to protect her—and rightly so—and he had warmed to Eli in the end. "He's fine," she said. "Totally fine."

He gave her a quizzical glance, so she explained. "I've come to collect my results."

"Oh, of course. Congratulations. If you'd like an extra pair of old eyeballs to review the data, I'd be happy to oblige."

She thanked him. Then her lungs deflated as Eliana, the busty head nurse, wrapped her in a mighty hug. Noga answered the barrage of eager questions and demands. Yes, she was well. So was Eli. And, yes, she'd visit more often.

Her curiosity satisfied, Noga took the stairs to the next floor and pushed through the doors of the Medical Genetics Institute.

"Hi, Katya," she said to the Russian with the shock of blond hair and—even Noga could tell—too much mascara at the front desk. "My results are in."

"Identity card?"

Noga handed over her blue identity booklet. Katya typed a few keys and pursed her lips at the monitor. For the purposes of data security and to satisfy hospital procedures, the data was transmitted on a secure medical network from the private lab to the institute.

Katya said, "USB."

Noga opened her laptop bag and handed over her flash drive.

A sudden worry jolted her. She had worked on her doctorate for so long that she hadn't thought about the day after. She'd get a job at a pharmaceutical company, she supposed, or dream up another research project and return to the scrabble for funding. A university post didn't appeal to her much, although Hannah, her doctoral supervisor, would probably love for her to join the faculty. One challenge at a time.

Katya handed back the USB.

"Thanks!"

Noga opened her laptop on the chair in the waiting lounge and plugged in the disk.

The lab data consisted of a simple text file of comma-separated values. Each row represented a test ID and flags indicating the presence or absence of the genetic markers she had specified. In her case, the flags represented the Cohen gene sequences—known as the Cohen Modal Haplotype, a pattern of six Y-STR markers, or short tandem repeats, on the male-only Y chromosome.

She loaded the file into EPSS, the statistical analysis program she had used to simulate her expected results.

A wheel icon circled on the screen as the processor cross-referenced the test results with the demographic data she had collected and ran the merged data through the statistical engine.

The moment of truth. The culmination of two years of her life.

A few agonizing seconds later, the findings displayed on the screen in graphs and bar charts.

In her pilot experiments, the lines and bars had stood out in tidy, colorful rows, clearly supporting her hypothesis that the Cohen gene appears only in Jews of priestly descent, proving that all priestly Jews descended from a single male ancestor. For fun, she'd call him Aaron in her paper, after the biblical Aaron, son of Amram and brother of Moses.

The actual charts from her final experiments, however, made her heart skip a beat.

That's strange.

The graphs on the screen were almost identical to her pilot experiments' results. Her main thesis still held water but there was noise, a large clump of outliers that had the Cohen genetic markers, and ninety-eight percent of them belonged to one group.

That doesn't make sense.

She performed a t-test to confirm whether the outlier group had statistical significance. It did. She could not write off the noise as diagnostic errors. The rogue results were not outliers at all.

She turned the data over in her mind. Her cheeks felt cool and the roots of her hair prickled, as though she was about to faint. The data could mean only one thing.

No, she thought. That's impossible!

CHAPTER 9

"What do we do now?" Samira asked.

Good question. Moshe had perched on the edge of his desk and shared the bad news with the Dry Bones Society management. He had gone head-to-head with rivals before—both in business and in his private life—but the government was a different story. A collision with that unmoving continent would shatter their fledgling organization to smithereens. Moshe would have to change course.

"The government's doors are closed to us for now," he said. "We'll have to be patient." This was his fault. He had raised their hopes and set them up for disappointment.

"Patient?" Shmuel said. "What if those doors never open? We could all starve by then."

"No one's going to starve," Irina said.

"That's right," Moshe said. "We have money for the cafeteria and dormitories so long as donations keep flowing."

"What about health care? Private doctors don't come cheap. And there's only so long we can shack up in shared housing."

Or support our non-resurrected families, Moshe added to himself.

"You're right," he said aloud. "We need new ideas. Any suggestions?"

Samira put up her hand first. "We could ask doctors to volunteer."

"And," Irina said, "we can ask pharma companies to donate medical supplies."

"Good. Good. That will help."

Shmuel said, "I suppose we could put together a magazine, and sell advertising. It'll be tax deductible and good PR." He shook his head, obviously not thrilled about chasing after advertisers.

"Excellent. Maybe an online magazine? Or a YouTube channel. We could interview the new arrivals and share their stories. We've had some interest in our cause overseas."

Rabbi Yosef had filled him in on his meeting with their new American ally before he slipped out to cash the check. Ten thousand dollars would not last forever and he did not want to pin their survival on a single donor.

"OK, friends, let's get to work."

The team dispersed to their new tasks.

Moshe moved behind the desk and slumped over, his head in his hands.

Begging for donations. Selling advertising. Not the sexiest ways to get by, but they'd have to work with what they had.

In the call center, telephones rang as lost souls called in.

Shmuel had not been entirely wrong. Each day their expenses piled up but the donations were not keeping pace. As the dead returned from the more distant past, fewer of them had the means to contribute, and living Israelis felt less connected to them. The Society would need new revenue streams to survive the long haul.

And no matter how many donations came pouring in, Moshe was still not able to draw a salary and keep his family afloat, never mind pay for a fancy wedding. He had placed all his hopes on Minister Malkior and paid the price.

A throat cleared and he looked up. Savta Sarah stood in the doorway, her sad eyes filling her glasses. "I saved you a plate of food," she said. "Seeing that you were too busy to eat."

Moshe's mood improved the moment the scent of stuffed cabbage and meatballs reached his nostrils. "Thank you, Savta."

She placed the plate on his desk along with a set of disposable cutlery, sat down, and watched him eat.

"We moved into an abandoned apartment building after the war," she said, slipping, as she did, into the past.

She meant the War of Independence. Moshe had heard the tale before. He and Irina had visited the two-room apartment on Bostanai Street in Katamon, where Savta and her husband, of blessed memory, both penniless Holocaust survivors at the time of the war, had lived ever since.

"After a while the government notified us that we could register our apartment with the Land Registry. One of the neighbors offered to go to the ministry and fill in the forms on our behalf." She emitted a bitter laugh. "Two weeks later, Edith from the first floor came to me in tears. 'He's demanding rent!' she cried. 'Calm down,' I said. 'He can't do that— it's your apartment.' 'Not anymore,' she said. 'He registered the entire building in his own name!' She was right. The crook had registered all eighteen apartments in his own name." Savta Sarah shook her head at the man's chutzpah.

"The clerk at the ministry was no help at all. 'Sorry,' she said. 'There's nothing we can do.' *Nothing we can do?* Ha! I found out who her boss was. I went home. I got all dressed up, put on my makeup. I waited for her lunch break and then I walked right into her manager's office and sat down."

She crossed her legs, placed her hands on her knees, and spoke with her nose high in the air, reliving the moment. "'Mr. Kramer,' I said. 'You are a fine gentleman. Surely you can help our neighbors, all of them poor and honest citizens.' He said no. He said that the crook had done nothing illegal, and there was nothing more he could do. '*Mister* Kramer,' I said. 'You *can* and you *will*. I'm not leaving your office until you have corrected this injustice. And what's more, I intend to have a word with Mrs. Kramer and I'm sure she will have an opinion about what you can and cannot do.' I didn't know

Mrs. Kramer—but I would have found her. In the end, I didn't need to. Within a half hour, Mr. Kramer had set the paperwork aright. And that crook, well," she grinned, "he fled Jerusalem and never came back."

She chuckled at her own tenacity, then looked Moshe squarely in the eyes.

"If there's one thing I've learned, Moshe dear, it's that there is always something you can do. You just need the balls to do it."

With that, she got to her feet and strolled out of the office.

Moshe chewed his stuffed cabbage in silence. As always, Savta had a good point. But how did one take on the government?

He got to his feet, abandoning his meal, walked out of his office, and leaned on the divider wall of Shmuel's cubicle.

"How many members do we have?"

Shmuel looked up from his computer screen. "Several hundred. Maybe a thousand."

"That will have to do."

A sly smile curled Shmuel's mouth. "Why? What are you planning?"

"We're going to war."

"With the government? How?"

"By hitting them where it hurts most."

CHAPTER 10

Ahmed had expected rivers of honey and wine, a private palace, and a seat of honor at the Heavenly banquet. After all, he had bought a ticket to Paradise. But when he had awoken in the Mount of Olives Cemetery, a gray-haired Russian called Boris had shipped him off to Hell. The angels had made a huge mistake but today Ahmed would correct that error.

He piled gray bricks onto a wheelbarrow and wiped his brow. The damned souls around him got about their tasks. Dark skinned and light. Round eyed and squinted. He was not like them. He didn't belong here. But every day he climbed the scaffolding with them, delivering bricks and mortar. He didn't speak much. He didn't step out of line. He had seen what happened to those who did.

A tall Nigerian had argued with the foreman on Ahmed's first day in the afterlife. When the muscular African had thrown down his hard hat and strutted off the construction site, a large demon in a gray suit had followed him. The Rottweiler, as the others called him behind his back, had arms as thick as trees and a neck to match. Two minutes later, the Rottweiler had returned, dragging the Nigerian by the scruff of his neck, and dumped him on the ground in a pile of pain. The other workers had strapped a stick to his broken arm and returned to their tasks.

Ahmed did not belong in Hell. Hasan had promised him Paradise. Paradise and forgiveness. Ahmed's mother had made him share his room with his cousin from Ramallah, who had visited for a few days. *He'll be a good influence, make a man of you.* She was always saying that, ever since his father had moved out to live with his new wife five years ago.

But Hasan had discovered the copies of Penthouse inside Ahmed's mattress. A disgrace, Hasan had said, to defile himself with infidel women. A mark of shame on his family name. His father would hate him if he ever found out. There was only one way to cleanse his blemished family honor, only one way to purify his Jew-loving soul.

Ahmed had boarded bus number eighteen, his backpack stuffed with rusty screws and ball bearings dipped in rat poison, and he had pressed the detonator button. The explosion had shredded his sinful flesh and transformed him into a *shaheed*. A palace awaited him, as well as a harem of virgin brides and a seat of honor at the Heavenly feast.

Every morning, a minibus shuttled him from the bleak warehouse to the construction site. The streets through the window resembled the Jerusalem of his earthly life, the way the world of dreams mixed together memories of his waking hours, only this nightmare had lasted two months. Every night, he lay on the camping cot in his tarpaulin cubicle beneath the high tin roof of the warehouse and he prayed. He prayed that tomorrow the angels would correct this terrible mistake. Every morning, he awoke to find his prayers unanswered.

He could bear the injustice no longer. He wheeled the barrow of bricks onto the wooden plank over a clump of steps, then made for the one they called Damas, a coal-skinned demon taskmaster. Ahmed laid the wheelbarrow at his feet, brushed dirt and dust from his calloused hands, and cleared his throat.

"What?" the taskmaster said, aiming his constant scowl at Ahmed. The yellow hard hat made his skin look even darker.

"Sir," he said, in Hebrew. "There's been a mistake."

"Spit it out!"

Two Romanian workers glanced their way and Ahmed tried to ignore them. "I'm not supposed to be here," he said, speaking as softly as possible. "I was supposed to go to Paradise."

Damas glared at him for two seconds "Paradise?" he said. "Who told you that?"

Ahmed felt the press of eyeballs around him. *Let them stare. I am a* shaheed. *I am above them all.* "My cousin Hasan promised me that if I—"

"Let me guess," Damas interrupted, "that if you killed some Jews you'd get seventy virgins?" He pulled out a worn notepad from his shirt pocket and turned the pages.

Ahmed's heart did a double-flip. *Yes!* Damas, for all his scaly ways, had to answer to the angels. He'd set things right. Ahmed should have spoken up long ago.

"Let me see," Damas said, scanning the notepad. "What is your name—Ahmed?"

"Yes, I am Ahmed!"

Damas frowned. "There is no Ahmed here," he said. "But I have a Stupid. Is your name Stupid?"

The taskmaster glared at him while Ahmed tried to make sense of the question. Then the Ethiopian burst out laughing. Others laughed around him too. Hot blood rose in Ahmed's cheeks. The souls of migrants and vagabonds, lowly scum and infidels, they all laughed at the *shaheed* in their midst!

Damas recovered from his fit of laughter and clapped him on the back. "Let me tell you about promises," he said, with sudden solemnity. "When I was a little boy in Ethiopia, the wise men promised us a Jerusalem of Gold. I left the village with some older boys and we started our holy journey on foot. We walked through war and poverty, thieves and slavers. Twelve of us set out; only two survived to see the glorious State of Israel. And what did we find here? A hero's welcome? A Jerusalem piled high with gold? A life of honor and luxury?" He spat on the ground. "A Jerusalem of trash and cat piss, of street sweepers and janitors, of people who treated me like crap and told me how they had saved me from the jungle."

He scowled at the gathering crowd. "What are you all looking at? Back to work!" The men scuttled away.

"Did you see that?" he told Ahmed. "I found my promised land. I earned it the hard way." He held up his hand. Two of his fingers ended in swollen stumps. "Now I tell them what to do and nobody messes with me."

He gripped Ahmed by the shoulders. "Take it from me, Stupid. Don't believe their promises. There is no Paradise, only Hell."

CHAPTER 11

Alex Altman spotted his target at the Delek gas station on the corner of Pat and Golomb.

The thirty-something in brown chinos, a button-down shirt, and a blue crocheted *kippah* leaned against the side of the blue Ford Focus. *Fresh meat.* The car, eight years old but in good shape, matched the photo from the ad that the owner had posted on Yad2, a website for secondhand vehicles.

Let the show begin.

"David?" Alex said.

David looked up and turned a paler shade of white. People reacted that way to the ponytail, the earring, and the large biceps covered in Russian tattoos, the badges of honor Alex had acquired in multiple Soviet penitentiaries. They told law-abiding citizens not to mess with him. Alex always chose a public meeting place for his magic shows to give the target a false sense of security.

David swallowed hard. "Shalom," he said. Hello. He had a British accent, and had probably bought the car brand new using the tax break for new immigrants.

Alex circled the car. He ran his fingers over the fresh rubber feelers on the tires and the line of chipped paint on the back bumper. New treads and minor scratches. Nothing serious.

"Accidents?" he asked.

"None."

"Keys."

"Inside."

Alex climbed into the driver's seat.

"Code?"

David told him and Alex punched the numbers into the immobilizer keypad. The car started quietly. Eighty thousand kilometers on the odometer. The tachometer gauge hovered at a thousand revolutions per minute and didn't waver. No engine issues either.

Alex closed the door. "Get in."

David hurried around the car to the passenger seat and strapped on the belt.

It's showtime!

Alex stepped on the accelerator, launching the car onto Golomb toward the City Center and pressing David back in his seat. The gears changed smoothly, with no audible grinding.

Magic is five percent distraction and ninety-five percent preparation, and Alex had done his homework.

He pressed his foot to the floor, flying past the speed limit. "How much?"

David clung to the edge of his seat as the car sped down the thoroughfare. "Eighteen thousand," he said.

David had done his homework too. Eighteen thousand was the Levi Yitzchak list price for the car. A fair price, but a poor first offer. David was not much of a bargainer.

Alex weaved between cars. *Make that ten percent distraction.*

"I'll give you nine," he said.

David didn't laugh. He didn't tell Alex to stop the car and take a hike. In fact, he probably felt grateful for the offer, because, like all good magicians, Alex had pre-selected his target from the crowd.

Yesterday, within minutes of posting the ad online, David had received five phone calls. Each potential buyer had offered five thousand shekels "and not an agora more."

Compared to those offers, Alex sounded generous. Alex knew this, because all five callers–including the older man and the woman with the sexy voice—were his stage assistants.

"According to the pricelist—" David began but Alex cut him short with a laugh.

"Forget that. Nobody pays the list price."

He gunned up Gaza Road. By this point, most sellers just wanted to flee the car before Alex crashed the vehicle into a pole, but David said nothing. Brave guy.

A part of Alex pitied him. This David hadn't done him any harm. But as far as magic tricks went, David would get off lightly. Over the years, Alex had performed many feats of magic on behalf of the Organization, and some still haunted his dreams.

Alex swung a right onto Keren Hayesod. Time to close the deal, and David needed a little extra push. Alex knew what made people tick. These Anglo immigrants always felt that they were being screwed over by the locals. Nine times out of ten they were right, but things would go a lot smoother if Alex let him feel that he'd won the bargaining game.

"Nine thousand and two hundred shekels," Alex said. "Final offer."

David exhaled a deep breath. "*B'seder.*" OK.

Alex pulled up outside the post office on Emek Refaim, and extracted a wad of two-hundred-shekel notes from his pocket. David's eyes widened as Alex counted out the bills, but he didn't ask any questions. He could guess what sort of person walks around with that amount of cash.

"Registration," Alex said.

David opened the glove compartment and fished out the certificate.

Alex pulled a piece of paper from his back pocket. "Sign here." The document appointed Alex as power of attorney regarding the sale of the car. "And write down the code too. Good." He dumped the cash in David's hand. "I'll take care of the transfer of ownership. Don't let me keep you."

The Brit took the hint and almost strangled himself on the seatbelt strap in his rush to get out of the car.

Alex kept the motor running and turned up the air conditioning. He did not get out of the car or enter the post office. He glanced at his wrist watch. There was no need to rush. Yesterday he had posted an ad of his own on Yad2 and arranged to meet an eager buyer at this very spot in another ten minutes. Within the space of a half hour, Alex's street magic would have earned him ten thousand shekels, without ever having the car registered in his name. *Now you see it, now you don't.*

His phone rang.

He knew the caller's number by heart, although he wasn't careless enough to add the number to his list of contacts. That number meant trouble.

He answered but did not say hello.

"I have a job for you," said the deep voice on the phone.

A jar of acid shattered in Alex's gut. The last job Mandrake had assigned him had almost broken him.

"I already have a job, remember?"

"I know, my friend. But this job requires… your special brand of magic."

Refusal was not an option.

Alex said, "I'm on my way."

CHAPTER 12

At 6 AM on Wednesday, Moshe broke the law. From the sidewalk of Kaplan Street, the Knesset building peeked above the bushes like a broad, flat fortress, and Moshe had prepared for a long siege.

Dry Bones Society volunteers offloaded equipment from two minivans: placards, fliers, empty packing crates, folding tables, and a large supply of bottled water. Irina and Samira climbed ladders and tied a large banner to the perimeter fence, while Shmuel oversaw the construction of a makeshift platform. The banner read, "LET US LIVE!" and volunteers handed out black shirts emblazoned with the words, "I AM ALIVE TOO."

Moshe had asked Galit, Rabbi Yosef, and Rafi—anyone with a valid identity card and something to lose—to stay away. Savta Sarah had put up a fight. "An army marches on its stomach," she had said. Moshe had accepted her food but refused to put her in harm's way or to involve any of them in the illegal demonstration.

The police had given him no choice. He had filled in the Urgent Protest Application form on the Israel Police website, only to receive a call an hour later notifying him that his request had been denied because his identity number belonged to a dead man.

By the time the first vehicles arrived, the picket line had formed along the sidewalk. Their signs read, "EQUAL RIGHTS FOR ALL" and "OUR BLOOD IS ON YOUR HANDS." Shmuel led the chant on a megaphone. *Ha'am. Doresh. Zedek chevrati!* The People. Demand. Social justice!

Soon, the picket line extended around the street corner.

"How many do we have so far?" Moshe asked Irina. She was handing out fliers.

"I don't know," she said, "but we just ran out of shirts."

"How many did we print?"

"Five hundred."

Moshe whistled. The turnout was better than he had expected. By the time the television vans arrived, the line had become a throng of demonstrators that choked the sidewalk. Then the luxury cars with tinted windows finally trickled in— members of parliament getting a late start to the day. The masses of angry, disenfranchised men and women overflowed into the street and surged around the vehicles. The drivers, with dark glasses and earpieces, honked their horns and crawled toward the safety of the Knesset compound.

Shmuel handed Moshe the megaphone. "It's time," he said.

Moshe nodded and climbed the wobbly platform of packing crates, those butterflies flapping madly in his belly. A pre-recorded address was one thing; speaking at an illegal demonstration before rolling cameras was quite another.

He glanced at his audience and the air fled from his lungs. "Dear God," he gasped. The roads and sidewalks were a sea of people as far as the eye could see. Thousands had answered his call—were there even that many resurrected Israelis? Their chants settled to an expectant murmur as they waited to hear his voice.

"Welcome, friends." His voice sounded deeper than usual on the megaphone and his words echoed off the crowded hills. "Thank you for joining us here today." Cheers spread across the swells of humanity. He waited for silence. "We have gathered here today not to disturb the peace, but because we have no other choice. Many of us here today have been blessed with a second chance at life. We want to be a part of society again. To work. To build. To live with dignity."

Another cheer rose in the mass of supporters. "LIVE WITH DIGNITY," they chanted. Moshe's pulse quickened but the inner butterflies fell into formation. The thrill of the crowd had an intoxicating effect that focused his attention. He was no longer nervous. When he raised his hand for silence, the crowd obeyed. It was time to get to the point.

"But the current government," he continued, "has rejected us." The people booed. "They tie our hands with red tape. Well, my friends, they can't hold us back any longer." A cheer. "We demand—"

The wail of a police siren interrupted his speech. A large black van with the police emblem—a Star of David within a laurel wreath—on the hood, waded through the crowd toward the platform and then blared its foghorn. A uniformed officer wearing a large shiny police hat stood through an opening in the roof. "Mr. Karlin," the man roared into a megaphone. "This gathering is illegal. Disperse at once."

Angry voices erupted in the crowd. A school of dark uniforms swam through the demonstrators toward him. He had a few seconds before they reached the platform.

"We will disperse," Moshe said. "Once the Minister of the Interior fulfills his promise and recognizes us as legal citizens with all the rights and—"

The siren wailed again. "Mr. Karlin, you are not above the law. Disperse your people at once."

A thousand trusting faces looked to him. They had answered his call. They had kept his terms of non-violence and zero damage to property. The least he could do was stand up for them.

"You're right," Moshe said into the megaphone. "We're not above the law. We're *below* the law. You deny us our right to demonstrate and exclude us from society, and so you have no right to silence us or—"

He did not finish the sentence. Iron hands gripped his legs. His feet slipped from beneath him and the megaphone flew from his hands. He landed hard on the asphalt. Four uniforms pinned him to the ground as he struggled.

"Let me go!"

A sweaty officer snarled over him. "Resisting arrest, are you?"

Then he slammed his baton down on Moshe's face.

CHAPTER 13

Boris waited in the parked van outside the Karlin residence on Shimshon Street and considered his future. The boss had called in an outsider to infiltrate the Dry Bones Society, a task that Boris should have handled himself. A wise man would prove his worth while he could still draw breath.

The sound of munching from the passenger seat grated on his nerves.

"Didn't your mother teach you to chew with your mouth closed?"

Igor stuffed a handful of puffed maize into his mouth from a jumbo bag of Bamba. The other men called him the Rottweiler, and now his dog breath stank of peanuts.

He grunted. "Never knew her."

That figured. The collapse of the Soviet Union had unleashed hordes of motherless ex-army thugs on the world, many of whom had found a new home in the Organization.

A white Kia Sportage pulled up outside the Karlin home and a dishy woman with dark hair got out. She unlocked the door of the house and stepped inside without even looking their way. Mrs. Karlin had returned home, and Moshe Karlin now had something to lose. Family and friends were weaknesses and Boris had taken care to accumulate neither.

Not even Igor. In the five years since the Organization

had assigned Igor to him, this was the first time Boris had inquired about his childhood. The thug had muscle for brains but caused no trouble if you kept him well supplied with Bamba to munch and bones to break. The less you knew, the less you cared; the less you cared, the longer you lived in this business, and Boris planned to live to a ripe old age.

He caught glimpses of the woman as she moved through the house. In the kitchen, she took a mug from a shelf and poured a cup of coffee.

Igor crumpled the empty bag of Bamba, tossed it out the window, and slapped peanut flakes from his hands. "Want me to get her?"

Boris shook his head. "First we watch and learn. Then, when the time is right—"

A movement on the sidewalk cut his words short. A hedge between the houses shook. Then a head appeared above the hedge and peered over the leaves. The head had a messy mop of oily hair and a face dark with stubble. The man dashed around the hedge in a rumpled shirt and dirt-stained jeans, and scuttled toward the Karlin home, his back bent in an exaggerated and failed attempt at stealth. The tramp pressed his back to the wall and stole a quick peek through the kitchen window.

"Well, well, well," Boris said. "It seems that Mrs. Karlin has a secret admirer."

CHAPTER 14

Avi Segal brushed off his jeans and sucked in a deep breath. *You can do this.* He hadn't spoken to Galit since she had stood him up under the *chuppah* two months ago.

The love of his life had left him for a zombie. That had hurt, and in a fit of rage he had sworn that he would never have anything to do with the Karlins again. But Galit had never left his thoughts. Not for a moment.

He shifted from one foot to the other on the threshold of the Karlin home. The house had been his home until Moshe had returned from the grave and stolen Galit from him a second time. This was all Moshe's fault, but now Avi would take back what was his.

He pressed the buzzer. High heels clacked in the entrance hall and the door opened.

Her welcoming smile faded when she laid eyes on him. "You have a lot of nerve, showing up here."

Avi needed to talk fast. He didn't ask for permission to enter. Inside she might throw dishes at him and her aim had improved.

"I love you, Galit. I need you. Don't tell me you don't feel the same."

"You have got to be kidding me."

"Moshe did this to us. Can't you see? He's vile. Unnatural.

He should be six feet under. How can you live under the same roof as him?"

She gave a derisive laugh. "No, Avi. You did this. With your lies." Her eyes glanced at his clothing, and derision turned into revulsion. "What's happened to you?"

Yes! Sympathy. Make her feel sorry for you.

"My parents threw me out," he said. He had slept on their living room couch through the summer, but they had turned him out when he had failed to find a job.

"Get off your lazy bum," his mother had said. "We put half our savings into that wedding, and even that went down the drain." He had run out of credit there.

"Last night," Avi told Galit, "I slept on a bench in Gan Sacher."

Pity flickered in her eyes for a moment before they hardened. "Good," she said. "You deserve worse. Is that why you're here—to leech off us again?"

The word "us" pierced his gut like a dagger, but the truth was he had nowhere left to go.

She made to close the door.

"Wait. Listen, I made mistakes, I know. Please, give me another chance."

"You're crazy. You should never have come here. I don't want to see you again. Ever."

As the door swung shut, Avi blurted, "I'll tell him!"

The door cracked open and Galit shot him a frightened look. "Tell him what?" she said but she knew only too well.

He had not meant to threaten her but she had given him no choice.

"He still doesn't remember how he died," Avi said. "I'll tell him."

Galit took a step back. "You wouldn't dare."

Avi stuck out his chest. The balance of power had shifted in his favor. "I don't want to but I will if that's what it takes. What will he think of you then?"

He had her now. A few words to Moshe, and he'd never want to see her again. Avi would do it to get her back, to save her from herself.

She lifted her nose in the air. "Then you're a liar *and* an idiot," she said, tears distorting her voice, "if you think that threats will make me take you back."

She slammed the door.

"You're making a big mistake, Galit!" he yelled. "Galit, please!"

Crap! He had blown it. What was he thinking? He pulled at his hair. Now she feared him *and* hated his guts. He had lost her for good.

This was all Moshe's fault. If not for Moshe, she wouldn't feel this way.

Avi slunk away from the house and crossed the street. He needed to find something to eat and a place to sleep tonight. More than that, he needed a plan to turn his life around.

He didn't dwell on it for long. As he walked past a parked brown van, a sliding door opened, two large hands pulled him inside, and the door slid shut.

CHAPTER 15

Boris turned on the ceiling light of the van. Igor had cleared the interior of seats, covered the floor in plastic sheeting, and tinted the windows black, adapting the vehicle for the smuggling of goods and, presently, the interrogation of captives.

From the low bench at the back, Boris sized up the tramp. The man kicked and flailed in Igor's cement lock. Igor grunted and wrinkled his nose. Boris smelled it too. Their visitor hadn't showered in days. *Let's cut to the chase.*

"What do you want with Moshe Karlin?" he asked.

"None of your business."

Boris glanced at Igor, who straightened his arms, pressing the man's neck forward and wrenching his shoulder blades back, until the man cried out.

"I'll decide what's my business or not. Is Karlin a friend of yours?"

"No," the tramp said. "I hate his filthy guts."

"Then why are you at his house?"

"Galit," he said. "His wife. She was mine. Until Moshe came back from the dead."

Galit. Mrs. Karlin now had a name and Boris had stumbled upon a love triangle. How touching.

The tramp hung limp in the strongman's grip. "He used to be my best friend," he continued, suddenly eager to talk. "But he took everything from me."

Boris knew an opportunity when he saw one. "Tell me all you know about the Karlins," he said.

"Why should I?"

The tramp had a short memory, but Boris decided to humor him. "Do you want to destroy Moshe Karlin?"

The tramp looked up at him and his face contracted with loathing. "More than anything."

"Then," Boris said, "it seems we have something in common."

CHAPTER 16

"Hello," Moshe called through the steel bars of the holding cell. Down the corridor and out of sight, police boots clicked over the grimy square floor tiles.

An hour ago, he had woken up on the coarse blanket of a low metal cot. The only other furnishing, a metal shelf, hung from a chain on the wall. His calls for attention had received no response.

With the swing of a baton, he had lost his hard-won liberty. His possessions too. The officers had emptied his pockets of his keys, his phone, and his pocket pack of tissues. He had never felt so helpless. Even Boris's forced labor camp had provided at least the illusion of freedom. In this bleak detention cell, a man could rot.

Late afternoon light seeped through the small barred window high on the wall of the corridor. Only a few hours had passed since his brutal arrest outside the Knesset compound. Unless he had lain there unconscious for a whole day. Or days? Did Galit know of his arrest? Had she tried to reach him? She must be worried sick. He had to call her, but his jailers had not answered his cries, never mind offered him a phone call.

Footfalls echoed down the corridor and grew louder. A policewoman came into view. Finally!

"Officer," Moshe said. "Excuse me."

She waddled along and passed his cell without even glancing his way.

"Please, ma'am. I need to call my wife."

Her back disappeared down the corridor.

How long were they going to hold him? Was he going to meet with an attorney? What was the punishment for arranging an illegal public gathering? Surely he had the right to a fair trial. Or did the deceased have no civil rights? Without rights, law enforcement was just one more violent gang out to get him.

He sat down on the hard cot and tried to be patient. He massaged the tender swelling where the baton had connected with his skull. His stomach growled. They'd have to feed him eventually. They couldn't just let him starve, could they?

The demonstration had drawn the attention of the authorities, all right, just not the kind of attention he had intended. He had not expected the road to victory to be short and level, but now he thought of little Talya and her dark curls. He had read her Winnie the Pooh before bed last night. Who would read her a bedtime story tonight? Was Galit wondering why he hadn't come home? He had only just won his way back into their lives. Was he willing to lose them again?

Regulation boots clicked on the tiles again, and this time the policewoman halted outside his cell. Moshe looked up. Dinner time already? She was not holding a tray of food.

He stood up and decided to say nothing. *Stay calm. Be polite.* The change of tactic seemed to work, for the policewoman jingled a chain of keys in her hand.

"Somebody likes you," she said.

She unlocked the gate of the cell and led him down the corridor. A heavy door of thick bars clicked open as they drew near. Did he have a visitor? Would they tell him to change into a prison uniform, then lead him to a long row of booths, where Galit would stare at him through reinforced glass while he spoke to her using a telephone receiver? Moshe had seen that in a movie.

There was no orange uniform or meeting hall at the end of the long corridor, only a counter and another officer, who handed him a manila envelope that contained his keys, phone, and tissues. They were releasing him. His shoulders relaxed and he inhaled the sweet, clear scent of approaching freedom.

Galit was waiting for him in a reception hall, clutching her handbag. She ran to him, and her embrace had never felt so good.

"I came here as soon as I heard," she said. "They wouldn't tell me anything."

Moshe glanced about the room and recognized the foyer of the Talpiot police station. He had accompanied Irina there in a failed attempt to figure out her identity. The same two receptionists with dark ponytails sat behind the reception desk, but they didn't seem to notice him. Moshe didn't mind—he had enjoyed enough police attention for one day.

"Let's get out of here."

Galit had parked her Kia Sportage on the street and she drove him home.

"How much was bail?"

"Nothing," she said.

That sounded suspicious. "Aren't they going to charge me with anything?"

She shrugged. "They didn't say anything. I didn't even know you were being released."

Gears changed softly within the vehicle as other gears turned in Moshe's mind. Had his lack of a valid identity card aided in his release? Had his continued incarceration required too much paperwork? *Somebody likes you*, the policewoman had said. What did it matter? He was free.

"The others," he said. "Were they arrested too?"

"Only you, as far as I know. I saw it on TV. I saw them jump on you."

They had made the news. Excellent.

A tear trickled down her cheek. "I couldn't reach you on your phone."

"It's over now," he said. "We live in a liberal democracy.

They can't just lock people up indefinitely." Behind bars he
had felt less certain of that.

"I thought I had lost you again."

"You won't. I won't let that happen."

"Promise me."

His arrest had distressed her harder than he had expected.
He had gotten off lightly this time. Next time, he might not
be so lucky. He'd have to make sure there would not be a
next time. His career of civil disobedience would have to end.

"I promise," he said.

Back home, Moshe hugged Talya and paid the babysitter.
At least his little girl knew nothing of his short incarceration.
He turned on the TV and switched channels. The news
broadcasts didn't mention the demonstration.

"I don't get it," he told Shmuel on the phone. "We should
have gotten more coverage."

Shmuel seemed frustrated too. "I asked Eran. The editors
didn't think we're newsworthy. A load of crap, if you ask me.
Larger powers are at work here and they're burying our story."

"Or," Moshe added, "maybe they're right and people just
don't care about us."

"Ten thousand people cared this morning."

"Ten thousand?"

"That's Eran's estimate. They can't all have been Society
members. And donations at the office have tripled."

"We'll need more than money to change the system."

"What other option do we have—declare an independent
state?"

The conversation stuck with Moshe during dinner. After a
mass demonstration, all they could show for their efforts
were a few hours of jail time and a spike in contributions.
Moshe was not about to start a civil war. Without new ideas,
Moshe and his fellow resurrected would remain in social
limbo for the rest of their second lives.

"Moshe?" Galit called his name for the second time. He
had spaced out at the dinner table. Talya sent him concerned

glances and, ever since their reunion at the station, Galit had eyed him as though he was in danger of collapse.

"Sorry," he said. He forced a smile for Talya's sake. *You've worried them enough.* "Just thinking about work."

"The Dry Bones?" Talya said, and giggled.

He patted her curls. "And getting drier every day."

Moshe had set up a non-profit and the cash was flowing, but he couldn't draw a salary or apply for a marriage certificate. He couldn't lead a normal life.

It's not personal, the minister had said. *It's politics.*

The buzzer sounded.

"Don't answer that!" Galit said, her eyes wide.

"It's OK, Galit. I'm sure they won't arrest me twice in one day."

Moshe wiped his mouth on a napkin and went to the door. Unless, he added to himself, Shmuel was right and larger forces were at work. Was that how the government wore down opponents, by interrupting their dinner and dragging them back to the cells?

The man in the peephole wore, not a police uniform, but a dark suit, with dark glasses and an earpiece. Moshe's skin tingled. Had Minister Malkior sent undercover agents this time? Secret Service? Moshe's little peaceful demonstration had opened a Pandora's box of enemies.

Moshe swallowed hard, stood tall, and turned the handle.

"Moshe Karlin?" said Dark Glasses.

"Yes."

Dark Glasses walked right in, followed by two of his clones. They spread out in the hallway and scanned the interior of the home.

The leader spoke into his sleeve. "Clear."

Then a third man in an expensive suit rolled into the room like a well-preened, middle-aged penguin. A penguin with a greasy comb-over. He needed no introduction. His smug grin, familiar to Moshe from the Channel Two news and the front pages of Israel Today, belonged to the most notorious career politician in Israel.

Isaac Gurion gave Moshe's hand a meaty double-handed squeeze. "Moshe Karlin," he said. "We meet at last."

CHAPTER 17

Moshe and Isaac Gurion sat on his living room couch like old friends, while the Secret Service guards kept watch and Galit led Talya upstairs to bed.

"I sympathize with your struggle," Isaac Gurion said, his face a picture of great torment. "The difficulties you and your kind have experienced are as many as they are unbearable. This business with the Minister of the Interior is unacceptable. You deserve to live and work with honor as equal citizens."

Moshe wanted to rub his eyes and pinch his leg. This was exactly the kind of attention he had hoped for. But the savvy politician obviously had an agenda of his own.

"What do you have in mind?"

"You need friends in the right places. Friends with power. The power, for instance," and he shot Moshe a mischievous grin, "to release a friend from wrongful imprisonment."

So Gurion was behind Moshe's mysterious release, and now Moshe owed him. Every favor would require payback.

"Friends like you?"

"Exactly."

"And what do you want in return?"

Gurion seemed both surprised and insulted by the question. "Your friendship, of course." He sighed and raised his hands to the heavens, a humble man set upon by insurmountable difficulties. "Elections are in a month and we'll need all the friends we can find to ensure that our new party, Upward, can finally fix our country's problems. Judging by your event this morning, you have a lot of friends. Fifteen thousand, by the police's estimate."

Fifteen thousand! Shmuel's count had been far off.

"And," Gurion continued, "according to what I hear, you make new friends every day. How many new asylum seekers arrive each week?"

"Asylum seekers?" Had Gurion confused the Dry Bones Society with another social cause?

Gurion's eyes sparkled and he swiped his hand in the air as though reading words off an invisible campaign banner. "*Refugees from Death*. We'll need some way to refer to your Society members. So tell me, what is your growth rate?"

Moshe swallowed hard. Rabbi Yosef was closer than he to the numbers on the ground, but he would be wise not to understate the size of their unique demographic. "More each day," he said. "I don't have the exact figures, but our growth is exponential."

"*Exponential?*" Gurion licked his lips. "Well, good friends should stand together. We'll right the wrongs of society and forge a better world. Together we'll be unstoppable."

"We'll settle for identity cards," Moshe said. "We don't have any grand plans to change the world. We're not politicians."

"And you won't have to be. You won't have to sit through boring Knesset meetings either if you don't want to. We'll each stick to what we do best. You carry on with your good work and I'll sort out the red tape. What a great partnership. As I said, we'll be unstoppable."

"Unstoppable," Moshe repeated and laughed. After spending the day behind bars, that sounded too good to be true.

Gurion mistook his silence for hesitation. "Think of it, Moshe. Think of all the good you could do."

"Right now I can't even open a bank account."

"So we'll fix that. Our first order of business will be to secure full and automatic citizenship for all asylum seekers."

Moshe felt as though he had just won the lottery and wanted to jump on the couch like a lunatic. *Don't appear too eager.* "I'll need to consult with my colleagues."

"Of course, please do. But I'll need an answer by tomorrow evening," Gurion said, getting up. "Elections are around the corner."

CHAPTER 18

Ahmed returned to the Devil's warehouse that evening, his mind bubbling over with doubt. Groups of sweaty workers swarmed beneath the fluorescents of the warehouse, rushing to eat and shower before lights out.

Don't believe their promises, Damas had said. *There is no Paradise, only Hell.*

The demon taskmaster's words would not let go. Had Hasan lied to him? Had he known that Ahmed's mission would lead to eternal damnation, not unending bliss? No. That couldn't be true. Hasan had assisted many others on the path to *istishhad.* And why would he knowingly send his cousin to a world of suffering?

He pushed through the flap of his tarpaulin cubicle, retrieved his tin mug from beneath the cot, and joined the long line for dinner.

The demon had lied. Ahmed deserved this fate. He had not believed with a whole heart. Even as he pressed the detonator button, he had not truly expected to wake up in Paradise. He had wanted to save his family from shame and for his father to think kindly of him. Paradise existed but it belonged to martyrs of pure mind and clean hands.

Yet Hasan had known that his cousin was no saint. He had promised Ahmed that the mission would purge him of his sins.

The bald cook ladled thick soup into Ahmed's mug. The sludge smelled of lentils and too much pepper. Ahmed blew into the mug to cool the soup on the way back to his tent, then halted. Beside an open cubicle, a man knelt on a towel, his feet bare, his bearded face and stained turban pressed to the ground.

Do my eyes deceive me?

Ahmed drew near and waited for the righteous man to finish his prayers.

"Sir," Ahmed said. "How has a righteous man come to be here?"

The man turned tired eyes to his questioner. "What do you mean, my son?"

Ahmed drew closer and whispered, "In this Hell. I thought I was the only believer among these damned souls."

A bemused smile crept over the man's lips. "This is not the Purgatory of *Barzakh*," he said, and he stroked his beard. "Although our lot is not much better." The man's Arabic had a foreign edge, but he seemed to know what he was talking about.

"Then where are we?"

"Talpiot, Jerusalem."

"Jerusalem? We're not dead?"

The smile fled and patience leaked from the man's voice. "No, we are not dead. Not yet." He rolled up his towel and tucked it under his arm. "The lights go out soon," he muttered and trudged off. "I have no time for fools."

Ahmed froze to the spot. Sweaty laborers streamed around him. The streets had seemed familiar because they were. He had died, that much was clear. He had awoken in neither Heaven nor Hell, but in the Jerusalem of his first life.

"Lights out in ten minutes," Damas roared from the railing at the far end of the warehouse.

Ahmed snapped out of his trance and raced for his tent. He gulped down his soup and ran for the shower line.

He had just crawled beneath the rough blanket of his cot

bed when the large fluorescents clicked out. His heart thumped like a drum. He was not in Hell; he was home.

Outside the flaps of his cubicle, the footfalls died down, replaced by the creak of bedsprings and then a chorus of snores. Ahmed pulled back his blanket and got out of bed, fully dressed. He padded through the gloom of the warehouse. The corrugated door of the building slid sideways on its track, the squeaking of rusty wheels piercing the silence of the black vault like a siren. He looked over his shoulder, expecting the dark taskmaster to emerge from the shadows. He listened for the heavy steps of the Rottweiler. Seeing and hearing nothing, he stepped outside.

The stars burned overhead in the boundless canopy of heaven. A plastic bag floated in the moonlight on a gentle summer breeze. Distant cars hummed along hidden streets. Ahmed was alive and his future lay out there.

He slid the door shut behind him and slipped into the night.

CHAPTER 19

"I have a confession to make," said the young man in the black T-shirt. He had introduced himself as Ben to the circle of new members at the Absorption Center of the Dry Bones Society on Thursday morning.

Yosef stifled a yawn. He wanted to listen with empathy. Each new member of the Society had a life story in need of sharing and a soul in need of healing, but the events of the last few days had kept him awake at night. He too felt the need for confession.

Ben continued. "I'm not dead. I mean, I haven't died yet. Not physically, anyway."

He told of a childhood of delinquency and drugs, of running away from home and life on the streets.

"When I heard about your program—about starting anew each day—I thought I'd give it a try."

Yosef nodded. The confusion of his own early years was reflected in Ben's story. Over the last few days, that confusion had returned in full force.

Yosef had partnered with Rev. Adams and cashed his generous check while, at the Ministry of the Interior, Moshe had struggled against Rabbi Emden, Yosef's former mentor and guiding light. The next day, Moshe had spent the morning in jail. Yosef could ignore the cognitive dissonance no longer.

Was he still on the right side—the side of justice, of God?

The meeting concluded with the singing of "*HaTikva*"—the national anthem—and Rabbi Nachman's "Narrow Bridge," and the new arrivals dispersed to the dining hall for breakfast.

Yosef collected the song sheets and leaned against the doorjamb, staring at the empty circle of plastic chairs.

Sitrah Achrah. The Great Council's verdict rang louder in his ears each day. Had he succumbed to charms of the unholy Other Side?

A hand touched his shoulder and he jumped. "Sorry, Rabbi," Moshe said. "I didn't mean to startle you. Can you join us?"

"Of course."

The Society's informal cabinet waited in Moshe's corner office: Moshe, Shmuel, Rafi, and Irina. Savta Sarah was busy ladling porridge and frying eggs in the dining hall.

Moshe closed the door and leaned against his desk. "Isaac Gurion came to our house last night."

He told them of the politician's offer.

"That's just what we wanted," Irina said.

"More than we wanted," Moshe said. "If they do well in the elections, which seems very likely, we'll get seats in Knesset."

Shmuel folded his arms over his chest. "How many seats?"

"I don't know."

"Did he mention any ministerial portfolios?"

"No, but he seemed open to negotiation. I suppose we could push for the Ministry of Interior."

"Ha!" Irina said. "Malkior will regret double-crossing us."

"This goes beyond identity cards," Moshe said. "We could make a real difference and not just for ourselves—for the whole country."

They exchanged ecstatic glances, in disbelief at their sudden good fortune. The intoxicating scent of new possibilities wafted in the air. Perhaps Yosef had been right to throw in his lot with the Dry Bones Society after all.

"Rabbi Yosef," Moshe said. "When I first came back, you said that the Resurrection was one of many prophecies about a future world of peace and justice."

All eyes in the room turned to Yosef and the blood drained from his cheeks. "The Messianic Era," he said. "When the Messiah King, son of David, will arrive."

Shmuel guffawed. "Messiah King," he said. "The days of hereditary kings are long gone."

"You're right," Moshe said. He turned back to Yosef. "But putting the monarchy aside, what else does tradition say about that time?"

Yosef racked his memory. The midrash had made some pretty extravagant claims about the Future To Come.

"There will come a time of plenty and wonder," he said. "The knowledge of God will cover the earth as the water covers the sea. God will rebuild Jerusalem and pave her streets with diamonds and rubies. He will bring an end to death, and the righteous will feast together beneath a great canopy made from the skin of the Leviathan."

"The Leviathan?" Irina said.

Yosef swallowed. "A giant sea creature, like the fish that swallowed Jonah."

A roomful of eyes glazed over in the awkward silence.

Moshe cleared his throat. "Rabbi Yosef, are there any other opinions among the rabbis—something a bit more, ah, mundane?" Moshe had become familiar with the nature of the rabbinic thought. Few principles were free of vigorous debate.

"There's Maimonides," Yosef said. "According to him, the Messianic Era will involve neither miracles nor wonders, and only one thing will change: the nations of the world will no longer subjugate the Jews, who will be free to serve God and study His Law without distraction."

"Sounds like the Israel Defense Forces to me," said Irina. "And freedom of religion."

"Yes," Yosef said. "But Maimonides agrees that the Messiah will rebuild the Temple."

The excitement in the room cooled considerably.

"The Temple?" Irina asked.

He swallowed hard. "A great synagogue on the Temple Mount. But with, um, sacrifices."

She wrinkled her nose. "*Animal* sacrifices?"

"Um, yes," Yosef said. The idea of slaughtering bulls and sheep and sprinkling their blood on an altar made him queasy as well. Solomon's Temple had held more romantic appeal as an abstract, distant symbol. "But according to one opinion," he added quickly, "the Third Temple will involve flour offerings only."

The tension in the room eased.

"Right," Shmuel the cynic said, "all the Messiah has to do is convince the Waqf to hand over the Temple Mount and demolish the Dome of the Rock to make room for a synagogue. Piece of cake."

Moshe shrugged. "Anything else?"

"The Messiah will bring peace to the land. 'The lamb will lie down beside the lion.'"

The heads of those present nodded slowly, a gesture that meant either full agreement or "keep dreaming, pal."

"Well," Moshe said. "The Messiah's got his work cut out for him."

"Isaac Gurion isn't your messiah, Rabbi," Shmuel said. "Have you seen the platform of his new party?"

"I haven't been following the elections," Yosef admitted. From the looks on their faces, that went for the others too.

"His Upward party is playing the anti-religious card. Conscription for the ultra-Orthodox. No more stipends. Hard to see him building a synagogue on the Temple Mount."

Moshe said, "Then the religious parties can't steal him from us, as they did Malkior."

Irina laughed. So did Yosef, although that truth hurt as well. Partnering with evangelical Christians was bad enough; now the Dry Bones Society was joining the list of an anti-religious political party too.

"Messiah or not," Moshe concluded, "he's the only game

in town. Who's in favor?"

Despite his misgivings, Yosef raised his hand and the motion passed unanimously.

"Shmuel, we'll need another press conference. Irina, please handle the logistics. I'll call Gurion. I suppose I'll need to write another speech."

As the team scattered to their tasks, Yosef remained in his seat.

First Rev. Adams, now Moshe. Everyone was asking Yosef about the Messiah.

A messiah is born in every generation, taught the Sages of Blessed Memory. He waits anxiously for the Redemption, when he will reveal his true identity to the world. Yosef could do with his guidance right now.

He had expected the Messiah to be among the sages of the Great Council, but instead of welcoming the resurrection as the first stage of the budding redemption, the council had, quite literally, demonized the resurrected Israelis. But didn't the redeemer always arise in unexpected circumstances? Ruth, King David's ancestor, was a Moabite convert, and Perez, an even earlier forebear, was conceived thanks to the illicit pairing of Judah with Tamar, his former daughter-in-law. Perhaps Christian charities and anti-religious parties were suitable partners in the messianic enterprise after all.

"Yosef, are you OK?"

Moshe glanced at him from behind his desk, his phone at the ready.

"I wish the Messiah would reveal himself already."

Moshe smiled. "He's out there somewhere."

Yosef nodded, and made for the call center. He needed to order more chairs and bunk beds for the dormitories, and to review the new schedules that Samira had prepared for the volunteers on cemetery watch.

He glanced out the window of the call center at the foot traffic on Jaffa Street. *He's out there somewhere.* The thought gave him some comfort. Somewhere in the Holy City, the Hidden Messiah waited with formidable patience. Waited for what exactly—a phone call from Elijah?

Yosef peered at the cubicles of the call center and an idea popped into his mind. If the Messiah was truly out there, Yosef might be able to find him.

CHAPTER 20

Noga pushed through the glass doors of the Frank Sinatra cafeteria at the Hebrew University's Mount Scopus campus, and hoped that she was wrong. Terribly wrong.

In 2002, Arab terrorists detonated a bomb in the crowded cafeteria during summer examination season, killing six women and three men, and injuring a hundred. The materials in Noga's bag were explosive in a different sense, but soon they would shake up the entire Middle East.

She scanned the faces of the students who held trays while they waited in the buffet line, but she found no sign of her lunch date. No surprises there; Noga had arrived ten minutes early.

Finding a quiet spot at the end of the cafeteria, she laid her shoulder bag on the table and watched the younger students. She had come a long way since her lonely campus years. Finally, she had completed her research and found a guy. She loved her life. Contentment fluttered within reach. But the data in her bag threatened to crush that life underfoot.

The doors of the cafeteria opened and a couple of students entered. The guy with messy hair laughed as he spoke to a girl with glasses and shoulder-length curls. They collected trays and got in line.

Acid churned in Noga's stomach and she couldn't think of

food. She had hardly eaten last night during her celebratory dinner with Eli at 1868, a gourmet restaurant on King David Street. She had not told him about the anomaly in her research results. Information could be dangerous in the wrong hands and she did not want to trigger a relapse.

That's why I landed up here, in the hospital, Eli had told her in the secret garden. *To meet you!* The man who had spoken was not the Eli she loved, but the madman she had fled. He had claimed that Noga was part of God's grand plan for the End of Days. Now the data in her bag seemed to support those grandiose claims and Noga did not want to add fuel to that fire.

But how else could she explain the data? Empirical facts didn't lie. She had pored over the results, trying to find her mistake. If she could only convince herself that she was wrong, then her new, perfect life would survive another day.

A woman in a white blouse and practical brown trousers sat down beside her. "Noga, dear." Hannah dropped her satchel on the third seat and reached out her hand.

That was Hannah. Never a kiss or a hug, only the formality bred from years of competing in a male-dominated academia. No makeup either, only cold hard facts and a dab of old perfume.

"I'm starved," Hannah said. "Let's get some food."

"Go ahead. I'll pass."

Hannah shrugged and joined the line. She returned with a tray of spaghetti bolognaise, a bottle of sparkling water, and a plastic saucer of red Jell-O for dessert.

"And the winner is?" she said, and laughed. She sliced her pasta into neat parallel lines like a plowed field, and the sagging skin at her jaw trembled as she gobbled her food. "I remember the day I compiled the results of my doctoral thesis. Those days were different. No emails and attachments, just pages and pages of notes. Calculations by hand. We even did some of the testing on ourselves—don't tell a soul. A drop of this here, a sprinkle of that there. Thank the gods for the lab. And computers!" She shoveled another mouthful of spaghetti. "But I won't bore you with all that. Nu?" she prompted her student. "Does our Y-chromosomal Aaron exist?"

"On the whole, yes. But I found something else. Something unexpected."

Hannah's jowls wobbled, her fork suspended in the air. "Significant?"

She meant statistical significance. "Yes." Noga reached into her bag for the printouts and laid the sheets on the table.

Hannah glanced at the line charts and squinted at the labels. She stopped chewing. Then she put down the cutlery and studied the pages in both hands.

She gave Noga a sharp, suspicious look. "Is this some kind of prank?"

"No, of course not. I found it hard to believe too. That's why I wanted to check with you first."

Hannah stared at the sheets again. "Do you have the raw data with you?"

Noga pulled out her laptop, nudged it from hibernation, and turned the screen to face her professor. Hannah jabbed at the mouse pad and scrolled through the rows of figures.

Five torturous minutes later, Hannah pushed aside her half-eaten meal and sagged in her chair. Noga had never seen her mentor look so lost.

"Gods, Noga," she said. "Do you know what this means?"

A pent-up breath burst through Noga's lips. She had not misread the data. But if the results were accurate, they only raised more questions.

"Hannah, how can this be?"

"Beats me. But one thing's for sure—this will change our world forever."

A shiver ran down Noga's spine. *Change our world forever.* She had heard those words before. The man who spoke them had ranted about the approaching Redemption and how she, Noga, had a role to play. But that man no longer existed. Noga had seen to that.

CHAPTER 21

"Do you mean to tell me," said Fievel, the Russian with the tidy parting, greasy mustache, and old-fashioned accent, "that you speak into the little box, and your friend will hear you across the street?"

Irina stood before a dozen students and held up her cellular phone for display. "Or on the other side of the world," she said.

"Without wires?" the man said. "Astonishing!"

He used archaic Russian words and a peculiar sentence structure that Irina now associated with the late nineteenth century. Fievel had fled the pogroms that had swept over the Pale of Settlement after the assassination of Tsar Alexander II only to die of malaria in the swamps of Ottoman Palestine.

Irina taught the course every morning in a classroom at the Absorption Center down the corridor from the Dry Bones Society. The number of participants grew each session, and many of the recent new arrivals spoke the old brand of Russian. Some had yet to change out of the white spa gowns issued to them by the DBS volunteers who picked them up at the cemeteries and street corners of Jerusalem, Tiberias, and Safed. The newly resurrected were easy to spot.

Irina couldn't decide what surprised the arrivals more: their new lease on life or how drastically the world had changed. Modern technology seemed to them like black magic, and some of the poor souls had required a lot of convincing to get them to board the shuttle bus.

The educational classes at the Society included Transportation (or "how to cross the street"), a crash course on Modern Hebrew, and her current class, Technology, during which Irina displayed the wonders of mobile phones, televisions, and computers. Most had trouble wrapping their minds around the Internet, a topic that she now left for her advanced course.

"That's all for today," she declared. "Time for lunch."

They filed into the new mess hall. Savta Sarah stood beside the tables of steaming food, as the hungry students helped themselves to disposable plates and cutlery and piled on stuffed cabbage, meatballs, baked chicken, and, of course, goulash. The arrivals had no difficulty at all appreciating her cooking.

They'd be OK, all of them. With time, they would adjust to their new world. They would learn a trade and make friends. Some would find love. And soon, if the merger with Gurion's Upward party worked out, they would each receive a shiny new identity card as a graduation gift.

Irina joined the line, filled her plate, and found an empty table.

One poor soul would never graduate. Two months after Irina's return, she still remembered nothing of her former life. She had stopped studying the eyes of strangers for that flash of recognition. With no history and no name, she'd remain in the limbo of the Absorption Center forever. Her past was a sealed tomb and so she looked to the future, but forging a future with no past felt like reaching for the heavens with no solid ground beneath her feet.

Savta Sarah sat down at Irina's table. As usual she had not dished up for herself. "Nu? Any luck?"

"Nope. I'm still Irina."

Moshe Karlin's grandmother-in-law tutted. "Any boyfriends?" She had a way of getting to the point, and Irina liked her straightforward approach.

She shook her head. During her first weeks, she had grown close to Moshe and even nursed the hope that they would become more than friends. But Moshe loved his wife and Irina had stood down. She wasn't the kind to break up a family anyway; she'd have to build a life of her own. How? She had no idea. With luck, she'd find love the way that Moshe had with Galit—at first sight across a crowded room.

"I could make a few inquiries for you," Savta said. When Irina chuckled, she added, "I've made a few matches in my time. You're a pretty young woman. You'll be easy. Gita was a different story. Did I tell you how I set her up?"

"No," Irina said. She was about to find out.

"Gita had buck teeth and a lazy eye. Her sister, Bluma, however, was a rare beauty. Their mother, my cousin, passed away when they were young girls—her health never recovered after the War."

The War, Irina had learned, was how Savta referred to the Holocaust.

"Bluma would have no problem finding a man, but Gita, what would become of her? Doctor Schneider's son was a decent young man and a medical student at the Hebrew University. So I made an appointment at Doctor Schneider's visiting rooms and took along both Gita and her pretty sister. 'Doctor Schneider,' I said. 'Your son is such a fine young man. Surely he would be interested in meeting one of my lovely nieces?' I put Bluma up front. The doctor agreed to send his son over to our home the following evening. Bluma, regrettably, was not able to join us that day." Savta winked. "She had an urgent meeting far away. But two weeks later, Gita and the young doctor-to-be were engaged."

Savta chuckled at her own audacity.

"Thanks, Savta. But I'm in no rush."

Savta shrugged and looked over her shoulder. Another group of hungry students had arrived in the dining hall, and she bustled off to feed them.

Irina finished her meal and dropped the disposable plate in

a large bin at the door.

She had fifteen minutes until her next class, so she headed for the call center to contact the Ministry of the Interior and double-check the arrangements for Sunday. The press conference would be larger than the first and they still had to work out the finer details of how to determine the identities of people long dead. The paperwork would be a challenge.

As she stepped into the corridor, she noticed a man standing outside the Dry Bones Society and staring at the lettering on the door. Tattoos covered his muscular arm—a circle of Russian characters around a Star of David—and his hair fell to his back in a loose ponytail. An unexpected thrill flared in her core. Now there was an interesting story waiting to be heard.

He turned as she approached and held out her hand. "*Dabro pah-zhah-lah-vaht*," she said. Welcome.

He turned to her and his lips parted. His eyes widened and his skin turned as white as paper.

"I'm Irina," she said, when he didn't respond. The newly resurrected often expressed shock and signs of disorientation, but she had yet to meet one with tattoos.

The introduction seemed to break the spell. He shook her hand. His grip was strong but cold.

"Are you OK?" she said.

"Have we met before?" he asked.

That thrill flared again. Not a spark of recognition—as far as she remembered, she had never met the man before—but perhaps something else? *Like an electric current*, Moshe had said of the moment he had first spotted Galit across a crowded Jerusalem nightclub. He had walked up to her and they had hit it off with an exchange of witty banter.

Irina couldn't think of anything witty to say now. The best she could come up with was, "Now we have."

CHAPTER 22

Alex washed his face in the bathroom sink. His hands trembled. He had asked for the men's room as soon as the girl led him into the Dry Bones Society. Otherwise, he would have fallen apart.

The girl lives!

Months ago he had received a call with that information but he had not believed the report. Knowing what he knew—having done what he had—how could he? The informant had not lied. But how could this be?

Mandrake had sent him to learn the magic tricks of this Dry Bones Society, and Alex had drawn the expected foregone conclusion. The dead never came back. These so-called resurrected people were collaborators in a large-scale hoax. But now the girl had turned everything he knew about the world on its head. This was no parlor trick.

Irina was no lookalike, either, or secret identical twin. Alex knew people, what they were feeling and thinking, often better than they knew themselves. He used this sixth sense to great effect for the Organization and his special talent was why Mandrake had selected him to sniff out the Society. Alex had known the girl well—perhaps too well—and this Irina tilted her head the same way, spoke with the same voice, and bore the same beauty spot on the side of her neck. No. This was no sleight of hand.

She remembers nothing. Not even her name. The informant had gotten that right as well. If she had remembered him, she would have fled the moment she had set eyes on him.

Was she planning to avenge herself? Was she holding her cards close to her chest, drawing him into a trap? After what she had experienced, he wouldn't blame her. But he dismissed the theory. Although he had almost fainted at the sight of her, the girl had seemed almost glad to meet him, and few people could control their visceral reactions so completely.

No, only one explanation remained—she truly didn't remember him. Good for her. But lost memories might resurface, and if they did...

His shoulders twitched, and he doubled over. Thankfully, he had the bathroom to himself. He splashed water on his face again and stared at the tough guy in the mirror. *Get a hold of yourself!*

He needed to go out there again, look her in the eye, and decide how much she really knew. If she remembered even a bit of her old life, he knew what Mandrake would command. Would he be able to go through that again? The first time had bent him, and driven him into semi-retirement. A second might break him for good.

He drew three deep breaths. The bathroom had two toilet stalls but he had used neither, so he flushed the one and stepped out the bathroom door.

She was waiting for him outside with a broad, friendly smile.

"Did you return this morning?" she asked.

"Return?"

"Come back to life?"

"No," he said. "I'm not one of those." To find out the truth, he'd have to play his real identity, or as close as possible. If anything was going to trigger a flashback, he wanted that to happen sooner rather than later.

She leaned in and lowered her voice. "It's OK," she said.

"We get a lot of visitors like you. Some are just curious. Others want to join the Society. You don't have to have died to want a fresh start."

He swallowed the ball of emotion that swelled in his throat. Was she hinting at their past? Was she goading him into a confrontation? He studied her large green eyes. Those eyes had haunted his dreams, but today they contained no trace of rebuke.

She looked away. "I'm sorry," she said. "That's me pushing my nose where it doesn't belong. Let me show you around. This is the call center."

She waved at the rows of cubicles manned by people with headsets. "The calls are from volunteers and donors mostly. The new arrivals usually get picked up on site."

Alex nodded his head and looked around. There was a kitchenette and a corner office with large windows.

"That's Moshe's office," she explained. "Moshe Karlin, one of the founders of the Dry Bones Society. Want to see the Absorption Center?"

He nodded.

They walked down the corridor and she showed him the classrooms, the dining hall, and the meeting room with the circle of plastic chairs that they used for their group sessions. He asked questions and she answered. She glanced at him often but without malice. If the gracious reception was an act, her performance was flawless.

"I have to give a class now," she said, and she touched her hair absently. "Funny," she said, with a bemused smile. "I still don't know your name."

"Alex," he said.

She seemed to turn the name over in her head. Any moment, he expected her to shudder and convulse with fear, to stab him with an accusatory glare.

Instead, she smiled. "Nice to meet you, Alex."

CHAPTER 23

That evening in the marble lobby of the luxury residential tower on Jaffa Road, Noga waited for the elevator and prepared to break the news to Eli.

The golden doors whooshed open and she stepped inside the mirrored box. After Hannah had confirmed the facts, she could keep the discovery a secret no longer. Would the revelation shove Eli back into the sinking sand of his old delusions?

An ephemeral black floor number projected on the golden lintel and climbed upward as the elevator rose.

Or had Eli been right from the start? She had dismissed his apocalyptic rantings out of hand, and yet now her laptop held the seeds of peace in the Middle East. Was that coincidence or Providence? Had God sent Eli to usher in the End of Days? Would Noga also play a key role in that cosmic drama? Had God caused Eli's accident, as he had claimed, in order to bring them together?

As the floor number reached P for Penthouse and the doors whooshed open, she made her decision. No, she could not hide this from her partner in life. She'd roll the dice—lay the facts before him—and hope that he'd hold it together.

She punched the code into a keypad and the lock clicked open, but when she turned the handle and pushed, the front door of the apartment stuck. Something was blocking the entrance. She peered around the edge of the door. A dozen packing boxes littered the hall.

Are we moving? Eli had said nothing about that.

She pushed harder, shifting the nearest moving box until she could slip through the crack. Each box had a white address tag taped to the top. New York, USA. Manchester, United Kingdom. Durban, South Africa. She didn't recognize any of the names. What was going on?

The trail of boxes led through the kitchen, down the corridor, and ended at the door to Eli's private sanctuary. Noga had discovered the room on her first visit to the apartment, when Eli had lain in a hospital bed at Shaare Zedek. She had avoided the room ever since. The shrine housed a collection of old weapons and personal items—mementos from Eli's imagined past and the pseudo-evidence that had fed his delusions. His presence in that room could only spell trouble.

She stood at the threshold. In the sunken den at the center of the room, Eli scribbled an address on another sealed package with a black marker, then looked up at her and smiled.

"Hey."

"Hey. What's going on?"

He hefted the oblong package in both hands and climbed the steps to the door. "Cleaning out some junk. Coming through!" He brushed past her. Nails and picture hooks marked the pale empty spaces on the walls where the artifacts had once hung.

She followed him to the kitchen. "You sold them?"

He lowered the package onto the kitchen island, beside another similar package. "People will buy anything on eBay. That's probably where I got them myself." He patted the oblong package. "This one might cause trouble in customs. A full-size claymore. A sword," he added in answer to her blank stare. "Very old, very sharp sword."

A few days ago, she would have welcomed a clearance sale of his bizarre collection. Today she wasn't so sure. "You're not keeping any of it?"

"Nope. Why would I?" His eyes narrowed. "Is everything all right? How did your meeting go?"

She placed her laptop bag on the counter beside the packaged sword and slumped onto a kitchen stool.

He moved behind her and massaged her shoulders. "Did she find a problem with the results?"

His hands felt good on her stiff muscles. "Not exactly," she said. "The main thesis still stands, but there's a glitch."

He released her shoulders and sat down beside her. "What kind of glitch?"

"The Cohen gene is real; it appears in all the Jewish participants who claimed priestly descent."

"And?"

Noga drew a deep breath. She wanted to hold onto this moment, possibly the last before her perfect life crumbled, the way it had in the secret garden at Shaare Zedek. This time she would be to blame, but there was no stopping now.

"Another group has the haplotype," she said. "In large percentages. Too large to dismiss as outliers or statistical errors. And in the same proportion as Jewish priests to Jewish laypersons."

"And the lucky group is?" he prompted.

"Arabs," she said. "Or at least those that live in Samaria and Judea. Palestinian Arabs."

Confusion crumpled his brow. "Are you sure the data is good?"

"I triple-checked. So did Hannah. There's a clear Founder Effect."

She didn't need to spell out the ramifications. If Palestinian Arabs originated from a closed group of Jewish ancestors, then she had uncovered the key to peace in the Middle East.

She gazed into his eyes, searching for the old flicker of madness and bracing for another rant about the End of Days.

But Eli didn't rant or rave; he didn't laugh at her either. Instead, he touched her arm. "I'm so sorry," he said.

"Sorry for what?"

He gave her a sympathetic smile. "That your thesis didn't

work out."

She had to laugh. "Are you kidding me? My thesis did *work out*, but along the way it proves that Palestinians Arabs are actually Jews. Don't you see? Think of what that means. This changes everything."

He frowned. "You set out to find the Cohen gene. If it shows up among Arabs, then doesn't that disprove your theory?"

She brushed his hand from her arm. "No, it doesn't!" He was being unreasonable.

He looked away. He wasn't kidding. "What's the alternative—that Palestinian Arabs just happen to be Jews? That's convenient. Now they'll hug us instead of trying to kill us? The end to the conflict? Peace in our time?"

"Yes!"

"Come on, Noga. Palestinians are Jews? How does that even make sense? The simpler explanation is that the theory is wrong. Occam's Razor says that the simplest explanation always—"

"I know what Occam's Razor is," she snapped. Now he was being mean, and his stubborn, self-assured manner was driving her insane. "You're ignoring the facts," she said, in the calmest voice she could muster. "This is shared genetic heritage, not some conspiracy theory. Genes don't lie."

He stared at her, a sadness in his eyes. "Let me tell you about facts," he said. He patted a package on the kitchen island. "This is an authentic crusader sword. A gift to me from William of Ibelin. He sang pretty well but only when he was drunk, which was often. He limped on his right leg ever since of the Battle of Hattin, where he barely escaped with his life. In the year 1187."

He pointed to another long package on the floor. "That's an oriental rug made by Yusuf of Acre, a Turk and the best carpet maker I've ever known. He traded that rug for an old mule I had, let's see, just over three hundred years ago."

With a sweep of his arm, he indicated all of the waiting packages. "These are all physical facts. Can't deny their existence. But what do they mean? To me they used to be memories collected over the course of a very long and eventful life." He grinned at her. "Did you know that Moses was a terrible dancer, or that King Ahab had dark curls and a cleft chin?" His grin faltered as he blinked back a tear. "It's all garbage. All this stuff, like the memories, they're all just strands in a thick web of lies that I told myself to give my life meaning." He turned to her and laid his hand on her arm again. "I don't want you to go through that."

She wriggled free of his grasp. "This is different," she said. "These aren't false memories propped up by random objects. This is a sound theory based on empirical evidence."

Eli gave a bitter laugh. "This time is always different."

He stared at the tangerine dusk through the French windows of the living room. "Messiahs crop up every other century. Their followers are experts at finding signs and omens. 'This time the Redemption is here for real.' The result is always the same. Disappointment. Disillusion. Often, death too. The greater the anticipation, the more destructive the devastation that follows. When will people learn? When will they stop betting everything on magical solutions and just accept the world as it is?"

He glanced at her and touched her cheek with the palm of his hand. He wasn't angry or upset, only tired. "Trust me on this," he said. "I've been there."

CHAPTER 24

Ahmed listened to the whisper of the morning breeze outside and the groan of his empty stomach within. He lay on the cold stone floor of an empty cave. Surviving the night had been the easy part; the day would be harder.

He sat up on his elbows, careful not to bang his head on the ceiling of the cave. Long ago, many hands had chiseled the crawl space into the bedrock of the hillside. The ancients had laid their loved ones to rest on the stone shelves cut into the walls, along with provisions for the afterlife. Over the years, tomb robbers and, later, archaeologists had cleared out the gifts and the bones.

As a child, a friend had dared Ahmed to sneak into one of the gaping mouths of the old tombs. He had climbed the rocky incline between his village of Silwan and the old cemetery on the Mount of Olives, more concerned about slipping on loose stones than disturbing the old spirits within. As a child adventurer, he had entered this tomb in daylight, standing tall on two feet. As an adult fugitive, he had crawled inside on all fours in the dark of night. This time, the demons lurked outside the tomb.

The old grave made a fitting home for a dead man. He had spent his first day of freedom cowering inside, the visible world shrinking to the rectangular mouth of the cave. He watched cars move between the stone houses and leafy trees of the City of David across the Kidron Valley. A woman in a hijab hung clothes on a line. Any moment he expected the mouth of the cave to darken, filling with the muscular bulk of the Rottweiler. But the day had passed without incident. He had devoured his last crusts of bread and emptied his plastic bottle of water. If he didn't leave the safety of the tomb while he still had strength, he would starve and make the tomb his home forever.

According to the old Muslim in the warehouse, this world was neither Heaven nor Hell. God had flung him from death back into the land of the living. Boris and Damas—even the Rottweiler—were men, not demons. He could not escape demons, but he might evade men. And in the real world, one place might still welcome him.

He crawled through the dust to the opening and peeked over the stony ridge. In the valley below, a white car parked next to the low square building at the Gichon spring. Satisfied that he was not being observed, he crawled outside, then rose to his full height and stretched his back. He peed into a patch of wild grass—dark yellow pee—and wiped his hands in the dirt.

Then he made for the quiet dirt road at the edge of Silwan, picking his way along the hillside and sliding down the bulge of bedrock. He strolled along the street, another dusty laborer late for work. Across the valley, a construction drill rattled. He turned this way and that, and looked over his shoulder. No one was following him in the jumble of lopsided homes and apartment buildings. The streets had no names, but he knew them by heart.

Two minutes later, he stopped before the spot where his childhood home had stood. The house looked nothing like he remembered. Tall, solid walls stood proud in a clean layer of gray paint. An impressive wooden door sealed the entrance.

Of course. His home was long gone, demolished by Israeli bulldozers, the fate shared by all the homes of suicide bombers. He had not considered that before he had boarded the bus with his bag of explosives and ball bearings. He had not told his mother about his plans for martyrdom. Some wealthy family had built over the ruins of his childhood. Perhaps they would know where he could find his mother. He clutched his stomach and leaned on the wall for support. Maybe they'd spare him a heel of bread.

The sound of scraping down the street caught his ear. A child walked toward him, dragging a stick in the dirt. He waited for the boy to pass and disappear down the street before he knocked on the door.

He was about to knock a second time when the door cracked open. An old woman in a black *niqab* peered at him with suspicion. Then her old eyes widened in the opening of the veil. She grabbed his arm, pulled him inside, and closed the door.

"Ahmed!"

She knew his name, and he knew her voice.

"Mother?"

He had not recognized her in the full head covering. His mother had always worn modest wraparounds of white and brown. She removed the *niqab* and looked him over, her braids of frizzy hair streaked with gray. The lines of her face had deepened and the skin hung looser, but the same glowing smile brightened her face.

She hugged him tight, and the first loving human touch in his new life felt so good, it pushed him to the edge of tears.

She held him out for inspection. "My little boy." Was that pride in her voice or heartbreak? He had abandoned her to become a martyr.

"I prayed for you to visit me in a dream," she said. "But I never thought I'd see you again." She shook her head and wrung her hands.

Ahmed didn't know how to explain his visit so he didn't, and changed the subject to his more pressing needs. "Mother," he said. "May I have something to eat?"

"Of course."

She sat him down at a marble table in a large, clean kitchen with every modern appliance, and soon he gorged himself on a fresh pita stuffed with his mother's homemade hummus and fried strips of lamb that she warmed in a microwave.

She watched him eat, her eyes drifting to his matted hair and filthy clothing, and concern clouded her face.

Ahmed washed the meal down with a glass of Coke. "This house," he said.

At the mention of her house, her features brightened. "When you... left, the soldiers destroyed our home." The event did not seem to upset her. "But then they built me a new house. Wonderful, isn't it?"

"Who built it for you, Mother?"

She leaned in to whisper. "A gift, Hasan said, from the governments that honor the families of our noble martyrs. Forty thousand shekels in cash too!"

"Forty thousand?" Ahmed had earned half that much in a year. He had died a martyr but his mother had received the palace. But now, he had come home.

"I missed you so, my Ahmed."

"I missed you too."

She leaned in again. "Tell me," she said, a gleam in her eye. "How are you enjoying Paradise?"

Ahmed inhaled his Coca-Cola and coughed.

"The banquet of the martyrs?" she continued. "The righteous prophets. And your wives!" She touched her palm to her cheek. "The noblest beauties in all the world, for sure!"

Ahmed cleared his throat. How could he tell his mother that, not only had he not seen Paradise, but he had passed through Hell?

"Silly me," his mother said. "So many questions. It is enough for me just to see your face again." She glanced at the front door and that troubled look returned to her face. "I'm sure you're eager to return to the afterlife. You can answer my questions next time."

"Next time? Mother, I want to stay here with you."

"Here?" A hint of annoyance had entered her voice. "That cannot be. You died a martyr, Ahmed. The people honor me.

They call me *Um-Shaheed.* They invite me to social events and public gatherings. I sit with the leaders and dignitaries. They give me money and I want for nothing." She sent another fleeting glance toward the front door, and her voice dropped to a hiss. "You're not supposed to be here. You should be enjoying your eternal reward in Paradise, not visiting your mother and looking like a starving tramp, all covered in dirt." Then she remembered herself and gave an embarrassed laugh. "You should be on your way."

She swept crumbs from the marble tabletop with her hand and took his empty plate to the sink. The street outside loomed large and terrifying.

"But Mother, I have nowhere to go."

"Nonsense!" She pulled him out of his seat and herded him toward the door. "You have your palace and your wives." She opened the door, looked up and down the street, and shoved him outside. "Enjoy your eternal reward," she said, as she closed the door and blew him a kiss, "and don't forget to visit your mother."

CHAPTER 25

Sunday morning, Moshe died and went to Heaven. Dazzling lights blinded him, not the spiritual glow at the end of an afterlife tunnel, but the glare of spotlights and the flash of press cameras in a packed auditorium at the Ministry of the Interior.

Minister Malkior sat beside him onstage while Isaac Gurion gave forth at the podium, his voice booming from speakers. He spoke of thousands of resurrected Jews and their needless suffering, of cutting bureaucratic red tape, and welcoming back long-lost family.

Moshe had a powerful friend, and there was no limit to the good they could do together.

Galit beamed at him from the front row, seated among the top brass of the Dry Bones Society, and ahead of the many rows of reporters. The idea of a career in politics had not overjoyed her at first.

"Are you sure you want all that attention?" she had asked him after Friday night dinner at home. He was asking a lot of her. Politics would shove them both into the public eye, and ever since his brief incarceration Galit had remained tense and pensive, looking over her shoulder every time they left the house.

"It's a great opportunity," he had said. "Think of all the

good we could do. Besides, I can't see any other way to get citizenship in the near future."

That argument seemed to win her over. "Promise me we'll get married right away."

"Of course. I'll book the first hall that's available."

"Forget a hall," she said. "Let's have a quiet ceremony here at home."

Moshe chuckled at her sudden eagerness. "What about your parents?" They'd need time to fly out from the USA.

"They'll get over it."

"And now," Isaac Gurion concluded at the podium, "the time has come to correct this injustice, by granting those poor lost souls recognition as citizens with all the associated rights and responsibilities."

He turned to the table where Moshe sat. "Minister Malkior, will you do the honors?"

Malkior waved his silver pen in the air like a magic wand, and signed the document on the table to the background music of flashing cameras. He gave Moshe a broad grin and shook his hand as though he hadn't double-crossed him last week. They faced the cameras, hands still engaged, for the photo op—the Minister of the Interior shaking hands with Moshe Karlin, the magnanimous Isaac Gurion standing behind them, his arms spread like sheltering wings.

Malkior picked up the microphone on the table. "I have a surprise for you, Moshe," he said.

The floor fell out of Moshe's stomach. Malkior's last surprise had involved a knife in the back.

"While we were drafting this letter of intent, our friend Mr. Gurion got busy pushing our new legislation through Knesset. This morning, the proposal passed its third reading."

Gurion shifted back to the podium. "The new law grants asylum and automatic citizenship to all new arrivals. I call it"—he paused for dramatic effect—"the Second Law of Return."

Applause broke out from the audience. Moshe glanced at the beaming faces in the front row. Shmuel clapped his hands and gave him the thumbs-up. *We've done it.* Tears welled in Moshe's eyes.

"Anticipating this," Malkior said, "I went ahead and had this made for you." He reached into the inner pocket of his suit jacket. Instead of a dagger, he withdrew a blue booklet.

Moshe opened the crisp, new covers and studied the freshly minted identity card within. *Moshe Karlin.* He had kept his old identity number. "Thank you." He shook the minister's hand and let him give him a side hug.

Gurion spoke into the microphone again. "We have another surprise for you, Moshe."

This was his cue to join his benefactor at the podium.

"I've gotten to know Moshe very well recently," he said. "He risked everything to help his brothers and sisters in need and I'm proud to count him as my friend. Our country needs more Moshe Karlins, and so I'm excited to announce that he and the worthy folks at the Dry Bones Society have agreed to join our list and run with Upward in the upcoming elections."

A commotion rippled through the audience and cameras flared again.

An aide adjusted the microphone for Moshe while he extracted his cue cards, and the hall fell silent.

"This is a truly historic occasion," he said, his voice echoing back on the speakers, deeper and more confident than he had expected. "On behalf of our resurrected brothers and sisters, I would like to thank Member of Knesset Isaac Gurion for his friendship and Minister Malkior for his quick and effective cooperation. Thanks to you both, thousands of men, women, and children are now able to lead dignified and productive lives. We at the Dry Bones Society look forward to working closely with you in future for the betterment of not only the resurrected but of all citizens."

Gurion opened the floor to questions. A multitude of hands shot into the air. Gurion picked one.

A disheveled man with reading glasses and a press card hanging at his neck stood up. "When will identity cards be issued?"

Moshe had rehearsed the expected questions with Gurion the previous night, and that one had topped the list.

Moshe leaned into the microphone. "Starting from tomorrow, the Ministry of the Interior will open special service desks to receive the resurrected. Details are on the Ministry of Interior website."

Gurion selected a female questioner. "How will the resurrected prove their identities?"

"Good question," Moshe said. His smile won a few laughs from the crowd, and he relaxed. "Those with pre-existing identity numbers will be matched with the photographs on record. There are still a few glitches to work through. The computer systems don't support multiple birth dates yet." Another round of chuckles. He was getting the hang of this. "Those without identity numbers—whose first lives predate the State—will need to provide details of their former life: dates and places of birth and death. Checks will be made— photo analysis and fingerprints—to ensure the applicants are not already in the system."

Gurion picked a third questioner. "What positions on the Upward list will the Dry Bones Society occupy?"

Gurion stepped in to answer. "Three, and then twenty through twenty-four."

The reporter raised his eyebrows. A recent poll had given Upward seventeen mandates in the upcoming election. Even with the resurrected vote, only Moshe would sit in Knesset. That didn't bother the Society much. Gurion's party had pushed through the Second Law of Return.

"I have one more surprise for Moshe," Gurion said, bringing the questions to a close.

Moshe glanced at him. Gurion had not mentioned this in their preparations.

"As you know, Moshe, we look out for our friends, so please accept this gift as a token of our appreciation." He handed Moshe a black box tied with a blue ribbon. "Go ahead, open it."

Moshe did. Inside, on a bed of soft velvet, sat a large gold watch.

"Every man of action needs a good timepiece," Gurion continued.

Moshe closed the heavy metal links over his wrist. The brand new Omega felt lighter than his grandfather's ancient Rolex. Moshe reminded himself to redeem the family heirloom from the pawn shop in Talpiot when he could afford to. The old vulture at the shop would not return the watch without a mighty negotiation. Luckily for Moshe, he had a secret weapon: Savta Sarah.

"Thank you." Tears threatened to surface again.

Gurion gripped Moshe by the shoulders and pulled him close for another photo op.

Moshe smiled for the cameras. He had nothing to worry about now; he had powerful friends.

CHAPTER 26

Noga stared at her laptop through the veil of steam from her coffee cup on the kitchen island. She had to prove Eli wrong. The data *did* support her thesis. But no matter how she arranged the charts, the conspicuous cluster of Palestinian Arabs with the gene markers of Jewish priests would not disappear. Erasing the pesky results was out of the question—she would never sacrifice her scientific integrity.

Background chatter came from the television in the living room. A Channel Two correspondent reported on early poll results. Election fever had gripped the country. Noga aimed the remote and the television screen went dark. She hated politics.

She stared at the charts and ran her fingers through her hair. The Arabs in the study were Jewish. They had to be. Hannah, her advisor, had reached the same conclusion. Noga's thesis stood strong. Her paper would appear in academic journals and, incidentally, solve the intractable Israeli-Palestinian conflict, making Noga both a world-renowned scientist and a national hero. How convenient, indeed.

Extraordinary claims, Carl Sagan had said, require extraordinary evidence, and the puzzle still lacked one critical piece—a working theory that explained how this mind-boggling reality had developed.

She exhaled a tremulous breath and her shoulders slumped.

"Thanks a lot, Eli." His devil's advocate questions had toppled her fairytale palace of cards. His counter-theory ignored the main thrust of the genetic data but still gnawed at her conscience.

Had her personal bias slanted her analysis? Was she simply not prepared to throw away two years of sweat and tears? If Eli was right, then the End of Days had arrived indeed—for her doctorate.

Was that so far-fetched? Every day, conspiracy theorists connected unrelated facts to support outlandish claims. Science had names for their logical fallacies: confirmation bias; confusing cause and effect; ignoring a common cause. Being human. Noga could easily have fallen into the same trap.

She had feared for Eli's sanity but could she be the one who had succumbed to delusion?

Her body convulsed as she laughed. She doubled over and tears seeped from the corners of her eyes. Tears of loss. Tears of relief. *You idiot!* She had been so convinced that she had stumbled onto an epic discovery! *This time is always different,* Eli had said. The list of failed messiahs proved that only too well.

She straightened on the kitchen stool and gulped her bitter coffee. So be it. *Dust yourself off and start again.*

She opened an Internet browser, typed two words into the search bar—"false messiah"—and clicked the link for Wikipedia.

"Wow," she said aloud.

Eli had not exaggerated. Messiah claimants had cropped up almost every century. Simon Bar Kokhba had led a doomed Jewish rebellion against the Roman Empire in the second century. Moses of Crete in the fifth. Most of them had met violent deaths. David Alroy, twelfth century, was murdered in his sleep. His contemporary, the Messiah of Yemen, had told his opponents to cut off his head in order to prove his claim. And on and on. Most of the names didn't ring a bell.

She *had* heard of Sabbatai Zevi. In 1666, after stirring up hope and controversy throughout Europe, Zevi arrived in Constantinople intending to conquer the globe without bloodshed and don the sultan's crown. The sultan promptly threw him in prison and gave him an ultimatum: convert to Islam or die. Zevi chose Islam and cast the Jewish world into black despair.

Some communities refused to accept his failure. A Polish Jew by the name of Jacob Frank claimed to be his successor but led his followers to Christianity. The Dönmeh sect of Turkey follow Sabbatai Zevi to this day.

Noga's heart did a double-flip. Her academic mind had discerned a pattern in the historic details, a recurring theme that united the failed messianic eras of the past but did not apply to the present day. This time really was different.

She laughed again. *Here you go again.* After only a few days of messianic mania, she still struggled to shake free. How had Eli managed to escape a lifetime of delusion? Her admiration for him grew.

At the sound of bare feet down the hallway, she switched back to EPSS, her statistical software.

Eli padded into the kitchen in pajama trunks. "Good morning." He kissed her on the cheek.

"Morning."

He fixed a cup of coffee behind her. The last few days he had been kind enough not to mention her thesis, but her vain stubborn streak had not been ready to concede defeat.

"Oh, crap," he said behind her. "I'm late." He ran back to the bedroom, returning in jeans and sneakers and pulling on a shirt as he rushed for the door.

"Late for what?"

"To pick up the bike," he said.

The bike. Eli had covered the coffee table with marketing pamphlets for Harley Davidson's latest and greatest.

"Hey," she shouted after him. "Don't forget—"

"I know," he said, preempting her. "I'll wear a helmet."

He blew her a kiss from the front door and slipped into

the elevator.

She sighed. Boys and their toys. At least his retail therapy seemed to have whetted his appetite for life.

Her phone jingled and she answered on the first ring.

"Hannah," she said. "I've been meaning to call you." She wanted to share her doubts with her advisor, but she didn't get a chance.

"Noga, dear," the professor said. She sounded unusually flustered. "I've found it."

"Found what?"

"The explanation for the results of your study."

Hannah must have figured out their mistake on her own. "Me too," she said. "I owe you an apology."

"An apology?"

"For misleading you."

"Misleading me? Not at all—you were *absolutely* right, and now I've found the key to the whole mystery."

Noga's heart fluttered. "What did you find?"

"I can't explain on the phone. You'll have to see for yourself. What are you doing tomorrow morning?"

"Nothing yet."

"Good. I'll pick you up at eight."

CHAPTER 27

Sunday evening, Alex pulled up at the Lev Talpiot Mall in his black Skoda Octavia, his heart banging against his ribs. He needed to lie to his boss—his boss and his oldest friend. Not a lie, really. An omission.

She's alive!

Once the shock had subsided, relief had set in. *She's alive!* Redemption glinted on the horizon. But soon that relief turned to dread. Mandrake must never know of her existence. If he did, Alex knew what he would command, and he couldn't go through with that again.

No. He had to close the case. To lock the door, melt the key, and never think of her again.

He parked the car in the loading zone at the side of the mall and raised the hand brake. Cops knew better than to tow cars parked in this particular loading zone. The street reeked of garbage and cat piss. A dark staircase cut into the side of the building, but no security guard manned this entrance of the mall.

As Alex reached the top of the stairs, moonlight traced an open-air corridor that ended in doors of tinted glass. The sound of toppling bowling pins met his ears as he drew near. He pushed through the doors, entering a space filled with soft light, cigarette smoke, and lounge music. To his left, a

Sephardic greaser in a leather jacket leaned over a pool table and dropped a yellow ball into a corner pocket. On his right, men in matching polo shirts rolled bowling balls down eighteen lanes to the applause of crashing pins. League night.

The Talpiot Bowling Center had belonged to an entrenched Israeli mafia clan until Mandrake had arrived in their turf and taken over their monopolies on recycling, vending machines, and protection rackets. Within a month, Jerusalem had fallen under the magician's spell.

The blonde at the front desk blew bubbles with her gum and studied her nails. Her tank top left little to the imagination. Silver trophies and special edition bowling balls crowned the low wall behind her.

"Evening, Anna," he said in Russian. "Is he in?"

She nodded. Easy on the eyes and devoid of curiosity, Anna did her job well. She even made phone calls to car sellers when required.

He went around the counter, behind Anna, and into a walk-in closet lined with shelves of bowling shoes. At the back, he glanced at the camera in the corner where the wall met the ceiling, and knocked on the door. A bolt shifted and the door opened.

Vitaly, with his bald head and scarred face, wore his trademark black jeans and T-shirt. He bolted the door behind them. "He's busy," he said, and returned to his game of solitaire at a round card table. A gun poked out the back of his jeans. Mandrake always carried a pack of playing cards and the habit had rubbed off on his foot soldier.

Alex settled on a chair in the corner, opposite the closed door of the Boss's office. Camera feeds displayed on a wall: the shoe closet; the front door; the street. Other locations of strategic interest across the city displayed on yet more screens: a dark alley; an old warehouse; a knot of loiterers with cigarettes outside a bar. From these rooms, the Boss ruled his empire.

The safest bet was to turn Mandrake's attention away from the Dry Bones Society. If he had no further need for them, he would never find out about the girl.

The office door opened and two heavyset Chinese men in business suits exited. Mandrake had extended his tendrils far and wide since the old days in the USSR. Alex didn't know half of the Organization's activities and that suited him well. He knew too much already.

Vitaly let the visitors out and bolted the door, then motioned for Alex to enter.

Alex closed the door behind him. A manager's chair of padded leather lay empty behind a bulky oak desk.

"Sit, my friend," said a voice behind him. He turned. Mandrake slouched on the leather wraparound couch. Wearing a black button-down shirt and black trousers, he puffed on a cigar.

Alex sat down on the edge of the couch.

Large, intelligent eyes studied Alex over a huge sensitive nose. The shaved head glowed beneath sunken spotlights.

"A drink?" Mandrake nodded toward a bar cabinet of polished wood. "A smoke?"

"No, thanks."

Mandrake cut to the chase. "So what have we learned about this Dry Bones Society and their magic tricks?"

Alex leaned forward on the couch. "No magic tricks," he said. "They're for real."

The intelligent eyes scanned his own. "Sasha," he said, a note of disappointment in his voice. He was the only man who called him by that name. "You surprise me. Dead men returning to life? We have been magicians too long to believe in magic *or* miracles."

Alex felt his stomach tighten. He hadn't expected the news to go over easily. "Call it what you like. It's real."

Mandrake laughed, leaned over, and tapped ash into a tray on a side table. "I did some homework too, I hope you don't mind. This Moshe Karlin threw together a demonstration last week, and got locked up for his efforts. Now he's playing politics. He's a clever trickster, but he's a trickster still." The eyes locked on Alex. "Has he tricked you as well?"

"There are signs," Alex said. "Physical signs. They have no belly button."

Mandrake dragged on the cigar, still staring.

"Like I said," Alex continued, "this is no trick. We should keep clear of them. My work is done here."

Mandrake blew a smoke ring in the air. "You're so sure of this. Why?"

Alex swallowed. There was no avoiding it. "The girl is with them," he said. "I met her. That's how I know."

The eyes didn't blink. "And how did she take to your reunion?"

"She doesn't remember a thing, not even her name. Goes by Irina now. She works at the Society."

"Could this Irina be another girl?"

Alex stared at his hands. "It's her."

Mandrake took another long drag. "If her memory comes back…"

"I doubt it. We spoke for a long time and I used my real name. They're no threat for now, unless we draw their attention."

Mandrake blew another ring and watched it disappear into thin air. "We cannot take that chance, Sasha. Take her to the Doctor."

Alex shifted on his seat. "I told you, she doesn't remember anything." His attempt at keeping her safe had backfired.

Mandrake stubbed out the cigar in the ashtray. "Take her to the Doctor, and we'll know for sure."

CHAPTER 28

Monday morning, Avi marched down Jaffa Road, propelled by indignation. The time had come to take matters into his own hands.

Pedestrians rushed along the sidewalks of downtown Jerusalem, as waiters arranged chairs and tables outside cafés.

"We can help each other," Boris had said. The Russian Mafioso had drilled him about Moshe Karlin and his plans. He had given Avi a cell phone and pocket money, and told him to pass on any new information. Together they would destroy Moshe Karlin. Five days since that promise, Moshe Karlin's star had risen only higher.

On the fuzzy television in his dingy downtown studio apartment, his old nemesis had shaken hands with politicians and fielded questions from reporters. The event gave Moshe and his undead friends new rights and influence, pushing Avi's revenge further away than ever.

With a valid identity card, nothing would stop Moshe from marrying Galit and shutting Avi out for good, and so he had sprung out of bed that morning with renewed purpose. He could wait no longer for Boris to deliver. Time was running out.

A crowd of people blocked the sidewalk, so he stepped into the road to walk around them, then froze to the spot.

What the hell? The human line stretched all the way to Queen Shlomzion Street.

He turned to a man at the edge of the crowd. "Is this the line for the Ministry of the Interior?"

"Yes," the man said, "But it's moving." He had a strange accent and wore a T-shirt that fell to his knees. He was one of *them*. The man smiled and put out his hand. "My name is Nikita. Are you also a returnee?"

"No," Avi snapped, wiping the smile off the man's face.

Avi trudged to the end of the line. *Bloody freaks.* He had set out early to avoid the crowds, planning to get inside the Ministry and cause havoc by shredding application forms and cutting computer cables. If he had to, he'd start a fire. That'd show them. The next news broadcast would have Moshe Karlin apologizing for the violent behavior of his followers.

The line inched forward.

This is ridiculous. At this rate, he'd wait an hour before he even entered the building. The undead had spawned like tadpoles. Another twenty stood in line behind him now. Their gleeful smiles made him want to retch.

Enough! He stepped into the road, abandoning his spot in the line, and marched to the head of the human python.

A mustachioed security guard raised his hand for him to wait while a young woman berated him. "What do you mean I can't go in?" she said. "I need to renew my passport."

"Ma'am," the guard said. "Today we're open only for resurrected."

"But this is urgent. I want to talk to your superior."

"You're welcome to," he said, "but this comes all the way from the top. You'll have to come back tomorrow." He glanced past Avi at the growing line. "Or next week, by the look of it."

"This is pathetic," the girl yelled.

"Yeah," Avi joined in. "We have rights too." The girl glanced at him and smiled.

"Sorry, friends," the guard said. "Please move along."

The girl stepped aside. "The country's gone mad," she

said.

"You're right," Avi said. He gave her a wide grin. He'd like to take her out for breakfast. Judging by her fancy skirt and collared blouse, she'd pick up the tab.

She brushed a strand of hair behind her ear. "These resurrected are taking over."

"Oh, no they won't," he said. "Not if I have anything to do with it."

A light bulb flared in his head. *That's it!* All thoughts of romantic breakfasts evaporated. He walked off, leaving the girl standing there, and pulled out his phone.

"Boris," he said, when the call connected. "I know how to take down Karlin."

CHAPTER 29

Yosef snuck into the corner office at the Dry Bones Society and glanced out the large windows to make sure no one was eavesdropping. The Society headquarters had been unusually quiet the last few days, the members busy with the press conference at the Ministry of the Interior and now with the issuing of identity cards, and Yosef took advantage of the situation to work on his own private mission.

He opened his laptop on Moshe's desk and loaded the spreadsheet he had created. The first worksheet contained a list of names he had gleaned from the Talmud and Midrash. He connected to the Internet, browsed to the Bezeq Online Directory, and searched for the first name on the spreadsheet: Menachem. A blue ball traced circles on the screen while he waited.

A table of results displayed. Twenty thousand six hundred and thirteen matches. Yosef swallowed hard. He would have to narrow his search. He typed "Rabbi Menachem," hit the Search button, and the table updated. Three hundred and sixty-five matches.

Still too many. He narrowed the geographic region to Jerusalem. Thirty-six results. *Thirty-six!* The number restored his enthusiasm. Thirty-six names, like the Thirty-Six Hidden Saints of Jewish legend.

The mission might succeed sooner than he had expected.

He exported the search results, pasted them into a new worksheet, and selected the first row.

Although the Talmud discouraged Calculating the End—attempts at predicting the onset of the End of Days—many sages had succumbed to the temptation. The dates often fell only a few years hence. The Redeemer would arrive in the year 1034. No—1043 is the appointed time. Or perhaps 1111? Surely by 1204. Just a little longer, a few more years. The dates came and went, but the Messiah remained as bashful as ever. 1646—last call! The Hind of Dawn pranced forever just beyond the rise of the next hill.

Theologians speculated about his chronic tardiness. The Redeemer would appear once all of the souls in the Divine Store had incarnated, or when all sinners repented their evil ways. If all Israel kept two Sabbaths, the Messiah would arrive. If only the students of the saintly Baal Shem Tov had joined him in prayer, the Messiah would have revealed himself. If all the great sages of the generation had only met, their joint holiness would have forced the Son of David from hiding.

The Messiah would appear as a king, a leper, a lowly beggar. He would possess wondrous knowledge and insight. Hidden since the Six Days of Creation, he yearned for the Deliverance and suffered with each passing moment. The ninth day of *Av*, the day of the Temple's destruction, would be his birthday, and Menachem his name. No, Efraim. Or David. Nehorai!

Yosef dialed the first number on the phone on Moshe's desk. He had to start somewhere. The receiver trembled in his hand as the number rang. Would this call kick off the Redemption? He imagined the fateful conversation. "Reb Yosef," a sonorous voice would say. "What took you so long? The appointed time has arrived! We have much work to do."

With each ring his heart palpitated.

"Allo," said a woman's voice, high-pitched and frail.

"Is that the home of Rabbi Menachem Azulai?"

"May his name be a blessing," said the woman with not a little agitation.

"My apologies," Yosef said. "And condolences. Goodbye."

Yosef put down the phone and marked the row in the spreadsheet with an X. One Rabbi Menachem down, thirty-five to go. He dialed the next number.

A smattering of guilt marred his anticipation. There would be hundreds of Davids, though not quite as many Yannais and Nehorais. Each call nibbled at Dry Bones Society funds, and each minute on the phone was a minute stolen from his duties as the Society's first full-time salaried employee. But he had to try. The resources invested in this quest would yield dividends infinitely valuable for the Society and for humanity as a whole. The Messiah was out there somewhere, and Yosef must find him.

"Yes?" The man on the phone sounded young and energetic.

Yosef's heart skipped a beat. "Rabbi Menahem Azriel?"

"This is he." The voice turned suspicious.

"My name is Rabbi Yosef Lev of the Dry Bones Society. Have you heard of us?"

"I study full time," said the voice of Rabbi Menachem Azriel, a note of evasion sneaking into his voice. "I don't have money to spare."

Many career Torah scholars lived off government stipends. If they were caught working off the books, they were likely to lose their stipend and receive draft papers from the IDF.

"I'm not collecting donations. I just want to ask you—"

"Whatever you're selling," the voice interrupted, "I'm not interested."

"I'm not selling anything. Please, just listen. The Resurrection has started. You might have heard about us on the news."

A silent, pregnant pause. "Ahh, yes," said the voice. "I'm glad you called."

Yosef's heart threatened to stop beating. God had guided his hand, like Abraham's servant at the well of Haran, and led him to the young Redeemer on only his second attempt!

"I have a message for you," the man continued. Yosef stopped breathing too. Then the voice on the phone yelled and Yosef jumped. "Go to Azazel, you satanic bastards, and don't call me ever again!"

The line went dead.

Yosef rubbed his ear, which still rang with abuse. He marked the second row of the spreadsheet with an X and moved the cursor to the next.

The door of the office opened, and Yosef froze at the laptop, a criminal caught red-handed. "Yes?"

Samira smiled at him from the doorway, wearing a green *hijab*. Although eligible for an identity card, she had remained behind to man the call center. Members of her former family worked at the Ministry and she feared their wrath should they spot her.

"Rabbi Yosef. A man is here to see you."

Had Reverend Adams returned to check on his investment? Yosef had hoped to hand over their dealings with the Flesh and Blood Fund to Moshe. How did the reverend always know when Yosef was alone in the office?

The man who stepped up beside Samira, however, was not Reverend Adams. He wore an impeccable suit, a spotless bowler, and a well-trimmed, stately beard. "Reb Yosef," Rabbi Emden said. "Hello, my old friend." His pearly teeth sparkled. "How good it is to see you again."

CHAPTER 30

That morning, Noga feared for her life. The old, beaten-up car barreled down a bumpy, winding road at breakneck speed. Through the dusty window of the backseat, stony hills rose and fell as the vehicle snaked through Samaria, the Wild West north of Jerusalem.

A storefront with Arabic signage whizzed by, then a donkey led by a man wearing a *kaffiyeh*. A sign at a crossroads pointed right to Ramallah. Were the holes in the signpost the work of rust or bullets?

The Arab in the driver's seat had a thicket of black hair and stubble on his cheek. He had not bothered with a seat belt and drove as though he had not yet discovered the brake pedal.

Hannah sat beside her and gripped the armrest. She had picked up Noga that morning on Jaffa Road and driven north past French Hill. Passing the army checkpoint, she had pulled up on the side of the road where the old car with blue Palestinian plates waited. After Hannah introduced the Arab driver to Noga as Khalid, her "new friend," the two Israeli women had climbed into the backseat.

The car rounded another bend in the road that tied Noga's stomach in a knot.

A few years ago, three Israeli teenagers—Eyal Yifrach, Gilad Shaer, and Naftali Fraenkel—had hitchhiked home from the Etzion Bloc south of Jerusalem. The car had yellow Israeli plates, but when the driver veered from his declared destination of Ashkelon, Gilad called the police hotline on his mobile phone. The tape of the call ended with shouting in Arabic and automatic gunfire. Three weeks later, a search team located the boys' corpses in an open field north of Hebron.

Noga gripped the torn upholstery of the backseat. She hoped that Hannah knew what she was doing.

"Here," said Hannah. She handed her a piece of black cloth with a large hole at the bottom and a smaller one at the front. A hijab. She had got to be kidding.

"Put it on," she said. She had already donned her own black headdress, which covered her head and shoulders and exposed only her face. The secular academic and bra-burning feminist looked like an old beggar woman. "If anyone sees that we're Jewish," she added, "people could get killed."

Yes, Noga thought. *Us!*

She put the hijab on, which felt lighter than it looked and created a very frail sense of security.

A hilltop with the tidy red roofs of a Jewish settlement rose in the distance and then disappeared as they turned right. The car climbed a dirt road among scattered stone houses and then halted in a cloud of dust inches from a large olive tree.

Khalid got out and strolled into the Arab village, and the women followed.

A little Arab girl chased a hula hoop, barefoot in the dust. Three Arab men glared at the two women from a cement porch. A number of shanties of corrugated iron leaned between the houses. Noga's theory about the Jewish roots of Palestinian Arabs seemed even more ridiculous on the ground. Nothing seemed farther removed from the Jewish city blocks and suburbs of Jerusalem and Tel Aviv than this primitive village community. She wanted to leave the place right away.

"Hannah," she whispered. "I think I might have misread the data."

"Shh. We're there."

Khalid stood at the threshold of an old stone hovel. Hannah pushed through the door of overlapping curtains and disappeared within. Noga glanced at their Arab guide, who scanned the surrounding hills, his mouth tight. Was he guarding them against hostile Palestinians or making sure there were no witnesses to alert the authorities as to the whereabouts of two abducted Israeli women?

With no choice but to follow Hannah, she pulled the curtains apart and stepped inside. The interior looked more like a tent than a stone house. Carpets covered the floor and walls and formed a low canopy overhead. In the corner, a young Arab woman in a flowing burka tended a tin pot on a gas burner, which filled the air with the aromas of lentils and onions. Noga almost didn't notice the old man on the rickety chair. He sat very still in a thin hand-spun gown, his eyes closed, gnarled hands on his lap, a brown length of cloth wrapped around his head.

She joined Hannah on a low bench at the old man's feet. Khalid crouched beside the old man, touched his shoulder, and whispered in his ear. The old man stirred and glanced at the visitors through rheumy eyes.

"He's the patriarch of the village," Hannah whispered in Noga's ear. "That's his great-granddaughter in the corner. Khalid," she said to their guide. "Please ask him to tell us what you told me."

The Arab whispered in the old man's ear again. The old man spoke in a soft frail voice, his thin lips trembling. Noga didn't understand the man's Arabic, but she didn't need to.

"My mother," Khalid translated, "would light candles every Friday at dusk. I never knew why. One day, when I was a young man and already a leader of the clan, my grandfather became very ill. He called me to his bedside. 'Khalid,' he said. 'The time has come for you to learn the truth. Pass this secret to your grandson, as my grandfather did to me.'"

The old man's breath came in short, quick gasps as he re-lived the memory.

"He asked me to come close so he could whisper in my ear. 'Our clan,' he said. 'All of us. We are Jews!'"

CHAPTER 31

Ahmed staggered down a dirt road in Silwan. A woman in a hijab grasped the hand of her young son and crossed to the other side of the street. He must look like a monster: his hair gray with dust, his clothes rigid with dirt and dried sweat, and reeking of garbage.

Hunger had drawn him from his dry hillside tomb to the trash bins at the edge of the suburb. No longer fearful of Boris or his henchmen, he climbed into the large bins and scavenged for food. He gobbled moldy bread crusts and scraped bits of oily tuna from discarded tins. He emptied the last drops of cola and water from old bottles and cans into his parched mouth.

He felt like a monster too. Anger simmered in his belly. Nobody cared about him. His father had abandoned him years ago, and now his own mother had forsaken him for a new life of comfort and prestige.

His rage focused on neither of them, though. Only one person occupied his mind now: Hasan. His cousin, with his wavy dark hair and easy, careless gait, had pushed him to *istishhad* by threatening dishonor and promising Paradise. Hasan had arranged the mission and sent him to his death.

Ahmed pounced on a little boy on the street and grabbed him by his shirt. "Hasan Hadawi," he demanded, taking out his frustrations on the wide-eyed bystander. "Where is he?" He already knew the answer. Hasan lived in Ramallah, out of reach of penniless, filthy monsters. To his surprise, the boy pointed up the hill. "The garage," he said. Ahmed loosened his grip, and the boy slipped away and fled.

Hasan was in Silwan. Ahmed climbed the dirt road, his muscles tensing. Damas had been right: Paradise was a lie, and now Hasan was going to pay. Ahmed would clamp his hands around Hasan's neck and squeeze, and as his life's breath slipped away, he'd ask him why. Why had he deceived him, why had he destroyed Ahmed's simple, worthless life?

Music echoed off the haphazard cinderblock apartment buildings as he rounded the hill—a song with a sensual maqsoum rhythm.

As the road curved, a cement hangar came into view. The music carried, loud and clear, from the speakers of a yellow topless sports car that bathed in the afternoon sun. A bass guitar thrummed while a synthesizer climbed and fell playfully, and Dana Halabi sang.

Ahmed's mother had banned the provocative Kuwaiti diva from her household. The man who slouched in the driver's seat of the Mercedes had no such qualms. His wavy hair pressed against the headrest and his legs crossed at the ankles over the dashboard.

Ahmed padded toward the car, acid boiling in his belly, his fingers twitching.

"*Hos hos hos*," Dana Halabi sang. Shh, shh, shh. "*Bos alaya bos.*" Look at me, look.

In the hangar, two scruffy thugs bent over a backgammon board, immersed in their game.

In the car, the man's head wobbled to the beat. An iPad lay on his lap, and on the screen, the young singer belly danced in a skimpy pink dress. She lay on a bed and sent meaningful glances at the camera. Then she posed on the deck of a yacht, gyrating her hips and hosing the vessel down, and drenching her clothes in the process. Ahmed could smell the man's cologne. He had the same wavy hair as Hasan, but longer and with strands of gray.

Shh, shh, shh. Look at me, look.

He reached out his hand and tapped him on the shoulder.

The man twisted around to glance at Ahmed and shrieked. The iPad flew into the air, landing on the passenger seat, and the music cut out. The man dived over the door of the car into the dirt, where he curled into a little ball of fear in the dust and shielded his head with his forearms.

Ahmed blinked in disbelief at the terrified man at his feet. Then he laughed.

The man peeked between his raised arms. His hair had streaks of gray and he had lines on his forehead, but the man was indeed his cousin. Hasan scuttled away, toward the two thugs who approached the commotion, then got up, straightened his loose white-collared shirt, and squinted at the dust monster. "Ahmed, is that you?"

Ahmed wiped the tears from his eyes as his laughter subsided, and nodded.

Hasan laughed too. He leaned on his knees and caught his breath. "*Halas*," he said, "you almost gave me a heart attack." He walked over and embraced his cousin. "It's OK, boys," he told the confused thugs. "This is Ahmed, my little cousin." He rubbed Ahmed's head.

The thugs shrugged and returned to their game.

Despite himself, Ahmed enjoyed the reunion with his cousin. "Were you expecting me?"

Hasan's smiled faded. "Not you in particular," he said. "But one of the martyrs was bound to turn up. The dead are rising. It's on the news."

"The dead are rising?" The words pushed all other thoughts from Ahmed's mind. He was not alone.

"More each day. They hang out at Clal Center." The dead were rising and they had a meeting place.

Hasan wrinkled his nose. "Man, you smell bad. Let's get out of here." He waved at the passenger seat. "Step into my office."

Ahmed walked around the sports car and got in. He needed to learn more about the rising dead.

Hasan pressed a button and the engine purred to life.

Cool air blew in Ahmed's face. He spotted a water bottle inside the door. "May I?"

"Go ahead."

He downed the bottle of clean cool water in one long gulp.

The Mercedes cruised down Silwan, climbed the City of David, and hugged the walls of the Old City. The road dipped down again as they passed Mount Zion.

"Nice car," Ahmed said. He had never sat in a sports car before. The leather seats cushioned his body in a soft embrace. Ahmed had blown himself up but his mother had gotten the palace, and Hasan had inherited Paradise. The anger simmered within again.

"Latest model," Hasan said with pride. "Bluetooth. GPS. The works."

"The suicide business pays well."

Hasan did not notice the bitter edge to Ahmed's voice. "It has its perks," he said. "Not as glorious as you *shaheed*s."

"If suicide is so glorious, how come you never tried it?"

"Me?" He seemed truly surprised at the question. "Nah. We each have a job. Mine is to find and dispatch guys like you. Yours is to blow up."

The engine growled like a tiger as the Merc crossed the valley of Ben Hinnom, then accelerated up Hebron Road.

Hasan seemed to relax more as they drove. Had his cousin wanted to treat him to a ride and a private chat or to remove Ahmed from his home turf? He parked at the Haas Promenade overlooking the Old City and eyed Ahmed. "You look like crap."

The questions that had crowded Ahmed's mind over the months surfaced again. "Did I kill many people?"

"Lots." Hasan clapped Ahmed on the shoulder. "Don't look so sad. You did well. Sons of pigs and monkeys, the lot of them. Killers of prophets. You showed them. You're a hero."

Ahmed didn't feel like a hero. The gastric juices bubbled in his stomach. "Aren't you going to ask me about Paradise— about my palace and wives?"

Hasan chuckled and lowered his eyes to the steering wheel.

Then Ahmed understood. "You knew all along, didn't you? It's all lies. There is no Paradise."

"Quiet," Hasan said. He looked over his shoulder. "You can't go around saying things like that. It sounds like heresy, and you know what happens to heretics around here."

"I want my life back."

"You can't. You must never go back to Silwan."

Ahmed's suspicions had been on target. "Why not?"

"You're a *shaheed*. You're a hero. You died for the faith. Your sins are forgiven. All the little boys want to be like you. The little girls too. You can't come back from Paradise and say 'I want a refund.'"

Ahmed lost his ability to speak. *He doesn't believe. He sends boys and girls to die on the streets but he doesn't believe his own promises of eternal reward.*

As a little boy Ahmed had received a plastic Kalashnikov for his birthday. A martyr's death had seemed so noble and just. Death would turn him into a superman. And now Hasan wanted him to help cover up the lie.

"How am I supposed to live?"

Hasan looked him in the eye. "I have another belt. My last one. When they built that wall we had to move to knives and vehicle attacks."

Had he heard correctly? "You want me to die again?"

"Think of it, cuz. You'll be a *shaheed* twice over. Nobody has ever done that before. You'll be the father of all *shaheeds*."

"You're crazy." Hasan had aged since their last meeting, but he had not learned anything.

Hasan gave a short laugh. "What else are you going to do?"

Ahmed had no answer to that. He opened the door and got out.

"Listen to me," Hasan called after him. "It's the only way. Hey, where are you going?"

"To a better place," Ahmed said, and he walked away.

CHAPTER 32

Yosef closed his laptop. He felt the urge to offer the padded manager's chair to his visitor. On the other side of Moshe's desk, Rabbi Emden sat ramrod straight but said nothing.

"Some coffee, Rabbi Emden?"

"No, thank you."

Why had his mentor visited him and why, of all places, at the Dry Bones Society, the society that, according to the Great Council, was in league with the unholy Other Side? Did he intend to pressure Yosef into abandoning the Dry Bones Society as he had pressured Minister Malkior?

Yosef dug his fingertips into the armrests. He believed in their cause, reverends and all.

The distinguished rabbi removed his bowler hat, lowered his eyes to the desk, and pursed his lips. He looked humble, even contrite. "I owe you an apology, my friend, for not reaching out to you since our meeting with the Great Council."

Whatever Yosef had expected, it had not been an apology. "There is nothing to forgive," he said. "You could not associate with us after their verdict. I understand that."

"Do you?" Rabbi Emden gave him a quick, penetrating look. "I failed to return your calls, even though I knew of your troubles at the school. When you needed a friend most,

I did nothing."

Yosef winced at the memory. A posse of Chassidic men had delivered the ultimatum to his house and then, the next day, the letter of dismissal from Rabbanit Schiff, the principal of Daas Torah Primary where Yosef had taught second grade. His support of the friendless resurrected had cost him his livelihood, and ostracized his family from much of the ultra-Orthodox community.

Would Rabbi Emden entice Yosef away from the Society with the offer of a new job?

"I want us to be friends again," the rabbi continued. "Can we be friends?"

"Of course!" Yosef's grip on the armrest slackened. The rabbi had checked his politics at the door and entered in his personal capacity. He had come to build bridges, not demolish them, and Yosef snatched the extended olive branch like a drowning man clamping onto a lifesaver in a stormy sea. Messianic questions weighed him down and he longed for the buoyant certainty of the rabbi's guidance.

Rabbi Emden produced a grateful smile. "Thank you."

A mad hope sprung in Yosef's heart. Had the distinguished rabbi decided to join their struggle? Had he seen the righteousness of their way? His optimism rocketed skyward. Had a messianic sixth sense alerted the rabbi to Yosef's secret phone calls? Had Rabbi Emden arrived to unmask his true identity and take over the reins of the Society as the rightful Heir of David?

"Now that we are friends again," Rabbi Emden continued, "I must confess that I am in need of your help."

Yosef's anticipation deflated like a balloon. What could the esteemed rabbi possibly need from him? "Of course," Yosef said. "Anything!"

The rabbi ran his tongue over his lips. "I understand that the Dry Bones Society has joined with Upward." The turn to party politics sank Yosef into murky confusion, which must have registered on his face, for Rabbi Emden elaborated. "Isaac Gurion's new party."

"Yes, that is true," Yosef said.

"Gurion is a godless man," Rabbi Emden said, "and a sworn enemy of religion. We cannot let his party take hold of the country."

"What are you asking, Rabbi?"

Rabbi Emden's eyes sparkled. "Join us, Yosef."

"Join who?"

"Torah True!"

Torah True, the leading ultra-Orthodox party, obeyed the Great Council. Torah True had convinced Minister Malkior to renege on his agreement with the Dry Bones Society, only to be double-crossed, in turn, when Gurion had entered the fray.

"I don't understand," Yosef said. "The Great Council called us the *Sitra Achra*. Now the Council wants to join forces with demons?"

"Not demons," Emden said, and gave a good-natured chuckle. "*Demon*-strators. The sages of the Council saw your protest before Knesset and have heard of your suffering. A host of Jewish souls such as that surely contains sparks of holiness."

"And now they have the vote." The words slipped out Yosef's mouth without passing his brain. How dare he question the Council's integrity? Shmuel's sarcasm had rubbed off on him.

Emden lowered his eyes again but didn't seem to take offense. "You are right, of course. This is politics. We cannot let the secularists rule the country. They will desecrate the holy Sabbath, and dishonor the Torah. The voting box is the only way to safeguard Tradition."

"And," Shmuel's voice said in Yosef's mind, "to keep the money flowing into the Council's coffers." The man across the desk was not truly a friend, only another politician.

Yosef studied the chipped edge of the wooden desk. He had lost his job, his unquestioning belief in the rabbinate, and now his role model. Shaking his head, he said, "Gurion got them the vote. The Society won't turn on him now."

"Then give them a reason, Yosef. You are the spiritual leader of the Dry Bones Society. Guide them to the side of holiness. You have the power—wield it. This is your religious duty. Do you want the government to fill with Torah sages or pork-*fressers*?"

Yosef stared at the desk. "I've met many resurrected people," he said. "Not all are religious. Some aren't even Jewish. God seems to like them all the same."

"Nonsense!" Emden's patience was wearing thin, but he returned to his cajoling tone. "Don't turn us down, Yosef. This is your last chance at redemption."

Yosef squeezed the armrests. "That isn't the redemption we've been waiting for."

The smile fell from Emden's face. He collected his hat and stood to his full height. "I came to speak with you as a friend," he said, placing his hat on his head. "Friends treat friends with kindness and consideration. But reject that friendship, Yosef, and the gloves will come off."

CHAPTER 33

Noga's coffee cup trembled in her hands as she sat opposite Hannah in Café Hillel on Emek Refaim. After the Samarian village, they had visited an Arab settlement in Judea where they had heard a similar confession, and long after the two Israeli women had left the West Bank, the revelations still shook them.

The discovery burned inside her, demanding that she run through the streets to share the news. So this was how Archimedes must have felt. At least she hadn't been lazing in a hot tub when the breakthrough had hit. And she still had a few questions to answer before she'd run naked through the streets of Jerusalem.

"We need to write a paper," Hannah said, infected, apparently, by the same urge. She stared into space and sipped her coffee. "The country has to know. The *world* has to know. This changes everything."

"I still don't understand how it can be," Noga said. She kept her voice low, so as not to be overheard by the couple at the next table. "Entire Arab villages, entire tribes–how can they be Jewish? It's too convenient, too easy. It doesn't make any sense."

Hannah leaned in. "There's a precedent. In the fifteenth century, Jews in Spain were given a choice: convert to Christianity or die. Thousands converted rather than leave the country where their families had lived for centuries. But many of these forced converts remained Jews in secret, and the Spanish Inquisition hounded these suspected *Marranos*, burning them at the stake."

She took another gulp of coffee. "Israel, Palestine, Judea, Samaria—call it what you like. Jews have lived here for over three thousand years. After King Solomon's death, the nation split into the Kingdom of Israel in the north and the Kingdom of Judah to the south. The Assyrians conquered the northern kingdom in 722 BCE, exiling those Ten Tribes and scattering them throughout the ancient world."

Noga thought she saw where Hannah was going. "But," she said, "if they're the Ten Lost Tribes, they should be somewhere else, not here in Israel."

"That," Hannah said and smiled, "is what most people think, and in this case most people are wrong. When we look closer at the historical record, we see a different picture. The Assyrians didn't exile entire nations, only the ruling elite—the powerful families and leaders who could coordinate rebellions and national revivals. They didn't bother with the simple folk—the farmers, villagers, and the poor."

The pit in Noga's stomach opened again.

Hannah continued. "Khalid's ancestors claim to have been here for many centuries," she said. "Before the British, the Ottomans, even the Crusaders and Muslims. When the Muslims invaded in the seventh century, they gave the native Jews the same ultimatum that the Spanish had: convert or die. Like the *conversos* in Spain, most chose to stay in their ancestral homeland and convert to the dominant faith in public, while still safeguarding their traditions behind closed doors."

She placed her coffee mug on the table. "Genes don't lie, Noga dear. They are Jews."

"The Ten Lost Tribes," Noga said, as though in a trance.

Hannah nodded. "People have been searching for the Lost Tribes across the globe when they were right here all along, under our noses."

Noga abandoned her coffee. She should feel elated. Hannah had vindicated her research. With one logical connection, they had discovered the elusive Ten Lost Tribes and traced a path toward lasting peace in their time. But this boon for the Jewish People spelled disaster for her personal life. *Why me? Why now?*

Hannah emitted a brief ironic laugh.

"What?"

"It's funny," she said. "According to an old Jewish tradition, the Ten Lost Tribes are destined to return at the End of Days, or the Messianic Era." She waved her hands in the air to express her disdain for fanciful ancient superstitions and chuckled again. "And guess who is supposed to rediscover them?"

"I know that one," Noga said, surprising her mentor. She had uncovered that factoid a few months ago, when she had researched the End of Days in order to better understand a cute but delusional patient she had met at the Shaare Zedek Medical Center. Her heart squirming, she said, "Elijah the Prophet."

CHAPTER 34

A rush of déjà vu made Moshe's skin tingle. Once again, he stood under the *chuppah* canopy on the grassy knoll between the Ramat Rachel Hotel and the event hall.

A trumpeter played the Carpenters' "We've Only Just Begun" as the sun sank behind the buildings, casting a soft golden glow over the long white carpet that ran between the rows of chairs dressed in white. The same venue, the same band, the same bride and groom. Savta Sarah's catering too. He might have traveled back in time to his first wedding eight years ago.

Only the guests were different. They trickled in from the buffet gardens and filled the rows of chairs. Not Galit's extended family like last time—her parents and brother had not been able to get on a flight from New Jersey in time—but the familiar faces of the Dry Bones Society. The unfamiliar faces belonged to the many VIPs of the Upward party list. The sheer number of guests had forced Moshe to opt for a wedding hall instead of the quiet home ceremony Galit would have preferred.

Isaac Gurion settled in the front row, cocktail in hand, beside a well-powdered Mrs. Gurion, and surrounded by an entourage of assistants and bodyguards. He nodded at Moshe and winked. The well-connected politician had twisted a few arms in the Chief Rabbinate to expedite the marriage permit.

Moshe inclined his head and smiled. Rabbi Yosef shifted on his feet under the *chuppah* and filled the wine glass on a side table. This was the first wedding ceremony he had conducted and his nerves were showing. Rafi and Shmuel, Moshe's witnesses, hovered at the edge of the wedding canopy. Rafi was doubling as his best man, the role that Avi had filled at Moshe's first wedding.

Times had changed. Only two months ago, Moshe had rushed to Ramat Rachel to stop Avi from marrying Galit on this very spot. Would Avi try to disrupt his wedding tonight?

Moshe scanned the crowd for the old thorn in his side. Spotting no intruders, he glanced at his new gold watch. The ceremony should have started five minutes ago. *Where was she?* Galit had left Avi waiting under the *chuppah*—would she stand Moshe up as well? He had lost her before without warning. Would that bolt of lightning strike him down twice?

Moshe adjusted his blue suit jacket and tie and dismissed the concern. *Don't be paranoid.*

On cue, the trumpeter played a new song, a traditional wedding ditty, and there she was. Galit stood at the end of the white carpet in her elegant white evening gown. She smiled at him through the wispy veil. Little Talya led the way in a frilly bridesmaid's dress, strewing rose petals from a miniature wicker basket. Moshe blew his daughter a kiss and she smiled from ear to ear.

Galit climbed the steps of the *chuppah*, beaming at him through the veil, and circled her groom, the train of her dress sliding over his shoes.

For all the similarities, this wedding was different. The bride and groom were older and wiser. Moshe was, literally, a new man. But the differences ran deeper than mere time passed. He had almost lost her, he had fought against all odds to win her heart again, and the effort had thickened the tendrils of love that bound them together. They were one living organism. Nothing would part them again.

Behind the rows of seated guests, Irina stood and smiled

beside her Russian friend. With his ponytail and bulging biceps, Alex had set off mental alarm bells, but when Irina had told him how her new friend had helped out at the Society and arranged for her a pro-bono appointment with a neurologist, Moshe had relaxed. Irina could take care of herself. With all his recent political activity, Moshe had had even less time to devote to her and he was glad that she had Alex's support.

Talya sat on a chair, her legs dangling, beside a teary Savta Sarah. Moshe glanced at the rows of friends and well-wishers as Galit stopped beside him and her hand found his.

Rabbi Yosef started the ceremony, and Moshe savored the moment. *This is it. This is what life is all about—moments of joy with family and friends.* Those fleeting happy times drove everything he did—not the cameras or even the salary. He had to hold onto these moments and create more of them. Which reminded him—on Wednesday he was scheduled, finally, to see that cardiologist.

A large, dark figure passed behind the crowd and a sudden dread pulled at Moshe's insides. Had he seen the hulking form of King Kong, Boris's muscular henchman, or was the vision just a trick of his mind? Had the slave master sent his crony to exact revenge for Moshe's disruption of his graveyard recruitment? Moshe should have seen this coming.

He squeezed Galit's hand but she only smiled at him. His muscles tensed, ready to rush her from the *chuppah* to safety, while he scanned the mass of wedding guests. The oversized mobster did not march down the aisle toward them, nor was he lurking among the bushes.

Moshe wiped sweat from his brow and shivered. He'd have to do something about Boris and his slave machine, and not only in order to ensure the safety of his loved ones. While Moshe celebrated his own personal happiness, many innocents languished in chains.

He'd have a word with Gurion after the election. The politician had connections at the police, and cleaning up a criminal operation would carve another glorious notch into his political belt.

The ceremony continued without mishap. Moshe sipped the wine, placed the ring on her finger, crushed the glass beneath his heel, broke bread, danced and posed for photos, but throughout the evening the dread lingered in the shadows of his mind. Let Gurion handle Boris. Moshe had kicked a sleeping tiger once and lived to tell the tale. He should avoid a second confrontation or he could lose everything.

CHAPTER 35

"Are you sure this is the right place?" Irina asked.

The three-story apartment block on Rav Berlin Street did not look like a medical clinic, and the doctor's name did not appear on the façade of grimy Jerusalem stone. A row of tall rustling trees created a reassuring sense of suburban calm.

"This is his private consultation room," Alex said. He held the gate of the yard open for her. Despite the tough-guy exterior, Alex behaved like a gentleman.

They had spent a lot of time together since their first meeting at the Society last Thursday. He had accompanied her to the press conference on Sunday, and early Monday morning, he had worked with her at the Ministry of the Interior, helping applicants fill out their forms and find the right desk. Some of them could neither read nor write Hebrew. That afternoon, during their lunch break of packed sandwiches, he had offered to take her to see the doctor.

Her memory loss fascinated Alex, but not only her memory loss. His lips trembled when he spoke with her and he moved with a self-conscious stiffness, which whispered that his interest in her went beyond mere intellectual curiosity.

She smiled to herself and walked through the open gate, down the short path of flat stones, to the door of the building. Alex pressed the buzzer for apartment number one and the door clicked open. As the building was situated on a hillside slope, they had to descend a gloomy stairwell to get to the first floor. Their footfalls echoed in the dank and cramped space.

"Are you sure I can't pay him?" she asked. She had brought a few hundred shekels and a Dry Bones Society credit card just in case. Having no identity, she couldn't apply for an identity card and thus she couldn't register for state health insurance. Luckily, she had not needed a doctor since her return. In fact, during the past few months she had been so busy trying to survive and, later, helping new arrivals at the Society that the idea of consulting a neurologist had never crossed her mind.

"He's an old friend," Alex said. "And he owes me a favor."

Alex stopped at a door on the lower floor. No name. No number. He knocked, then entered and turned on a light.

They stood in a plain rectangular room. Sunlight seeped through slatted windows on one side and fell on two simple chairs of steel and plywood. Pale rectangles on the walls remained where once pictures had hung. The small square floor tiles reeked of disinfectant. In the remains of an old kitchen at the back, gas pipes protruded from the wall. Irina clutched her handbag to her chest. This was not your typical waiting room.

A door opened and a short man in a white cloak and thick black-framed spectacles glared at them. A bald patch glistened on the top of his head. He waved them inside without a word.

A large dentist's chair dominated the center of the chamber, and a tray of medical tools sat atop a long set of drawers. *That's more like it.* But the unusual mix of medical equipment gave her pause. Did neurologists use dentist's chairs?

"Sit," the doctor said in Russian. He was not a man of words.

DAN SOFER

She made for the dentist's chair and a layer of thick plastic sheeting crinkled beneath her sandals. This was probably the most unusual doctor's room she had ever visited, although, to be fair, she remembered nothing of other medical visits.

The doctor sat on a squeaky-wheeled chair and searched among his equipment. Alex leaned against the wall and folded his arms. She was glad he had come with her.

The doctor leaned over her. "Look up," he said. He flashed a light in each of her eyes.

"Alex tells me you're a neurologist," she said, in a lame attempt at small talk.

The doctor raised his eyebrows at her, so she pointed toward the set of drawers behind her. "The dentist's drill," she said. "And the chair." She had noticed many other long, pointed tools but didn't know their names.

Alex spoke. "Dr. V has many qualifications and many talents."

The doctor gripped her wrist and glanced at his watch. "Both involve extraction," he said, a crooked smile twisting his thin, chapped lips. "As a dentist, I extract teeth. Today we will extract memories. Ready?"

Irina inhaled a deep breath. Today was the day. Her first memory. Her first glimpse at her former life. She nodded.

"Good."

There was a click and a mechanical groan. The chair shuddered as it flattened to a reclining position.

The doctor grasped a round sticker attached to a thin wire and pressed the sticker to her right temple, then attached a second sticker to her left temple. The doctor arranged her hands on the armrest and a strap tightened over one of her wrists.

"Are you sure that's—?" she began but the doctor cut her off.

"For your safety," he said.

She glanced at Alex for reassurance and he nodded. The doctor buckled a strap over her other wrist and did the same for both her ankles. She couldn't move.

She said, "Is this is really necessary?"

The doctor straightened on his seat. "Old memories can be very traumatic. This way you won't injure yourself. Breathe deeply and stay calm. OK?"

Irina drew a long, deep breath and tried to relax. She was prepared to go through almost anything to get her memory back. The doctor had dodgy rooms and unorthodox methods, but he might be able to help her.

He turned on a lamp behind her. "I will show you a few objects, and you will tell me if they look familiar. OK?"

She nodded.

He raised his arm in the air. In his hand, he held a stuffed teddy bear.

She smiled. She had almost expected a dead fish or a writhing snake. "Nothing," she said.

The bear disappeared and he held up a poster of the Eiffel Tower. "No." She shifted on the chair. This would be easier—and far more comfortable—with a computer and without the straps.

The next item made her giggle. He held a kinky bra of black lace in his hand, while he scrutinized her eyes. She shook her head and stifled another giggle. Alex studied the floor.

The next few objects helped her overcome her giggle attack. A knife with a long, thick blade. A photo of a dingy alleyway with broken trash bins and shattered windows. What strange things to show her.

"No," she said for what seemed like the hundredth time. None of the objects or photos had registered in her memory.

The doctor glanced at Alex and Alex nodded his head.

"We will try another approach," the doctor said. He leaned over her and pointed beneath his right eye. "Look here. Good." He narrowed his eyes. "Don't take your eyes from mine. Don't speak or move until I tell you."

Hypnosis, Irina realized, with mild disappointment. The first attempts had failed.

"As you follow my instructions," he continued, "nothing

in the world can prevent you from falling into a very deep and pleasant sleep."

This probably wouldn't work. Had she ever undergone hypnosis? She didn't think she was the susceptible type.

"Now, take a deep breath and fill your lungs." He lifted his hand into the air and her lungs filled. "Now exhale." He lowered his hand and her lungs emptied. He repeated the procedure twice, her breath deepening each time.

She swallowed a yawn. The doctor was good. She felt very relaxed.

"I'm going to count from five down to one. As I do, your eyelids will feel heavy, drowsy, and sleepy. By the time I reach the count of one, they will close and you will sink into a deep hypnotic slumber. Deeper than ever before."

Whatever. She'd humor him. What did she have to lose?

He raised his hand above her head and pointed into the air. "Five," he said. "Eyelids heavy, drowsy, sleepy."

He lowered his hand a notch. "Four. Those heavy lids are ready to close." His eyes filled her mind. Only his eyes existed. She blinked.

"Three. The next time you blink, that is hypnosis coming over you." The hand dropped slowly. His eyes bored right through her.

The hand fell out of sight beside her head. "Two," the voice said. "They begin closing, closing, closing, closing, closing them, close them, close them. They're closing, closing, closing. One."

Fingers closed over her elbow. A hand grasped her head at the base of the skull and shoved her head forward. "Sleep now!"

Her eyes closed.

She waited.

Hearing nothing, she waited some more.

Fingers clicked and she opened her eyes. The doctor stood over her. Over his shoulder, Alex watched her. They said nothing for a while. *It didn't work.*

"Sorry, Doctor," she said. "I don't think I'm a good candidate for hypnosis." She sniffed the air. "What's that burning smell?"

The doctor didn't answer. He leaned in and plucked a round white sticker from her temple. She had forgotten about the wires. A wisp of smoke rose from the underside of the pad, which had charred to black. He detached the other pad and removed them from sight.

Strange. She hadn't felt any burning.

"Retrograde amnesia," the doctor said to Alex. "She truly remembers nothing of her former life." He spoke as though she wasn't in the room.

"Will her memory ever return?"

The doctor shook his head. "This is caused by a lack of blood flow to the right temporal lobe, the seat of long-term memory. It is usually the result of head trauma."

Alex nodded as though that made sense.

Irina spoke up. "But I haven't hurt my head."

The doctor turned to her. "Not now," he said. "Before your death."

"Oh. Right." She had received a blow to the head toward the end of her first life. That ruled out cancer as her suspected cause of death and pushed car accident to the top of the list. Or some other violent end. She shuddered, and suddenly she wanted very much to get far away from the doctor and his dingy consultation room.

The chair groaned and shuddered toward an upright position and Alex unbuckled the leather straps, then helped her out of the chair. He escorted her up the stairwell and out of the building.

Her temples itched. When she touched them, her fingers returned with a patina of dark, crusty flakes like burnt bread. Or singed chicken.

Alex held the gate open for her. "Disappointed?"

"I suppose."

He grinned. "Don't be," he said. He seemed to be in a good mood, despite the failed attempts at recall.

The prognosis hit her. "I'll never get my memory back,

will I?"

He gave her a sympathetic frown. "Look on the bright side. You have a new life. A clean slate."

Moshe had said the same thing to console her on her first day. Irina slipped her arm in his and they walked to Alex's car together. Men were strange creatures.

CHAPTER 36

Ahmed ignored the stares as he walked up Jaffa Street. He had shaken the dirt from his soiled clothes as best he could, but some passersby made faces and blocked their noses. His own nose had grown used to the stench of trash, and he wore his stiff clothes and foul smell like armor in enemy territory.

Israeli society had not always been enemy territory. He had worked among the Jews at the Rami Levi supermarket in Talpiot without fear. He had unpacked crates, mopped floors, and laid out fresh vegetables for customers to buy. Yigal, his boss, had joked around with him in Arabic, asked after his family, and let him take Fridays off. All that had changed the moment Ahmed had stepped onto a crowded bus and pressed the detonator hidden in his sleeve.

The tired façade of Clal Center loomed over Jaffa Street: two floors of large cement squares topped by thirteen more, all stained with soot. Dark bands separated the floors, windows dotted by air conditioning units. The old building looked like a prison. Once inside, he might not be able to escape. Would they kill him on sight to avenge their murdered friends and family, or torture him first? Or would they take him in as one of their own? Ahmed the killer had died. Was there hope for the new Ahmed?

The cramp in his stomach cast the deciding vote.

He crossed the street. A handwritten sign on the door read, "Dry Bones Society. Third floor." The resurrected met at Clal Center, Hasan had said, and they had selected a fitting name.

An arrow pointed the way inside. One look at the elevator convinced him to take the stairs, but the third floor corridor was quiet. Too quiet. Had Hasan sent him into a trap? Was this Dry Bones Society a second killing field for martyrs who refused to stay dead?

He passed a door with a sign that read, "Absorption Center."

"You," said a commanding voice and Ahmed jumped. An old lady poked out the door, stared at him, then waddled over. Her eyes grew very large behind her thick glasses. "Hungry?"

He nodded.

She grinned. "Follow me."

She led him to a large room within the Absorption Center. Steam rose from a long line of silver trays on a counter. The scent of cooked meat and rice almost overpowered him. His limbs trembled. The sight was too much. He wanted to charge ahead and bury his face in the food. Had he finally reached Heaven or was this another cruel trap? The food would disappear on touch. Or he would choke, the Jews having laced the delicacies with poison.

The old lady placed a clean plate in his hands. "Go on," she said. "It's kosher. *Glatt* kosher. The classes break for lunch soon, so dish up before there's a line."

Ahmed didn't need a second invitation. He piled chicken thighs, rice, and steamed vegetables on the plate, then added the juicy cuts of meat dripping with thick gravy.

"Easy does it," she said. "You can come back for seconds."

He shoved handfuls into his mouth, then settled for a table and cutlery. So far, he had not dropped dead. If the old crone had poisoned the food, he would enjoy a very tasty final meal.

The old lady poured him a tumbler of sweet juice, and sat down opposite. "What's your name?"

He paused mid-bite. Should he lie to his generous hostess? Even if she threw him out, he would have gobbled more food in the last few seconds than he had in the past few days.

He said, "Ahmed," trying and failing to mask his Arabic accent.

The old lady nodded and pulled out a mobile phone. "Hello, dear," she said into it. "Another one just came in. Yes. In the dining hall."

Had she called security? He shoveled food into his mouth faster in case he had to dash for the exit.

"I'm Sarah," she said. "You'll want to have a shower, trust me. There's plenty of donated clothes to choose from, and I expect you'll want to stay in the dormitory."

"Dormitory?" Had she offered him a place to live?

"One floor up," she said, and pointed at the ceiling. "Nothing fancy, but it's a place to stay and close to the Absorption Center."

A tear trickled down his cheeks. The old lady was willing to accept him, alive and whole; Ahmed had found a new home in the most unlikely of places.

"That is," she added, "until you can process your identity card and make your own way in the world."

He swallowed hard. Once his old identity became known, they'd cast him out for sure. He would have to avoid that.

The old lady peered at the door behind him. "There she is."

Ahmed heard soft footfalls and turned around. The figure that stood beside their table was not a security guard, but a pretty young woman. She wore a green hijab and gave him a demure welcoming smile.

"Ahmed," the old lady said, "this is Samira. She'll take care of you."

CHAPTER 37

Is this really happening?

A number of young professionals buzzed around Moshe Wednesday evening while he waited on a comfortable armchair in the Channel Two studio. One attached a microphone bud to his shirt. Another applied a makeup brush to his cheek. Yet others adjusted spotlights wrapped in umbrellas and positioned large mounted cameras.

Beside him, Dani Tavor reviewed a sheaf of papers on the conference table while an attendant styled his wavy gray hair. Liat Arbel sat next to him and gave him a brief smile. They looked older in real life, although, to be fair, Moshe had first seen the father-and-daughter duo on the small screen fifteen years ago.

Liat brushed a strand of hair from her face. "Nervous?" she asked him.

"A little."

She smirked. "We'll try to go easy on you."

Fat chance of that. The famous duo, Dani and Liat, were known to grill their guests on the weekly television panel like plucked chickens on a rotisserie. In his previous life, Moshe had fantasized about appearing on this Israeli answer to The Oprah Winfrey Show to discuss the unrivaled successes of Karlin & Son. Moshe's current reality had surpassed even that fantasy.

Heat up the grill. Moshe didn't mind. Negative publicity was publicity too, and he represented a non-profit that aided the weakest, poorest, most miserable minority in society. How bad a picture of him could they paint?

"Five seconds," said a man with a tablet computer and a wireless earpiece.

The makeup crew fled and the famous duo sat up in their chairs. Moshe did the same.

"Welcome," Dani said into the gaping mouth of a tele-prompter camera. "Unless you've been living under a rock this past week, you will have heard of the wave of new immigrants that have reached our shores. Unlike other immigrants, however, these have arrived not from another country, but from another life, or, as some would say, another world. With us in the studio is Moshe Karlin of the Dry Bones Society, the organization that he established to cater to the needs of this new demographic of resurrected men and women. Welcome to the show, Moshe."

"Thanks."

Liat took over. "You've had to face a lot of opposition and not a few setbacks over the first few months, haven't you?"

"Yes," Moshe said. He'd have to move beyond monosyllables soon, and needed to find an excuse to plug the Society's toll-free donation hotline.

Liat continued. "Many doubted the truth of the so-called Resurrection, calling it a hoax. Until recently, the State didn't recognize your people or their rights."

"That is true," Moshe said, jumping on the opportunity. "In addition to the inherent trauma of coming back to life, they aren't able to function in society—to find jobs or get medical attention. Many still have no food or shelter. We rely heavily on donations to assist newcomers. Our volunteers visit cemeteries across the—"

"But now," Dani said, cutting him off, and Moshe felt the full force of his trademark piercing look, "you've had many successes. The Second Law of Return gave you citizenship and, it seems, preferential treatment at both the Ministry of the Interior and the National Insurance Institute, which now overflow with resurrected men and women applying for identity cards and health insurance. And, of course, there's your recent foray into politics."

"Yes," Moshe said. "Thank God, we've made significant progress."

"Thank God, you say. And yet you have joined with Isaac Gurion's new political party, Upward. Isaac Gurion is running a very anti-religious campaign."

Moshe took a sip from his complimentary bottle of mineral water and placed it back on the table. He had expected comments like that. "The resurrected come from all parts of society. Religious. Secular. Jewish. Arab. We help them all and we hope that our new friends will enable us to do more good."

"Do you think," Liat asked, "that the rest of us should feel... threatened?"

Moshe had not expected that one. He hoped his mouth hadn't dropped too low. "Threatened?" he repeated. "Why should you? Our society will only gain. Lost loved ones are returning home. We've added talent and working hands to the economy, not to mention their many years of experience and insight."

"Yes," Dani said. "But each job taken by a Dry Bone—for lack of a better term—is a job lost to a First Timer. The Ministry of the Interior has been closed to them for days, and our medical services have only so much capacity. Would ordinary citizens be right to feel disenfranchised?"

Moshe's fingers reached for the buttons of his shirt. The grill had heated up. "That's a temporary spike. The load on the Ministry will ease up soon enough. The State will need to invest in infrastructure, that's true, but that will only stimulate the economy further. Most industries in Israel suffer from a lack of workers, not unemployment. We'll no longer need to import foreign workers."

Dani didn't seem to have heard him. "And now," he said, "with your new political clout, it's understandable that a few people might be concerned."

Liat said, "Not just a few. Twenty thousand. See for yourself."

The screen built into the table lit up. Hordes of people crowded Kaplan Street outside the Knesset building. At first Moshe thought this was footage of the Dry Bones Society demonstration, but these protestors wore yellow shirts with black nuclear hazard signs. The placards in their hands read "Zombies Go Home!" and "Life is for the Living!"

"This came in an hour ago," Dani explained. "Citizens in Jerusalem have taken to the streets in protest."

Moshe didn't buy the spontaneous demonstration narrative. Someone had to have printed the yellow shirts and coordinated with the police officers, whose cruisers watched from the corner. A thicket of bearded men in the black cloaks of the ultra-Orthodox held their own picket signs aloft, which read "Demons Be Gone!"

"What are they chanting?" Liat asked.

Dani said, "Sounds to me like 'Undead Stay Dead!'"

One man stood above the crowd and led the chanting. The demagogue shouted hatred into a megaphone as the camera zoomed in.

Moshe shuddered and his face drained of blood. He knew the man with the megaphone, and so he knew who had printed the shirts, arranged the crowds, and turned the country against him. Their paths had crossed before only too often. His name was Avi Segal.

CHAPTER 38

Noga led the blindfolded man from the bedroom into the corridor. He didn't reach out with his hands to feel for obstacles. Eli trusted her completely. *Good.* She would need a double dose of that trust tonight.

"Almost there," she said. She led him to the dining room and struggled to untie the scarf around his head.

"So," he said, smiling, "are you going to show me why you locked me in the room for the last hour or what?"

"Patience, Smart Ass." The knot unraveled and the scarf fell from his eyes. "There!"

He blinked at the set table and lit candles.

Noga clasped her hands together like a Queen Ester who had entered the royal court uninvited, her life depending on the king's reaction. Raise the golden scepter and she lived. Otherwise, off with her head. Noga needed a good reaction right now, especially knowing what she had lined up for later.

"Wow!" he said. He turned to her and his eyes widened further. "Wow again!"

She had used his credit card and selected a minimalist red evening dress for the occasion. Matching lipstick and half an hour with a blow-dryer and voila! A romantic dinner for two. The phone call to Oshi Oshi had provided a platter of his favorite tempura sushi.

He seated her first, then poured wine into the two glasses. "My birthday is a few months away," he said.

"I know," she said. They split their takeout chopsticks and dug in.

"What's the occasion?"

"You'll see."

He grinned and dipped his sushi in the tub of soy sauce.

"I've got a surprise for you too," he said.

"You do? What kind of surprise?" His last surprise had almost wrecked their relationship in the secret garden of Shaare Zedek.

"That depends on you," he said. "What do you prefer—the Bahamas or the Caribbean?"

"Come again?"

"There's a big and beautiful world out there," he said. "We should see it. Let's take off a few weeks and go on a cruise."

"A cruise?" A thrill ran through her body.

"Mm-hmm," he said, chewing his food. "Norwegian and Princess do both lines. Which do you prefer?"

We're going on a cruise! "Um," she said. "Both sound good. You choose."

Noga had never dreamed of going on a cruise—expensive vacations had never made it onto the menu—but Eli was going to make those dreams come true all the same.

She slammed the brakes on her enthusiasm. If the evening went according to plan, the cruise would have to wait. Was she making a huge mistake?

In the hospital, Eli had been the closet lunatic, she the voice of reason. How the tables had turned! She had double-checked her facts and rehearsed their delivery. She had shed every ounce of doubt and made her decision. Eli would hear the whole truth tonight, and to implement her decision, she needed Eli's support, not just to hold her hand, but to play an active role, the role she had dismissed months ago as a delusion.

"Everything all right?"

She put down her chopsticks and wiped her mouth on an

Oshi Oshi napkin. She had to tell him now; the stakes were too high.

"Eli," she said. "Remember that time in the hospital, in the secret garden? You gave me a rose and a jewelry box."

"How could I forget," he said.

"You asked me to listen without interrupting. To hear you out."

"Yeah," he said. "And then you threw the box at my head and stormed out."

She managed a nervous smile. "I need the same of you tonight," she said. "The 'hear me out' bit," she added quickly. "Not the storming out."

He raised his eyebrows and the smile faded from his face. He had guessed what this was about. "OK," he said. He loved her and he'd listen, just as she had.

The Jerusalem skyline darkened through the French windows in the adjoining living room. No turning back now.

"I owe you an apology," she said. His eyebrows bunched with confusion. She had hoped that the opening would pique his interest and soften the impact of her words. "I went with Hannah to Samaria yesterday," she continued. "We met with the heads of Arab clans. Their traditions back up the genetic data from my thesis. They're Jewish and they know it. And now Hannah has figured out why."

Eli stopped chewing and watched her in silence.

"They're like the *Marranos* of Spain—they chose conversion over death or expulsion—but they've been here since the First Temple. Eli, they're the Ten Lost Tribes of Israel."

Eli blinked but said nothing, so she plowed on.

"You were right about the false messiahs. There were loads of them and they caused so much damage. But they all appeared during times of turmoil and suffering. Bar Kokhba after the destruction of the Second Temple. A whole bunch of messiahs during the Crusades. Sabbatai Zevi after the Khmelnytsky pogroms that wiped out a third of European Jewry. Those messiahs arose during desperate times. These are not desperate times. We live in a democracy with supermarkets and medicine, technology and reality TV. This time really *is* different."

He drew a deep breath and exhaled. Were the facts getting through?

"Two months ago in the secret garden, you told me that you were Elijah, that the End of Days was here and that we had a special role to play together. It sounded crazy then—it still does—and I walked out on you, I know. But what if you were right?"

He gazed at her with sad, tired eyes.

"I'm sorry I doubted you, Eli. But I'm ready to make that up."

Still not a word.

"Well?"

"Are you done?"

"Yes, I'm done." His calm silence had frayed her nerves and was driving her insane.

"I'm not going to throw anything at you," he said.

A nervous gasp of air escaped her lips. The rogue was playing with her, deliberately keeping her in suspense when he was behind her all the way.

"I'm not going to storm out either." His smile faded. "But I don't want you to suffer the way I did."

"Suffer?"

"I know what it's like. The certainty. The all-consuming obsession. It wasn't easy to break free. You saw that for yourself."

Noga exploded. "Have you heard a word I've said? These are hard facts—undeniable data points—not some conspiracy theory. My thesis supervisor wants to go public and write a paper."

"And in the past," he said, in an annoying singsong, "people sold their homes to join the Son of David in the Holy Land, only to lose everything." He paused to calm down. "I heard you out, Noga. Now, please, listen to me. Delusions are delusions because they seem so real. Let her publish her papers. Her colleagues will laugh her into isolation and her career will come to a sudden and embarrassing end. Don't make the same mistake I did."

The chopstick in her hand snapped in two. She didn't realize she had been holding it. She had expected resistance, but Eli was completely ignoring the facts. He wasn't thinking rationally. Or was he right—was she the irrational one?

"I know it's hard to hear this," he said, "so don't act on it yet. Please. Cool off for a week or two. Think it over. Don't stick your neck out for some rosy chance to save humanity. That never ends well."

CHAPTER 39

It started with a single tomato. Moshe had just sat down behind his desk at the Dry Bones Society Wednesday morning when Shmuel burst in.

"Disrespectful bastards!" he said, and waved his fist in the air.

Moshe jumped to his feet, then exhaled a long, relieved breath. The spatter of red that plastered the side of Shmuel's face and trailed down his shirt was a rotten tomato, not blood. "Who did this?"

"The horde downstairs."

Moshe made for the cubicles of the call center, where a press of Society volunteers peered out the windows. Down below, a dozen picketers danced in a circle on the wide sidewalk between the tracks of the light rail and Clal Center. Three of them stood beside a vegetable crate and hurled soft tomatoes at a woman who approached the entrance of the building.

Yesterday's demonstration had not blown over as quickly as he had hoped. "Kids," he told the volunteers dismissively. "Delinquents. They'll grow tired of it soon."

They nodded and exchanged embarrassed grins, then got back to their cubicles. Avi had sparked the protest but he didn't have the staying power for a protracted campaign. The news outlets would soon lose interest and return to their coverage of the elections. He hoped the demonstration would disperse soon. He had to leave for his cardiologist appointment in a half hour.

Moshe patted Shmuel on the shoulder. "I'm sorry you had to experience that," he said. "You can't create real change without making a few enemies. We must be on the right track." Shmuel nodded and headed for the bathroom to get cleaned up.

Moshe got back behind his desk and returned to the draft of his speech for the campaign event Gurion's team had arranged. Moshe was not scheduled to speak, but he should prepare for that eventuality.

"Isaac Gurion," he typed, "has been a friend to the helpless in their time of need."

He made a correction: a *true* friend.

He had just started to polish the language of the speech when the blare of a megaphone broke his concentration.

"They've taken our jobs," said the booming voice, and the crowd answered with an angry murmur. "They've invaded our lives."

Moshe knew that voice. He got up and returned to the window overlooking the street. "Dear God."

The scattering of demonstrators had grown into a swarm that covered the sidewalk. The volunteers at the window beside him were no longer grinning.

Avi stood on a wooden crate. "They're not natural," he said. "They're zombies. Undead. They feed on the living. They call themselves the Dry Bones Society. Well, you know what we do with dry bones? We snap them!"

The rabble cheered and punched the air with their fists. "Break the dry bones!" they chanted. "Break the dry bones!"

Moshe turned as the doors of the Dry Bones Society burst open, and three girls stumbled inside. Red juice and mangled tomato flesh plastered their faces, hair, and clothing, making them look rather like Hollywood zombies. Irina and a few others dashed over to help them.

"Everybody stay calm," Moshe said, uttering the words most likely to cause panic. "I'll call the police." He turned to Shmuel and whispered, "Lock the doors. Delay the shuttles for now." Shmuel nodded and got to work.

Moshe strode to his office and closed the door. He didn't call the police. He called Isaac Gurion.

"Isaac," he said, "they're outside the building. Masses of them. They're getting violent."

"I'll call the commissioner right away."

"Thank you."

Moshe eased back in his chair and thanked God for powerful friends. He listened to the chant of the angry mob below, unable to compose his thoughts, never mind his speech. He glanced at his golden watch, then called the cardiologist's office to defer his appointment.

When he heard the bleat of a police foghorn, he raced back to the window. Two cruisers blared their horns and cut through the crowd. Three uniformed officers got out of a marked van and pushed toward the wooden crate. They raised their batons and gripped Avi by the legs, toppling him to the ground.

Moshe smiled. Avi would wake up in a prison cell like Moshe had, only Avi didn't have powerful friends like Isaac Gurion to open the door.

"It was Avi, wasn't it?" Galit said over dinner at home that evening.

He had not wanted to trouble her with the details. Avi had caused her enough suffering.

She put down her fork. "I saw him on the news. I should have warned you."

"Warned me?" Talya sat out of earshot on the living room couch and watched a cartoon.

"He came by the house last week."

Moshe stopped chewing his spaghetti. "What did he want?" He knew the answer only too well. Avi wanted to take over his life again, the life he claimed Moshe had stolen from him, the hypocrite.

"I didn't want to alarm you," she said. "He's full of lies. Promise me you'll stay away from him."

"That shouldn't be hard. The police arrested him. He won't be bothering anyone for some time."

"Promise me you won't speak with him." Tears streamed down her cheeks. The ordeal had shaken her harder than he had expected. Good thing he hadn't mentioned the rabble's promise to break the dry bones. Or had she heard that on TV as well?

"All right," he said. "I won't." That promise should be easy to keep.

There came a loud knocking at the door. Moshe and Galit locked eyes.

"Don't."

"It's not him."

Moshe walked over to the door and put his eye to the peephole. He recognized the security guards and opened the door.

"Isaac, welcome. Please, have dinner with us."

Talya jumped up when the first dark agent stepped inside. "Is that a real gun?" she said and pointed at the shoulder holster that protruded from his suit jacket.

Isaac Gurion declined the dinner invitation. He wrinkled his brow and pouted his lips. "Can we speak in private?"

Galit herded a disappointed Talya upstairs to bed and the two men settled on the living room couch.

"Thank you for your help today."

"Don't thank me yet. I have some troubling news." The politician frowned, as though loath to share the tidings. "We did some polls, as we often do. The zombie meme is spreading."

"We're not zombies."

"I know that. But, as you can imagine, the idea arouses very unpleasant reactions in voters."

The walls wavered around Moshe, the same sense of vertigo he had experienced on the phone with Dr. Malkior's secretary the morning the minster had abruptly cancelled their press conference. The ground was slipping away beneath his feet again.

"How many voters?"

"Enough. We need to cancel your appearance at the event tomorrow, to distance the party from the Dry Bones Society for now. Until the negative sentiments settle. This is a temporary measure, I assure you."

"How long?"

"As long as it takes."

Was this goodbye? Moshe was developing a healthy distrust for politicians, and his tingling doublespeak feelers indicated that Gurion wasn't telling him the full story.

"I'm sorry, Moshe. I wish things were different. This isn't personal," he added. "It's just politics."

CHAPTER 40

Thursday morning, Ahmed strolled down a narrow lane of small, round cobblestones. Potted plants lined the storefronts of Mazkeret Moshe, the labyrinth of quaint alleys behind Clal Center. Leafy trees glowed in golden sunlight while birds sang songs of hope. Beauty filled the world when a pretty girl walked at your side.

After his first meal at the Dry Bones Society on Monday, Samira had shown him the storeroom of secondhand clothes, and then his new bed—one of four simple bunks in a cramped dormitory room. He placed his box of clothes beneath his bed and enjoyed the first steaming-hot shower of his new life. Samira signed him up for carpentry classes. She checked up on him often and they shared most of their meals together. He had made his first new friend and, although their Arabic chatter drew some concerned glances in the dining hall, Ahmed finally felt comfortable in his new home.

That morning he had summoned the courage to ask Samira to go with him for a walk. They had ducked out through the parking bay beneath Clal Center to avoid the hateful demonstrators on Jaffa Street, and strolled through the maze of old stone courtyards and enclosed gardens.

A warm, fuzzy sensation buzzed in his chest as they walked. He no longer looked over his shoulder for Damas or the Rottweiler. He had left his suffering far behind, and allowed his worries to fade away until only he and Samira remained, like Adam and Eve in the Garden of Eden.

Samira tucked a strand of brown hair into her hijab. "Shall we sit here?" She pointed to a wooden bench in a courtyard.

Water flowed from the mouth of a fountain shaped like a jumping fish, and splashed into the basin at the center of the yard. Stone rabbits crouched at the edge of the flowerbeds.

"I always wanted a rabbit," she said. "When I was young we never had any pets."

"Me neither."

The air filled with the sounds of bubbling water and whispering trees.

"It's so peaceful here," she said.

"Yes," he said. "It's good to get out, to get away from them." He chuckled. He shared his room with a crazy man who ranted in Old French and three sullen and bearded Jews. Ahmed kept to himself.

"Them?"

"You know. The Jews."

Her smile faltered, and his world darkened. He would do anything to bring back that sweet smile.

"I had a baby," she said. "In my old life. A little girl. But my husband was a jealous man. He forbade me to work or even to leave the house. He spread lies that I had... that I had sinned with another man. My father," she said. "My father..." She turned to the heavens and wiped a tear from her eye.

"It's OK," Ahmed said. "We don't have to talk about it." He could guess the end of the story. Arab girls disappeared all the time. Indecent girls. Arab men as well. Collaborators, all of them. Nobody talked about the honor killings but everyone believed the rumors of their guilt. They had deserved to die. But what if, like in Samira's case, the rumor was false?

"When I woke up," she continued, "I had nowhere to go. This was before the Dry Bones Society. Only Rabbi Yosef was prepared to take me in, a dirty, homeless Arab girl." She looked Ahmed over. "And Moshe Karlin saved me from slavery, even though he didn't have to."

"Slavery?" he asked.

She glanced down and rubbed the palm of her hand. "A labor camp in Talpiot. We worked odd jobs for a few days. Our task master was a cruel Ethiopian."

Ahmed's heart skipped a beat. "An Ethiopian missing two fingers?"

Her eyed widened. "You know Damas?"

"I was his slave too!" They laughed.

Ahmed inhaled quickly, almost choking on fresh air. He had kept his past bottled up so tight, it felt good to open the lid and release the pressure. "After two months in that hell," he said, "I escaped. I slept in an old tomb for a week before I came here."

"You escaped?"

"Yes, like you."

"We didn't escape. Moshe bought our freedom with a lot of money. Aren't you afraid?"

Ahmed stretched his arms over the back of the bench. "They've given up on me by now."

She nodded her head but worry still cast a shadow over her features. She cared about him, and he wished that their walk would last forever.

"What about you?" she asked.

"Me?" He gave her a questioning glance and she lowered her eyes again.

"How did your old life end?"

A ball of dread lodged in his throat. After all the Jews had done for her, the truth would horrify her. He could make something up—that he had saved a child from a speeding truck, or even that he had slipped on a banana peel at work—but he did not want to lie to her.

"I can't... I don't want to talk about it," he said.

She nodded quickly and her eyes glistened again. "I understand," she said. "We don't have to talk about it." The hint of a terrible death had awakened her sympathy for him. No, she must never find out.

"This is a new life," she added. "A fresh start."

Ahmed liked the sound of that. "Yes," he said, that warm, fuzzy feeling returning. "A fresh start."

CHAPTER 41

Moshe's dreams shattered on the morning news. The screen mounted on the wall of the Dry Bones Society showed Isaac Gurion speaking into the microphone at the offices of his Upward party.

"I am excited to announce a new partnership," he intoned in his authoritative baritone. Avi Segal stood beside him in a green suit, a self-satisfied grin threatening to split his face in two. "Mr. Segal's presence high on our list is another sign of our commitment to the hard-working middle class—the salt of the earth and the core of our society."

Moshe folded his arms. His cheeks cooled. He should have seen this coming. The winds of public opinion had shifted and Gurion's "temporary distancing" from the Dry Bones Society had become—literally overnight—the new backbone of his election campaign.

"That double-crossing bastard," Shmuel grumbled beside Moshe.

But there was more. The camera zoomed out to reveal a clump of ultra-Orthodox rabbis onstage, grinning and stroking their beards. Among them, Rabbi Emden stood erect in his satin suit and tidy bowler, and flashed his pearly whites at the press.

"And," Gurion continued, "I extend an equally warm welcome to our new friends at Torah True. Together we will guard all that our country holds dear and keep back the unnatural scourge that threatens our timeless traditions."

"Hypocritical creep," Shmuel said. "Isaac Gurion in bed with the rabbis. Who would have believed it?"

"Stranger things have happened," Moshe said. He should have seen that coming too, but the double betrayal had added insult to injury.

He glanced at the assembled Society members around him in the call center. The chant of "Death to the Dead" drifted through the window from the street below, but softer than before. The numbers of the picketing mob had dwindled. Apparently, they had more important matters to deal with now such as campaigning for the elections.

Phone operators groundhogged the cubicle dividers, concern imprinted on their faces.

"No need to worry, my friends," Moshe said, loud enough for all to hear. "Calls are still coming in. Resurrected men and women still need our help and donors are still opening their checkbooks. Let's get back to work."

Heads disappeared into cubicles and Moshe turned to his management team. "Let's talk in my office."

"Are we in trouble?" Irina asked, when the door had closed.

Moshe perched on the edge of his desk. "Time will tell."

"At least we have the identity cards," Rabbi Yosef said, finding, as usual, the silver lining. "That was the main reason we joined with Gurion."

"I suppose you're right." Moshe tried to hide his disappointment. Gurion had whetted his appetite for more than mere citizenship. *Think of all the good you can do*, he had said. *You could make the world a better place.*

"Let's not be naïve," Shmuel said. "I don't think this Segal character is going to live and let live once he's in Knesset. Rights can always be revoked. We could lose everything we've gained with another stroke of a pen."

There came a knock on the door and a new volunteer

leaned into the room. "Sorry to interrupt," he said. Ben wore a black T-shirt and a pale, worried expression as he glanced at the room's occupants. "There's a problem at the Ministry of the Interior."

Moshe's heart lurched. *Here we go.* "Have they stopped issuing identity cards?"

"No," Ben said. "But they closed the special counters. 'No more special treatment.' Things are going to take a lot longer."

Moshe swallowed his sigh of relief. "Thanks, Ben. Let us know if anything else changes."

Ben nodded and closed the door behind him.

"See what I mean?" Shmuel said. "This isn't the end."

Rafi shook his head and scowled, but Irina clenched her jaw. "Forget Gurion," she said. "We'll find another partner. There must be other parties that will work with us. What about Malkior?"

Shmuel gave a short, mirthless laugh. "Gurion promised him the vice presidency. The Ministry of the Interior is in his pocket. The rabbis too and they hated us to begin with. And with all the bad press we've had, no one else will touch us with a ten-foot pole. We're stuck."

Once again, Shmuel was right. Their situation was hopeless.

Savta Sarah leaned against the large window of the office, her arms folded over her chest, and stared at Moshe. A smile curled the edges of her lips, and for a change he knew what she was thinking. Her steely nerve had rubbed off on him. Perhaps "hopeless" was not the right word.

"We have one other option," Moshe said.

He had the room's undivided attention. His suggestion was so bold, it required an introduction and a dab of drama.

He pulled his blue identity card holder from his back pocket and turned it over. "This is nice," he said. "It helps me open a bank account and wait in line for a doctor. But in the end, it just makes me a part of the system." He dropped the card back onto his desk. "And the system stinks."

He glanced at his team. "I've had enough of crooked politicians who change their values like underwear and create new parties every other day. I'm sick and tired of having to pull strings just to get society to respect my basic rights. And I bet voters are sick of all that too."

At the back of the room, Savta Sarah's smile widened.

"They deserve better. *We* deserve better. And this is where we can make a difference. We're not just a bunch of ex–dead people. We are the past and the present. Religious and secular. Jews and Arabs. Our lives ended and we can see them for what they were, warts and all. And from this new vantage point, we can build a better future. A future with integrity and dignity, equality and harmony." He smiled at Rabbi Yosef, who swallowed, no stranger to the themes of the messianic era. "To fix the mistakes of the past."

Moshe inhaled the magical hope his words had conjured. The promise of a bright new future hung in the air and glittered in the eyes of his audience.

"That's a wonderful speech," Shmuel said, breaking the spell. "But how are we going to replace the system without powerful friends—without *protekzia*?"

Here it comes. Moshe straightened on the edge of the desk. "By becoming our own powerful friend."

Savta Sarah beamed at him from the back of the room.

"I don't understand," Shmuel said. "You want us to run in the elections—independently?"

"Why not? We have a message and a platform. We have new members joining every day."

Shmuel laughed. "An election campaign is going to require a crap load of money."

"You're right. Luckily for us, we have a new supporter with very deep pockets." He winked at Rabbi Yosef, who swallowed again. The rabbi was still not comfortable dealing with Rev. Henry Adams and his New Evangelical Church of America. He'd get used it.

"But," Shmuel said, spluttering at the lunacy of the idea. "Even if we have the money and the numbers to win a few seats, elections are less than two weeks away. How are we supposed to throw together a winning campaign in two weeks? We don't have that expertise."

Moshe had hoped that Shmuel would raise that question. "As it happens," he said, "I know someone who will be perfect for the job."

"Oh, really? And where did you find him?"

Moshe grinned. "Who said anything about 'him'?"

CHAPTER 42

The renowned sage opened his eyes. A sky of clear, dazzling blue filled his visual field, framed by the branches of leafy trees and what appeared to be a tall monument. Large arcs rose high in the air to form a lattice of metal spires. Never before had he seen such a structure—an object of great architectural beauty and no doubt the life's work of a master smith—on any of his travels or among the pointy domes of Fustat.

He brought his hands to his face and studied them, wrinkled and weathered as usual. Then he touched his beard and face, his head, chest, and thighs. His physical body was intact but without a single shred of clothing. No funerary shrouds, not even a turban for his head!

This was not the World of Souls, the immortal spiritual realm in which Active Intellects merged with the Mind of God, for there were no bodies in that world of pure thought.

This must be the Resurrection. Ha!

The deduction amused him. His detractors had accused him of denying the resurrection of the physical body, despite his inclusion of the belief in his Thirteen Principles. Even after he had elucidated his views on the matter in his letter to the Jews of Yemen, still his critics condemned him as a heretic. *A disciple of Aristotle*, they said. *A rationalist*. This'll show them!

He turned over. The hard ground beneath him was covered in identical hexagons as gray and as smooth as fresh mortar. There was nothing new under the sun, as Ecclesiastes wrote, but the artisans of This World had honed their methods since his death.

He got to his feet and took a few wobbly steps.

How long had he slept in the dust? Had the Son of David arrived?

Was his son Abraham still alive? According to his son's calculations, the Redemption would begin only a few decades hence, and, although he had warned his son against Calculating the End, now he hoped that his son's predictions had been accurate.

A dull pain throbbed in his skull. Headaches resulted from excess humors in the body. As a respected healer, he would have prescribed peppermint tea and the avoidance of dairy products, but as he glanced about the stony hillocks, he found no tea decanters, only a street of black pitch and a table.

A young man with blond hair sat at the table, which was draped in a white sheet with blue hexagrams. The man looked up from a black tablet of shiny obsidian, smiled, jumped from his seat, and rushed over.

"Welcome, Honored Rabbi," he said in Hebrew, not Arabic. How curious.

The young man helped him into a fluffy cloak as soft as fine wool and as white as snow, and tied the garment with a white sash.

"Here." The man dropped two white pellets into the palm of his hand.

"What, may I ask, are these?"

"For your headache. Swallow them." He held out a glass of water. The glass was extremely thin and transparent, and crackled in his grasp like parchment but did not shatter. Curious! He washed down the pellets and returned the paper-glass cup. No, this wasn't the World of Souls and yet it was not quite the world he had known either.

He cleared his throat. "Where are we?"

"Tiberias."

"Of course." He had instructed his son to bury him in the Holy Land. Abraham had fulfilled his father's wish, although he would have preferred Jerusalem. Perhaps the sultan had not permitted a burial in the holy city.

"And how long have I…?"

The man completed his question. "Been dead? Over eight hundred years."

"Eight hundred years!" His spirits sank. His son had passed from the world long ago. Or would he meet him again in this new life? "My son, Abraham…?"

The young man seemed to know what he was asking. "I'll ask the Head Office about him."

"Head Office?"

"Yes. In Jerusalem."

"The sultan's court?"

The man chuckled. "There is no sultan here. This is the Jewish State."

"The Jewish State!" Jews had regained control of the Land of the Forefathers. The Son of David had arrived. He cleared his throat. "Are you the Son of David?"

Another chuckle and a shake of the head. He held the black tablet to his ear, then quickly pocketed the item. "You have many questions," he said. He seemed to be reciting a well-repeated saying. "We'll answer them as best we can in time. Meanwhile, have some breakfast." He pointed to a box of pastries on the table. Then he wandered off to a nearby tree, pressed the black tablet to his ear, and talked to himself. Curious indeed!

Were the denizens of the future world all insane?

He recited a blessing and gave the pastry a tentative bite. It was very sweet but quite delicious. The pain in his skull subsided. He sat on a vacant chair of thin, shiny material that bent under his weight but didn't break, and was neither wood nor stone. Fascinating!

In the Days of the Messiah the laws of nature would remain unchanged. He had reached that conclusion after a lengthy analysis of the sources with the aid of reason and philosophy. Men could discover new materials, however, and learn to bend them to their will. Of course. He knew there must be a logical explanation.

The young man returned and placed the tablet on the table. "The Head Office doesn't have a record of your son, Rabbi, but he might still be out there."

"But you said that this Head Office is in Jerusalem?"

"I spoke with them. On the phone." He looked at the small tablet.

"Phone?"

Molding new materials was one thing, but conversing across great distances—how could that be?

The young man opened his mouth to explain but a loud roar made him glance at the road of black pitch. A roaring beast sped by in a flurry of noise and smoke. Not a beast—a chariot, for he had glimpsed a woman through a window of the shiny exterior.

"What...?" he mumbled to the young man. "But where is the horse?"

"There is no horse, Rabbi. That's a car. Don't worry about it, Rabbi. They'll explain everything at the Head Office."

"But how?"

The man scratched his head. "Think of a boat. A boat has no horse but moves on the water."

"Yes, but a boat has sails. The wind pushes the boat."

"Think of this as a boat on wheels."

Metal boats on wheels. Pellets that cured headaches in minutes. Paper-glass. Tablets that carried a man's voice between cities in an instant! What would they show him next—metal boats that floated in thin air?

Ha! Some ideas insulted reason and were truly impossible. The thought gave him some consolation. This world was not so different after all. It just needed a little getting used to.

"I would like very much to meet with a philosopher," he

said, "to learn the wisdom of this New World and—"

A sudden rumble from the heavens stopped him mid-speech. The noise, which resembled thunder, grew louder but the sky above was cloudless.

Then he saw it. High overhead, an object advanced through the sky—slender and with wings and a tail. Sunlight glinted off the shiny exterior. That was no bird.

"Don't worry, Rabbi. That's just an airplane."

"An airplane?" He had a bad feeling about this.

The young man scratched his head again. "It's like a metal boat that flies through the air."

Maimonides gasped and clutched at his beard. "Oh, no," he said. "Not that too!"

CHAPTER 43

Noga had never been in a stretch limousine before but she was quickly getting used to the idea. She relaxed on the soft couch of beige leather as the vehicle glided over speed bumps with ease and the workaday world of mere mortals zipped by through tinted windows.

Eli handed her a glass of champagne and raised his in the air. "Here's to a great vacation."

The yellow-orange liquid shifted lazily below the rim of the glass as the immense car moved. She sipped the bubbly dry wine. The champagne was a first for her and, she expected, many more firsts awaited her on this trip.

Two days after her failed romantic dinner at home, the tension in the air had dissipated. She had honored his request—her laptop remained closed on the coffee table and she avoided all talk of Jewish Palestinians and the End of Days—and she had not objected when their week of "cooling off" had become a two-week cruise on the Mediterranean, the nearest departure date available.

And so Noga found herself in a limousine to Ben Gurion Airport, where they would soon board a short flight to Barcelona. Life was good when you had free time and an unlimited budget. She could get used to that too.

Noga took another sip of wine. "Are you trying to impress

me?" she said. The wine, apparently, was having its desired effect.

Eli caressed her with his dark eyes and smirked. "Always. Have I succeeded?"

Sip number three. "Getting there."

They turned off Road Number One toward Ben Gurion Airport.

Her phone tinkled, so she placed her wineglass in the sunken holder on the side table of polished wood, and fished for her phone in her handbag. A text message had arrived from Hannah. "Need any help with the paper?" Noga turned off the screen and dropped the phone back in her bag.

"Everything all right?" Eli asked.

"Yeah," she said. "Nothing urgent."

Eli's arguments had made more sense as time passed. Some Jews and Arabs shared a common ancestor. Big deal. Some local Arabs believed they had Jewish roots. So what? In the Bible, Abraham had fathered both Isaac and Ishmael, before either Jews or Muslims existed, and all humans descended from one genetic Eve. Their common ancestor might lie much further back in history, and so long as the facts had a competing explanation, she had best keep her messianic speculations to herself. She'd reply to Hannah later. The paper could wait. A deal was a deal, and Noga was on vacation.

The car slowed as they approached the airport entrance road. The windows slid down and a security guard with a machine gun peeked inside, nodded his head, and waved them in. At a traffic circle, they turned toward Terminal One. That didn't seem right.

Noga was familiar with the airport. Her old classmate from Hebrew U, Sarit, had convinced her to fly with her to Eilat one weekend in search of eligible single men. Instead, they had shared the hotel pool with loud Arab kids and aging Japanese tourists.

"I thought we were going to Barcelona."

"Mmm-hmm."

"Isn't Terminal One for domestic flights?"

"Among others." Eli smiled his rakish smile.

Her heart sank. She was pretty sure that cruise ships did not pass through the Straits of Tiran to get to Eilat. A born planner, Noga did not like being kept in suspense. "I don't understand."

"Patience, Noga. You'll see."

The limo bypassed the parking lot and proceeded to a gate with another armed guard. After a short conversation with the driver, the guard opened the gate and waved them through.

Noga sat up on the couch. "Oh my God."

The limo drove along a wide expanse of tarmac and crossed two landing strips before pulling up beside a small jet, the kind she associated with celebrities and heads of state. A uniformed pilot and flight attendant stood at attention beside a short retractable staircase.

Noga flopped back on the couch. "OK," she said. "I'm impressed."

Eli chuckled. "My dear," he said, "we're just getting started."

CHAPTER 44

Thursday evening, Avi entered his parents' apartment in Wolfson Towers to the ululations of his mother. Even his father gave him a hug. "Well done, my son. Or should I say, Member of Knesset Segal!"

Avi savored the hero's welcome, then plopped onto the living room couch, leaned back, and clasped his hands behind his head. After being screwed over so many times, finally Avi had come out on top. *So this is how it feels to be Moshe.*

His mother brought out a tray of cakes and mint tea.

The only sour face in the room belonged to Ronen, Avi's brother. "So what ministry will Gurion give you?" he asked, his pale lips quivering with spite. "Chief Garbage Collector?"

Avi grinned. Ronen was jealous. For once in his life, his snooty older brother had to share the limelight, and his obvious discomfort was the icing on Avi's cake. "Who cares?" he said. "I'll get a fat salary and a pension for life, which is more than you get at the Philharmonic."

Followed the Segal family tradition, Ronen played the violin at the Israeli Philharmonic Orchestra, and he had secured the coveted post only thanks to his father's connections. The tone-deaf Avi had been a source of chronic disappointment to his parents. Until now.

"You need to serve two terms to get a pension," Ronen

shot back, "and I bet you won't last that long."

"Enough of that, boys!" their mother chided. "Let's all be happy for Avi. This is a wonderful achievement."

"Achievement?" Ronen seemed insulted at the suggestion. "He's only aping his dead old friend. Moshe throws a demonstration, Avi throws a demonstration. Moshe joins with Gurion, Avi joins with Gurion."

Avi wanted to deck Ronen right then and there. "Moshe is out," he shouted, "and I'm in. All right?" There was no arguing with that fact.

"Calm down, Avi," his mother said.

"For now," his brother added.

"Ronen!"

Their father leaned forward on the armchair and rubbed his hands together. "Don't settle for any of those minor ministries," he said. "Go for Defense, Finance, Interior, or Foreign Affairs."

Ronen laughed. "Foreign Affairs! He can't string together two words in English."

Avi shifted on the couch. He was positioned to sit in the next government and already his parents' expectations had climbed a few rungs higher. "I'll see what's on the table after the elections. Gurion has to save the big jobs for other parties in order to create a coalition."

In truth, Avi had not discussed the matter with his party leader. He'd be grateful with Deputy Minister of the Environment if it came to that. The main thing was to be in the game. Besides, a minor position would free him to pursue his ultimate goal: Galit.

He had been stupid to threaten her and had written off his mistake to homelessness and desperation. Never mind. After the elections, she'd come to her senses and welcome him back with open arms.

Avi accepted a steaming cup of sweet tea and bit into a slice of his mother's honey cake.

The thrill of victory faded. Finally, he had outsmarted Moshe, but after standing in his shadow so long, a thread of nostalgia pulled at his heart. There was an annoying grain of truth in Ronen's words. Moshe had guided his actions and haunted his thoughts for ages. Without him, his mind was an empty shrine. If Moshe were in his shoes, what would he do next?

"There's one thing I don't understand," Ronen said. "Karlin had the Dry Bones Society to rally behind him, but you—how did you pull off that demonstration?"

Avi's face grew hot. He had not told anyone about Boris and his thugs. Although the Russian had never spelled out what he did for a living, his line of work did not involve helping old ladies cross the street. *Who cares?* Boris and his minions had served their purpose. Once Avi took office, he'd shake them off like an old coat. The thugs had befriended Avi Segal, the miserable tramp, but they wouldn't dare mess with Avi Segal, the Member of Knesset.

He washed the cake down with his mint tea. "My dear brother," he said, his voice greasy with sarcasm, "you underestimate me."

CHAPTER 45

A young woman entered the Dry Bones Society Friday morning, her high heels clicking on the floor tiles. She wore a business suit of elegant cream with a matching Louis Vuitton bag, and her blow-dried hair dusted her shoulders as she gazed about the call center.

"I missed the old place," Sivan said.

Moshe looked on with pride. The spunky girl with the faded T-shirts and torn jeans had grown up since leaving Karlin & Son. Avi had fired her after Moshe's death, having invented an affair between Moshe and his attractive employee in order to win over Galit. Moshe had learned all this only weeks into his second life, and Sivan had tried to help him set the record straight.

"Welcome home," he said.

She shook hands with Rafi, whom she knew well from her days at Karlin & Son, and Moshe introduced her to Shmuel, Rabbi Yosef, and Savta Sarah. "Sivan is the VP of Marketing at a high-tech company in Malcha."

"She's a bit young," Shmuel said, as though she wasn't in the room.

"And I'm a bit old," Savta Sarah said.

"Young for what?" Sivan asked.

Moshe had not gone into the details on the phone. "For a

new challenge," he said. "Let's talk in my office."

Moshe perched on the edge of his desk and Savta Sarah closed the door.

"I saw you on TV," Sivan said, taking a seat in the visitor's chair.

"Then you know all about the Dry Bones Society."

She nodded. "I saw the anti-zombie demonstrations too. I'd say you have a bit of a PR problem." They all smiled at the understatement. "I assume that's why you called me in— to consult."

"More than that," Moshe said. He clasped his hands together for the big revelation. "What are our chances if we were to run independently in the upcoming elections?"

Her mouth dropped open. "Independently?"

"We've been double-crossed too many times to rely on politicians. We need our own clout to make a difference. And to do that we'll need a killer campaign manager."

She laughed. "You weren't kidding about the challenge bit."

"She's not up to it," Shmuel said.

Moshe understood his resistance. Until now, Shmuel had led the Society's public relations efforts, and he was not about to hand over their fate to a pretty face in a fancy blouse. He had not seen Sivan handle tough drivers on the dispatch CB radio. The delicate exterior hid a featherweight prize fighter. But Moshe didn't have to defend her bona fides.

"The hell I'm not," she said. "I took a young start-up from zero customers to market domination."

"And which start-up was that?"

Her cheeks flushed. "Ridez."

Blood drained from Moshe's face. He had heard that name from Avi. "Some kid made an app for ordering taxis," he had said, "and our drivers jumped ship."

"Wait a minute," Rafi said. "Isn't that the company that..." He had enough tact to trail off.

"That put Karlin & Son out of business," Moshe said. "Yes."

The room fell silent. Sivan had avenged her unfair firing by joining a rival company and blowing Karlin & Son out of the water. Was that why, at first, she had not returned Moshe's calls after his return? Was that why, later, she had agreed to help him out?

Moshe continued. "That proves her abilities." Sivan gave him a repentant smile and her shoulders relaxed. "And this time," he added, "I'd prefer to have her on our side. So what do you say—what are our chances?"

Sivan inflated her lungs and stared at the wall. "There will be a lot of hurdles," she said. "But you have a clear advantage."

"Which is?"

"You're an unknown. People here never vote *for* a candidate—they vote against the other guy who disappointed them last time, and they do this by choosing someone else."

Moshe smiled. She had a point.

"And you're already well positioned," she continued. "A secular leader, a rabbi to draw in the religious vote, and Rafi for the Sephardic community. Savta Sarah takes care of both women and retirees. That means you will all need to appear high on the list."

Rafi said, "Sure."

"Of course," Savta Sarah said.

Rabbi Yosef squirmed but nodded his consent.

"Great. And you'll need to rebrand."

"Rebrand?" Shmuel said.

She nodded. "You have to appeal to the general population, not just the resurrected. You'll need to adjust your messaging."

Another good point. The Dry Bones Society had served them well, but the Society's name did limit their target market.

Sivan brushed a strand of hair behind her ear. "And, as it happens, I have the perfect name for your new party."

She told them.

"Wow," said Rabbi Yosef.

"I like it," Moshe seconded.

Savta Sarah grinned. "It's *sexy!*"

Even Shmuel couldn't hide his excitement. "It hints at hope and a clean slate, but speaks to everyone."

"So," Moshe said. "Does this mean you'll take the job?"

Sivan glowed with enthusiasm. "Hell, yeah."

CHAPTER 46

Friday night, Yosef sat at the head of his Shabbat table, staring at his bowl of chicken soup. The good news strained to burst out of him.

He had not managed to update Rocheleh before candle lighting. The planning session at the Dry Bones Society had stretched on for hours and he had returned home with minutes to spare before he had to head out to open the synagogue.

One should not plan weekday matters on the Sabbath, the Sages taught. But this wasn't really planning, was it?

"I have some good news."

At the other end of the table, Rocheleh looked up from her soup. Uriel glanced at him, but Simcha, Ari, and Yehuda continued their contented slurping.

"We're going to run in the elections."

"Who will?"

"The Dry Bones Society. Well, it's no longer the Dry Bones Society. We're rebranding. Moshe will announce the new name on Sunday."

Rocheleh returned to her soup, displaying little interest in the new branding. Over the past few months, she had softened and no longer raised her voice at him. She had made peace with their new status at the fringes of the ultra-

Orthodox community. Their boys had not been expelled from school and the sky had not fallen. He suspected that the steady income from the Dry Bones Society, along with the brand new dishwasher, the company car, and the weekly cleaner, had played a large role in their new household tranquility. Their new means had allowed her to quit her teaching job in order to become a full-time housewife.

"There's more," he added. "I'll be number two on their list."

That got her attention. "Why you?"

"For the religious vote. That's what Sivan said. She's our campaign manager. After Moshe, I'll be the next in line to sit in Knesset."

Uriel perked up at that. "You'll be in the government— like the Prime Minister?"

Simcha said, "*Aba*—does that mean you'll get your own card?"

He extracted a wad of wrinkled soccer cards from his pocket and fanned them out. A bearded rabbi stared out from the surface of each laminated rectangle.

Yosef had no idea how they selected the rabbis for their cards. "Maybe."

"Awesome!"

"Please, *Aba*," Ari said. "Can you get us some of your cards? Please! Please!"

Yosef chuckled at the excited little faces, so proud of their father.

"Settle down now," Rocheleh said, then glanced at Moshe. "Don't get their hopes up, Yosef."

She was right. Once again, gusts of optimism had carried him away. There were a lot of "ifs" in his glorious future, as well as a short and difficult campaign. Did he even belong among the country's lawmakers? The thought made him tremble.

He turned the family's attention to the weekly Torah reading and the meal continued as usual.

Later, after the boys breathed deeply in their beds and he

had loaded the dishwasher, Rocheleh led him by the hand to their bedroom.

In the dim glow of the shuttered night lamp, she pulled off her head covering and her hair fell to her shoulders. They sat on the edge of the bed, her hands clasped in his.

"You have a good heart, Yossi," she said. "You are an honorable man. Politics is no place for honorable men. They will eat you up for breakfast, without salt."

"But if the honorable men stay away, how will politics ever become honorable? How will we make the world a better place?" Moshe's idealism had infected him. He thought of Rabbi Emden's betrayal and threats. "The rabbinate is rotten," he continued. "They only care about power and money; they have forgotten their moral duty. 'In a place where there are no men,' the Sages say, 'be a man.'"

"Shh…" She placed her finger on his lips, and argued no more.

His own mind argued for her. Power corrupts. Had his comfortable new salary—a salary he had received thanks to messianic Christian donors, no less—whetted his appetite for more?

Then she pushed him back onto the bed and all thoughts of money and power fled.

CHAPTER 47

Sunday morning, Samira stood before a dozen strangers in the circle of plastic chairs. Blood pumped noisily in her ears. The Absorption Center was unusually quiet. Most members of the Society had gone to witness the historic press conference in the call center down the corridor, leaving her to receive the new arrivals.

"My name is Samira," she said, her voice quavering. She had never addressed a gathering of her peers before. In her old life, her husband had forbidden her to work outside the house, and she had grown accustomed to hiding behind walls and veils. In this new life, however, she had discovered an inner strength.

"Rabbi Yosef asked me to fill in for him," she continued. She had often assisted the rabbi with the sessions, translating his words into Arabic, but today, for the first time, she led the group. She managed a smile. In their faces, she saw fear and confusion. She knew those emotions only too well, and now she had the skills with which to guide them across that narrow bridge.

"Whatever you experienced in your previous lives," she said, in Hebrew and then Arabic, her voice finding confidence in the rabbi's words, "wherever you're from, you've left all of that behind. This is a fresh start. We are all the same now. We are family. Around this circle, every day, we tell our life stories and we listen. Share as little or as much as you like."

She broke the ice by telling her own story. Then, one by one, the men and women arose and shared theirs. When the last had spoken, she handed out song sheets for the Israeli anthem—"HaTikva"—and Rabbi Nachman of Breslov's "All the World Is a Narrow Bridge." She sang and they followed along on the printed sheets. Some used the Hebrew sheets, others the Arabic. Many preferred the transliteration in Latin letters. As the session concluded, she felt that she had crossed a long, narrow bridge of her own.

Ahmed watched her from the corner as the new arrivals handed in their song sheets and dispersed to the refreshment tables. She drew near.

"You did very well," he said.

Her cheeks warmed and she looked away. "Thank you."

"I have something for you."

In his hand he held a wooden creature with almond eyes, a rounded nose, and long ears.

"It's a rabbit," he explained. "I made it for you in carpentry class. You said you had wanted a rabbit. I'm sorry it's not better. I'm still learning."

A flutter arose in her belly along with the urge to hug her new friend. No one had ever made a gift especially for her. "It's beautiful," she said. "I love it."

After an awkward moment, they made their way to the refreshment table and he poured her a glass of orange juice. Ahmed made her feel special and understood. She could tell him anything, and over the last week she had. If all the suffering she had endured had led to Ahmed, perhaps her death had not been in vain?

She sipped her drink, gripping the pile of sheets under her arm. "You are welcome to join us next time," she said. Ahmed still avoided the group sessions.

His smile faltered. "I don't think I'm ready."

"That's OK," she said. She understood, having clung to

the shadows for months, fearful of her family, fearful of her own reflection. The hurt of a traumatic first life took time to heal. "It's not easy," she said. "I know. I keep delaying my application for an identity card. I think I'll be stuck here forever."

"That sounds good to me," he said.

"What—to be stuck here?"

"With you, yes."

She glanced away again, smiling despite herself, and adjusted the hijab over her hair. The flutter returned. He had told her that he loved her. "Yes," she said. "That would be good."

CHAPTER 48

"I have to go," Alex told the girl who called herself Irina. "I'll be back later." It was the first lie he had told her, and his last.

They stood in the corridor of Clal Center outside the Dry Bones Society. Society members streamed around them toward the call center for the big announcement.

He had struggled with his demons ever since their visit to the Doctor last week. Irina remembered nothing; she was off the hook. Alex had no cause to contact her again. That morning he made his decision and had stopped by only to see her one last time.

"It'll only take a minute." Irina feigned anger. "Don't be selfish."

He *had* been selfish but not in the way she thought. Every moment he lingered, he put her in danger, and if anything happened to her a second time, he would not be able to forgive himself.

"I have to work," he said. That much was true. He had neglected his street magic, pulling in only a third of his usual revenues for the Organization. Mandrake had said nothing yet, but eventually he would put two and two together, and then Irina would become a problem again.

"I forgot," she said. "Some of us have real lives. What is it that you do that's so important anyhow?" Until now, the topic of his employment had never come up.

"Cars," he said." Buying. Selling. Fixing." Also true, technically. He did not want to lie to her again.

"Your cars can wait, Mr. Mechanic. We're making history today." She gripped his hand and pulled. The touch of her fingers melted his last thread of resistance. She towed him into the office, and they joined the press of bodies in the call center.

TV cameras were trained on the raised podium. Moshe Karlin stood at the microphone and shuffled cue cards. Behind him, a white sheet covered a rectangular object on an easel, like a painting awaiting auction.

"There he is," Irina said. The joy in her voice stabbed Alex inside. Moshe had taken her under his wing like a little sister, and she would be forever loyal. Alex could identify with that, but her reverence for the man made him jealous, another sign that he had taken this too far. He must leave now, for her sake.

The Dry Bones chief was harmless enough. He had given Alex suspicious glances at first but accepted him as Irina's friend. Karlin was an honest man. Honest men were easy to handle. You always knew what they would do next. Mandrake didn't share that predictability, and that was why he always came out on top. If the Boss ever moved against the Society, Karlin wouldn't last long.

Which was another reason for Alex to leave. The less he knew, the better. His involvement could only cause harm.

Karlin spoke into the microphone. "Friends," he said. "Recent events have taught us that to survive in this new world we cannot rely on others, however good their intentions." A murmur of bitter agreement rose from the crowd.

"To change society for the better—for the better of all citizens, not just the resurrected—we must make a stand for our values. Stand tall, stand proud."

A man cheered at the back. "Yeah!" The mood turned from bitterness to inspired activism.

"And so," Karlin continued, "I am glad to present to you

today the new face of our organization."

He turned to an attractive young woman with salon hair and a designer business suit. She pulled at a string and the white sheet fell from the easel. A poster displayed a single short word. The bold blue letters leaned forward as though racing ahead into the future. The word was "Restart."

Hands clapped. Some whistled their approval. Irina glanced at Alex and nodded her head. "It's great, don't you think?"

He had to agree. The name was modern, punchy, and a big improvement on the Dry Bones Society.

"Our country needs a restart," Karlin declared, and cheers broke out again. "To clear out the corruption and decay of the past. To build a better tomorrow for our children and grandchildren—for all of us."

Irina cheered as well. While she stared ahead, her hand found Alex's. Emotion rippled through his body like a shock wave. Her touch pushed him back in time to a moment of happiness, the moment he thought he had lost forever. How could he walk away now?

Karlin waited for the excitement to settle. "To achieve this," he said, "I am happy to announce that Restart will run in the coming elections."

The crowd went wild. Irina jumped on the spot and then hugged Alex. A gasp escaped his mouth and he smiled like a fool. She beamed up at him, mistaking his joy for hers. He couldn't turn his back on her again. And now, he wouldn't have to.

He excused himself and made for the bathroom. Checking that the stalls were empty, he dialed a number on his phone. Moshe Karlin had given him the pretext he had needed to stay close to her a little longer.

"Check the news," he said, when his boss answered. "Karlin might be of use to us after all."

CHAPTER 49

"This is heaven," Noga said, and Eli was inclined to agree.

They stretched out on rented recliners, while gentle waves lapped at the shore of white sand. The Mediterranean sun warmed his skin and dried his swimming trunks. Only a dozen other vacationers had discovered the hidden cove, and they frolicked in the refreshing waters.

That morning their cruise liner had docked at Santorini. Whitewashed cottages and blue domes gleamed on the cliffs high above the caldera, the flooded mouth of the volcano that had sculpted the Greek Island. When they disembarked, a chartered motorboat was waiting to whisk them away to the secluded beach.

"'Heaven is a place on earth,'" he said, quoting the '80s song and making Noga laugh.

He lifted his head from the recliner and gazed at the girl beside him. Sunlight glinted in the drops of seawater on her goosefleshed skin. Her one-piece bathing suit rose and fell to the rhythm of her breathing. A gentle sea breeze caressed the locks of hair below her wicker sunhat and carried the holiday scent of coconut oil.

He basked in the awe of her beauty, pure and natural, like the sea and the sand and the sky. But that beauty ran deeper than a pretty face and slender body. He had come to rely on her honesty and razor-sharp wit. She spoke her mind even if he didn't like what she had to say, not out of spite but because she cared.

Sure, she enjoyed the luxury and pampering as much as the next girl, but he was more to her than a bank account. After all, when she had first fallen for him he had been a crazed and friendless invalid. No, Noga truly cared.

And so do I. The hairs on his arms prickled at the realization. For the first time in his real life, he cared about someone.

The large, dark lenses of her sunglasses turned to him and she smiled, bemused. "What?" He had been staring at her, a foolish grin on his face.

"Nothing," he said. "I'm just… happy."

Her lips parted as her smile widened. She shifted on the recliner and returned to her suntanning. "Let's stay here forever," she said.

"I wish we could." He wanted to seal this moment in a jar for eternity, but he couldn't. The black, clawed hand of dread closed over his heart. For the first time in his life, he had something to lose.

"Nothing lasts forever," he continued. "Not even islands. Take Santorini. People lived here for thousands of years until one day the mountain exploded and sank into the sea. A whole civilization wiped out in an instant. The ash cloud spread for hundreds of miles and hung in the air for weeks."

"How do you know all that?"

How indeed? In his mind's eye, a little boy stepped outside a mudbrick home as heavy, gray clouds crawled from the horizon and covered Goshen, shrouding the villages in gloom, and seeding stories of miraculous darkness and cities that sank into the sea. He could still taste the ash in the air.

"I read it somewhere," he said. His mind still played tricks on him, conjuring false memories of the ancient past and zombies on the streets of the present. Noga's theories about the Ten Lost Tribes had not helped him separate fact from delusion. He had to hold onto reality at all costs; reality was all that had kept Noga in his life.

He leaned back on the recliner, returning to the sun and the soft crashing of the waves on the shore. In a few hours, he and Noga would return to the boat and move on. A few hours of heaven was more than any mortal could hope for.

CHAPTER 50

Avi yanked open the sliding door of the old warehouse in Talpiot and marched inside. He wanted answers. Just when things were going his way, the eleven o'clock news had spoiled his morning.

Fluorescents suspended from the rafters illuminated the warehouse, which reeked of singed metal and stood empty except for a large glass cube the size of an elevator in the center. A lanky Ethiopian crouched beside the cube and applied the flame of a welding gun to a corner. As Avi approached, the Ethiopian stood, extinguished the flame, and lifted the welding mask from his face.

"Where's Boris?"

With a toss of his head, the Ethiopian indicated the supervisor's office in a corner two floors up.

Avi made for the metal staircase. The stairs clanked underfoot. Boris had given him the address of the warehouse for emergencies. Today was an emergency and if his so-called partner didn't fix things, there'd be hell to pay.

He marched along the narrow walkway and burst through the door of the corner office. Boris looked up from behind a cheap desk. His large Russian bodyguard stood at the wall behind him, his tree-trunk arms folded over his chest, making Avi reconsider the wisdom of his visit, but only for a moment.

"You said you'd destroy Moshe Karlin."

Boris peered at him beneath droopy eyelids, unmoved by the accusation. "I said that *we'd* bring him down together. And what of it—Gurion dropped him for you, didn't he?"

"Moshe started his own party. He's running in the elections as an independent."

The gray-haired thug grinned. "And there I thought you were upset that he married your old girlfriend."

Avi's thoughts scattered. "What? When?"

"Ramat Rachel, Monday last week." He chuckled. "You didn't know?"

Avi's throat constricted and he couldn't breathe. That scumbag Moshe had stolen his tactic and brought the wedding forward. Only this time, the ploy had worked.

Boris seemed to soften at Avi's loss for words. "Your friend is more resilient than we thought, but I wouldn't worry about his little experiment."

The Russian's dismissive attitude sparked Avi's temper. "Then start worrying—they say he could win seats in the next government all on his own. You have got to stop him."

The grin faded from the Russian's face. "I don't *got* to do anything."

"Oh, yes you do, Boris." Avi puffed out his chest. "I'm Isaac Gurion's rising star, remember. I'm going to be a member of Knesset. You clean up this mess. I can't get my hands dirty."

Boris stared at him. "What do you want me to do—kill him?"

Avi almost swallowed his tongue. He had punched Moshe in the face and threatened his life, but he had never actually intended to murder him. Boris, however, wasn't joking, and Avi had the sudden urge to pee. "Jeez, no. No, don't kill him. Just destroy his party."

"And how do you propose I do that?"

Another silence. Moshe had been the brains behind Karlin & Son. He had always had a plan. Ronen was right—Avi had only followed in Moshe's footsteps, and now Moshe was outmaneuvering him again. It wasn't fair.

"How should I know? You're the criminal mastermind. Think of something."

Avi had gone too far and he knew it. But Boris didn't set his thug on him. He didn't throw him out either. Instead, he drew a deep breath, leaned forward, and clasped his hands over the desk.

"Growing up in the Soviet Union," he said, "you learn a thing or two about power politics. When the Bolsheviks took control of the country, they didn't use physical force alone." He tapped his temple. "They invaded people's minds as well, and their memories, causing confusion and uncertainty. Soon people had difficulty predicting the past."

Invading minds. Predicting the past. What was he going on about? "What are you trying to say?"

The Russian's mustache wriggled. "It's simple," he said. "If you want to rule the future, you have to change the past."

CHAPTER 51

A week later, Noga stepped out of the golden elevator and into the dark yet familiar penthouse on Jaffa Road. Motors hummed as the blinds parted, revealing the Jerusalem skyline in orange sunset hues through the large French windows.

Eli wheeled their bags inside. "Home sweet home," he said.

Home. The cruise had surpassed her wildest dreams of the perfect romantic vacation, but she was glad to return to the place where she belonged, here with this man who made dreams come true. She wrapped her arms about his neck and he dropped the bags.

"Let's celebrate," he said, a mischievous twinkle in his eye.

She laughed. "We celebrated every day of the trip."

"Why stop now?" He scooped her up in his arms and made for the bedroom. Their bags remained in the hall all night.

Early the next morning, she fixed herself a cup of coffee and flopped on the living room couch. A muffled car horn blared from the street below. Monday morning and not a care in the world.

She aimed the remote at the TV and switched channels, settling on a rerun of Friends on the HOT Comedy Channel.

Her laptop lay shut on the coffee table. With the scant Wi-

Fi access on the trip, she hadn't bothered to check her email. She hadn't even powered on her phone, and now she dismissed all sixty-one notifications. At some point, she'd have to wrap up her doctoral paper, but she could muster little motivation to sum up her failed experiment. At least she'd get her piece of paper.

Hannah might need some convincing. Or had she stepped back from her messianic theory as well? Probably. Eli was right—no serious academic would commit career suicide over a few equivocal data points.

On the screen, Joey bet a hundred dollars that he and Chandler knew more about Rachel and Monica than the girls knew about them. Where was Phoebe?

Doctorate finally in hand, Noga would have to decide what to do with the rest of her life. She was leaning toward doing another degree. An ironic laugh escaped her lips. She was becoming like Sarit, her old friend from Hebrew U. They hadn't spoken in ages. Romance trumped girlfriends. Of all people, Sarit would understand that. Noga would call her later.

In the Friends universe, Ross pointed at a score board on a chair. The couples had tied and started a thirty-second lightning round of questions. The stakes had risen: if the girls won, the guys would get rid of their pet rooster and duck; if the guys won, the girls would switch apartments with them.

Noga's laptop beckoned to her from the coffee table. She opened the lid, nudged the screen to life, and scanned her inbox. Two hundred new messages, mostly adverts and newsletters. Hannah had emailed her three times.

Friday, the day after they had left in the limo: "How is the paper going? Call me. I have some ideas to discuss."

Monday, last week: "Send me your first draft ASAP. The university has approved a discussion paper slot for their website. The print journal closes for submissions next week. On second thought, the university journal is too small a platform for this sort of paper. We should submit to Nature Genetics."

Nature Genetics! Noga's pulse quickened. Hannah wanted to submit their paper to one of the most esteemed peer review academic journals in the world. During Noga's cooling-off period, her advisor had only heated up.

Another email, Thursday last week: "Are you OK? Can't reach you by phone. Did you get my messages?"

Noga should have at least told her she was going away. Her fear of confrontation had caused her mentor unnecessary worry.

She dashed off a reply. "Sorry for not responding earlier," she wrote. "Went overseas on short notice. Will call soon."

Eli padded down the hallway behind her. She hit send and closed the laptop.

"Hey," he said. He kissed her on the ear and moved to the kitchen. "What are you watching?"

"Friends."

"Funny name for a movie."

She turned to look at him. He wasn't joking. "How can you not know Friends?"

He shrugged. "I must have been sick that day."

Oh, right. Messianic delusions were a full-time job, and the old Eli had spared little time for petty entertainment. She relented. "It's about a group of guys and girls who share apartments near each other. This is a great episode. Joey and Chandler are playing a game of 'Who Knows Each Other Better' against Rachel and Monica. If the guys win, they switch apartments with the girls. If the girls win, the guys have to get rid of their pets."

"Their pets? That's a bit harsh."

"A rooster and a duck."

"Oh. And who's that?"

"That's Ross. He's facilitating."

"It's his apartment?"

"No, Monica's—just watch already."

Eli sat beside her and sipped his coffee.

In Monica's living room, the girls failed to answer the question "What is Chandler's job?" The boys got to keep their pets and won the better apartment. The credits rolled.

How would Noga fare if she were to play that game with Eli? Not very well.

"What *is* Chandler's job?"

"Some hi-tech thingy."

Noga switched channels. The camera panned over a sprawl of low buildings, the familiar campus of the Hebrew University.

"We return to Professor Yakov Malkovich," said the voice of the Channel Ten reporter.

A bespectacled old man hunched behind a large desk in an office plastered with certificates and awards. His bush of untamed white hair defied gravity, standing out in haphazard tufts as though he had spent hours pulling at the ends. He spoke with a wild enthusiasm and waved his hands.

"We have measured elevated levels of magnetism in the air," he said. "Perhaps the result of a recent solar flare, which appears to have had a peculiar effect on human remains, although we have yet to reproduce the regeneration in the laboratory. We are calling on volunteers from the undead community to assist with our research."

Did he say "undead"?

Eli shifted on the couch.

"Professor," the balding reporter said. A smirk pulled at the edge of his mouth. "The last time we spoke you claimed that these self-professed resurrected men and women were part of an elaborate hoax. Does this mean that you've changed your mind?"

At the word "resurrected," Noga's intestines tied in a knot.

The professor's lips trembled. "It's hard to argue with an empirical phenomenon. We just need to understand it better."

The camera switched to Clal Center on Jaffa Road, a few blocks down from their apartment complex. A mass of angry protesters covered the wide sidewalk. What were they chanting? "Death to *Zombies*'?

"Meanwhile," the reporter narrated, "other reactions to

the new demographic have been less welcoming."

Noga had noticed a crowd on the street a few days before their trip, but had found a detour to get around them. Just another political demonstration, she had thought.

The reporter held a microphone to the mouth of a young woman with long, brown hair and spectacles. She wore a yellow shirt with a black nuclear hazard sign. "They're not natural," she shouted above the roar of the crowd. "They're taking our jobs and overloading public services. The dead should stay dead. Life is for the living."

Another protester faced the mike—a man with black curls. "My neighbor died five years ago," he said. He spoke with a heavy Moroccan accent. "Scared the crap out of me when he got in the elevator with me." He shivered. "Still gives me the creeps, and now he kidnapped my cat, I swear it. She's probably dead by now, poor thing. The undead did it. They eat the brains." He nodded his head. "They're screwed up, man. It's them or us."

Eli snatched the remote from her hand and the screen went blank.

"Put it back on."

He got up. "Enough TV for one day. Let's go out."

She glared at him. He was trying to change the subject. "Did you know about this?"

He waved it away with his hand. "Election propaganda," he said. "It doesn't mean anything."

"*Doesn't mean anything?* Dead people are walking the streets." She touched her forehead, which was cold and damp, and her breath came in shallow, rapid bursts. "Eli, you heard the professor—this is real. This is the freaking end of the world!"

Eli tried to laugh. "The old guy with the crazy hair? Being on TV doesn't make him a scientist. It's all scripted, a publicity stunt for a new zombie movie."

"That was Channel Ten, Eli. It's not a joke."

He raised his hands in a conciliatory gesture. "OK. I'm sorry." He sat down beside her and took her hands in his.

"Maybe it's true; maybe it isn't. I don't know. It doesn't matter. All that matters is us."

She pulled her hands away. "What are you saying—that we should just get on with our lives, with this going on outside?"

"Why not?" Annoyance hardened his voice.

The implications rose in her mind. Hannah was right and Noga had made a big mistake. "My research," she said. "This can't be a coincidence. I have to call Hannah." She reached for her phone but he grabbed her wrist.

"Don't, Noga. Please, just don't."

"We can't just turn a blind eye."

His nostrils flared. "We can," he said, raising his voice. "And we will."

She broke free of his grip, got to her feet, and stepped away from him. "What's gotten into you?" She no longer knew the man on the couch. He had known all along. Was the cruise just a distraction to hide the truth from her?

"You can't help them," he said. "No one can."

Tears crept into her eyes and her voice cracked. "We have to."

"I'm done with humanity. Let them figure it out themselves."

Noga recognized that voice. Elijah had spoken, not Eli. But had the prophet forsaken his mission?

"You were right, Eli. I'm sorry I didn't believe you before, but we have a role to play now. Both of us. Together."

He shot her a fiery glance. "Then you're on your own. I won't have anything to do with it."

Noga's legs turned to jelly. He had moved from "us" to "you," and once again, their future teetered on the brink. But this time, the stakes were far greater than her own personal happiness.

His stubborn words sparked a blaze within her too.

"Fine," she said, and she marched to the front door. She pressed the button for the elevator, then folded her arms over her pajama shirt, waiting for him to apologize and beg her to stay. He didn't.

The doors opened, so she stepped inside. Then, spotting their bags, she pulled her suitcase into the elevator after her. *That'll show him.* But Eli just stared ahead at the view through the windows, his jaw clenched.

She pressed the button for the lobby. "You know what your problem is?" she said, as the doors closed. "You only care about yourself."

CHAPTER 52

Yosef arrived bright and early Monday morning at the call center of the Dry Bones Society—of Restart, he corrected himself. Over a week into the campaign and he still hadn't adjusted to the new name. Today, he would take a break from campaigning and return to another urgent task. With the elections only three days away, he could neglect this task no longer.

"Good morning, Rabbi," Samira said.

"Good morning, Samira."

She smiled at him and nodded at the wall. The mounted TV screen displayed his own talking head. He hadn't adjusted to that either.

His TV self wore a new suit and freshly trimmed beard. "Starting anew each day," he said, "is what Rabbi Nachman of Breslov taught and this is what Restart is about."

"How are we doing?" he asked Samira, more to change the subject than to gain information. During the mad flurry of activity in the first week of the campaign, he had starred in infomercials and interviews. The lecture circuit had taken him to synagogues around the country, and during that time he had handed over the management of the Absorption Center to Samira and Irina. They were doing a great job.

"More new arrivals every day," she said. "The fifth floor is filling up."

"I'll speak with Mr. Adams about expanding the dormitory," he said. He preferred not to use the title Reverend. "And the campaign?"

Her smile widened. "Sivan said that attendance at the rallies is much higher than expected. The polls give us twelve seats."

"Incredible," he said. Sivan had orchestrated a powerful campaign.

He headed for the corner office and closed the door behind him. The speaking tour had taken Moshe south today and freed up his office.

Yosef settled behind the desk, opened his laptop, and found the spreadsheet of telephone numbers.

So far, he had called over two hundred Menachems, Efraims, and Davids. Their responses had ranged from mild amusement to irritation. Some had shouted abuse in his ear.

But he had to continue. How could he sit in Knesset when the Son of David was out there? Yosef would gladly vacate his number two slot in the Restart list for the Lord's Anointed. Each day brought new questions that Yosef could not answer. In Knesset, that list of questions would only grow in number and importance.

Yosef scrolled down the list to where he had left off, and selected the first Nehorai. As he dialed the number, the door of the office cracked open.

Irina stood on the doorway. "Rabbi Yosef, you're on TV."

"I know. I've seen it a dozen times."

"Not this one," she said. "We didn't put this out, I'm sure of it." From the drawn look on her face, he knew that the broadcast was not good news.

He put down the phone and followed her out of the office.

His face appeared on the screen, all right, but in a photograph on the Channel Two news. The shot showed him grimacing as he got out of a car. Not the most flattering likeness.

The female news presenter gave her viewers a scandalized smile. "More bad news for Restart, the controversial new party formerly known as the Dry Bones Society."

Yosef had to laugh at the blatant attack on their new brand. These media people had no shame. As she continued to speak, however, he stopped laughing and the hairs on the back of his neck stood erect like the fur of a startled cat.

Restart was in deep trouble, and it was all his fault.

CHAPTER 53

Adrenaline pulsed through Moshe's bloodstream as he waited in the wings of Turner Stadium. In the corridor that soccer teams used on their way to the field, Sivan's amplified voice echoed from the stage outside. By now, he knew her introductory speech by heart.

Galit squeezed his hand. "Ready to conquer the world?"

"Beer Sheba will do for now," he said.

Sivan had booked the Beer Sheba Theater for his election rally a week ago. Two days ago she moved the event to the city's main stadium. The crowds had grown with each city they visited, and the unofficial capital of southern Israel had beaten all their early attendance forecasts.

Sivan's voice rose as she mentioned his name, and the cheers of countless people carried into the tunnel.

"Here we go."

Holding hands with Galit and little Talya, he marched outside, into the morning light, across the field, up a few steps, and onto the stage.

Sivan stood beside the microphone, smiling and clapping. The mass of supporters roared, filling the field and grandstands. Moshe waved at them. Restart banners hung from railings. Restart placards and flags dotted the human sea like white horses. Their goodwill surged through his body and sharpened his senses. The rush was addictive. *So this is how pop stars feel.*

He reached for the microphone and the cheers settled. Moshe no longer needed his cue cards.

"Friends," he said. "Thank you for joining us today. I know why you're here. You're here because, like us, you know we need change." On cue, the crowd murmured agreement.

"For too long," he continued, "we have endured corruption and cronyism. For too long, we have let cynical politicians divide us. Religious and secular. Rich and poor. Established and immigrant. Ashkenazi and Sephardic. And, more recently, first-timers and the resurrected. The time has come to put those divisions aside and come together as one nation. The time has come to restart our society!"

Voices cheered. Hands reached for the heavens. Flags waved. A chant rose: Re-start! Re-start! Re-start!

Moshe lifted his hands in the air like the conductor of the largest orchestra in history. He was born for this moment. A full minute later, the chant subsided and Moshe got on with his speech. He urged them to go out and vote tomorrow and make that change a reality. The crowd broke into song again and at the climax, Moshe collected his family and walked off the stage. On the way out, he leaned over the barrier fence and shook hands with supporters.

Reverend Adams waited in the wings. "Great job, Moshe," he said. He gave his hand a mighty shake and clapped him on the back. "I didn't understand a word, of course, but the crowd said it all. How are we doing?"

Moshe turned to Sivan.

"Over thirty thousand," she said in English. "Our best turnout yet. At this rate we're projecting twelve mandates."

"Mandates?" Rev. Adams was still new to the intricacies of Israeli politics.

"The one hundred twenty seats in Knesset are divided up proportionally to each party according to the number of votes received. We passed the electoral threshold easily."

The reverend's smile dropped. "Twelve is far from a majority."

"There are too many parties for that. The largest party gets to form a coalition government and divide up the ministries. At twelve seats, we're sure to be included in the coalition."

"I see." The broad, toothy smile returned.

Moshe said, "You're welcome to join us on our next stops, Reverend."

"I'm afraid I can't. I have to check up on some of our other investments. Which reminds me—Moshe, may I have a word?"

"Of course."

They stepped aside. "About our new arrivals. How far back in time are we now?"

Moshe cleared his throat. "Eighth century, last I heard. But I'll check with Rabbi Yosef."

"I see." The reverend seemed disappointed but then brightened. "I'm glad that we'll be well positioned by the time we do reach that *critical time.*" He gave Moshe a meaningful glance. "You keep that seat in Knesset warm until it's needed."

"Of course."

Rev. Adams nodded and strode off, his briefcase-carrying assistant trying to keep up.

Moshe exhaled a deep breath. Rabbi Yosef would not be happy with that arrangement. They'd cross that bridge when they reached it. If Jesus did show up, he might not want to sit in Knesset, and if he did, well, he was a Jewish social activist, wasn't he? Moshe could do with all the help he could get.

"What did he want?" Galit asked.

"Just looking out for an old friend. What's our next stop? Sivan?"

Sivan held her phone to her ear and shook her head. She did not look happy.

"We have to head back right away," she said when she put down the phone.

"I thought we had a few more stops in the south."

"Not anymore," she said. "We have a problem, Moshe. A very big problem."

CHAPTER 54

Alex parked outside the Technology Park opposite the Malcha Mall and wondered what Mandrake was up to. They had never met at this address before.

He walked around the security boom at the entrance where a guard checked the trunks of cars before waving them in. As a pedestrian, Alex got a free pass.

He headed for the main set of office buildings in the center of the complex. Straight paths of paving stones crisscrossed the tidy squares of trimmed grass like electronic circuits on a silicon chip. Man-sized Hebrew letters and metallic orbs littered the grounds. He weaved between the oversized sculptures, a small, vulnerable creature inside a cold, heartless machine.

"Stay close to Karlin," his boss had instructed when Alex had informed him of Karlin's intention to run in the elections. "I want to know his every move."

And so Alex had found his excuse to stay close to Irina. She had Moshe's ear, and what she learned she shared with Alex. He had fooled himself into believing that the arrangement would last forever.

Maybe Mandrake would change tactics after the elections; maybe not. But the summons to the Technology Park the day before the elections had shattered his sense of security. Once again, he had failed to predict his old friend's next move, and his future was up in the air.

He passed the offices of the Open University, entered Tower Four, and took the mirrored lift to the eighth floor. A sign on the wall pointed the way down the clean, carpeted corridor toward the offices of Magitek.

Mandrake had probably chosen the name.

He pressed the intercom button at the glass door.

The blonde at the enamel white front desk looked up from her phone, and the door clicked open. Anna had traded her tank top for a white blouse but had kept the gum. She motioned to the side with her head. "All the way to the end. He's waiting."

Alex cut through a long, wide hall of cubicles. Young men peered at computer monitors and jabbered into their headsets excitedly in English, French, and Russian, frantic worker bees in a hive of human activity ten times the size of the call center of the Dry Bones Society.

Was this a new scam or a front for the Organization's other criminal operations? Alex had glimpsed only the tip of the iceberg of Mandrake's activities and, once again, he sensed the immense bulk that lurked beneath the surface.

At the end of the hall he found a white enamel door. A security camera eyed him from above like a sphinx. He must have answered the silent riddle correctly, for the door clicked open as he neared and he walked right through.

Mandrake stood in a plain white antechamber, a tall, bald man, the bulge of his muscles visible beneath his button-down shirt.

"Welcome to the future, Sasha," he said in his sonorous voice and smiled. "What do you think?"

Alex pointed a thumb behind him at the call center. "A new trick?"

"Binary options," Mandrake said.

"Never heard of it. Is it real?"

Mandrake's eyes glittered. "More than real—it's magic. Money disappears in one country and reappears in another.

Poof! Today, we can reach the entire world from one computer. It takes a little imagination but then again, true power has always lived here"—he tapped his forehead—"in the mind."

"And I thought revenues were down."

"Oh, no, my friend. Business has never been better. So long as people have hope for the future, they are easily parted from their money. I want to show you something."

His boss made for the far wall of the antechamber. Alex followed, and breathed at ease. Perhaps the visit had nothing to do with Karlin and the elections.

Mandrake paused at a framed mirror and combed his imaginary hair. "Mirror, mirror on the wall," he crooned.

Whoosh!

Alex took a hurried step back as the wall slid sideways to reveal a rectangular black portal.

Mandrake turned to him. "Cool, hey? Facial recognition. Only the prettiest get to go inside."

They walked through the portal. The room beyond the hole in the wall was the negative image of the call center. Black walls, dull blue light, and silence. An array of huge screens covered the walls, similar to the video feeds on the walls of the secret office at the back of the Talpiot Bowling Center, but the number of feeds had grown substantially. Computer terminals lined the walls. The swivel chairs stood empty.

"Our new headquarters," Mandrake said with a flourish of his large hands. He plopped onto a circular couch in the middle of the command room, put his hands behind his head, and admired his handiwork.

Alex joined him. "Congratulations. It's beautiful." Mandrake was sharing a milestone with a close friend. Alex was not like the other hands in Mandrake's employ. They had a special relationship. Or did Mandrake make all his captains feel that way?

Mandrake chuckled. "The bowling alley couldn't contain us much longer. Not enough cable, for one thing. Information is the key, my friend. It flows from this building to the world and back. And the world looks to us. To Jerusalem, the Eye of the Universe."

The poetry was lost on Alex, but his boss didn't explain.

"I'm proud of you, Sasha," he said. "You followed your instincts and the girl led us to Karlin's inner circle. Now I think it's time I met this Karlin."

Alex tried not to swallow. Meetings with his boss were not the kind one scheduled in an appointment book. The attendees could not refuse. Often, they did not survive. "When?"

"Tomorrow."

He couldn't be serious. "Tomorrow is election day."

"The perfect time to reap what we have sown."

Alex did not like the sound of that. "OK," he said. "I'll make the arrangements."

Let him have Karlin. Anyone who messed with the Organization had it coming. So long as the girl remained safe, Mandrake could do with Karlin as he wished.

CHAPTER 55

Irina opened the door of Moshe's office but nobody seemed to notice. The top brass of Restart—Shmuel, Sivan, Rafi, Rabbi Yosef—huddled behind Moshe and stared at the computer screen on his desk. Judging by the pensive looks on their faces, the situation was bad. Very bad.

She had walked over to the call center at lunch time looking for Alex, who hadn't returned yet from his work commitments that morning, when she had noticed the anxious team through the window of the corner office. Had the campaign rally at Beer Sheba gone awry?

"What's happened?" she asked the room at large.

No one answered, so she joined them behind the desk. The recording of a Channel Two newscast played on YouTube. A terrible photo of Rabbi Yosef was displayed beside a female presenter.

"Rabbi Yosef Lev," she said with scandalized relish, "former primary school teacher and number two on the Restart list, is an alcoholic. According to a close friend and confidant of the rabbi, he was fired recently from his teaching job, and although the school did not press formal charges, a representative confirmed that they had deemed Rabbi Lev unsuitable to work with children."

Irina shuddered. Rabbi Yosef—an alcoholic? *Unsuitable to*

work with children—the phrase implied that he was a pedophile too! *Never!* The kind rabbi stared at the screen, shaking his head and pulling at the ends of his beard.

The screen cut to a familiar angry mug. The subtitle read, "Avi Segal, Upward Party."

"These zombies are eating up the living and overrunning our country." His mouth contorted with disgust. "Now it seems that they're molesting our children too. They belong behind bars. That Restart has the nerve to run in the elections is an insult to the entire nation."

The camera cut to the news desk. The presenter's smile widened. "More scandal for the beleaguered fledgling party— as if that wasn't enough!" The photo of the rabbi became a shot of Moshe, his mouth open in mid-speech, his eyes half-shuttered. "Our investigative reporters have discovered that, shortly before his death, the leader of Restart, Moshe Karlin, had been thrown out of his home by his wife, who suspected him of cheating on her."

Sivan leaned in, clicked the mouse, and the video froze. "I know the story about Moshe is a sham. We can deny that rumor without any problems. Rabbi Yosef? Sorry, but we have to know."

The rabbi spread his hands in supplication. "I've been sober ten years."

"And the kids?"

"Heaven forbid! I taught them about the Resurrection— that's what caused the trouble with the principal. Then they fired me for working with the Society."

"Good. Then we'll fight back. We'll do a press conference right away. Shmuel, speak with Eran. Moshe and Rabbi Yosef, be ready to rehearse your messages. I think we can put a positive spin on this."

A positive spin? That sounded like a miracle.

Shmuel laughed his bitter laugh. "How will you do that?" he said, mirroring Irina's thoughts.

"Restart is all about correcting mistakes. A recovered alcoholic makes a great poster child. Moshe, we'll need Galit at your side when you make your statement."

Moshe nodded. "What's the damage so far?"

"Our telephone poll started an hour ago. Results should be in soon. Even with our denials and spin, there will be damage. This could cut our votes in half."

Moshe gave her a grim nod.

"But spin will only go so far," Sivan said. "We need to hit back and hard."

"What do you mean?"

"We need dirt on Gurion. Or Avi—he'll make an easier target. He lies and cheats in his sleep. We won't need to dig very deep. We can start with his ex-girlfriends."

Moshe wriggled on his seat. "I don't think we should go there. We're running a clean campaign. These are exactly the kind of sleazy tricks we're promising to root out."

Sivan put her hands on her hips. "Which do you prefer: a clean campaign or a winning one?"

Moshe's mobile phone rang. He gave them a meaningful glance and got to his feet. "Reverend Adams. Yes, I saw the news." He paced the room.

Don't let him cut us off, Irina prayed. *Please.*

"No, of course not," Moshe said into the phone. "A smear campaign from our rivals. We're preparing a response right now. I understand. Of course."

He put down the phone and slumped into his chair.

"Are we still afloat?" Sivan asked.

Moshe nodded. "For now. But our benefactors are uneasy about associating with adulterers and drunks. I'm sure he won't like us jumping into a mud fight either. OK, everyone, battle stations."

"How can I help?" Irina asked him, as the others filed out of the room. Poor Moshe. She knew how much he cared for Galit, how he had struggled to win her back and clear his name. The returning accusations must really hurt, and to have them aired on television? Unbearable!

Moshe managed a brave smile. "You're already helping. Thanks for holding the fort. Restart couldn't go on without you."

"And Samira," she added. "Arabic is in high demand these days. We'll get through this."

"I know. We've been through worse, right?"

Irina left his office on a wave of renewed energy. She'd spread the word. The false rumors must be circulating in the Absorption Center by now and the Society's morale would need a boost.

Opening the door of the call center, she almost collided with Alex. He must have heard the accusations on the radio, because he looked pale and tense.

"It's all a lie," she said.

His eyes widened. "What is?"

"What they're saying about Rabbi Yosef and Moshe."

"Oh, right. Yeah, I heard. It's terrible."

"I hope they pull through," she said.

He pulled her close and stroked her hair. "I hope so too."

CHAPTER 56

Ahmed steeled himself to face his worst fear.

At the opposite side of the circle of chairs, Samira listened with interest to each speaker. She sensed Ahmed's eyes on her, met his gaze and gave him that warm, encouraging smile. Basking in that smile, he could brave anything.

He fidgeted with his song sheet. The heavyset man beside him folded and unfolded his tanned arms, muttering to himself and smelling of soap.

People passed by the window in the door, fellow Society members on their way to lunch. Perhaps the session would end early and save Ahmed the torment. Would his fellow Society members guess his evil deeds? Would his guilt show on his face?

Two seats down, a bearded man with olive skin stood. "Mustafa is my name," he said. Ahmed had trouble understanding the strange Arabic dialect.

"Three young wives," Mustafa said, "ten olive groves, and a hundred head of sheep I had. Broke bread with Abd Al-Malik, the great caliph, when he visited the walled city." After bragging about his wealth and connections, however, he started to sob. "Then I awoke in this land of terrible sounds and devil-wagons. I hid in tunnels beneath the road for a week, scavenging and stealing, God forgive me. Then a young man found me in the trash bins and led me here. A thousand blessings upon you all, my daughter."

When Mustafa sat down, Soap Man stood and jabbered away in a foreign tongue.

Samira looked about the room. "Does anyone understand him?" She repeated the question in Hebrew and then in English.

"Romani!" Soap Man said. "Romani!"

Samira motioned for the distressed man to sit. "We will find someone who can speak with you, sir."

The comforting tone of her words seemed to calm him and he sat down. Samira smiled at Ahmed and her eyes glittered.

Ahmed's turn had arrived. He glanced at the door for salvation. A man passed by the window and glanced at him—the balding older man he had seen with Moshe Karlin. There was no escape now.

He rose to his feet and a dozen pairs of eyes set upon him.

"My name is Ahmed," he said. His voice sounded strange to own his ears. He wiped his clammy hands on his jeans. Samira nodded, encouraging him. In the other faces he found understanding and acceptance. "I died ten years ago. My life was not special. But my new life is. I thank God, Who led me here, for the people I have met and the experiences I have had." Samira swallowed and her eyes glittered again. He was talking about her, and she felt the same way about him. "I hope," he continued, "that in the future—"

The door flung open. The balding older man who had appeared at the window stormed into the room, and he had eyes only for Ahmed.

"Murderer!" he yelled.

Ahmed stiffened. *He knows!*

Samira turned to the source of the commotion. Others rose and shifted out of the man's path as he shoved a chair aside and cut through the circle toward Ahmed.

"Murderer!"

"Shmuel," Samira cried. "Wait!"

Shmuel clamped two beefy hands around Ahmed's neck. Ahmed fell backward, his chair slipping away. The old man landed on his chest, winding him and pinning him to the floor. The hands tightened about his neck. Ahmed couldn't breathe.

"Murderer!" the balding man cried again, raining spittle on Ahmed's face. He struggled but the man was too heavy and furious.

Then the man was yanked back, his hands slipping from Ahmed's neck. He sucked in air and scrambled to his feet.

"Let me go!" Shmuel kicked and flailed but Soap Man and the Mustafa held him back. "You killed us," Shmuel yelled at Ahmed, tears in his voice. "You blew us up. On the bus. You ruined our lives!"

Samira turned to Ahmed, her eyes wide with disbelief. "No, Ahmed. This is not true. Tell him."

Ahmed opened his mouth to lie. He wasn't a murderer. Some other boy had pushed the button, not him. He wanted to see her warm smile again, but he had lost it for good.

So he ran for the door and fled.

CHAPTER 57

That evening, Yosef slunk into the grocery store on Emek Refaim Street and kept his head down. After the exhausting hours of PR work, he never wanted to step in front of a video camera again. Daylight was fading by the time he headed home, but Rocheleh had insisted that he stop by the local grocer for odds and ends, as many stores would close tomorrow for Election Day. Fortunately, his wife had not been exposed to the slanderous reports on television.

While he selected zucchini from a tub in the vegetable section, a fat woman in a wooly shawl fondled the sweet potatoes in the next tub and gave him sharp looks. Did she recognize him from the mug shot on Channel Two? Her eyes seemed to shout, "Drunken pervert! Shame on you!"

He bagged his zucchini, selected two cartons of three percent milk, and waited in line at the till. The scanner beeped as Gavri swiped the barcodes. Yosef sank his head further into his shirt collar, a feeble attempt at avoiding conversation with the chatty store owner. He wanted to crawl into a hole and hibernate until the next millennium. The embarrassment caused by the accusations accounted for only part of the heartache.

The gloves will come off, Rabbi Emden had warned him, and off they had come. Yosef had expected a reprisal. The rabbinate had lashed out at him before—they had terminated his teaching job at Daas Torah Primary and he had felt the full force of their political maneuvers at the Ministry of the Interior.

But this time the betrayal was personal. Rabbi Emden had stood by him in his darkest moments, when Yosef had opened his heart and bared his soul. The media had not revealed the identity of their source, but only one "close friend and confidant" had heard his sacred confessions.

Yosef could absorb the financial and political blows; he could even forgive them. But now Emden had turned their years of emotional intimacy into a political weapon. Yosef had never imagined that his spiritual mentor would stoop so low, and the loss of his dearest friend and confidant hurt like a jagged tear in his soul.

Yosef stepped forward as the checkout line progressed and Gavri scanned the barcodes. *Beep. Beep.*

Having his good name dragged through the mud on television and losing his spiritual guide had seemed like enough of a beating for one day, but the afternoon had delivered the knockout punch to Yosef's peace of mind.

No matter what the world threw at him he had found comfort in the Resurrection. Over time, a pattern had emerged. Like Moshe and Samira, the growing mass of returnees had suffered tragic and untimely deaths. The Resurrection allowed them to pick up their life stories from that abrupt intermission and read all the way to the happy ending. From Hannah and her seven sons in the Hanukkah story who, rather than betray their faith, had died as martyrs at the hands of the evil Emperor Antiochus, to the victims of terror today, the Resurrection was turning those rivers of bitter tears into the sweet dew of fresh life. The returning dead not only validated ancient Biblical prophecies, they demonstrated God's justice.

Then, that afternoon, Shmuel had staggered into the call center, broken and shaking, and Yosef's rosy theology had crumbled to dust. Why would God revive a suicide bomber—an intentional mass murderer—along with his victims? What was the Resurrection if not compensation for the righteous? Or had Yosef misunderstood even that? And so, at a time when he most needed guidance, Yosef found himself lost, under attack, and utterly alone.

Yosef placed his groceries on the conveyer belt of the checkout counter.

Gavri weighed the vegetables and scanned the other items. *Beep. Beep.*

Yosef placed a fifty-shekel bill on the counter.

"Ready for the big day tomorrow, Rabbi?"

Yosef gave his questioner a suspicious glance. Was this a sarcastic hint at the rabbi's political demise or a good-natured ice-breaker? The fat woman with the evil eye waited in line behind him, and he'd prefer to avoid further public ridicule.

"It's in the voters' hands now," he said.

"Voters?" Gavri seemed to have tasted salt in his coffee. "Who cares about the elections? Tomorrow, the Messiah is coming."

Yosef's breath caught in his chest. "He is?"

"Sure. Everybody knows." Gavri waved the fifty-shekel note at him. "I think, Rabbi, that since you became a politician, you lost touch with the people." The store owner chuckled at his own joke.

Was Gavri pulling his leg? "What messiah?"

"No one knows his name or where he's from, but tomorrow morning he's going to make his big announcement."

"Where?"

"At the Kotel. Where else?"

Yosef turned to the shoppers behind him in the line. They nodded their heads. How had Yosef not heard of this? He had spent hours calling rabbis throughout the city in search of the Son of David, when the tidings of the Messiah had waited for him at the corner grocery store.

Gavri dropped the change into Yosef's hand, the tinkle of coins sounding like the rain of jackpot money at a casino. "Thank you, Gavri!"

"You're welcome, Rabbi. Next customer."

Yosef stumbled out of the store like a sleep-walker. The long-awaited Messiah would appear tomorrow at the Western Wall. Nothing else mattered.

CHAPTER 58

In a parking garage beneath Jaffa Road, Eli pulled on a black leather jacket and a pair of matching riding gloves. The winged Harley Davidson emblem gleamed in the cool fluorescent light on the matte black chassis of the Sportster Iron 883.

Once settled on the leather seat, he placed the black helmet over his head. One long stay at Shaare Zedek had sufficed, and Noga had insisted on the safety equipment. But tonight he was not going to think about Noga. Tonight he was going to forget all about her.

He squeezed the clutch, lifted the shift lever to neutral with his boot, and thumbed the starter. The V-twin engine growled to life. He clicked the remote, and the gate of the private parking bay rolled upward. Easing back on the throttle, he launched up the ramp and onto the street.

He slowed briefly at the light, then tore along King George Street. On Emek Refaim, revelers buzzed between the neon signs of Burgers Bar, Kaffit, and the Magic Carpet. The distractions he sought tonight would require a double dose of adrenaline, so he gunned down Pierre Koenig toward Talpiot.

Noga loved Eli Katz, so he had held his delusions below the waterline of his consciousness, and waited for them to drown. But just when that part of his mind had stopped struggling, Noga had changed her mind. Now she wanted Elijah back.

Did she expect him to switch his identity like clothes? She had piled on her arguments like cement bags, weighing him down again with the fate of the entire world until, last night, he had collapsed under the load. To hell with Elijah. To hell with the Redemption. He wanted out.

When she stormed out of his apartment with her suitcase that morning, he had waited for her to return. Let her cool off; she'd come crawling back soon enough. But she didn't. Fine. Her choice. Let her waste her life trying to save humanity if she liked. He was done with mankind. Good luck to her and good riddance.

On a seedy Talpiot street corner, a dozen young women in short skirts lined up at the door of a nightclub. A yellow mushroom cloud filled a poster on the wall. The sign above the door read Hangar 17, and the pulse of the dance beat within reverberated on the street. Bingo.

Eli pulled up on the sidewalk, took off his helmet, and got in line. The girls chatted, all makeup and perfume. A brunette glanced at him and smiled. He returned the smile, and followed them past the bouncer and inside.

Purple light flickered to the beat of trance music in the dark hall, illuminating figures on the dance floor and gallery like lightning. The dancers raised their arms and swung their heads. Smoke billowed at their feet and the sweet scent of alcohol wafted in the air. In a corner, a couple kissed. They had the right idea—live for the moment.

He placed his jacket and helmet on a bar stool and hit the dance floor, weaving among the couples. Some of the dancers had dressed up. One guy had an axe wedged in his hat. His partner had an arrow through her head. *Strange.* The country had celebrated Purim months ago.

At this point, he remembered that he didn't quite know how to dance. During the many years of obsessing over messiahs, apocalypses, and computers, he had not picked up that skill, so he improvised. He lifted his arms in the air and shifted his feet, closed his eyes, and moved his shoulders.

He opened his eyes to discover that a tall blonde was dancing with him. A star exploded on her black T-shirt. She had tied her hair up, the ends sticking out of her head like sunbeams. Her green eyes flashed at him. She had a very pretty smile. She leaned in to say something but her words got lost in the music, so he waved for her to join him at the bar.

"What are we drinking?" He had to shout to be heard.

"Breezer," she told the bartender. "Peach."

"Make that two." Eli had never had a Breezer before but tonight he was eager to taste something new.

When the drinks arrived, they clinked the bottles together and took their first sip. Rum. Very sweet rum. There was a time when rum was his drink of choice, in an age of sea travel and discovery—but he decided not to follow that reverie.

"What did you say on the dance floor?" he said.

"What are you dressed as?" she said.

A definite pickup line. He glanced over his black shirt and jeans. He'd have to make something up. "What's the theme?"

"The End of the World."

He laughed. "I like it." With all the zombies and weirdness lately, the theme seemed oddly appropriate. The bar managers had a sense of humor.

He said, "I'm a prophet of doom," and she gave him the thumbs-up. He took another sip. The sweetness was growing on him. "How about you?"

"I'm a supernova."

"I'll bet you are."

She held his gaze and smirked. "You don't remember me, do you?"

Oh, crap. Where had they met? "Sure I do," he said. "Remind me anyway."

"Café Aroma. On Emek Refaim. You were the big tipper who got away."

She took a long swig from her bottle and he remembered.

The waitress with the intelligent green eyes had sat down at his table and busted him for using The Magic to pour another cup of coffee from the empty milk pot.

He had brushed it off as a magic trick and offered to teach her the secret. When she rushed inside to fetch his check, he dropped a fifty on the table and disappeared. Seconds later, the Thin Voice spoke to him—he remembered that clearly— and the next day he had landed up in Shaare Zedek.

A shiver traced his spine. *That really happened, didn't it?* He took another sip. "I owe you a private lesson," he said, taken off guard by his own audacity. He glanced at the bottle in his hand. *This is great stuff.*

The green-eyed girl held his gaze. "I'm not working to-morrow. Election Day." Her cheeks dimpled as she smiled. "I've got all night."

Eli knew an invitation when he saw one. "Tell me," he said, flashing his charming smile. "Do you like motorbikes?"

CHAPTER 59

"Let me get this straight," Sarit said to Noga. "Your hot, rich boyfriend took you on an amazing cruise, and now you ditched him because... because he didn't agree with your thesis? See—that's the part I'm not getting."

Noga slouched on her friend's puffy couch. "It's more complicated than that. I'd show you the data but I left my laptop at his place."

She had not made an inventory of her belongings before storming out of his apartment. When the golden elevator had opened on the lobby, she had stayed inside, waiting for him to call the elevator back up, fully expecting him to come running after her.

Ten minutes later, she fished clothes out of her suitcase, changed out of her pajamas, and dragged her suitcase through the lobby and down Jaffa Road until she collapsed in a sobbing heap outside Sarit's apartment in Nachlaot.

On the couch, Noga told Sarit the details of her research results, Hannah's theory, and their adventures in the West Bank. "The key to peace in our time has just landed in our lap," she said. "We have to tell someone."

She still remembered the anger in Eli's eyes. *I'm done with humanity.* She felt as frightened as she had that day in the hospital when the comatose patient had grabbed her arm and spouted his deranged claims.

"OK, so you want to go public with your research and win the Nobel Peace Prize or whatever. Still, I don't understand—why did you leave him?"

"Because he didn't want to help."

Sarit laughed. "Noga, you've got to admit that your plan here does sound a little, you know." She waggled her eyebrows.

"A little what?"

"Loony? Nuts? Insane? Ah, yes—*crazy*, I believe that's the scientific term. Certifiable. Stark raving mad. Wasn't that the reason you broke up with him months ago—because he wanted to announce the End of Days?"

Noga sucked in a deep breath. "What if he was right all along? What if we *did* meet for a reason and he really *is* Elijah, and together we were meant to find the Ten Lost Tribes and announce the Messiah? Dead people are walking the streets, for Heaven's sake—is this any less believable?"

Sarit slapped the arm of the couch. "I told you he was for real!"

"You were joking. I didn't believe him either, even after I saw his apartment. You should have seen it—he had this room full of mementos from the last thousand years."

"There you go—that's your proof, isn't it?"

"Well, not anymore. He sold everything on eBay. I think he did it to please me."

"I've got it! Problem solved." For once, Sarit's indefatigable optimism seemed like a lifeline, not an annoyance. Over the years she had dragged Noga to dance classes and charity evenings and other thinly disguised singles' events. Noga had regretted all of them but now she hoped against all odds that her friend held the answer to her problems. "Here's what you do," she continued. "Go back to him. Let him think it over. In time, maybe he'll come to see it your way. *Or not.* What do you care? Either way, you get the penthouse."

"I don't care about the penthouse and I don't want to go back. He's... changed. The old Elijah may have sounded insane but at least he cared about something besides himself."

"He cares about you, doesn't he?"

"I'm not so sure anymore."

"So does that mean he's available?" Noga swatted her with a stiff cushion. "Just asking. Anyway, after dating you, I don't think I'd meet his high standards."

Sarit got up and the couch creaked. "Take it easy, girl. Watch some TV. I'll make hot chocolate and we'll be miserable together. Like the good old days."

Noga sneezed. The dusty couch was triggering her allergies. The good old days sucked.

What would Elijah the Prophet do now? According to Eli, he had possessed a holy intuition and a bag of miracles. She had neither. She needed to share her data with someone in a position of power. They'd know what to do next.

Then she'd have to find an apartment and a job. One mission impossible at a time. Sarit was right—she needed a rest. Tomorrow, she'd pick herself up; tonight she'd wallow in self-pity.

A kettle whined in the kitchenette. Noga slid the remote from the mug-stained coffee table and turned on the immense TV on the small wooden stand that looked ready to collapse.

A studio panel deliberated the elections polls. She had almost forgotten about the elections. Would she even bother to vote tomorrow? One of the new parties wasn't doing so well. A chart showed their projections drop from twelve seats to zero, despite a televised apology.

An honest-looking man in a suit threw his arm over the shoulders of a bearded rabbi. "Restart is all about starting over," the man said.

"Welcome to the club," Noga said.

He gave the rabbi an admiring glance. "Rabbi Yosef has been sober for ten years and was unfairly dismissed from his job. The other allegations made against us are also unfounded."

Sarit returned to the couch and handed over a mug of hot

chocolate.

Noga asked, "Who're they?"

Sarit performed her stunned fish impression. "Have you been living under a rock? That's Moshe Karlin of Restart, formerly the Dry Bones Society."

"The Dry Bones Society?"

"The non-profit that takes in those resurrected people. Pretty freaky, hey?"

"He's running in the elections?"

"Yeah. Handsome guy, I know, but don't bother—he's taken. Pretty wife too. Maybe he's your messiah?"

"You think he's the Messiah?"

"Yeah, why not? Although with all the scandals, he probably won't get any mandates."

Then you can do that on your own, Eli had said. A plan formed in Noga's mind and gave her new hope.

CHAPTER 60

"Oh my God," Lia said. "This place is amazing!"

The green-eyed blonde took in Eli's living room as the blinds opened and the night skyline of Jerusalem glittered through the French windows.

She had climbed onto his Sportster Iron 883 and clung to him as the bike shuddered down the bumpy Jerusalem streets. He had let her wear the helmet.

At the penthouse, he pulled two glasses from a cupboard and poured generous helpings of red wine and joined her at the window. The Old City glowed golden in the distance.

"Thanks." She took a sip. "This is good. What is it?"

"Shiraz."

She raised her glass. "Here's to new experiences." The glasses clinked and they swallowed more wine.

"You have this whole place to yourself?"

"Mm-hmm."

The penthouse had a seductive charm. How had he never taken advantage of that before? Noga, the first girl to visit his bachelor pad, had gone there alone to investigate his prophetic claims while he had lain in a hospital bed. She had broken up with him all the same.

Lia's large green eyes drank him in. "Don't you get lonely up here?"

Eli considered the question. Loneliness had never been an issue and yet he had rushed to fill the vacuum Noga had left. "I suppose I do."

"You don't have to be lonely anymore." She kicked off her sandals and dropped ten centimeters in height. Slipping her hand in his, she led him away from the window, and a knot tied in his stomach.

At the couch, she took the wine from his hand and placed both their glasses on the coffee table.

"You must be good at what you do."

Was he? Eli Katz had failed at leading a normal life, and Elijah had failed at bringing the Redemption, and neither of them had prevented Noga from walking out.

Lia's eyes twinkled in the glow of the LED lighting of the kitchen. "Success is very exciting."

She pulled a pin from the plaits above her head and blond hair spilled over her neck and shoulders.

The knot in his stomach tightened. What if Noga walked in right now? There would be no turning back. Would he ever see her again?

Lia's sweet perfume filled his head as she leaned in, her eyes closed, her lips parting.

"Wait," he said. "There's something I need to tell you."

CHAPTER 61

Yosef rushed home Tuesday morning straight after prayers. Today was the most important day of his life but he couldn't tell a soul. Not yet.

In his bedroom, he found his wedding suit in the closet and removed the plastic cover of the dry cleaners. A messiah is born into every generation and can reveal himself at any moment, and so Yosef had kept the suit at the ready for years. Two months ago, he had adjusted the trousers ahead of his fateful meeting with the Great Council of Torah Sages. Instead of greeting the Messiah, however, he and Moshe had fled the Great Synagogue of Kiryat Belz, an angry ultra-Orthodox mob at their heels.

Today would be different and that certainty warmed his bones. Gavri the grocer had shared with him the word on the street. While Yosef had wasted time cold-calling potential messiahs across the city, the true Messiah had whispered his arrival date to the city folk. Instead of attempting to force the End of Days, Yosef should have waited patiently and kept his finger on the spiritual pulse of the Nation of Israel, for, if not prophets, they were the children of prophets, and their holy intuition did not err.

Deciding to skip breakfast—who could think of food on this historic morning?—he combed his hair, grabbed his black fedora, and headed for the front door.

"It's just an election," said a voice as he marched through the living room. Rocheleh sat at the kitchen counter with her coffee and newspaper, her hair covering wrapping her head. She eyed his clothes. "There's no need to get all dressed up."

He had not shared Gavri's tidings with his wife. She would not hold the messianic promises of the local grocer in high esteem.

Yosef gave her a sheepish grin. "They might need me for a press conference later." That was true enough. Why annoy her with optimistic theories when he could delight her later with joyous facts?

She shrugged her shoulders and returned to her newspaper.

Yosef clicked the remote on his keychain to unlock the brand new Hyundai i35 on the sidewalk. The company car— the first issued by the Dry Bones Society—had replaced his broken down old Subaru, and the engine started every morning without protest.

He turned right onto Yehuda Street, cut through the German Colony, and parked outside Horev Primary School. He was third in line when the voting station opened.

"Save us from the zombie menace," said a young man at the gate. "Vote Upward." Like his friends, the young activist wore a yellow T-shirt with a black nuclear hazard sign.

Yosef just smiled and pulled his hat over his eyes. He bounced on the balls of his feet like a man in dire need of the bathroom. When his turn came, he left his blue identity book at the table of observers and dashed behind the voting booth. He placed a white paper scrap with a large Hebrew letter *Hey* for *Hat-chel*, or Restart, in his envelope, which he dropped through the slot of the voting bin.

Having fulfilled his civic duty, he got back in his car and made for the Old City, painfully aware that now he was officially shirking his professional duties. He had not told Moshe about the Messiah either. Moshe had enough on his mind on Election Day, and his absence at the Dry Bones Society would not change their inevitable defeat at the polls. And if the Messiah didn't show, Yosef would have added one more disappointment to an already depressing day.

But this morning the Messiah was going to show. He had to. The exiles were returning to the Land and the Resurrection was progressing in full force. All that remained was to rebuild the Temple and bring peace to the land—easy tasks when compared with raising the dead.

Cyndi Lauper sang "She Bop" on the car's speakers. Moshe had given him the disc of her greatest hits to replace Yosef's stretched old cassette, seeing that the new car only had a CD player. The jumpy pop song filled the sunny Jerusalem air with the thrill of adventure and discovery, although, to be honest, Yosef had no idea what the song was about.

He crossed the short bridge over the Hinnom Valley and climbed toward Mount Zion. In the jam-packed visitors' lot, he parked between two tour buses, then ran for the gates of the Old City. He passed beneath the tall arch of Zion Gate, the imposing walls around the arrow slits pockmarked with bullet holes, and jogged down the inner road that led from the Armenian Quarter.

The alleys and cobbled squares of the Jewish Quarter grew thick with tourists, seminary students, and locals. Quite a turnout for Election Day. The throng reminded Yosef of the surging crowds that formed during Passover, Shavuot, and Sukkot, the three pilgrim festivals when Jews flocked to Jerusalem from all over the world. The rumor of the Messiah had reached many more ears than he had imagined.

When he reached the stairway that descended toward the Western Wall Plaza, the pedestrian traffic came to a standstill. A quarter hour later, he had only reached the bend of the staircase.

The golden Dome of the Rock rose behind the Wailing Wall. The long massive slabs of weathered stone were all that remained of Herod's immense Temple complex.

In the Western Wall Plaza below, a tightly packed mass of people—men and women, black-hatted and bareheaded—

covered every inch of floor tile from view. Yosef had never seen the plaza so full or so quiet.

The throng of waiting Jews extended down the steps to a security inspection booth. Men with backpacks. Women with strollers. Yosef descended one step as the line inched forward and the Western Wall Plaza dropped out of view behind the barrier wall of the staircase.

Yosef glanced at his wristwatch and panic shot through him. This would take time. Far too much time. A mere hundred meters away, the Messiah was about to announce his arrival, but Yosef was stuck behind a wall, waiting in line!

CHAPTER 62

Moshe grinned at Galit over the breakfast table. "Time to conquer the world," he said.

He felt surprisingly optimistic. The PR sessions had gone well yesterday and should calm voter concerns about the moral integrity of the Restart list. Voters weren't stupid. They could smell trumped-up and politically motivated charges a mile away. And Restart only needed a few seats in Knesset to be a viable coalition partner.

Galit, on the other hand, did not share his optimism. Avi's televised accusations had hit her hard, making her toss and turn in bed. That morning, she had hardly tasted her toast and eggs.

She gave Moshe an imploring glance through puffy eyelids. "Don't go out today, Moshe," she said. "Please."

He laughed. "If we don't go out and vote, how is Restart going to win any seats? Besides, the team needs me at the office to boost morale. After yesterday's drama, the media will be watching our every move and who knows what last-minute fires we'll have to put out."

"I have a bad feeling about this, Moshe. Let's stay home. You heard their hatred on TV. People could get violent."

Violent? What had gotten into her? He got up, walked over, and hugged her. "It's an election, not a civil war. What's the worst that can happen—we don't get into Knesset?"

She stared into his eyes. "What if Avi makes up more accusations?"

"Then I'll respond right away. He's done his worst. He's out of ammunition now."

Galit did not seem convinced.

The doorbell rang. "That must be Noa," Galit said and went to open the front door. They had arranged for the teenager down the street to stay home with Talya for Election Day. Galit let her in and explained when to wake Talya, what to feed her for breakfast, and how to keep her occupied. Good luck to her with that. Their daughter packed enough energy to power a small city for a week.

Moshe freshened up in the bathroom, put on a new collared shirt, and knotted his tie. He sketched out a congratulatory speech in his head, but would pencil in the number of seats later. The official vote count would be available only late that evening.

He prepared a consolation message for his followers as well, just to be on the safe side.

Galit slipped into a green dress. "How do I look?"

"Delicious. Maybe we *should* stay home today."

Finally, he had succeeded in making her smile. Today would end well, he could feel it.

He fished his car keys from the drawer in the hall but when they stepped outside, a large black Mercedes idled on the curb.

The driver wore a dark suit and sunglasses and held the back door open. He would have passed for one of Gurion's secret service agents, except for the ponytail.

"Good morning, sir," Irina's tattooed friend said.

"Morning, Alex. What's the deal?"

"The VIP service," the Russian said and grinned. "For our upcoming Member of Knesset."

CHAPTER 63

"And then," Eli said with the manic enthusiasm of a man who had stayed awake all night, "she said that I don't care about anyone. She got in the elevator and left."

Lia, the blond bombshell, hid a yawn behind her hand. She had been very understanding. They had not kissed. They had not even cuddled. Instead, he had told her his story, and once he had gotten going he had not been able to stop. He had never experienced such an outpouring of emotion. A lifetime—a very long lifetime—of repressed guilt and failure had extinguished the fire in his soul, but these cathartic flashes had made the old coals glow again.

Her eyes became sleepy slits as she rested her head on the couch. "But you *do* care," she said. They had been through this before a number of times throughout the night, but each time the insight burned brighter. "You care about *her.*"

"You're right!" he cried. "I do!" The realization shed light on his entire life, the way the morning sun rose over Jerusalem in the French windows of his living room and bathed the couch in warm beams. He laughed with abandon, an ecstatic lover or a madman. Or both. "Now everything makes sense!"

For the first time in centuries, he truly understood God's plan. His accident, and meeting Noga. Elijah the Prophet had neglected his mission because of a serious, if understandable, personal flaw, and the Boss, in His infinite wisdom, had set him straight.

Lia stifled another yawn. "She's a lucky girl."

Did she believe his story? Was she just humoring an insane and possibly dangerous stranger? With the dead walking on every street corner, anything was possible. Either way, she had listened with empathy and put her finger on the heart of the matter.

Her eyelids closed, then opened. "You should tell her."

"You're right!" Adrenaline pumped through his arteries. "I'll call her right away."

Lia sat up on the couch and massaged the back of her neck. "And I should probably go home and get some sleep."

"Yes, of course. Thank you. Thank you so much. I'll call a cab."

He saw her to the elevator door and folded a two-hundred-shekel note into her hand for the ride home.

"See you around, Big Tipper."

"You can count on it."

When the elevator doors closed, Eli found his phone and dialed Noga's number. He would start with an apology. This was all his fault. She was right, he had made a terrible mistake, and he wanted her back—no, he *needed* her back. He'd make everything right again. There was no time to waste. They had a lot of work to do.

Then a sound made him swear under his breath. In the bedroom, Noga's phone rang.

CHAPTER 64

Sweat trickled down Yosef's neck as he waited in line under the late morning sun. He stood halfway down the staircase to the Western Wall Plaza and could see the metal detector and bag scanner at the security gate. Any moment now, he feared, he'd hear the cheer of the crowd as the Messiah delivered his good tidings, while Yosef squirmed with frustration on the wrong side of the barrier wall.

The anticipation in the air made him tipsy and created an instant camaraderie among his fellow pilgrims. Yosef's cheeks hurt from smiling. He helped a mother in a long, white head-scarf lower her pram, step by step. A bearded man with a large white *kippah* grinned at him and nodded his head like a bobblehead dog on a car dashboard. After two thousand years of waiting, endless wandering and persecution, the moment of the Redemption had edged within sight. He only hoped he wouldn't miss the historic event by seconds.

Who was this mysterious messiah? Was he resurrected— had he passed right under Yosef's nose at the Dry Bones Society? The traditional texts had remained silent on this point. One thing was sure: seeing that the Resurrection had not reached the Roman period yet, this redeemer would disappoint Reverend Adams. *But enough guesswork!* The age of speculation had drawn to a close and the bright new reality would settle all questions.

Finally, he stepped through the metal detector, spread his arms for the security inspection, and joined the eager throng in the plaza. He waded through the crowd toward the men's section at the foot of the Western Wall, squeezing past Torah altars and trolleys of prayer books. Sweat glimmered on the faces of the men around him. How would he recognize God's chosen? Would he be bearded or clean-shaven, young or bent with years? What if two messiahs claimed the crown at once? Or three? Or twenty!

The sweaty faces eyed him with the same silent, bursting expectation. Yosef waded toward the towering, ancient stones.

Worst of all, what if no one emerged from the crowd? What if the Messiah had changed his mind and gone back into hiding for another two thousand years?

A gasp rose from the assembled Jewry and hands pointed to the sky. "There! Up there!"

Yosef craned his neck and shielded his eyes from the morning sun. On top of the wall and haloed in sunlight, stood a man.

White robes flapped around his thin frame in the breeze. Long locks of his hair glowed golden as they flowed from a white cotton beanie. He glanced down at them, gracing them with a loving, white smile.

Yosef trembled. Joy gurgled involuntarily in his throat, as ecstatic tears seeped from his eyes. *Yes! This is happening. In my lifetime.*

He had merited to gaze upon the Messiah. In hindsight, a shepherd's robe would have been more appropriate than his formal wedding suit, but his clothing didn't matter. Nothing mattered, except for the saintly figure overhead.

Excited whispers circled the gathering. "It's him! Thank God!" A large man in Chassidic garb beside him recited *She'hecheyanu*—Who Has Granted Us Life, the blessing for momentous occasions.

They gazed at their savior for what seemed like minutes,

when a man clambered onto a Torah altar below. His white cloak and head covering matched those of the Messiah on the Wall, only his beard was red and short. He raised his arms above his head.

"Friends and neighbors," he cried. "Behold your redeemer. Open your ears and your hearts to his message, and your eyes will behold *wonders*." He pointed to the Messiah on the Wall, then slid off the altar.

The Redeemer spread his arms over his flock, a compassionate, embracing gesture. "Friends and neighbors. The time has come. Your suffering is over. A healing sun rises upon you, and a new hope. Your eyes will behold wonders."

Friends and neighbors. Your eyes will behold wonders. The repeated phrases soothed Yosef's mind. There was a plan. The Messiah knew what he was doing.

"But first," the Redeemer continued, "let the blast of the *shofar* carry the tidings throughout the world." With a flourish, he pulled a short, twisted ram's horn from a pocket of his cloak, and then waved his arms in wild circles, like a man trying to regain his balance, while a thousand onlookers gasped.

The Messiah on the Wall found his footing again and smiled, and the crowd exhaled with relief. *Phew!* Yosef's heart returned to his rib cage. He wiped a fresh layer of sweat from his brow. *That had seemed close.* The Redeemer couldn't fall. Of course not. He just had a sense of humor.

High above, the Redeemer raised the ram's horn in the air, his body swaying ever so slightly. Yosef knew that rocking motion. He had performed that dance many times during his wasted youth, usually late at night and in dark alleys that reeked of his own vomit. Yosef dismissed the suspicion from his mind. *No, he's not drunk. It's just the breeze.*

The Redeemer pressed the shofar to his lips, drew a mighty breath, and blew hard, but for all his efforts the blast sounded like a camel passing wind.

The crowd exchanged bemused looks but hid their smiles. Another bit of humor to lighten the mood, that's all. But a dark pit opened in Yosef's stomach. *Something isn't right.*

The Redeemer tossed the horn over his shoulder. "Unbelievers will doubt us," he said. *Was he slurring his words?* The Messiah waved his finger in the air. "Do not fear them. When they ask you, 'Can he walk on water?' tell them, 'No.'" The crowd sighed with disappointment. He had promised wonders.

Then the Redeemer punched the air, as he cried, "Tell them, 'He walks on air!'"

The crowd cheered, eager to witness the miracle firsthand. Yosef's insides clenched. *No. Don't do it!* He looked about the flock, searching for another pair of concerned eyes, but all heads were turned to the heavens. Was he the only one who thought that this was a really bad idea?

Before a protest could form in his throat, the Messiah on the Wall stretched out his arms like a tightrope walker, extended one foot, and stepped onto thin air.

Yosef blinked. The walker leaned forward, resting his weight on the empty space above their heads. No glass or mirrors reflected in the sunlight. A bubble of childlike delight escaped Yosef's mouth. *He's doing it. Dear God. He's walking on air!*

"Behold the true Messiah!" Redbeard cried below, his cheeks bulging with an ecstatic smile.

A joyous cheer rippled through the masses. A voice cried out—Hallelujah!—and a dozen more followed.

Then the Messiah moved his other leg, stepping off the wall, and he fell like a stone.

CHAPTER 65

In the backseat of the Mercedes, Moshe held Galit's hand while the suburban scenery of Baka panned across the window. The driver's ponytail shifted as the luxury car negotiated the bumps.

Irina's new friend still made his skin crawl. If Rafi had wanted to treat them to a chauffeur drive, surely he would have picked them up himself? Or had Irina cooked up the surprise treat, not Rafi? If so, where was she?

Moshe chided himself for judging a man by his appearance. He'd need to learn that lesson fast if he wanted to survive in government.

The phone rang in his jacket pocket.

"Where are you?" Sivan asked.

"We're on our way to the voting station," Moshe said. "We'll head to the office right after."

"Good. Remember, you're registered for the International Convention Center. Yaron has a camera team at the voting box."

"Anything else?"

"Yes. The telephone poll came in."

"Great. Galit's here, I'll put you on speaker." Time to find out where Restart stood.

Sivan said, "Now remember, the poll went out just as the

story broke and before we could answer the rumors."

Moshe and Galit exchanged anxious glances. Sivan was trying to soften the blow, so the results must have been terrible. "Go ahead. We understand."

The car rose and fell over another speed bump.

At the end of the line, Sivan drew a long, audible breath. "Nothing."

"Nothing?"

"We don't get any mandates, according to the poll. We don't pass the electoral threshold."

Moshe felt the blood drain from his face. "But that's only three percent."

"Three point two five percent. Out of tens of thousands of participants, only a handful said they were definitely voting Restart."

Galit squeezed his hand. He pictured the sea of supporters in Beer Sheba and a dozen other cities. Had they all abandoned him so quickly?

"As I said," Sivan added, "that was before your response hit the media."

He masked his heartbreak with sarcasm. "I'm sure Channel Two gave that the widest possible exposure."

"We have to work with what we've got."

He thanked her for the update and tucked the phone into his pocket. Avi's false accusations had erased weeks of intense campaigning. They would be lucky to win a single seat in Knesset.

A Karlin never quits, his father had always said. When the Arabs forced Jews out of the Old City in 'forty-eight, Moshe's grandfather lost his business, but he started over from scratch. His own father had created a successful dispatch company from nothing. But how could Moshe undo the damage as voters already made their way to the ballot boxes?

A sharp pain flared inside his rib cage.

"Are you OK?" Galit turned to him with large, frightened eyes. He was clutching his chest.

The pain faded. "Yeah, I think so. It's been a stressful

couple of weeks." Had he rescheduled that cardiologist appointment? He had been reckless with his health, his eyes always on the future. If he ignored his health any longer, he might not have a future.

Galit slumped back on the seat and gave him a wan smile. "Maybe it's for the best, Moshe. If we're no longer a threat to Avi, maybe he'll finally leave us alone."

Avi, Avi, Avi. His ex–best friend had become the proverbial thorn in Moshe's side. He had stolen Moshe's wife in the past and now he had torpedoed his chances in the election. Judging by his recent behavior, Avi wouldn't be content to live and let live when in power. The new career in politics and the dirty campaign were just stepping stones to Avi's ultimate goal—Galit—and to get her, he'd have to do more than beat Moshe in the elections.

Out the window, the Great Synagogue towered over King George Street. They were traveling in the wrong direction.

"Alex, we're expected at the International Convention Center. We should have made a left onto Ramban."

The ponytail bobbed. "My mistake," Alex said in that lethargic Russian accent. "I'll double back as soon as I can."

Traffic slowed, then stopped. The line of cars ran on and on toward a distant red light. They had dived headlong into peak traffic.

Far behind them, a motorcycle horn bleated. His fellow citizens had set out to vote early so that they could enjoy the rest of the day at parks and beaches. Moshe wouldn't mind joining them. Instead, he would have to watch helplessly as his campaign imploded.

The light was still red. The growl of a motorcycle engine grew louder.

Moshe leaned forward to peek at the side mirror. The biker sped toward them in the emergency lane. The rider wore a full white helmet, thick jacket, and gloves, like an off-road racer.

The growl became a roar as the biker whizzed by their window. Then his brakes screeched and the rear wheel arced, spinning the bike ninety degrees and into the line of cars, where it halted in front of the hood of their Mercedes, blocking their path with the length of the bike.

The biker pulled out a large handgun and pointed it at their windshield.

"Oh my God!" Galit cried.

Without a word, Alex raised his hands in surrender.

"What the hell…?" Moshe blurted, although he knew exactly what the hell was going on.

They were going to die.

CHAPTER 66

Voices gasped as the messiah plummeted, and the men in his trajectory pressed backward to avoid the impact, squeezing the breath out of Yosef in the compacting crowd.

There was a sickening *crack.* The masses held their breath, waiting for their messiah to jump up with a smile and an "I'm OK!"

Instead, someone at the front puked.

Oh no!

The press of bodies eased as the crowd dispersed in a hurry.

Yosef stood frozen to the spot, a rock in a stream of panicked men. "Paramedics!" he cried, but none of them were listening. He turned around and stood on tiptoe to shout above the crowd. "Call the paramedics!"

The fleeing men flowed toward the turnstiles at the exit, but one of them ran for the Red Star of David van positioned beside the security checkpoint.

Yosef waded against the current, toward the towering wall until he reached the clearing that had formed at ground zero, like a crime scene cordoned off by yellow tape. Multitudes had flocked to greet the Messiah; fewer were willing to scrape him off the tiles.

In the center of the clearing, the former messiah lay in a

heap of twisted limbs, his white robes spattered with blood. The stench of half-digested food rose from a fresh puddle of vomit.

For the second time that summer, Yosef wished that he had learned first aid. He turned to the white-faced bystanders. "Is there a doctor here?"

A gray-haired and bewildered man detached from the edge of the clearing. "I'm an anesthesiologist."

"That'll do."

The man crouched over the mangled messiah, laid a trembling hand on the messiah's neck, then looked up at Yosef. "I think he's dead."

Yosef turned around. "Stand back!" he shouted. "Let them pass!" as the medics, carrying a folded stretcher, negotiated a path through the human obstacle course.

A paramedic pulled open the blood-stained robes and attached the pads of a defibrillator to the injured man's chest, while his colleague pumped his heart. They stood clear and the messiah's chest rose from the ground as an electric charge passed between the pads. The paramedics examined the still body again, then lifted him onto the stretcher and rushed him away on their shoulders. He might live yet.

Yosef wiped his brow on the back of his hand. He had observed paramedics at the scene of an accident two months ago. The leather-jacketed biker at the Mount of Olives Cemetery had rocketed up an access road and slammed into a truck.

That rider had survived too. Yosef had handed the paramedics a note with his own contact details, but had heard nothing since. He didn't even know the biker's name.

Yosef didn't know the name of the fallen messiah either, but he had believed in him all the same. *You old fool. When will you learn?*

He stood among the clump of dazed witnesses, who stared into space like lost children.

A finger tapped his shoulder. "You're Rabbi Lev, aren't you?" It was Redbeard, who had introduced the former

messiah. "Rabbi Lev," he repeated, "of the Dry Bones Society?"

Yosef nodded. He couldn't imagine how the man must
feel. "I'm so sorry," Yosef mumbled. "So very sorry."

The man gave Yosef's hand an eager shake, his cheeks
bulging as he smiled, his eyes large and radiant. "I'm Tom.
Tom Levi. We need to work together," he added, "you and
I."

"Work together? I don't understand."

It was Tom's turn to look surprised. "Why, to spread the
good tidings of course." He laughed. "What else?"

"You can't be serious." Yosef pointed at the blood-stained
floor. "Didn't you see what happened? He's badly hurt. He
might die."

Tom lifted his hand, palm up, like an ascending elevator.
"Then he'll just have to rise from the ashes. Everything that
happens is part of God's plan." He became very serious. "We
should talk about the Temple."

"The Temple?"

Tom nodded in the direction of the Western Wall. "The
Third Temple. We need to get rid of that golden monstrosity
and then—"

Yosef held up his hand. "I have to go now. I'm sorry." He
hurried toward the exit and away from the madman without
looking back.

"Nice to finally meet you, Rabbi Lev," the man called after
him. "We'll speak again real soon."

CHAPTER 67

Ahmed woke up that morning with a start. A ceiling of stone hovered inches from his nose, and the chill of bedrock seeped through his clothes, through the flesh of his back, and into his bones. His mouth tasted of dust. Outside, a valley breeze whistled.

Where am I?

Memories of the previous day rose in his mind: the balding older man kicking aside a chair as he charged toward him, shouting accusations; the pressure of his fingers on Ahmed's throat; the look on Samira's face before he turned and fled.

He had dashed down the streets of downtown Jerusalem, running blind, trying to escape the anguish in his head, until he found himself back in Silwan. He scrambled up the stony hillside, clambered into the old burial cave, and stretched out on a rough-hewn shelf. Like the previous occupants of the tomb, he was trapped.

When he closed his eyes, he saw her face, the disbelief, the disappointment, and the fear. He had lost her beautiful smile forever, and he wished he no longer existed. How long would it take for him to starve to death?

His stomach rumbled. Against his better judgment, his body wanted to live.

Why had he pushed that stupid button and stained his soul

for eternity? But had he not died, would he have met Samira? Was this God's punishment for evil men—to offer them Heaven on a silver platter, only to yank the platter away? None of the fires of Hell came close to that torment.

He lay there, suspended between death and life, and shuddered as he sobbed.

Damas was right—he was a fool. A fool to have believed Hasan's lies. An even bigger fool to believe that he could start over. No, he was worse than a fool. He was a monster. He did not deserve to live.

He would lie there until his body withered. The rats would find him first. The thought made him sit up and he bumped his head on the rocky ceiling. *Serves you right.* A coward even in death.

He slid off the shelf and crouched on the cave floor. The mouth of the tomb was a rectangle of blue sky. A hammer sounded in the distance, and cars rumbled on hidden streets. Arabs and Jews got about their daily business.

He crawled to the opening, and two small birds fled from a grassy outcrop as he poked his head out of the tomb.

The Kidron Valley sprawled below, the dry riverbed and the Gichon spring, beneath the City of David. But not a single soul in sight.

He staggered out into the open and stretched. Dirt and dry sweat plastered his body. His hair was thick with dust. He scratched a spider bite on his ankle. Above the tomb rose the Mount of Olives, the mass of grave markers like scales on the back of a sleeping dragon. How many sandaled feet had trampled that hillside over the centuries, building and burying, toiling and murdering—and for what?

He peed, dousing a clump of weeds in dark yellow fluid, then hobbled down the steep hill to the dusty streets of Silwan. He trudged along, dragging his feet in the dust like a zombie. Only one path remained to him.

He passed by the streets of his childhood and his mother's new house, and he climbed the unpaved incline.

The yellow Mercedes was parked outside the cement

hangar. Hasan's two thugs sat on crates and stared at their backgammon board. Another seductive melody blared from the speakers of the car to a maqsoum beat. *"Ma Tegi He-na?"* Why don't you come here?

Ahmed approached the luxury vehicle from behind. Hasan slouched in his usual position. On the iPad, Nancy Ajram danced in a fruit market. She wore a skintight red dress and ran her hands through her long curly locks. She gyrated her hips and sent suggestive glances at the camera as she carved watermelons with a butcher's knife.

A cold, cruel idea froze Ahmed's breath in his lungs. Lunging forward, he could seize Hasan's head in both hands and, with one mighty twist, break his cousin's neck with a satisfying crunch before his henchmen knew he was there. They would kill Ahmed but he didn't care. His life was no longer worth living.

Five cowardly seconds passed, but Ahmed did nothing. Instead, he touched his cousin on the shoulder.

Hasan flipped on the seat like an omelet in a frying pan. "You crazy bastard, Ahmed. You've got to stop sneaking up on me like that." He shook his head, laughed, and paused the music. "So, cousin, have you considered my offer?"

Ahmed stood over him and nodded. He said, "I'm ready."

CHAPTER 68

In the middle of the city center and in broad daylight, a biker pointed his long-barreled gun at the windshield of their car.

Time stood still and Moshe's senses sharpened. His heart pounded in his ears. His lungs inflated with his final breath.

He had watched enough Jason Bourne movies to know what would happen next: the *thump-thump* of shots fired through a silencer; the bullet holes in the windshield; the death dance of the trapped victims. Bourne would dodge the bullets and escape in the nick of time, but this was no movie and Moshe was no Jason Bourne, so he froze on his seat, squeezed Galit's hand, and braced for the worst.

The gunman didn't fire his weapon. Instead, tires screeched as a large brown van pulled up beside them in the lane for oncoming traffic.

It happened very fast. Thugs in ski masks poured out of the van. Galit's door opened and a masked man leaned inside, pressed the release for her seatbelt, and pulled her, kicking and screaming, from her seat. Her hand slipped from Moshe's. He lunged forward to grasp her waist but his seat-belt held him back. He disengaged the belt when his door opened and powerful arms locked around his neck and shoulders, yanking him out of the car and lifting him in the air.

He flailed his legs, trying to find traction or to wriggle free of the steel grip. The immense thug carried him off with ease as though Moshe was a baby and Moshe thought of King Kong, the Russian henchman from the slave labor camp.

Then Moshe floated in the air and landed hard on a metal floor. A sliding door banged shut, casting him into darkness.

Moshe scrambled to his feet, but the floor moved and he fell onto one knee. Outside, a motorbike engine growled. A light bulb ignited on the ceiling of the van, making him blink. Two thugs pinned Galit to the floor and wrapped her wrists in duct tape. Moshe dashed at her but something heavy collided with his arm and again he slammed into the metal floor. Pain seared through his shoulder.

A ski-masked giant crouched over him, his head blocking the glowing bulb. He pulled the mask from his head and the ugly mug of King Kong grinned down at him.

"Miss me?" the Russian asked, and he slammed a boulder-sized fist into Moshe's face.

CHAPTER 69

Eli woke up face down on his bed, still fully dressed, his brain pounding inside his skull. He was starting to regret last night and not just the drinking.

His phone read 12:04 PM. There were no missed calls on his phone, and the only missed call on Noga's was from himself. He plugged her phone into a charger. Even if she had decided to leave for good, she'd probably come back for her phone and laptop.

He trudged to the bathroom, his head exploding, his mouth tasting like glue. He popped two Acamol tablets, stripped, and stepped under a hot shower.

That morning he had passed out on a high, having rediscovered his true identity. Finally, he understood God's plan, and the revelation empowered him to both win back Noga and redeem the world. Wonderful.

Nothing dampened the human spirit like a hangover. He had surrendered his identity once before to find favor in her eyes. Was he ready to do that again? And if, this time, he was right, where was the Thin Voice? And where were his legendary miraculous powers?

He turned off the water, wrapped a towel around his waist, and sat on the edge of his bed. The pair of mobile phones lay motionless on the bedside table. Elijah the Prophet had summoned fire from Heaven and revived the dead. If he really was the famous prophet, surely some of those abilities remained?

He stared at Noga's phone, then closed his eyes. He imagined the Samsung Galaxy floating in the air, as weightless as a feather in a gentle updraft. He flexed the muscle in the center of his brain. In his mind's eye, the black tablet rose a centimeter above the table.

He opened his eyes. The phone remained grounded. His shoulders slumped. Then the phone rang.

He glanced at the display. Who was Hannah? The name sounded vaguely familiar. Was Noga calling from a friend's phone in order to locate her own? Or did she want to speak with him, to mend their bridges and come back home?

He answered.

"Noga?" said the voice of an older woman.

"This is her phone."

"May I speak with her?" The voice had the tone of restrained annoyance.

"Who's calling?"

"This is Professor Hannah Rechter, her doctoral supervisor. And who, may I ask, are you?"

"A friend," he said. He did not say "boyfriend." Their relationship status still hung in the air and the fewer details he shared, the fewer questions he would have to answer. "She left her phone here by accident," he added. "I'll tell her to call you as soon as she can."

The professor exhaled her frustrations into the receiver. "Please do. I've been trying to contact her for weeks!"

"She's been... distracted lately." The distraction had answered her phone. "But she'll be back on track soon."

"I hope so. If we don't submit soon, we'll have to wait months."

Eli put the phone down, the professor's urgency reigniting his own. He had to find Noga and not just to deliver the professor's message. Not even to patch up their relationship.

If Noga was right, he had a job to do, and his job was...

what exactly? Elijah had always known the where, the how, the why—the Thin Voice had whispered the details directly into his brain. Eli Katz, however, was lost. Clueless. But together, he and Noga might just figure things out.

He pulled on some clothes, gulped down a glass of milk, and collected his riding jacket and helmet. He pocketed an apple as well. This might take some time.

As he waited at the front door for the elevator, he bowed his head. *Boss, if ever there was a time for a hand up, it's now. Where is she?* He waited for the soft whisper, the sudden flash of clarity.

The doors opened on the golden elevator but he made no move to get in. What was he going to do—drive around the city hoping to spot her on the street?

The elevator doors closed. He dumped the helmet on the kitchen island, returned to the bedroom, and picked up Noga's phone. The screen wasn't locked. Ignoring the pinch of guilt for invading her privacy, he scrolled down her call history and found another vaguely familiar name.

CHAPTER 70

Yosef had hoped to sneak into the office unnoticed, but the call center of Restart, formerly the Dry Bones Society, had never looked so crowded. Or festive. Balloons and streamers in blue and white hung from the ceiling and windows. On the mounted TV, political commentators dissected the mounting exit polls. Party members and reporters chatted and glanced him over as he entered. Some members wore party hats.

"Where have you been?" their eyes seemed to ask. Was his guilt written on his face? The answer was as embarrassing as it was predictable: Yosef had believed. He had followed a false messiah, basing his blind faith entirely on the rock-solid authority of—wait for it—his local greengrocer. Thank God that he had not shared his messianic convictions with Moshe or with his own wife. Rocheleh was right; Yosef the gullible fool had no place in public politics. Was he even worthy of guiding a charitable organization?

"Hi, Rabbi!" Irina said. She knelt beside a large packing box at the entrance and stared up at the rabbi, who flinched preemptively at the expected interrogation.

Her cheerful countenance faltered. "Are you OK? You look pale."

"I'll be fine." He gave her a quick, feeble grin to back up his claim and made for the secure isolation of Moshe's office.

"Rabbi Yosef," called another female voice, and he stopped in his tracks. Sivan had spotted him from across the call center and strode toward him. He braced for the worst. *Here it comes.*

"I'm glad you're here," she said, breathless, and she looked over her shoulder at the sea of reporters. Her painted-on smile failed to hide her anxiety. "Where's Moshe?"

The question caught him off guard and he glanced around for their party leader. "I haven't seen him yet. Is something the matter?"

Yosef had a bad feeling about this. It wasn't like Moshe to abandon his team in times of trouble.

Before Sivan could answer, Irina joined them, the cardboard box in her arms. "Here's the confetti we ordered. Where do you want it?"

"In Moshe's office for now," the campaign manager said.

"How are we doing?" Yosef asked softly.

"Not good," Sivan said, still smiling at the packed room. "We should have hit back harder. That's what you get for running a clean campaign."

Yosef swallowed. This was his fault. His failings had crippled Restart. Rabbi Nachman of Breslov taught that one can start life anew each day, but a new today didn't erase a shameful yesterday.

"Pray for a miracle," she whispered and walked off.

Perhaps Restart would fare better without his prayers. He should resign and let them be. Not now, of course, like a rat abandoning a sinking ship, but after the elections. His presence drew calamity the way magnets drew iron filings.

"Let me give you a hand," he said to Irina, and reached for the box. At least he could help out with the manual labor without causing more damage.

"I almost forgot," she said. "There's someone here to see you."

"To see me? Who—Mr. Adams?" Yosef was in no state to host their Christian benefactor.

"No, a woman. She wanted to speak with you or Moshe.

She said it's important."

Had a messenger of the failed messianic cult beat him to the office? "Was she wearing a white cloak?"

Irina's eyes narrowed and she gave him a bemused smile. "A white cloak? No. Are you sure you're OK?"

"Yes. Of course. Never mind." His cheeks warmed. "I'll see her in Moshe's office."

Yosef placed the box of confetti in a corner of the office and settled behind the desk. The countless calls he had made at that desk to potential messiahs had achieved nothing. He would never find the Messiah—if he existed at all.

Yosef shuddered at his heretical thought. What if the Messiah was a myth—a futile exercise in communal wishful thinking, an imaginary fairy godmother for centuries of miserable Diaspora Jews?

For starters, Yosef should stop wasting time in trying to find him. In fact, he should stop accepting everything he read or heard. If he didn't grow up soon, he'd bring more disgrace to himself and those around him.

Irina opened the door for a pretty young woman with tied-up dark hair, and moved on to her other tasks. The woman approached the desk, her eyes large and expectant, her mouth drawn, and she put out her hand. After a moment's hesitation, Yosef shook her hand and beckoned for her to sit. Despite his numerous interviews with female reporters, physical contact with a woman other than his wife still made him uncomfortable.

What did this pretty young woman want with him? Had Avi Segal sent her to generate more scandalous rumors?

Two reporters glanced at them through the large windows of the office. He had better send the woman on her way as soon as possible.

"How can I help you, Miss…?"

"Shemer. Noga Shemer. I'm a doctoral student at the Hebrew University. My research—"

"Then I must refer you to Professor Yakov Malkovich," Yosef said, cutting her off. "He's already heading up a study

of volunteers from our Society at your university. I think he'll
be happy to discuss your research."

Miss Shemer glanced at the desk, and seemed taken aback
at the interruption and abrupt dismissal. "My research is
different and, in my opinion, of great interest to you."

Yosef felt ashamed at his curt behavior. He had no choice
but to hear her out. "I'm sorry. Please go on."

"My study aimed to find a genetic link between Jews of
priestly descent—the Cohen Gene."

"And did you find this link?" He still didn't see how this
was relevant to the Dry Bones Society.

"Yes. But I discovered something else, something unexpected. I won't bore you with the technical details but the
bottom line is this: I think I've found the Ten Lost Tribes of
Israel."

Yosef considered her words. According to Rabbinic
sources, Elijah the Prophet would reveal the Ten Lost Tribes
at the End of Days. Now this pretty young student claimed to
have discovered them in a test tube.

"The Ten Lost Tribes?" he repeated, and he tried to conceal his smile beneath his moustache. He folded his lips into
his mouth to stop them from trembling. After his experiences
that morning, her statement was just too much.

She studied his reaction in tense silence.

Trying to keep his voice level, he said, "And where are
these lost Israelites?" Had she spotted them between the
chromosomes in her lab, or perhaps the lost Jews had colo-
nized the moon?

"They're right here, Rabbi Lev." She lowered her glance to
the table again. "Among us. Palestinian Arabs are the Lost
Tribes."

His body shook with pent-up laughter. He did not want to
embarrass the girl but—Palestinian Arabs! A sobering
thought helped curb his sense of humor. First, the weirdo
messianic cult; now a pretty young pseudo-scientist. He
should hang a sign on the door: "Fools Anonymous. We buy
anything. All manner of crackpot theories welcome. Leave

reason at the door." *This is what you've become, Yosef: a magnet, not for calamity, but for lunatics.*

He drew a deep breath, stared at the ceiling, blinked back a tear, and counted to ten. Composed, he retrieved a yellow square from a pile of notepads. "As you can see outside, we're a bit swamped with the elections today. But please leave your name and number and we'll try get back to you later."

The girl stared at the sheet, then scribbled down her contact details and stood. "Thank you for your time," she said, her voice soft and defeated, and she left the room. She had read between the lines.

Try to get back to you, he had said; he had made no promises.

CHAPTER 71

A pain at the back of his neck roused Moshe to consciousness. He was slumped over on a hard chair in a dark place.
Daylight seeped through the filthy slats of windows high on
corrugated walls. The floor stank of old motor oil.

He wanted to massage his neck but he couldn't move his
arms. Thick duct tape secured his wrists and ankles to the
metal frame of the chair. He made to speak but his lips were
taped shut, and he breathed heavily through his nose. The
skin over his cheekbone felt raw and tender.

He turned at the sound of a whimper at his side. Galit sat
strapped to another chair, a line of silver tape over her
mouth, and fear glittering in her eyes.

Moshe had never intended to put her in harm's way, but
he should have seen this coming. Boris had done this. King
Kong had pulled him from the car and King Kong did Boris's
bidding. Moshe may have bought back his own freedom with
hard cash, but his Dry Bones Society had ensured that none
of the newly resurrected landed up in the crime lord's slave
labor machine. Fewer slaves meant less money. The backlash
had been slow to arrive but inevitable, and now Boris would
settle the debt.

Where was Alex? Their driver had raised his hands in the
air when the biker had trained his gun on their car. Had he

tried to resist when the thugs had pulled Galit and Moshe from the back seat? Moshe didn't recall hearing gunshots, but the abduction had happened so fast and King Kong had knocked him out.

The future rolled out in front of him. Boris could have had them killed in the car if he had wanted. No, he had something else in mind. Torture. Threats. A lesson Moshe would never forget. Would Boris hurt Galit or was she there only to remind Moshe of what he had to lose? No, he wouldn't hurt her, would he?

A pitiful snort of fear and remorse escaped Moshe's nose. He should have kept his head down and been thankful for his freedom. Instead, he had rushed headlong to save the world, and in doing so he had drawn a bull's-eye over his loved ones. Poor little Talya was probably wondering why they hadn't come home. But how could he have done nothing while Boris led other new arrivals into slavery?

Don't panic, Moshe. Stay focused. His first priority was to get out of there alive and in one piece. He'd tell Boris whatever he wanted to hear. Afterwards, in safety, he could figure out how to help others without jeopardizing his family.

Moshe looked around. He heard no movement. They seemed to be alone in the abandoned warehouse. A third chair stood empty beside a large circular table that had been toppled onto its side, the round surface painted red like a single bloodshot eye. Beyond the table, a thin line of daylight framed a door in the corrugated wall.

He pulled at his bonds, rocking the rickety chair on its metal feet. If he could dislodge the wooden surfaces, he might be able to free his hands and then—

A door creaked open behind them and fluorescent strip lights flickered to life overhead. Heavy footfalls drew nearer.

A tall bald man in black walked around the chairs and stopped before them. He turned his immense nose and large sensitive eyes to them, his arms folded behind his waist like a restaurant host eager to serve his guests.

"Welcome, Mr. Karlin," he said, with a distinctly Russian

accent. "Mrs. Karlin." He inclined his head. "We meet at last. Thank you for joining me on such short notice. I must apologize for leaving you alone for so long. You know how things are."

Moshe did not know how things were, but from the conciliatory tone he inferred that he might be released sooner than he had thought.

"I'm so very proud of you, Moshe," the man continued. "You don't mind if I call you Moshe, do you? Look how far you've come! From practically a slave to a contender in today's elections. Although," he wrinkled his nose, "the exit polls have not been very kind, have they?"

This comrade of Boris knew far too much about Moshe for his liking, and his tone of exaggerated friendliness did not put Moshe at ease.

The man seemed to read Moshe's discomfort on his face, for he slapped a large hand to his forehead. "I have such bad manners. My name is Mandrake." He bowed, then snapped his fingers. "Vitaly, if you will."

Another man stepped into view. Like Mandrake, Vitaly wore black and had shaved his scalp, but he was built like a tank and a long, jagged scar bisected his left cheek. When the henchman leaned over him, Moshe flinched, expecting another blow to the face, but the man peeled the tape from Moshe's mouth.

"That's better, isn't it?"

Moshe's lips stung from the hastily removed tape. "What do you want from us?"

Mandrake looked insulted. "You misunderstand me. *I* am here to serve *you*. I prepared this show especially for you."

Moshe was about to ask "What show?" when the door behind Mandrake rattled.

"Excuse me," Mandrake said, "but I think our other guests have arrived."

The door of the warehouse swung open, and three men walked toward them in a momentary nimbus of bright light. Moshe knew them all by sight: Gray-haired Boris in his usual

tweed jacket; King Kong trudging beside him.
  The third visitor made Moshe's blood boil.

CHAPTER 72

"Sit," Hasan said and Ahmed obeyed, settling on the simple school chair. Plaster flaked from the walls of the room, which stank of damp rot. No one lived there. This was no place for the living.

"Take off your shirt."

Again, he obeyed.

Hasan had led him to the empty apartment in Silwan, two streets down from the garage hangout, to prepare for his mission. Before his first mission, his skin had tingled and he had worried about being captured by the Israeli authorities. This time, he felt numb. He would do whatever Hasan commanded. Soon it would all be over.

Hasan pulled a pair of thick gloves over his hands and draped a stained sheet over Ahmed's shoulders. With the handle of a worn toothbrush, he stirred the mixture inside a plastic tub and applied the thick yellow paste to his cousin's hair. The chemical broth smelled of rotting fish, like the crates of offal Ahmed had lugged to the trash enclosure outside the Rami Levi supermarket in Talpiot.

Ahmed closed his eyes and focused on the gloved hands that pulled at his hair and worked the dye into his scalp, the last human touch he would experience in this life.

"No one has done this before," Hasan said. "A double

martyr. You will be a hero. No, more than that—a legend."

Ahmed opened his eyes. He would be neither. He no longer believed the lies. The mission would line Hasan's pockets but Ahmed would find neither glory nor Paradise. He sought neither of those now, only the black emptiness of nothingness.

Hasan placed the tub on the floor and plugged a blow dryer into a cracked wall socket. The machine whined and blew hot air over Ahmed's sticky head, then fell silent. The stench of singed hair hung thick in the air.

"What now?"

"We wait."

"Is this really necessary?"

"The Jews have wised up over the years. No one does buses anymore. Their wall has made moving explosives difficult, and the bus stations are full of soldiers. You can't walk around looking like a sad Arab kid."

Ahmed nodded. He waited in silence while Hasan leaned against the wall, smoked Peter Stuyvesants, and toyed with his fancy mobile phone. After a few minutes, he glanced at his shiny watch and stubbed out his cigarette. He dried Ahmed's hair with a towel and plugged another machine into the wall. The clippers groaned and vibrated over Ahmed's head as severed blond locks piled in his lap.

Hasan turned off the clippers, pulled off the sheet, and threw him a new black T-shirt. "Stand."

Hasan placed a harness over Ahmed's shoulders and tightened the straps about his chest. Bulging packs of explosives pressed into his ribs, covered in plastic bags stuffed with metal screws and ball bearings. Last time, Ahmed had hefted the payload in a shoulder bag; today his body was the bomb. Maybe this time he would stay dead.

Hasan helped him into a thin black jacket and threaded the detonator cable through the sleeve.

"Remember how it's done?"

Ahmed nodded. "Where do you want it to happen?"

His cousin shrugged. "Find a crowd during rush hour."

He glanced at his wristwatch. "You have enough time to get into position." He held up a mirror for Ahmed. "What do you think?"

Ahmed stared into the frameless, chipped square in his cousin's hands. A boy with a blond Mohawk stared back. The boy wasn't him; Ahmed was already dead.

CHAPTER 73

Tuesday afternoon, Eli stood outside a large blue door on Shilo Street and prepared to bare his heart. He pressed the buzzer. Pulling off a riding glove with his teeth, he combed his hair with his free hand. The other hand held a fresh bouquet of roses and the delicate aroma of new beginnings.

He had changed and Noga would forgive him—of course she would!

A gutter ran down the center of the narrow cobbled lane. Short metal poles of red and white guarded the grubby stone façades from passing vehicles. Nachlaot, a labyrinth of courtyards and stony alleys, had sprouted in the late nineteenth century, when Jews settled the hills outside the Old City walls in order to escape the cramped conditions within. Mishkenot Yisrael, Mazkeret Moshe, and Knesset Yisrael had followed. A century later, as the city expanded further, the hive of arched windows and haphazard balconies had fallen into decay until recent gentrification projects had revived the quaint neighborhood and sent property prices soaring.

Eli had not researched the neighborhood's history on the Internet; he had witnessed the evolution firsthand. His memories were real, not the creaking of an unhinging mind. Noga's research proved that.

A giddy sense of release flowed through him. No longer

did he have to repress his memories or deny his identity. He was Elijah of Tishbe, priest, prophet, and messianic harbinger. Granted, his prophetic intuition had fled along with his miraculous powers. He lacked the tools to fulfill that destiny and the sheer magnitude of the task scared him to his core. But despite all that, his all-night catharsis had unearthed an empowering insight along with a hidden vial of optimism for the fate of mankind. And so, he had never been both so ill prepared and yet at the same time highly motivated to complete his historic mission. The irony was not lost on him.

Behind the gate, feet thumped down steps, but the footfalls were too heavy to belong to Noga.

When the gate swung inward, a large woman blocked the path to the apartment building. Her small eyes moved from the flowers to his face, and the mouth on the pudgy face smiled, revealing a large set of buckteeth. The image of a chipmunk rose in his mind, a chipmunk ogling a mound of tasty acorns.

"You must be Sarit," he said. "I'm Eli."

"I know all about you," she said, and smirked.

Eli swallowed, hoping that at least some of what she had heard about him had been flattering. "Is she here?"

She leaned a flabby arm on the edge of the gate. "How did you find me?" The playful lilt in her voice implied that she had waited all day for his arrival. Her smile widened and Eli feared she might start gnawing at his head.

"With this," he said, and he retrieved Noga's phone from his pocket. "And the Internet."

She held out her hand, palm up, and he handed over the phone.

"Come on up," she said, and she sauntered toward the apartment block, rolling her hips.

He followed her up a flight of stairs, his heart thumping in his chest, and he rehearsed the speech he had prepared on the way. The words had a lot in common with his previous revelatory speech, the one he had delivered to Noga in the secret garden courtyard at the Shaare Zedek Medical Center. That speech had ended in disaster, but a lot had changed since then. He only hoped that this time she'd be more forgiving.

Sarit unlocked an apartment door and stepped into a small but homey living room. Well-thumbed novels crammed an IKEA bookshelf. In a small fishbowl, a guppy circled a water plant. A patterned rug led to a sagging couch, but no sign of Noga.

His hostess slipped into the kitchen, returned with a vase, and relieved him of the flowers. "Have a seat."

Eli settled on the edge of the couch, expecting Noga to emerge from the corridor any moment.

Sarit sat down beside him. "So," she said, brushing a lock of mousy hair behind her ear, "you're the one with the private jet?"

How much had Noga shared with her? "A charter," he said, and avoided her hungry chipmunk eyes. "I don't travel often."

Her head bobbed up and down. "Can I get you a cup of coffee?"

"No thanks."

"Something stronger?" Her voice had dropped to a knowing purr. Was she stalling?

"Is she here?"

"No," Sarit said, still grinning at him.

"Where is she?"

Sarit laughed as though he had asked her to dance on the ceiling. "I can't tell you that."

"Why not?"

"Because then you'll try to stop her."

"Stop her?" he repeated. "Stop her from what?"

CHAPTER 74

In Avi Segal's fantasies, he drove Moshe Karlin's car, owned his home, and lived with his wife. Moshe himself had not featured in these fantasies. In fact, the defining characteristic of Avi's romanticized victory was the complete and utter absence of his ex–best friend and, lately, political adversary.

But now, as he stood over the cowed figure tied to a chair in a dank warehouse, surrounded by Boris's henchmen, he couldn't resist rubbing Moshe's nose in his defeat.

"Moshe, Moshe, Moshe," he said. "I told you to stay away from her."

In the offices of Upward earlier that day, Avi had been busy sipping wine and high-fiving Gurion's campaign and media teams while the exit polls rolled in, when Boris had appeared in the doorway.

"We're busy here," Avi had hissed at him. "What do you want?" He could not be seen with the thug, who seemed intent on spoiling his moment of glory.

"I have a surprise for you," was all the Russian would say, and Avi had grudgingly followed him out of the building.

A surprise was an understatement! Tying Moshe to the chair seemed a bit too dramatic, but the message was clear: I win, you lose. For once, Moshe had run out of witty comebacks. *That'll teach him.*

He turned to tell Boris to let the runt go—Avi had places to go—when a whimper drew his attention to a second seated figure, bound and gagged, who peered at him with a mixture of fear and pleading in her eyes.

"Boris," he said. "What the hell is the matter with you? Let her go right now!"

Boris said nothing and made no move to release Galit.

"Aren't you happy with our little gift?" said a bald man in black. He had an enormous nose.

"Who the hell are you?" Avi was having none of this. He had powerful friends. As number nine on the Upward list, he would soon be a member of Knesset himself.

"My apologies," Big Nose said. "We have not been formally introduced. Mandrake." He gave a slight bow. "I make dreams come true."

What was this Mandrake smoking? Avi turned to Boris, who stared at the floor in meek silence. It was apparent that Mandrake called the shots in here, so Avi opened his mouth to tell him to free Galit, when Mandrake said, "Vitaly, will you do the honors?"

Another bald thug in black stepped toward Moshe and placed a long-barreled handgun to his temple.

"Wait!" Avi cried, his voice echoing off the corrugated walls. All eyes turned to him. "Don't... don't shoot him."

Mandrake peered at him with surprise. "I don't understand. Moshe Karlin is your enemy. Surely you want to be rid of him?"

Moshe blinked at Avi, his chest heaving. Galit stared, her eyes wide.

"I don't want to *kill* him!" This Mandrake was a real wacko. How had he gotten mixed up with these people?

"Oh, I see. Very well." Mandrake waved his hand and Vitaly stood down, the gun disappearing into his clothes.

Then Mandrake gave his head a slight nod, and thick arms grabbed Avi under the armpits, lifting him into the air, pushing his neck forward and his shoulder blades back, and he cried out in pain. Avi had experienced these sensations be-

---

fore, and so he knew that Boris's giant held him in a steely vise.

"Put me down, you idiot!" He had powerful friends. A seat in the government. They couldn't hurt him, could they?

Mandrake scratched his head. "You've put me in a tricky situation, Avi. You see, I have two horses in this race—you and our friend Mr. Karlin here. No point competing against myself. Your numbers are looking more favorable at the moment, so I had thought to keep you, but I suppose now you've given me no choice. Vitaly, if you will?"

Vitaly stepped forward, drew his gun, and aimed at Avi's head.

"No!" Avi cried, losing all sense of entitlement. "Please, no!"

CHAPTER 75

By the afternoon, the crowd at the Dry Bones Society had thinned as reporters left to cover parties that might actually win a seat in Knesset. Society members also slunk off one by one, each remembering that they had urgent things to do somewhere else.

Irina collected empty paper cups off the refreshment tables and the floor of the call center and tried to stay out of Sivan's way. The campaign manager stood in the middle of the room, her arms folded, and stared at the screen where a pair of political commentators analyzed the results. At first they had joked about Restart's lack of support; now they didn't bother mentioning the once-hopeful party at all.

"I don't believe it," Sivan muttered. "We'll demand a recount."

"Let them finish counting first," Shmuel said. "Not that it'll help any." He leaned against the window of Moshe's office beside Rafi, who stared at his feet. The rabbi hadn't left Moshe's office since he had arrived. Irina didn't blame him.

"Where is he?" Sivan had asked the same question all morning. It wasn't like Moshe to hide from defeat, but Irina didn't blame him either. He had bet everything on winning seats in the election, and without friends in the new government, their hard-earned gains would disappear overnight.

"Meatballs?" Savta Sarah said. She peered up at Irina, her eyes filling her glasses, disposable bowls of steaming food on the tray in her hands. "Stuffed cabbage?"

"No thanks, Savta."

"Cheer up, girl. While there is life, there is hope."

A caustic laugh escaped Sivan's mouth but she stayed glued to the big screen.

"Where is your boyfriend?" Savta continued.

Irina sucked in a deep breath. Another good question. Aloud she said, "He went to pick up Moshe this morning, but they haven't arrived yet. They're not answering their phones either."

Savta seemed taken aback. "That's not like Moshe—not to show up for work. Have you called the police?"

"They're probably sharing a beer in a bar somewhere," Shmuel said. "Which is not such a bad idea." The poor results had sharpened his cynicism.

"Savta's right," Irina said. "Maybe something happened to them."

Knuckles rapped on the door of the call center. A man stood on the threshold. He wore a black leather jacket and held a large bouquet of roses. Irina walked over to greet the stranger, who had obviously lost his way.

"Hi," he said. "I'm looking for Noga Shemer."

Irina shrugged and shook her head. The name didn't ring a bell.

The man frowned. Stubble peppered his manly jaw and thick locks of jet-black hair fell over his forehead. This Noga Shemer was a lucky gal.

"She was on her way here this morning," he said, "to meet a Moshe Karlin. She's about twenty-eight. Average height. Intelligent. Beautiful. Stubborn, at times." He smiled.

Irina remembered. "Oh, her! She waited all morning for Moshe, but he wasn't in so she spoke with the rabbi. She really is quite pretty." *You're rambling, Irina. Stop that.* "She left about an hour ago."

"Oh." His expression darkened. Broken stems stuck out

where some of the flowers had fallen off. He had obviously been searching for her a long time. Hope flickered in his dark eyes. "Did she say where she was going?"

"No."

He nodded, thanked her, and left.

She turned around to find that the others—Shmuel, Rafi, and Savta Sarah—had joined Sivan, and together they watched the screen with open mouths.

Enough was enough. "Guys," she said, "maybe it's time we turned that off."

"Shh!" they said as one.

Irina drew near. A bar chart was displayed on the television while the commentators jabbered in the background. Of the dozen colored bars, three rose above the others and one of them towered even higher. "What's happening?"

"We're in the lead," Sivan said without turning from the screen.

Rabbi Yosef emerged from the office and joined them.

"I don't understand," Irina continued. "I thought we had no votes."

"Those were the exit polls," Shmuel explained, his lower lip trembling. "These are the real results."

"What did we get?"

"Two seats so far," Sivan said. She turned to stare at the others and a maniacal smile broke over her face. "We're in!" she cried. They shouted. They jumped up and down and hugged like soccer teammates after a deciding goal.

"We're in! We're in!"

They were so busy celebrating the turn of events that they didn't hear the door open again. Sivan saw him first and gasped. A man leaned against the doorpost. Dirt stains marred his T-shirt, a fresh bruise his cheekbone. He staggered inside and Irina launched forward to help him. "Alex!"

CHAPTER 76

Moshe gulped air, his chest heaving. Moments ago, the hard, cool barrel of a gun had pressed against the side of his head. *Game over*, he had thought, as a dagger of pain pierced his heart and slashed his left arm. At least the bullet would end his life quickly.

Then Avi had cried out. Years ago, in a cold army position in the Judean Hills, Avi had thrown Moshe to the ground, saving him from a terrorist's automatic gunfire. Today, against all Moshe's expectations, Avi had saved his life again.

But now Mandrake had turned the tables.

King Kong held Avi in a neck lock, lifting him in the air like a rag doll, while Vitaly walked over and put his gun to Avi's head.

"No!" Moshe cried. "Don't!"

Mandrake's shoulders slumped like a frustrated teenager. "Moshe," he chided. "This is your moment. We're doing this for you. Your old friend here betrayed you and deceived you. He's done everything in his power to destroy both you and all that you've worked so hard to create."

Mandrake sighed. "I know what you're thinking. 'He just saved my life, so now I should return the favor.' Awkward, isn't it?" He gave an embarrassed chuckle. "Personally, I think he did it for the girl—your wife. She'd never forgive him if he let you die. But let me tell you a secret." His voice dropped to a whisper, but loud enough for all to hear. "I wasn't really going to kill you. You're far too valuable to me. You're a natural leader. Avi here, on the other hand, well"— he turned to Avi—"no offense, Avi, but you're an idiot. Nobody believes in you. Nobody is going to follow you into battle."

Mandrake paced before them, as though lost in thought. "Tell you what, Moshe, let me do you this favor, and then I'll let you and your wife go. Little Talya is waiting for you. I'm sure that young babysitter of yours must be very anxious by now. Just say the word. Vitaly will put Avi out of his misery and we can all go home. What do you say?"

Moshe looked at Avi. As much as Moshe detested him, he had no desire to watch his head explode. And Moshe didn't believe Mandrake's promises either. None of the captives would leave the warehouse alive. The psychopath was toying with them.

"Please, Moshe," Avi pleaded, misinterpreting Moshe's long silence. "I'm sorry." He convulsed with tears. "I never meant to hurt you. I'll give up politics. I'll leave the country. I'll do anything, just please don't kill me!"

"Say the word," Mandrake crooned, "and all your troubles will be over. You don't have to pull the trigger. You don't even have to say the words. Just nod your head. Nod your head and we'll understand."

Galit sobbed beside him. Whatever he answered, the result would be the same. So Moshe said nothing, and kept his head as still as humanly possible.

What did Mandrake really want? If Moshe could find that out, he could make a deal. But nothing the man did made any sense. How did you bargain with a psychopath?

"Moshe," Avi pleaded. He was bawling now. "I never wanted to kill you. I just wanted to be like you. That's all. Can't you see?"

Moshe could remain silent no longer. "Don't hurt him," he said. His voice sounded weak and foreign to his own ears.

His mouth had dried up. "Leave him alone." Then he closed his eyes and braced for the worst. Who would they shoot first?

A chair leg scraped on the cement floor and Moshe opened his eyes. King Kong was tying Avi to the third steel-framed chair.

Mandrake padded toward Moshe. "I'm disappointed in you, Moshe. You could have ended it all." He towered over him like a large bird of prey and smiled. "But between me and you, secretly I was hoping you'd do this."

He danced back a few steps and spun around on one foot. "Ladies and gentlemen," he cried like a circus ringmaster. "A warm round of applause for our brave volunteer, Moshe Karlin." With a wild flourish of his arms, Mandrake indicated the overturned tabletop. "The show must go on!"

CHAPTER 77

Alex stumbled into the call center of the Dry Bones Society. Irina gripped his arm and the rabbi wheeled over an office chair, and they eased him onto the seat. A half-dozen worried faces huddled over him and stared at his face with pained expressions. They had fallen for his act.

The black eye was real. After the street show on King George Street, he had stopped by his apartment in downtown Jerusalem, munched a tuna sandwich, and slammed his bedroom door into his face. The injury added an element of realism that nipped any doubts in the bud.

"What happened?" Shmuel and Rafi said at once.

"Where is Moshe?" Sivan said.

"We were ambushed," he said. "On King George Street. They took Moshe and Galit."

Irina gasped. Sivan swore.

"Who did?" Shmuel again.

"Men with guns. They wore masks." That much was true. "They shoved them into a van and sped off. One of them got away on a motorbike."

Shmuel and Irina exchanged meaningful glances. Did they doubt his story? Or had they run into these goons before?

"This is Avi's work," Sivan said. "Gurion wouldn't do anything as stupid as this."

"No," Shmuel said. "It's Boris." Sivan didn't know the name, so Shmuel explained. "We were practically his slaves in his labor camp until Moshe bought our freedom. After that, the Society saved new arrivals from falling into his hands."

"Organized crime?" Sivan put a hand to her forehead as though she had a fever. "You went up against organized crime? Perfect!" She turned to Alex. "What do they want—ransom money?"

Alex raised his hands in a gesture of helpless ignorance. Irina swept strands of hair out of his face and dabbed a damp tissue over his wounds. He *had* to deceive her; it was the only way to keep her safe.

"Thank God the press has gone," Sivan said, "but they'll be back soon."

"They will?" Alex said. The show was to proceed on the quiet, without public attention.

Sivan waved at the screen. "We're back in the game. Just when our numbers go up, this has to happen."

Alex glanced at the bar chart on the television screen, which showed Restart ahead of Upward and the other parties. He had to tell Mandrake. Surely this would change his plan for Moshe and Galit.

Rafi said, "We should call the police."

"Are you crazy?" Sivan said. "No one can know this. People are still voting out there. We have to get him"—she pointed at Alex—"out of sight. We'll go public once the voting ends."

"No!" The single word dazed them into silence. Rabbi Yosef had spoken for the first time. His forceful utterance seemed to have surprised him as much as them. "We can't just wait here and do nothing. We have to help Moshe. He'd do the same for us."

Irina and Shmuel nodded.

"What can we do?" Rafi said.

The rabbi blinked. "Try and find him? At least we'll know where to point the police. Alex, what color was the van?"

"Brown. A brown GMC."

Shmuel said, "So what are we going to do—drive around the city and hope we bump into them?"

"We don't have to." This time Rafi had spoken up. "Most cabbies still have CB radios. I'll put the word out to look for a brown GMC."

Sivan said, "And I'll speak with my friends at Ridez. They can broadcast messages inside the app. It's worth a shot."

"I'll take my cab out now," Rafi said. He mopped his dark, balding forehead. "Alex, which way were they heading?"

"Toward Talpiot," he said. He knew exactly where they were heading. He moved to get up. "I'll come with." If they were going to play the hero, he had better keep tabs on them.

"But you're hurt," Irina said.

"I can drive. And two cars are better than one."

"Three cars," the rabbi said. "I'll head out too."

"Oh, no you don't," Sivan said. "You're number two, remember. We need you to hold the fort and speak with the press. This place is going to explode soon. It's what Moshe would want."

The rabbi relented.

"I'll go with you," Irina told Alex.

Alex considered refusing. She might see things she wasn't supposed to, and he had to keep her out of harm's way. But how could he persuade her without raising questions that he couldn't answer?

"OK. Call if anything comes up," he told the others. "Wish us luck."

CHAPTER 78

Eli parked his Harley Davidson in the private garage beneath Jaffa Road and ran for the elevator. Wind and turbulence had decapitated most of the roses in the bouquet, and now he was running out of both flowers and options.

Noga had been at Sarit's apartment and the Dry Bones Society, but Eli remained two steps behind. He had called some numbers from her phone, but neither Hannah nor her adoptive parents had heard from her, and now she had disappeared from the face of the planet.

A new anxiety gnawed at his heart. Something had happened to her—something sudden and terrible. His stubborn refusal to help her had pushed her into the ever-waiting jaws of tragedy, and he had lost her forever.

The Thin Voice had not told him this; the whisper of Divine providence remained as silent as ever. Instead, his fears fed off a vague and very human premonition. But the premonitions of Elijah the Prophet meant business.

As the elevator climbed toward his penthouse apartment, his heart clung to one final possibility: that while he had sped along the streets of Jerusalem in search of her, Noga had returned home. To her *real* home, with him. Whether she had come back to make peace or to claim her stuff didn't matter; he didn't mind if she hated him, as long as she was alive and well.

Never delay, Oren had warned. His late former roommate in the neurology ward of the Shaare Zedek Medical Center had shared far more wisdom than, apparently, Eli had accumulated in centuries. But Eli had not taken that advice to heart in time. Happiness had fluttered into his life and he, with the carelessness of a jaded immortal, had left the window wide open.

The floor numbers incremented on the digital panel inside the elevator. She would be waiting for him when the door opened, and she'd greet him with conciliatory smiles and hugs—or a well-deserved slap across the face—either way, preemptive tears of joy welled in his eyes.

But when he punched in the code and the door clicked open, he found the apartment dark and empty. The blinds slid on their tracks and spotlights faded in as the Jerusalem skyline basked in late afternoon light. He placed the surviving roses on the kitchen island. Her laptop lay closed on the coffee table. He made a quick search of the penthouse, checking the bedrooms and bathrooms—even his den, the walls naked and forlorn. Selling his mementos had been a rash move, and he would never see them again. Would he see Noga again?

He dashed back to the elevator and pressed the button for the lobby, his feet twitching as he waited, like an edgy racehorse at the starting gate. As the doors opened, he rushed to the front desk.

"Tomer," he said, reading the watchman's name on the identity card clipped to his shirt pocket. Eli had never bothered to find out his name, a factoid he added to the growing evidence against his former callous personality. "Has Noga come by—today or last night?"

Over the past few months he must have seen her come and go, although in his line of work it was wiser not to ask too many questions about a tenant's casual visitors.

Tomer looked up from his book and raised his eyebrows, so Eli added some identifying details. "Long dark hair. Pretty.

About twenty-eight—and don't tell her I told you her age."

Tomer smiled but shook his head. "Not today, but Evgeni might have seen her last night. I can call him, if you like, but he's on his way here for the night shift."

Evening already? The late summer sunlight was misleading.

Eli swallowed his disappointment and his fear. "Thanks."

Had she snuck in undetected? Even watchmen took bathroom breaks.

He dialed Sarit on his phone. "Anything?"

"No," she said. "I called her folks again. Her professor too. Now they're worried as well."

The dark cloud of foreboding returned. Noga was in danger. More than ever, she needed him. But where could she have gone? "Are you sure she didn't mention any other places or people?"

"Nothing. She borrowed my disc on key, though."

"Your disc on key?"

"You know, a USB thumb drive. She didn't say why."

A theory kindled in his mind, a final desperate spark. *You stubborn girl.* "I'm heading out again," he said. "I think I know where she's gone."

CHAPTER 79

As the henchmen fastened leather straps over his wrists and ankles, Moshe realized his mistake. The round, upended table was no table at all, but an oversized archery target.

King Kong and Vitaly stepped back and admired their work. They had strapped Moshe, his limbs extended like the Vitruvian Man, to the target, the tender flesh of his belly over the bull's-eye.

A lever thumped and a spotlight in the rafters beamed a brilliant circle of white over the target, making Moshe blink and avert his eyes.

"Ladies and gentlemen," Mandrake cried in his stage voice, "another round of applause for our brave volunteer!"

Galit and Avi stared at Moshe in horrified silence, unable to comply, gagged and bound as they were to their chairs. Moshe's suit jacket hung limply on the empty third chair.

Mandrake turned to the two seated figures and palmed his forehead. "Silly me! Your hands are tied. But cheer him on. He'll need your moral support before the show is over. Go on!"

Galit and Avi made muffled noises through the duct tape.

"That's better." He clapped his hands twice. "To work, boys. We can't keep our audience waiting."

King Kong inflated red balloons with large gulps of air

and handed them to Vitaly, who tore lengths of adhesive tape with his teeth and stuck the balloons to the target. He positioned the first balloon below Moshe's left armpit, beside his palpitating heart, and the second balloon beside his left ear. Moshe had seen enough magic acts to know what would come next. They were just trying to scare him. They wouldn't really throw knives at him, would they?

"I apologize for my vulgar assistants," Mandrake said, like an old friend striking up conversation. "But the pretty young women were unavailable on such short notice."

The two assistants completed their preparations. King Kong scuttled aside, veins bulging on his forehead from the effort of inflating the balloons. Amplified sound rung in Moshe's ears from the plastic orbs on either side his head, and he felt the pressure of those under each armpit. Vitaly placed the final red balloon between Moshe's legs and uncomfortably close to his crotch.

"Hold it tight," Vitaly said. Moshe pressed his knees together, gripping the balloon between his thighs as tightly as his bound ankles would allow.

Satisfied, Vitaly hurried away and set a leather case on a low stool before his boss, then returned to the shadows.

"I don't like guns," Mandrake said. "So cold and impersonal. If you're going to kill a man, you ought to get to know him up close and personal, don't you agree?"

Kill—did he say kill?

Mandrake opened the case and extracted a long, sharp throwing knife. Galit moaned and shifted on her chair. Moshe glanced at her and put on a brave face. Mandrake wouldn't risk impaling him, would he? Moshe was his prized race horse. He planned to pressure Moshe for favors once he was in office. But Restart had dropped in the polls. Moshe would never set foot in Knesset and Mandrake must know that already. Was he expendable? Would his painful death be an example to Avi?

Mandrake held the blade horizontal, placed a single finger under the edge of the hilt, and balanced the knife in the air. "I know what you're thinking. 'I hope this guy can throw straight!'" He laughed at his own joke. "Rest assured, Moshe Karlin. I practice often, and I hardly ever miss." His eyes twinkled, and he laughed again, enjoying himself.

Moshe's legs began to shake against his will. The balloon slipped from between his thighs and bounced on the stained cement floor.

"Aw, did I upset you? Vitaly, please help our friend. This time, Moshe, hold tight." Vitaly emerged from the shadows and lifted the balloon into position again. Moshe clamped his legs together, the awkward position demanding a lot of effort, but when he glanced at the knife held so casually in Mandrake's hand, the tremors returned to his legs.

"Not so brave, after all, are we? Vitaly…"

Vitaly returned to the circle of light and taped the balloon in place.

"Don't be ashamed, Moshe. I understand how you feel. You're afraid the knife might cut you… over there. Of course! How thoughtless of me. Vitaly, see what you can do."

Vitaly disappeared behind the target and emerged holding a silver cooking pot, which he positioned over Moshe's nether region.

"Very good. But Vitaly, this is Moshe Karlin we're dealing with. Can't you find something a bit more… suitable?"

Vitaly made a show of scratching his head, then slipped behind the target again. This time he returned with a silver tea strainer and tested it on Moshe for size. The tiny strainer barely covered the button of his trousers.

"Much better!" Mandrake laughed again. His henchmen chuckled as well, while Vitaly attached the handle of the strainer to the belt of Moshe's jeans with a large safety pin. They had planned the routine ahead of time and were enjoying every moment. This was a joke. A prank. After they'd had their fun, they'd unstrap him and let him go. They would all go free.

Mandrake flipped the knife in the air and caught it by its sharp, silver tip. Vitaly scampered out of the way. White spotlight danced off the blade.

"Are you ready, Moshe? To be honest, I'm a bit nervous myself. I'm not used to performing in front of a crowd."

Sweat trickled into Moshe's eyes. He tried to weave a plan in his mind, but his thoughts scattered.

Mandrake raised the knife in the air, and Moshe's muscles tensed, the straps biting into his wrists.

Mandrake lowered the blade. "You're right," he said, his face contorted with sudden doubt. "This is scary. Too scary. Vitaly, please. A blindfold."

The henchman reappeared at Moshe's side and tied a red bandana over his eyes. The world went dark.

"That's better," Mandrake's voice said.

Vitaly's feet shuffled away. Moshe moved his head, trying to find an angle that allowed him to peek through. The sound of his own breath—quick and shallow— filled his ears, along with the pounding of his heart. He was afraid to move, afraid to speak.

"Ready?" Mandrake called, his voice loud and distorted through the balloons at Moshe's ears.

Ready for what—to die?

His muscles squirmed. *No. He won't do it.*

"Three!" Mandrake counted out loud.

He can't. Galit squealed and the feet of a chair scraped the floor.

"Two!"

He's just trying to scare me. More shifting noises and grunts of protest. Even Avi's growl had joined the commotion.

"One!"

Moshe froze. He didn't dare breathe.

Crack! Thunder exploded an inch from his left ear, the deafening sound of metal slicing through a balloon and plunging into wood.

CHAPTER 80

From the sidewalk opposite Clal Center, Ahmed scanned the windows of the third floor. Some of the faces he recognized from his stay at the Dry Bones Society. Most he did not. And none wore a green hijab.

People had stared as he walked past the Old City. At Jaffa Gate, a young woman in a green Border Police uniform had looked him over, her machine gun slung at her waist. Could she sense the explosives beneath his light jacket? Would she tell him to stop for inspection? He walked on without incident.

It was his hair. The mane of peroxide blond had made them stare. "Another weirdo kid," they must have thought. Hasan knew his job well.

Ahmed walked on and on until he reached the light rail shelter opposite Clal Center. Television vans pulled up at the corner and camera crews entered the building.

Election Day. A day of rejoicing for the Society. Their leaders were expected to enter the new government. Would Samira join the celebrations? Had she forgotten him already? Surely she despised him. How could she do otherwise?

And yet, here he stood, a lone outsider once again, hoping to steal a glimpse of the girl with the warm smile. Had he expected her to sit at the window, waiting for his return? To rush across the street in order to speak with him one last time?

He had tasted Heaven in this new life for one brief moment, and he deserved not even that. She was right to hate him. His evil actions had stained his soul forever. There was no redemption for him, only death.

Ahmed was running his thumb over the detonation button, when an old man bumped against him and almost set off the explosives.

"Pardon me," the old man said.

A group of commuters grew around him at the shelter. *Sons of pigs and monkeys. Killers of prophets.*

No. Hasan was wrong. Rabbi Yosef had taken Samira in, and Moshe Karlin had bought her freedom. Did they deserve to die?

With one flick of his finger, the fires would ignite. The screws and ball bearings would shred his flesh and shatter his bones, and the projectiles would mow down all those around him.

He shuddered at the memory of his first death. The shifting of the bus underfoot. The pain, momentary but excruciating. Then he had woken up an instant later, naked and alone on the Mount of Olives. Would Boris be waiting for him a second time?

No. This time, he would not come back, he was sure of it. He would not enter Paradise either. The promises of Heaven and eternal pleasure were fictions created by cruel men to get fools like him to do their bidding.

This time he would end his life but not for the promise of pleasure or to erase his shame. He glanced at the third-floor window of Clal Center one last time. *For you, Samira.* This time he would die to set her free of him forever.

CHAPTER 81

After her meeting with Rabbi Lev, Noga trudged down Jaffa Road in a daze, feeling numb and hollow. The rabbi had tried not to laugh in her face, but he had not been able to conceal the effort. She wanted to crawl under a rock and shut out the world. Eli had warned her that no one would listen. *So this is how he felt all those years.*

She hadn't eaten all day, so she stopped at a shawarma store and bit into a pita stuffed with slivers of steaming turkey. *Galgalatz* Radio played on speakers in the corners of the pokey fast-food joint, and the news broadcast summed up the exit polls. For a change, Noga followed the election results with interest. Restart had received no mandates. *Strange.* Their promise to sweep clean the political establishment was supposed to have won a lot of popular support. Were Moshe Karlin and Rabbi Lev the wrong partners for her after all?

The meal revived her spirits. No wonder the rabbi had dismissed her as a lunatic. She had rushed over to Restart without any hard evidence in hand. In his shoes, she would have done the same. The evidence lay on her laptop in Eli's apartment, and she was not going back there.

Although he hadn't quite lied to her, Eli had hidden the truth. Worse yet, he had let her walk out the door. He hadn't run after her to bring her back. She was a pudgy teenager again, the plain girl none of the boys had given a second glance.

He didn't want her? Fine. She didn't need him either. Let him keep her laptop and her phone. She'd replace them, just as she'd replace him. Let him rot in his penthouse with his money. She'd push on without him. The world needed to know, and she would tell all.

She poured *tehina* from a ketchup bottle onto her half-eaten shawarma. No matter which political influencer she turned to in the end, she would need her data. If she hurried, she might take care of that today.

She bunched up the shawarma wrapper, emptied her can of Diet Coke, and prepared to move on, when the news reader interrupted with another election update. The real vote counts were rolling in, and this time, Restart emerged with an early lead.

Noga laughed. The obituaries in the media had arrived prematurely; the party of resurrected Israelis refused to stay dead.

She tossed the empty wrapper into the trash bin and hit the street. Boarding the Red Line at City Hall, she found a seat at the back of the train.

Her hand found Sarit's flash drive among the change in her pocket, the remains of the money her friend had lent her. She'd obtain another copy of her research data from the hospital, transfer it to the USB, install her software on Sarit's laptop, write up her paper, and publish the discovery with Hannah.

The train slowed at the Davidka station outside Clal Center.

Soon, Rabbi Lev, you'll believe me. You'll have no choice.

A fresh group of passengers made their way down the carriage and found their seats. The punk with the blond Mohawk caught her eye.

Haven't seen one of those in years.

The strip of peroxide blond clashed with the olive scalp of his shaved head. Sweat glistened on his forehead as he moved down the aisle, his arms folded over his chest in his thin black jacket, his eyes roving, self-conscious.

She averted her eyes. *Poor kid*, she thought.

CHAPTER 82

Moshe felt the vibrations through the wooden tabletop as the knife shuddered in the target.

I'm OK! He hit the balloon!

In his dark, sightless world, relief turned to horror. *Oh my God—he threw it! He actually threw the knife!*

Mandrake laughed. "Ha-ha! That was close, Moshe. My hand is shaking. I wish you could see it. One down, four more to go."

Four more?! His body convulsed.

"No," he cried. *Think, Moshe, think! What will make this madman stop?* "Please let us go."

"We're just getting started, Moshe. Which one should I do next? Never mind—it'll be a surprise. Three!"

Galit and Avi bleated, trying to cry out despite the rags in their mouths.

"Two!"

Oh God, save me, please!

"One!"

Crack-thrung-ung-ung! The balloon at his right ear burst, the knife vibrating from the force of the impact.

"Two in a row! We're on a roll, Moshe. Whoo-hoo!"

Nnn-gggrhh-mmm!

Galit's groans turned to sobs. This was too much. He had

to make it stop. Did their torturer want to feel power over his victims? Moshe would give him what he wanted.

"Please, Mandrake, sir! Let them go. You can have me, but please, just let them go."

"What a man," Mandrake said, with awe. "Even in his final moments, he's thinking of others. Which reminds me, Moshe. Seeing that this might be our last opportunity to chat," he chuckled, "in this lifetime, I want to pick your brain. Tell me, one magician to another, how did you do it?"

He'd just thrown two knives at Moshe and now he wanted to chat? "Do what?"

"You know, that trick where you die and come back to life?"

Was he serious? "That's not a trick," he mumbled, knowing that his captor would not like his answer. "It just happens."

"I'm disappointed, Moshe. I thought we were friends. You'll have to learn to trust me. Luckily, I can help with that. Three!"

"No, please."

"Two!"

A familiar sharp pain seared inside his chest.

"One!"

Cr-rack! Thrung-g-g-g!

The knife buried into the wood between his legs, catching the edge of his trousers.

"Three in a row! I never get three in a row. Moshe, you're my lucky charm."

Moshe's stomach churned. His fingers felt cold, the blindfold wet with perspiration. The pain in his chest subsided, and he gulped air. How much more could he take?

"I know, I know. This doesn't seem fair, but think of Boris. You know Boris. Poor old Boris. He had a thriving business until you decided to play the hero."

Helping the new arrivals had involved a risk, Moshe had known that from the start, but he couldn't stand idly by as Boris roped thousands of unsuspecting men and women into slavery. Had he really thought that he could get away with it?

"Tell you what," Mandrake's voice said. "I'm a reasonable man. I'll give you one more chance."

"Oh, thank you. Yes. Please. I'll do anything you want."

Galit no longer whimpered. Had she passed out?

"Here it is. You can either die here in front of your lovely wife, or you can let us kill your old traitorous friend here, Avi Segal. A life for a life. What do you say?"

Moshe said nothing. He had been willing to do anything—to shut down Restart and the Dry Bones Society, to stay out of public life. To hand over his worldly possessions. But this—this was murder. To fight in self-defense was one thing, but to kill someone else to save his own skin?

"A quick death, I promise. Over in a second. You won't have to pull the trigger. Then you and Galit go home to sweet Talya."

Mandrake seemed intent on turning Moshe into a killer. Was that some evil rite of passage or just another deception? Would he carry out the order? Nothing was certain with this man.

Moshe hung his head.

"OK," Mandrake said. "It's your funeral. No hard feelings. I wanted to break my record anyway. Four in a row would be awesome. Just thinking of it makes my hands shake. Here goes."

Moshe braced his body for impact, sucking in air with feverish gulps like a woman in labor, his limbs shaking.

"Three!"

Moshe's head swam in the blackness. His mother glanced down at him and patted his hair. His father handed him a heavy silver watch. *This is yours now.* He rested his hands on young Moshe's shoulders as they smiled at the cameras outside the brand new offices of Karlin & Son. *A Karlin never quits...*

"Two!"

Galit met his eyes across the dance floor of Hangar 17. "You're late," he said to her. She smiled. "I got here as fast as

I could." Then her face crumpled with effort and she squeezed his hand. She lay on the hospital bed in the Shaare Zedek labor ward, perspiring with the effort, and he felt a rush of joy as Talya burst into the world.

"One!"

CHAPTER 83

Daylight faded over the Talpiot industrial zone as the black Mercedes cruised down Pierre Koenig. Alex had not had time to clean out the rental car before Irina had settled onto the passenger seat. Any moment now, she might blow his cover.

A loaded Glock lay in the glove compartment above her legs, and the trunk contained reams of plastic sheeting, a bundle of rope, and a pack of cable ties. He'd have trouble explaining away the equipment, which he had packed in case the abduction of Moshe and his wife veered from the script.

Irina dialed a number on her phone and thumbed on the speaker. "Any luck?"

"No," Rafi's voice said. "Nothing yet. I'll let you know as soon as we do." CB radio static roared on the other side of the line. Across the city, friends of the Yemenite driver, in cabs and shuttles, scanned the streets of Jerusalem for a brown GMC.

Alex had given an accurate description of the vehicle used by Mandrake's extraction team. Eyewitness accounts would surface later anyway.

Irina pointed to a side road of old, derelict buildings. "Let's look over there," she said.

He turned the wheel.

"That's it," she said. "Stop here."

They idled outside a nondescript warehouse of corrugated fiberglass.

"You know this place?"

"I wish I didn't. We lived here for a few days—Moshe, Samira, and I—after we left the rabbi's home. Our first job, or so we thought. We had a roof, two square meals, and a contract that made us their slaves. The place is a trap for refugees and illegals, anyone without the right papers. That's where we met Shmuel. Moshe got us out."

Alex grunted in sympathy and stared at the decrepit warehouse, yet another tentacle in Mandrake's ever-growing empire. He knew what Irina was thinking: Moshe had crossed the slave drivers before, so maybe they had returned to collect their dues. She was right, of course, but she had no idea just how long and grasping those tentacles had grown. Neither did Alex.

"No brown vans here," he said.

"Let's try the streets nearby."

They did. There was no harm in humoring her. Mandrake was holding Moshe and Galit far away, but Alex couldn't take her there. Not until Mandrake was done with them, and by then it would be too late.

Irina slapped the armrest in frustration.

It pained Alex to see her suffer. She cared for Moshe, her friend and guide in difficult times, and Alex was grateful for that.

Had Irina and Moshe been more than friends? Unlikely. Moshe was too clean and by-the-book. Again, he felt that stab of jealousy. One thing was sure: he did not envy Moshe Karlin now. Alex had advised restraint, but there was no guessing how far Mandrake would go. He had learned that lesson early on and a world away, in Korosten.

The linoleum floor and whitewashed walls of the People's Primary had reminded the young Alex of the hospital where his father had died. On his first night after lights out, the other boys had wasted little time in welcoming the newcomer.

"That's a nice suitcase," said the leader of the pack, a

stocky blond kid with crooked teeth. The night light, a naked bulb above the door, cast a ghostly glow over the long row of cot beds in the dormitory.

Alex hugged the case to his chest. "My father gave it to me."

The boy smirked and cast a glance at the thugs behind him. "And now you're going to give it to me, Jew-boy."

Alex had closed his eyes and tensed for the worst. He didn't remember the boy's name, but he'd never forget the expression of disbelief on his face when, three seconds later, his tormentor was sprawled on the shiny floor, touching a trembling finger to his tender, bloody lip.

A stranger stood over the pack, the cruel boys crumpled at his feet in varying states of pain. "That's no way to welcome our new friend," the stranger said, his bare hands pressed together in a polite gesture that was at once adult and ominous. The wolves scattered.

The savior remained at the side of his bed and grinned.

"How did you do that?"

The boy put a finger to his lips and winked. "It's a kind of magic."

Alex stayed close to him from that day on. They shared their meals and exercised together in the training yard. His name was Gennady but behind his back the other boys called him The Jew. Strangely, he seemed to like his nickname. Nobody messed with The Jew. Only later did Alex learn about knuckle busters and the virtues of lead piping hidden up a sleeve.

A year later, as Chernobyl burned and the authorities evacuated Korosten, the two Jewish boys set out on their own, leaving behind the world of cold institutions and hateful rules. They were thirteen years old.

As Gennady honed his repertoire of street magic, the two friends found early successes and had a few close brushes with the law. When the Soviet Union collapsed, opportunities for energetic men with the right skillset sprouted from the ruins. The local criminal networks, however, guarded their turf with iron fists and limited their expansion.

The Middle East beckoned, drawing them with the sweet scent of lawlessness, and the free one-way tickets offered by the Jewish State, an oriental fruit, ripe for the picking. They learned the new turf and language, and quietly set the stage for a new, improved show. In Israel, no one called them Jew-boys.

Irina's phone rang.

"Any luck?" Rabbi Yosef asked on the speaker. The hub-bub of voices in the background made his voice hard to hear.

"Nothing yet," she answered. "How are we doing over there?"

"It's a miracle!"

She glanced at Alex, an excited twinkle in her eye. "More mandates?"

"We're twenty seats ahead of Upward."

Twenty seats!

Irina's mouth dropped open.

"Everyone's asking for Moshe," Yosef said. "I can't hold them off much longer."

Irina ended the call. "This is amazing," she said, but then her enthusiasm turned to worry. "We have to find Moshe."

"You're right," Alex said. Had Mandrake seen the results? Would that change his plan? With Irina sitting beside him, Alex had no way of contacting his boss.

Irina's phone rang again. "Anything?"

"Yes," Rafi's voice said. "A driver saw a similar van heading west on Golomb, toward the city outskirts."

"We're on it." She ended the call. "Do you think they left the city?"

"Anything's possible." Alex doubled back onto Pierre Koenig and headed west. "It's worth a shot."

Ready or not, he thought, *here we come.*

CHAPTER 84

Eli dashed out of the large steel elevator and onto the fourth floor of the Shaare Zedek Medical Center. Memories flooded his mind at every step. Racing down the linoleum corridor in his wheelchair, Noga calling after him to slow down. At the water cooler in the kitchenette, eavesdropping while Moti, the therapeutic clown, had dissected Eli's psyche for the entertainment of a young nurse.

Nut case, the carrot-haired clown had said of Eli. *Trapped.* They had pitied him, and he had absorbed their worldview. Now Eli had come full circle.

He reached the neurology ward, half expecting to bump into Noga in her white cloak.

Eliana, the large Russian head nurse, stood at the information desk and looked over the shoulder of Nadir, the Arab nurse with the white hijab. They both looked up.

"Eli," Eliana said, smiling. "Welcome home." She glanced at the battered bouquet of roses in his hand—only three of the flowers remained intact—and gave him a bemused smile. "Is everything all right?" If Noga had spoken with her, she had not mentioned their recent split.

"Did Noga come by today?"

"No. Was she supposed to?"

The premonition reared its horrible head again. Noga was

in danger. He had to find her right away.

"I think so. She left her phone at our place, and I haven't been able to reach her. Can you call me if you see her?"

Bemusement turned into concern, and he knew what she must be thinking: surely Noga could call him if she wanted?

"We had a fight," he confessed. "And I owe her an apology."

Eliana handed him a notepad and he jotted down his number. "I'll call if I see her."

"Thanks."

Eli walked over to room 419C, his old room. Oren's bed lay bare and empty. *Don't delay*, he had said, urging Eli to make amends with Noga. His words were all the more relevant today.

Eli walked past the plastic divider curtain. A young girl lay in his old bed by the window, eating her hospital dinner on a wheeled tray, a white sanitary bandage wrapping her forehead. She looked up at him and paused mid-chew.

"Hi there," he said.

"Hello."

"This used to be my bed."

She blinked at him, probably wondering what the stranger with the black leather jacket and fistful of abused roses wanted. He pointed at the window with the steamed glass. "Have the crows come to visit yet?"

She shook her head. Of course not. The cruel birds had carried a message for him, a message that now, two months later, he finally understood. "If they do," he said, and he winked, "say hi for me."

Nadir sat alone behind the nurses' desk when he returned. He leaned against the desk. *Where to now?* Noga had borrowed Sarit's flash drive. She must have wanted to get a fresh copy of her research results in order to move forward with her mission without him. But the nurses hadn't seen her.

He cleared his throat. "Nadir, Noga came here a few weeks ago, right?"

"Yes. She came to collect her data."

"Did you help her with that?"

"Oh, no. She just stopped by on her way to the Medical Genetics Institute. All the data goes through there."

Bingo! "And where is that?"

She pointed upward. "Fifth floor."

Eli raced down the corridor to the elevators and pressed the button. After five frustrating seconds, he pushed through the door to the stairwell. He took the stairs two at a time, losing another rose in the process, and burst onto the fifth-floor corridor, gulping air like a drowning fish.

Following the signs, he rounded a corner and marched down a passageway of glass walls. The desks and counters within sat motionless in the gloom. When, finally, he reached the entrance of the Medical Genetics Institute, the glass doors held fast. A handwritten note taped to the door explained that the Institute had closed early for Election Day.

If Noga had been there, he had missed her. But why hadn't she returned to Sarit's apartment, and why hadn't she called?

Outside, a siren sounded—the all too familiar wail of an ambulance. The noise grew louder. A second wail joined the first, then a third.

The remaining flowers dropped to the linoleum floor.

Oh, God, no! Not Noga!

CHAPTER 85

"Four in a row!" Mandrake's voice cried, as another knife twanged in the wooden board, inches from the tender skin of Moshe's right armpit. He had flinched on impact, but less than before. The unrelenting tension had drained his adrenaline and numbed his reflexes.

The pain in his chest had become a constant pressure at his core. A warmth spread over his crotch, ran down his legs, and trickled onto the floor.

Let it be over. Kill me already.

"Vitaly," Mandrake said. "Let him have a look."

Feet shuffled, then fingers lifted the blindfold from Moshe's head.

Moshe blinked against the spotlight. Mandrake smiled at him. His bald head glistened under the fluorescents. "Look, Moshe." Moshe obliged. The black handles of large daggers protruded from the target on either side his head, under his right armpit, and between his legs. The last balloon hovered to his left, by his heart.

Galit sagged forward on her chair, her head hanging limp—had she passed out? Avi looked away, the twisted cloth digging into his mouth.

"We make a great team, Moshe, you and I, don't you agree? Think of what we can accomplish together, if only you'd let me help you."

Mandrake's glance dropped to Moshe's feet and he wrinkled his nose. Moshe glanced at the cement floor. A reeking puddle spread beneath him.

"Aw, Moshe. Did you pee your pants? It's OK. I won't tell anyone. This will be our little secret. Soon, it won't matter." He lifted another knife in the air. "One more to go, Moshe. What do you say—should we risk it? Is five in a row too much to hope for? Are we pushing our luck too far? What the hell." All concern emptied from his voice. "You're mine, Moshe, do you understand? Your life belongs to me." He wiped his brow on his sleeve, and smiled again. "Feel the tension—huh?"

Moshe closed his eyes. *Let it be over. Start the countdown.*

But Mandrake wanted to chat. "I can't lie to you, Moshe. I'm nervous. Look at my hand. Open your eyes." Moshe did as he was told. Mandrake held up his hand. The fingers shook. "This is scary. Too scary. I can't bear to watch it either." He rested the knife on the leather case, pulled a red kerchief from his pocket, and tied it over his eyes. "There, that's better." He felt around for the knife, found it, and raised it in the air by the tip. He faced a point off to Moshe's left.

A sudden gust of optimism lifted Moshe's spirits. He might survive this throw after all.

"Boss," Vitaly said.

Mandrake lifted his blindfold. "Ha! Silly me. Thanks, Vitaly." He corrected his position, lifted the knife, then rolled the blindfold back into position. "Help our friend with his blindfold again, won't you?"

The thug pulled the blindfold over Moshe's eyes, and the world went dark again.

This is it. He's done toying with me. It's all over now.

"Three!"

Moshe swirled wine in a glass at his fortieth birthday party. Among the buffet tables in the Italian restaurant at the Botanical Gardens, he searched for Galit. He wanted to raise a toast to her. He stepped outside onto the terrace overlooking the pond, and in the still night air, he heard her voice.

"Two!"

Walking down a dirt path through the trees and bushes, he saw them. The man leaned against a tree, his back to Moshe. A high-heeled foot ran up against the man's leg, exposing a woman's leg as it pressed against his thigh.

His wineglass cracked on the stony ground, and the couple broke apart like a flock of startled birds.

"Galit!" His voice was distant, incredulous. Galit stepped away from Avi and straightened her dress, a mixture of surprise and defiance in her large, pretty eyes.

"One!"

No! Pain exploded in his ribcage, and he clutched at his chest. As the cheating couple gaped, he collapsed to the ground, and the world faded to black.

CHAPTER 86

Eli rushed out the doors of the Emergency Department and onto the street. Hospital staff in luminous yellow vests pulled stretchers from the ambulances and wheeled them inside. Eli glanced at the bloodied civilians as they passed: an old man; a little girl; a young woman with brown hair. Noga was not among them.

"Out of the way!" a paramedic shouted and Eli stepped back, trying to identify the wounded at a distance.

"What happened?" he asked, but received no answers from the busy medical staff. His premonitions had given him little to work with. *Thin Voice, I need you now!* But the psychic silence continued.

The third ambulance emptied. Had they already wheeled Noga inside? Or did her absence mean the worst—that she was beyond help, her remains collected for interment by the bearded volunteers of Zaka?

He passed the security check to reenter the building and pushed through the double doors of the Emergency Room.

"You're not allowed in here," a nurse said.

"I'm looking for my girlfriend, Noga Shemer. Mid-twenties, dark hair."

The nurse shook her head. "You'll have to wait outside."

Eli retreated. He paced the corridor while medical staff

bustled around him.

He pulled at his hair. *You fool. After all the warnings and hints the Boss sent you, you let her slip through your fingers, and now it's too late!*

A familiar face exited ER, severe-looking and graying at the temples.

Eli ran to him. "Dr. Stern!"

The head of neurology turned at the mention of his name, and his eyebrows rose. "Mr. Eli Katz. You got here fast."

The doctor had treated Eli after his accident, and he knew Noga well. He would have recognized her among the injured. Eli tried to divine her fate from his pale blue eyes.

"Did you see Noga?"

Dr. Stern's eyes narrowed with confusion. "I told her today that I wanted to speak with you, although I didn't think you'd visit so soon. To be honest, I wasn't sure you'd respond at all."

The doctor had taken a very close interest in Eli's case, especially his speedy recovery and delusions, and now was probably not the time to mention his recent relapse. But the doctor had spoken with Noga.

"Is she OK?"

"Yes, of course." Dr. Stern followed Eli's glance to the double doors of the Emergency Room. "Chain accident on Road One," he said. "Horrible mess. A bus and seven cars, I believe, but there's no work for me there."

Noga didn't drive. Had she tried to leave the city by bus? The scenario didn't fit.

"She's not in there?"

"No. She stopped working here a month ago, as you know."

"When did you see her?"

"An hour ago, at the Genetics Institute."

Noga had arrived at the hospital in one piece. Thank God for that. She had bypassed the neurology ward and headed straight to the Medical Genetics Institute. But where was she now?

"She was upset," Dr. Stern continued. "The Institute had deleted her data, and she had to resubmit her request." He brightened. "Shall we talk in my office?"

"Another time, Doctor," Eli said.

He ran down the linoleum corridor, weaving between nurses and anxious civilians. Noga had been at the hospital very recently—and she might still be there. There was one place he hadn't checked.

CHAPTER 87

Noga slumped on the bench in the gloomy twilight of the secret garden, and shook her head at the ironies of life. Two months ago, she had met with Eli in the grassy courtyard of the hospital, expecting a declaration of love. Instead, she had received a deranged proclamation from Elijah the Prophet.

While he ranted and raved about the End of Days—and the special role he and Noga were to play in the imminent apocalypse—a part of her had died inside. She had fallen for a madman. Feeling stupid and naïve, she had stormed out, determined to prove him wrong.

And she had succeeded. The mountain of evidence she had gathered for the Eli Katz of flesh and blood had buried the immortal prophet in the depths of Eli's subconscious. In return, she got her dream boyfriend, a life of luxury, and a carefree future. There was only one small problem: she had been wrong.

If the Jewish Arabs outed by her research data had failed to convince her, the zombies on the streets left no doubt. The world she knew was ending, and now that she actually needed Elijah, he was nowhere to be found; she had killed him.

If she had accepted his story that day in the secret garden, she might have saved everyone a lot of trouble, and maybe

Eli wouldn't have turned into the selfish jerk who cared about nothing, not even her.

Noga sucked in air and her body trembled. She couldn't do this alone. Rabbi Lev had laughed her down, and soon, if she submitted the paper Hannah wanted her to write, the academic world would do the same. But she wouldn't crawl back to Eli either. To him she was a pretty face, a shiny trophy on his mantelpiece. He cared about her in a self-interested way—seeing her as an extension of himself—and not enough to make him change course. Not again.

The handle of the door squeaked. Noga sat up and wiped the tears from her cheeks. She didn't want the pity of strangers. But the intruder was no stranger.

Eli stood there, rectangles of amber light from the hospital rooms above projecting over his leather jacket. Her body tensed. Had he come to drag her back to his mantelpiece? In his hand he held a single, bent rose.

He drew near, sat down beside her on the bench, and looked up at the stars.

"You were right," he said. "I should have told you about the Resurrection. At first, I thought I was hallucinating. Then, I was afraid. If I was Elijah without my powers, I was useless."

Was this the truth, or was he telling her what he thought she wanted to hear? She said, "I'm not going to change my mind."

"I know."

"I'm not going to back down."

"That's OK," he said. "I'll help you."

She studied his eyes. "I thought you didn't care about humanity."

He stared ahead at the flowerbed. "I did, at first. But the centuries passed, and the world didn't move any closer to redemption. There were hopeful eras, sure, but they always ended badly. Little by little, I dried up inside. Humanity would never be worthy, so why bother? To hell with them all. It wasn't my fault. But you taught me something."

"Oh, did I?"

He gave her his charming, boyish smile. "As a matter of fact, you did." He read his thoughts off the still night air. "I wasn't just afraid of failure. I was afraid of losing you." He gave her a quick, self-conscious grin, then looked away again. "Humanity is just a word. Humanity doesn't exist; people do. I don't have to care about humanity. But if I care about one real person, maybe that's enough, maybe that makes the world worth saving. And by loving that one real person, maybe I'll learn to love the rest." He held out the dilapidated rose.

The emotion that had swirled within her bubbled over and she couldn't hold back. She leaned in and he wrapped his arms around her. He was back. Eli, or Elijah—it didn't matter. The rest was details.

He cleared his throat. "I was talking about myself, obviously. 'Learning to love yourself is the greatest love of all.' Hey! No tickling."

They sat there for a while together, then Eli pulled away. "We should get home. We've got preparations to make."

"We do?"

"Oh, yeah. And a messiah to anoint."

CHAPTER 88

Moshe came to, the sound of a woman's sobbing in his ears. His shoulders burned, as did his wrists, and the stench of pee assaulted his nostrils. The pain in his chest had subsided to a dull throb.

He opened his eyes—he could see! The red bandana hung at his neck, damp and limp. He was still tied to the round wooden target.

A fifth knife stuck in the wood, inches from his heart. Five in a row—Mandrake had broken his record, but there was no sign of the mad magician or his thugs. They must have turned off the spotlight on their way out. The show was over.

Bound and gagged, Galit and Avi sat on their chairs under the ghostly fluorescent light of the derelict warehouse, their heads hanging low.

When Galit looked up, her sobs became muffled cries of teary relief, and her shoulders shuddered. Avi glanced up at him with wide, wild eyes. Had they thought that he had died?

"Are they gone?" he whispered. His throat felt rough and parched.

The two seated prisoners looked about them and nodded. Had Mandrake left them to rot, or would he return any moment for his fancy throwing knives?

They had to free themselves and flee the place while they

could.

Moshe strained against his bonds, curling inward like a spider, but the straps on his wrists and ankles were leather belts threaded in brass buckles, and they held fast.

He pressed his thighs against the handle of the throwing knife between his legs. If he could just get hold of a blade…

No. His legs were too far apart, so he tried a new tactic. He shifted his weight from side to side, pushing against the flat edge of the blade with the inside of each thigh. After a dozen swings, the knife shifted out an inch and lurched downward. Now, to press the blade between his thighs…

The knife clattered to the cement floor. He had hoped to launch the dislodged blade closer to the other two captives, but this would have to do.

"Avi," he said. His ex-friend and nemesis looked up at him, sweeping the greasy fringe out of his eyes with a flick of his head. Or was that "former" nemesis? They had spared each other's lives, after all.

Moshe sent a meaningful glance toward the knife on the floor. "Shift closer," he said. "Topple over near enough and you'll get to the knife."

Understanding glimmered in Avi's eyes. He rocked on the chair, the legs lifting off the floor and edging toward Moshe.

"That's it. Keep going."

Avi rocked harder, inching faster toward the circular target, his nostrils flaring over the knotted cloth in his mouth.

"Easy does it."

The warning came too late. Avi lost balance and fell sideways, groaning as his bodyweight crushed his forearm between the metal frame of the chair and the hard floor. He writhed and wriggled, shifting the chair in useless circles, until he gave up, moaning and sweating.

So much for that.

Moshe glanced at Galit. She nodded, made a valiant effort to shift the chair with the tips of her toes, but made no progress.

I guess it's up to me.

Avi's failed attempt gave Moshe an idea. He leaned forward, then threw his weight back against the wood. It barely moved. *That won't work.*

He shifted to the side and soon he wished that he had not. The wooden circle rolled on its edge like a wheel, grating against the rough floor and turning him upside down before it slowed to a stop. Blood drained to his head, a dizzying sensation that made him want to puke. The fallen knife lay on the floor—now the ceiling—far off to the side.

He shifted in the opposite direction and the wheel rolled back, coming to rest two feet behind where he had started. His plan had not worked out, but at least he was right side up. The knife glinted on the floor.

One option remained. The new plan might just bring the knife within grasp. On the other hand, it might impale or crush him. Either result beat waiting for Mandrake to return.

He lunged forward, straining against the straps. The target tilted forward, then slumped back. Galit shook her head and groaned in protest. She didn't seem to think that toppling the heavy wooden tabletop onto his body was a good idea and she was probably right. But with only one path left to freedom, he had to take that chance.

He lunged forward again, a Samson straining at the pillars. This time, he leaned back on the rebound, adding momentum to the next forward swing and, for two fateful seconds, the table teetered on a fragile equilibrium before succumbing to gravity.

Oh, crap!

Galit shrieked. Moshe cried out as well, closed his eyes, and clenched every muscle in his body as the unforgiving floor of hard cement rushed up toward him.

The crash echoed against the warehouse walls.

Moshe opened his eyes. He lay, face down, in the newly formed crawl space between the overturned target and the floor, supported by the knives that their mad captor had lodged into the wooden target.

He laughed, a tense, happy-to-be-alive, teary laugh. "I'm

OK," he said. The knives had saved his life, and his spread legs had ensured that the base of the target had not crushed his feet.

But the sound of the falling target would not go unnoticed. He waited ten seconds, catching his breath, listening for the return of heavy footfalls. None came.

Although alive, Moshe lay suspended from the toppled target like a turtle under an oversized shell, unable to move.

He craned his neck. The loose knife lay directly below his shackled right wrist, but twenty centimeters of air still separated his grasping fingers from the key to freedom.

He threw his weight to the left, the target tilting like an unsteady table, then rocking to the right, the heavy wooden surface now pressing against the side of the knife legs, threatening to loosen the blades from the base and crush Moshe. His fingers had just brushed the knife handle, when pain flared in his right foot, which was now pinned beneath the edge of the table and the floor, and he cried out again.

Working fast, his fingers jabbed at the knife, at first rotating it out of reach—*no, please no!*—then caught the blade as it rotated back. *Yes!*

He shifted to his left again, pushing the floor with his right knee. The target rose off his foot and settled back onto the knife legs.

His fingers managed to hold the blade—barely—but they couldn't slice the straps from that angle.

Now what?

He ran the blade along his fingers and grasped the handle. He couldn't saw through the strap, so instead he inserted the point into the buckle and between the straps, pushing down on the handle, using the lower strap for leverage, teasing the tongue of leather out of the brass buckle.

Encouraged by his success, he inserted the point inside the buckle a second time, slipping the strap over the brass prong, and his wrist fell free to the floor. After some stretching and painful contortion, he unstrapped his right ankle, heaved the table upward, and tended to the remaining restraints. The turtle had slithered out of his shell.

He limped over to Galit and Avi, his limbs trembling. "You OK?" He pulled the gags from their mouths.

"Thank God!" Galit said. "I thought you were dead."

"They were messing with you all along," Avi said, from his painful position on the floor.

"What do you mean?"

"He didn't really throw the knives."

"But he did. I heard them. The balloons..."

"Vitaly stuck them in by hand. When you passed out, they did CPR, then split. They weren't trying to kill you, just scare you."

"Well, they succeeded." All of this, just to freak him out. Gagged and bound, Galit and Avi had no way of telling him that it was all a show. Mandrake was one seriously deranged criminal.

Moshe faltered on his feet. This was too much. If they managed to escape tonight, he would withdraw from public life. He had stood out from the crowd once and become a target for dark forces. For all his good intentions and honest desire to fix the country, few things were worth losing his life, and nothing was worth losing his family.

As he stood over the bound couple, knife in hand, a memory triggered in his mind, a dark moment that he had buried deep in his subconscious.

"We should get out of here," Avi said. "Before they come back."

"He's right," Galit added. Then, "What's the matter?"

The girl had pressed her high-heeled foot to the man's thigh, her dress rising up her leg.

"You were there," Moshe said. "Both of you. In the garden."

"What garden?" Galit said.

Avi hissed, "Moshe, we need to go. Now!"

"At the Botanical Gardens."

Galit and Avi exchanged glances and fell silent.

"Against the tree," Moshe continued. "He had his hand on

your waist, your leg over his."

Moshe's brain added one strange fact to another. The morning of his return, Galit had screamed and climbed the walls. She had not been surprised, but terrified.

Avi had given a nervous laugh at the offices of Karlin & Son. "Why did you come back?" he'd asked. "To haunt me?" Then, "You don't remember, do you?" *Remember what?* "Dying."

Galit had sat on the wall of the Tayelet overlooking the Old City. "Can you forgive me?" she'd asked. *There's nothing to forgive.*

Moshe towered over the chained couple in the abandoned warehouse. "You cheated on me," he said, choking on disbelief. "Before I died."

Galit teared up and Moshe felt as though he had died all over again.

"That's what killed me—that's what brought on the heart attack. And you both just stood there and watched me die."

Galit began to bawl and could hardly get the words out between sobs. "I'm so sorry, Moshe. I thought you had cheated on me!"

Moshe shook his head and squeezed the handle of the knife. He should have let Mandrake kill Avi—kill them both, for what they had done.

"She's right," Avi said. "It was my fault. I screwed everything up."

Moshe remembered Avi's earlier confession. "You just wanted to be like me?" His words dripped sarcasm like venom.

"I'll make it up to you, Moshe, I swear to God, if it's the last thing I do."

"You ended my life, Avi. And now you've ruined it." Galit's tears continued to flow, but he kept on going. "How are you going to make that up to me?"

Avi swallowed. "You're right. I can't. Do what you want with me—whatever it is, I deserve worse." He hung his head. What did he deserve? A knife in the heart, right here, right now? Moshe wanted that. Mandrake had wanted that too.

"But," Avi added, "don't take it out on her. I practically forced myself on her. It wasn't her fault."

Moshe stood there and the urge for violent retribution subsided. She had thought he had cheated on her. She had felt the way he did now. He drew three deep breaths, then got to work, cutting the tape that bound their wrists and ankles.

Galit stepped up to him and threw her arms around his chest, clinging to him, her body trembling. She looked up at him, a plea in her eyes. He put his arm around her and touched her shoulder, a reflex, mechanical gesture, unsure what he felt. He would not figure it out here.

A car engine growled outside and yellow light flashed in the gap between the warehouse doors.

"Quick, get a knife," he hissed to Avi.

Avi hurried to the overturned target, while Moshe pulled Galit by the hand and ran to the doors of the warehouse. Bringing knives to a gunfight, they'd stand no chance against Mandrake and his thugs, but if they hid behind the opening doors, they might escape into the night.

Or they'd surprise them and fight for all they were worth. He gripped the handle of the throwing knife.

Outside, car doors opened and closed. Avi joined them at the corrugated wall, a knife in each hand. Moshe put his finger to his lips for silence. He peeked through the crack of the doorjamb. A black car idled beside a dormant brown van. A man and a woman crossed the beams of the headlights. They peered into the windows of the dark van, then walked around it. The man wore a ponytail; the girl had the leafy blond hair of a fairy.

Alex and Irina! Were they walking into a trap? "Wait here," he whispered to the others.

"Don't go," Galit said, but he pushed the doors open.

"Moshe!" Irina cried and ran to him. "Thank God we found you. Are you OK?"

He blinked back the bright lights of the car and shielded his eyes with his arm.

"I think so. For now."

Alex joined her. A large bruise around his eye shone in the headlights. "The whole country has been looking for you."

"I doubt it."

"They have," Irina said. "We won the elections."

His heart thumped in his chest. Had he heard her right? "We got a seat?" That was amazing. Unbelievable. He had lost hope of Restart ever making an impact.

"More than one, Moshe. Far more. And there's something else you should know."

She told him.

"What?" Moshe said, trying in vain to wrap his brain around the words. His recent trauma had taken its toll.

She told him again and, for the second time that day, Moshe passed out.

CHAPTER 89

Eli punched in the code for the front door of his apartment, nausea spreading through his gut. On the bike ride home, he had not expected the Thin Voice to speak inside his head. The Divine whisper had remained adamantly silent for months; why would that change?

But now, as the door clicked open and Noga followed him into the penthouse with the calm confidence of a trusting disciple, he realized that, in a secret corner of his heart, he had hoarded a desperate hope of hearing that guiding voice in the nick of time. In other words, he still had no idea what to do next.

Noga found her laptop on the coffee table and tucked the device under her arm.

"OK," she said, primed for action. "What now?"

"We anoint the Messiah."

"And where do we find him?"

"Or her," Eli said, and gave an awkward laugh. She glanced at him, expectant. He swallowed. He licked his lips and opened his mouth, then closed it.

"You don't know, do you?"

He shook his head.

"But if you don't, who does?"

He plopped on the couch. "The Thin Voice usually tells

me what to do."

She sat down beside him. "The Thin Voice?"

"Only I can hear it, like my brain is tuned into God's will."

She nodded, but her mouth became a short, tense line. Apparently, she had not factored obstinate Divine voices into her new life's mission.

"I haven't heard the voice in months," he continued. "Not since the accident."

She shrugged. "Then we'll figure it out ourselves."

"It's not that simple. Even if we think we've figured it out, how will we know we're right? With the Thin Voice, there were no doubts. All my intuitions since then have been wrong."

She considered his words. "What was the last thing the voice said?"

"I was to anoint the Messiah on the Mount of Olives. But as I got there, I slammed into a truck."

"You didn't meet the Messiah?"

Eli searched his memory of that fateful morning. "There was a white car and two men. The one with the beard called the paramedics." Another memory surfaced. He hobbled out of the neurology ward, one arm supported by a crutch, the other in Noga's. His fingers brushed against a folded note.

"What?" Noga said.

"He must have left that note in my jacket pocket. It had his name and number."

"Do you have it?"

He shook his head again. He had crumpled the yellow note and tossed it into a trash can at the hospital elevator. "The name was Yossi. No, Yosef." He strained his powers of recollection. "I don't remember his last name."

"There are a lot of Yosefs out there."

"There was a girl too," he said. "She had short hair. Blond, almost white."

Noga perked up. "I met a girl like that at Restart, when I spoke with the rabbi. Rabbi Lev. Wait a minute." She opened her laptop on the coffee table and ran a search.

The website of a political party loaded and displayed the picture of a rabbi. Streaks of gray ran through his neat brown beard.

"That's him!" Eli read the name in the title. "Rabbi Yosef Lev." He laughed. That was quick. "Restart—that new party?" Eli never bothered with politics or elections. Only God selected potential messiahs and He whispered their names in Eli's third ear. But the messianic task called for a charismatic and popular leader, and Noga's theory was showing promise.

"Yeah," she said. "The exit polls weren't optimistic, but last I heard, they were bouncing back."

She grabbed the remote control and thumbed on the TV in the corner. A woman sat at a studio discussion table. "It was inevitable, if you think about it," Liat Arbel said to her father and co-host, Dani Tavor. "For years, voters have felt disenfranchised, so they turned against the Establishment."

"But the exit polls painted a different picture," countered the gray-haired analyst. "How do you explain that?"

The woman shrugged. "With all the party's recent bad publicity, nobody wanted to admit that they were voting Restart."

"So they lied to the pollsters."

"Sure."

A chart of election results displayed on the screen. "Wow," Noga said. "I don't believe it. Restart took the elections."

"Whatever the explanation," Dani said, "this is the first time an unknown party with an inexperienced leader has trumped all the other candidates in the elections. Who knows what's in store for our country? So far, the Prime Minister-elect is keeping us in suspense, shying away from the cameras all day. This evening, however, he has promised to deliver a message to the country from his home in Jerusalem."

A photo of a clean-shaven man filled the screen.

"That's him," Eli said. "The new prime minister—he's the other guy from the Mount of Olives."

"Are you sure?"

"Yes."

"One thing is certain," Dani continued on the screen. "Prime Minister–elect Moshe Karlin has his work cut out for him."

CHAPTER 90

That night, Ahmed strolled in the shadows, while the towering walls of the Old City bathed in spotlight.

The explosives chafed his ribs. On the train, as his thumb hovered over the smooth detonator button, he had wanted to escape into the black hole of death. But when he gazed into the eyes of his fellow travelers, he hesitated.

True, he was a monster. He was not worthy of life. Yet God had brought him back from the grave. Why? To torture him—to rub his nose in the suffering he had caused? Ahmed had tasted that purgatory. God might as well turn him back to dust. Or was God not done with him yet?

In any event, did he really think that his journey would end if he were to repeat his mistakes? There was no escape in this universe. His deeds today would greet him tomorrow. He knew that now. Promises of Paradise had not saved him from his actions and neither would his desire for oblivion.

"Hey, kid," the conductor called to him, breaking his trance. "Time to get off."

The train had reached the end of the line and the last passengers had alighted.

Time to get off. To Ahmed's ears, the words had emanated from Heaven.

He stepped off the train and into a new world. The old

Ahmed had committed terrible crimes and swallowed lies; he had not been worthy of Samira's smile. That Ahmed had died.

He left the Old City walls behind, passed through the City of David, and descended into the Kidron Valley. Silwan rose above him in the night, lights glimmering in the windows of the chaotic apartment blocks and houses.

He climbed the rocky hillside and crawled into the cool emptiness of the old tomb. Turning on a plastic flashlight, he extracted his arms from the straps and placed the explosive belt on the vacant shelf.

Then he left the cave and made for the trash heap at the edge of Silwan. Picking a trail through the fresh refuse, he chewed a crust of stale pita bread and spotted a discarded pizza box. When a tin can tinkled nearby, he turned and pointed his flashlight. The light revealed neither Damas nor the Rottweiler, but a young man in ragged clothes.

He shielded his eyes with a grimy forearm. "I don't want any trouble," he said in Arabic. The man sounded about Ahmed's age. "I'm just hungry."

Ahmed lowered the flashlight to the man's torn jeans, just another wretched soul scavenging for food. At least he wasn't alone.

"I'm Dara," the man said, his voice hungry for conversation too. "What's your name?"

Ahmed considered the question. "You can start life anew every day," the rabbi at the Dry Bones Society had taught. Now was as good a time as any.

"Walid," he said. The word meant newborn. "My name is Walid."

CHAPTER 91

As the light turned green, Eli pulled back on the throttle, and the Harley Davidson surged forward. Once again, he was back in the saddle and racing to anoint a messiah, but this time everything was different.

He made sure to wear his helmet, for starters, and traffic lights no longer gave him preferential treatment. Doubts plagued him, both about the target and the success of his mission. Without the Thin Voice, he was flying blind.

Strangely, none of this troubled him. On the contrary, the uncertainty exhilarated him. His sudden optimism had something to do with the pretty young scientist who clung to his waist. He might be flying blind, but he was not flying alone. He and Noga would figure it out.

They had to—the fate of billions depended on them, and humanity was worth saving.

He pulled up outside a minimarket on Emek Refaim, and purchased a rectangular bottle of Yad Mordechai virgin olive oil. The Machaneh Yehuda market closed at nightfall and his home olive press would take too long. This time he would not stand on protocol. Maybe this time, he'd finally get it right.

Anointing oil checked off the list, they zipped up their riding jackets, put on their helmets, and sped off into the night.

Eli had looked up the address on the Internet. He made a left into Yehuda Street before diving into suburban Baka.

When he turned into Shimshon Street, however, he squeezed the brakes. Black SUVs with tinted windows blocked the street and straddled the sidewalks. Men in black suits with close-cropped hair, earpieces, and hi-tech machine guns cast suspicious looks at the clump of curious neighbors and camera crews that gawked from a safe distance.

Eli parked on the sidewalk and stowed his helmet on the bike. Noga did the same. Then, hand in hand, holding a laptop and a bottle of oil, they walked down the street.

A black suit stared them down. "This area is off limits," he said, his tone not allowing for negotiation.

"We need to speak with Mr. Moshe Karlin," Eli said. "It's urgent."

The agent asked for their identity cards and told them to stand back while he radioed in their details.

Noga met Eli's glance. He knew what she was thinking: What were the chances that the Prime Minister–elect would let them in? Their names still meant nothing to him.

Eli drew a long, deep breath and closed his eyes. He focused on the muscle at the center of his brain. *Flex.* Let us through. *Flex.* Moshe Karlin will understand. *Flex!*

The guard handed back their cards. "You're not on the list. On your way."

Eli's attempt at Jedi mind control had failed.

"But we have an urgent message for him," Noga said.

The agent nodded toward the crowd of onlookers. "So do they. Now move along." He tightened his grip on the handle of his gun.

Eli touched her shoulder and she relented. They turned back toward the bike. *So close and yet so far.*

"What do we do now?" she said.

He understood how she felt. Frustration had been his staple meal for centuries. But this time would be different. This time the Redemption would arrive. It had to. God alone knew for sure, and He was keeping His cards close to His chest.

"Simple," Eli said, pumping his voice with a confidence he did not feel, at least not yet. "We'll have to get on that list."

CHAPTER 92

A week later, Moshe found himself on a cream armchair in an office lined with bookshelves and jammed with reporters and clicking cameras.

The President of the State of Israel, a red-faced, white-haired man, filled the other armchair. Through thick reading glasses, he squinted at the fancy document set on blue velvet in his hand, and recited the formal declaration with some hesitation and intonations of disbelief.

Moshe shared his sentiments. On his first visit to the President's Residence on Ha'Nasi Street, the president was appointing him to form the next government of the State of Israel.

In another life, the achievement would have overjoyed him. Today, Moshe would have preferred to avoid the limelight. Reaching for the stars seemed like a good idea until you got burned. But now he had no choice.

The president signed at the bottom of the declaration, they shook hands, and they smiled for the cameras. The president leaned in. "Good luck," he said and smirked. "You're going to need it."

"Not luck," Moshe whispered back. "I need a miracle."

They chuckled and patted each other on the shoulder.

Galit, looking fantastic in a new white evening dress, waited in the entrance hall among the Members of Knesset and reporters—a delectable lamb among the wolves. She smiled up at him, her lipstick glistening, and brushed a speck of dust from his suit jacket, which she had helped pick out along with the silk tie in stately blue.

He had recovered from their ordeal on Election Day and no longer flinched at her touch. The memory of his death had hurt him to the core, and he supposed their relationship would never quite be the same, but he couldn't blame her. Avi had deceived her—he had testified to that himself—and, for a change, his old friend had brought Moshe and Galit closer.

The time had come for healing. Healing and forgiveness. To accept the past and look to the future.

"Ready to conquer the world?" she asked.

He took her arm in his. "One small country is more than enough."

They made for the garden and passed a rotund man with a bad comb-over, who made a conspicuous point of turning his back to them.

Moshe tapped him on the shoulder. "No hard feelings?"

Isaac Gurion swiveled, his bloodshot eyes flashing like angry daggers. Recovering quickly, the older politician shook Moshe's hand but bared his teeth as he smiled. "None at all." He seemed to be trying to crush Moshe's hand in his meaty grip.

"Remember," Moshe added, "it isn't personal; it's just politics." And he left the career politician snarling on the carpet.

A podium with microphones waited for Moshe at the edge of the garden, as did a healthy crowd of dignitaries and members of the press.

Moshe extracted cue cards from the inner pocket of his jacket, while an aide adjusted the microphone.

"Feeling grateful and humbled," Moshe said, "I accepted the president's appointment today. My heartfelt thanks go to those who made this moment possible: our team at Restart, my wonderful wife and daughter, and of course, you—the people of our beloved state. I will do everything in my power to serve as prime minister for all citizens, even those who opposed me. Thank you."

He opened the floor to questions.

The aide selected one of the raised hands, and a weasel of a reporter stood. "Seeing that you have no political experience, Mr. Prime Minister–elect, were you surprised by the president's appointment to form the government?"

Moshe had expected snide questions, but he did not reply in kind, resolving to behave with the dignity worthy of his new role. "Not really," he said. "Restart received the majority of the seats in Knesset. The president didn't have much of a choice." His remark won a few laughs from the crowd.

From among the faces in the packed garden, Reverend Adams gave him the thumbs-up and winked. Moshe responded with a subtle nod. One day, his wealthy backer would call in his favors.

And not only him. Moshe scanned the crowd for a bald head and hooked nose, and prayed that Mandrake's thugs had not slipped past the security detail. *You're mine*, Mandrake had said. *Your life belongs to me!* The mafia boss had revived Moshe and let him slip away. From their encounter Moshe had drawn two conclusions: resurrected people can die; and, sooner or later, Mandrake would return with his own demands of the new prime minister.

Another reporter stood. "With sixty-one seats in Knesset, are you going to form—for the first time in our history—a single-party government?"

"No, that's not my intention. We need to work together to meet the challenges ahead. I call upon the leaders of all parties to join our unity government and work with us to build a brighter future for all. Thank you very much."

He took Galit by the hand and followed Alon, the head of his security detail, to the waiting cavalcade, where another secret service agent held the door of a black SUV.

They climbed inside.

"That went smoothly," Galit said, as the car pulled off and

the world passed by their window.

"Yes it did. Let's hope that's a sign for the future. Where to now?"

"Dr. Klein."

"Right." Dr. Klein. The cardiologist. One advantage to being prime minister–elect, Moshe discovered, was the ease with which specialists became available on short notice.

The SUV, one of five identical vehicles in the cavalcade, pulled off.

Another advantage was the security detail that stood between his family and organized crime. Moshe had better make sure he stayed in office.

People lined the streets, hoping to catch a glimpse of their new prime minister. Some waved Israeli flags and streamers; others hefted signs of protest. One placard read, "Undead Stay Dead." Among the crowds stood a vaguely familiar man with a long stately beard and what appeared to be a white DBS spa gown.

Moshe's invitation to the party leaders was sincere, and not just because he needed their political experience. As the shock waves of the Resurrection rippled through the country, tensions grew. Never mind forming a government, he'd be lucky to avoid civil war.

"Look," Galit said. She pointed to a large clump of demonstrators in white robes and headdresses. The large banner over their heads displayed an abstract portrait of Moshe and the words, "Welcome, King Messiah!"

Moshe swallowed hard. "Talk about high expectations," he said.

Moshe wasn't the Messiah. At least, he didn't think he was. He would have known if he was. Did he even believe in a messiah? Until recently, he hadn't believed in a resurrection either.

Galit squeezed his hand. "Piece of cake," she said.

Moshe laughed and shook his head. He didn't know about that.

Messiah or not, the time had come to get to work.

ALSO BY DAN SOFER

An Unexpected Afterlife
The Dry Bones Society, Book I
Readers' Favorite 2017 Silver Medal Winner
(Fiction, Religious Themed)

A Premature Apocalypse
The Dry Bones Society, Book III
Coming 2018

A Love and Beyond
Winner of the 2016 Best Book Award
(American Book Fest, Religious Fiction)

ABOUT THE AUTHOR

DAN SOFER writes tales of romantic misadventure and magical realism, many of which take place in Jerusalem. His multi-layered stories mix emotion and action, humor and pathos, myth and legend—entertainment for the heart and soul. Dan lives in Israel with his family.

Visit **dansofer.com/list-dbs2** for free bonus material and updates on new releases.

CPSIA information can be obtained
at www.ICGtesting.com
Printed in the USA
LVHW031707160119
604152LV00004B/797/P

9 780986 393259